NORTHROP HALL

NORTHROP HALL

Margaret Bacon

This first world edition published in Great Britain 2003 by
SEVERN HOUSE PUBLISHERS LTD of
9–15 High Street, Sutton, Surrey SM1 1DF.
This first world edition published in the USA 2003 by
SEVERN HOUSE PUBLISHERS INC of
595 Madison Avenue, New York, N.Y. 10022.

British Library Cataloguing in Publication Data

Bacon, Margaret
    Northrop Hall
    1.   Upper class families - England - Fiction
    2.   Domestic fiction
    I.   Title
    823.9'14 [F]

    ISBN 0-7278-5941-2

Typeset by Palimpsest Book Production Ltd.,
Polmont, Stirlingshire, Scotland.
Printed and bound in Great Britain by
MPG Books Ltd., Bodmin, Cornwall.

For Becky and Alex

One

'That is a very bad word, Rupert. We must wash out your mouth with soap water.'

'It's not fair,' he told her indignantly, cheeks flushing, eyes accusing. He quite liked the taste of soap actually; it was the injustice of it that maddened him.

'Papa said it yesterday. I heard him.'

'That's as maybe,' Nanny said calmly, as she led him to the washstand, placed a bar of Pears soap in a mug and poured hot water from the jug on to it.

'He was in the office with Mr Shaw and I was outside and I heard him. "We must consider closing the school," he said. "It's ridiculous to keep it open for so few children," he said. "*Bloody* ridiculous," he said.'

'That's twice you've said it now,' Nanny told him, glancing at his younger sister who was playing on the hearthrug as if absorbed in rearranging the furniture in the dolls' house, but with a telltale stillness about her which showed that she was listening to every word. 'So that'll need two soap rinses.'

'I didn't *say* it. I *quoted* it. A quotation doesn't count.'

'Twice,' Nanny repeated, fishing the soap, soft and slippery now, out of the mug.

She watched as he rinsed and spat into the blue and white china bowl. Twice.

Thirty years of always knowing best had armoured her with implacable righteousness; her employer would no more have thought of arguing with Nanny Stone than she would have disputed the ten commandments with Moses.

Children argued with her, of course; children did, and Rupert more than most, but none of it made any more impact on her than paper arrows on armour plating.

1

She had been there for as long as any of the children could remember, as much a fixture as the shutters on the windows or the tall, brass-knobbed fireguard on which she hung their clothes to air. She never had a day off and belonged in the nursery like the chimney piece.

She didn't change any more than the other fixtures; always dressed in a black bombazine dress with carved jet buttons, protected by an apron and stiff cuffs, her hair drawn back into a plait which was wound around her head, nothing about her varied. The seasons came and went, the weather altered, but Nanny Stone never changed. And her behaviour, her standards, her everything, was as predictable as her clothes.

She always followed punishment with religious admonition.

'Tonight, you must ask God for forgiveness,' she told him. 'Never forget that he sent his only son to save your soul.'

'Why didn't he come himself?'

'Because . . .' if she hesitated, it was only for a second '. . . because he was too busy. He had a lot of things to see to, being God. And that's enough of questions.'

'Why did he only have one son? I mean, my parents have four of us and they're just mortals.'

'Dicky Paste's father has just had another son and he's only an undergardener,' his sister pointed out from the hearthrug.

'Oh, can we go and see it? I like Dicky Paste. We used to go to see them with Teddy and Diana so it wouldn't be fair if we couldn't go by ourselves now, just because they're not here.'

'There is no cause to argue,' Nanny told him. 'I shall ask permission. And now we must get ready to go down and see your mamma.'

Reluctantly they reached for brushes and combs, clean boots and buttonhooks. This hour downstairs was the treat of the day, but that didn't make the preliminaries any less tedious.

There were four flights of stairs down from the day nursery. The top flight was steep so Nanny went carefully, holding on to the bannister and looking down at her feet. Laura, knowing her manners, hovered alongside, but the next stairs were shallower so she ran ahead with Rupert, eager to get into the drawing room. Soon she would be sitting by her mother,

2

smelling that sweet lavender smell, listening to fairy stories, or *Lob-lie-by-the-Fire* or *The Water Babies* or *Jackanapes*, or Mrs Gaskell or – oh anything. It didn't matter; it was all wonderful. And if you sat on the floor the carpet felt lovely after the nursery linoleum. On good days, there might be biscuits as well as stories, biscuits and lemonade which Cook made in a big glass jug. If it was a bad day there would be Grandmama. They waited by the door until Nanny caught up with them.

They saw at once that Grandmama had decided to join them; she was sitting by the fireside, casting her black and gloomy presence over their golden hour. But they knew how they must behave; they went across to her, each in turn planting a kiss on that cheek which was surprisingly soft so that you feared your mouth might sink into its folds.

Her grandmother's cheeks always reminded Laura of the dough which Cook sometimes let them play with if she was in a good mood, especially if their parents were away, when they seemed to spend more time in the kitchen and the maids would spoil them and say, 'Oh, you're a caution you are and no mistake' and even Mademoiselle would unbend and call them her little cabbages. There was a special sort of bread bun which Cook made, into whose soft surface she would let them press a glacé cherry; the uncooked dough felt just like Grandmama's cheek.

Duty done, they were free to run across to their mother, kiss her firm, pink cheeks and settle down for a story, Laura sitting on the floor, leaning back against her mother's knees, Rupert on a stool alongside.

From her armchair by the fireside old Lady Arndale watched them, her eyes so hooded that they seemed to be closed. Her grandchildren hoped that she slept, that she wouldn't spoil their hour by firing questions at them about their catechism or make them recite their tables.

But although she watched them, her mind this afternoon was not on her grandchildren. She was thinking about the school, now under threat of closure. Building a school for the estate workers had been the pinnacle of her achievement in establishing her family as landed gentry and she could not bear to see it closed.

There had been no school here, of course, when they had bought the estate in 1863; it had been much smaller then, only two hundred acres with four farms and a neglected hall set in an even more neglected garden. It belonged to a very distant relation of her mother and was going, as she kept telling her husband, for a song.

The husband she had married in Lancashire came from a wealthy old cotton family. Trade, alas, but very *old* trade, as her own mother had pointed out to her in mitigation, very well established trade, not the sort of trade you got nowadays. She herself was the only child of well-to-do parents who died shortly after she was married, leaving her a considerable inheritance. So, as she explained to her husband, there was no reason why they should not buy the estate. Why not move south, why not exchange the bleak Lancashire landscape for the gentler Gloucestershire countryside and the life of a millowner for that of a country gentleman?

He had taken a great deal of persuading. 'I invest in South American railways, I invest in banks and assurance companies and I get a good return. But what sort of return would I get on land, eh? Tell me that,' he had objected, his northern accent getting stronger as his doubts multiplied.

'The return on investment in land is of a different kind,' she told him gently, but with the firmness of one who came of a family who knew about such things. 'It is a social and perhaps political return, a return for which our children will bless you. We have the next generation to consider.'

She had known, of course, that it would be hard for him to resist the pleas of his beautiful young wife, especially now that she was pregnant.

So they had bought Northrop Hall and immediately set about embellishing it, adding a nursery wing and extending the servants' quarters. They modernized the existing building and even installed a lavatory on one of the half-landings for the use of women and children. The men would, of course, her husband insisted, go outside, as they had always done.

The estate was small but over the next few years they added three small villages, two hamlets and six independent farms. They also owned the church and the right to appoint the vicar as well as the clerk to the parish and the overseer of the workhouse. She would have liked her husband to enter Parliament but he drew the line at that, limiting his political activities to supporting the local candidate at election times, transporting all his estate workers to the voting station and making sure that they voted as they were bidden, though it was hard to be quite sure after that dreadful Mr Gladstone introduced secret ballot, which seemed to her a very sneaky and un-English way of doing things. She also saw to it that her husband gave large donations to their own party, in return for which he gained his knighthood.

She was the one most interested in gardens so it was she who had supervised the landscaping of the neglected grounds around the house, replacing overgrown hedges with a ha-ha to lengthen the view, introducing fashionable parterres and rose gardens, classical statuary, loggias and pergolas. In the great debate between formality and nature she came down heavily on the side of the former.

When all these improvements had been wrought, Lady Arndale was satisfied that their way of life was indistinguishable from that of the landed gentry who had owned their estates for generations, but she was aware that when it came to philanthropy they had the edge over her. True, she supported local charities, donated money for the Sunday School, helped the clothing society and the lying-in society, but more impressive than any of this was to found a school for the children of the estate workers. A school would be the final proof that they had arrived.

The decision to do so was timely, for her husband had just bought more land which included a tiny village whose three families no longer worshipped at their local church which was falling into disrepair. He didn't like waste of any kind so it seemed a good use of stone to have the church pulled down and rebuilt as the school his wife so fervently wanted in Northrop. He found just the right site for it, set back from the road, sheltered by a line of trees and with ample space for a playground. It did, of course, look exactly like the church it had once been, which occasionally confused antiquarian visitors to the parish.

5

Of all her duties as lady of the manor, supervising this school had given her the most satisfaction. The actual management of it was, of course, left to the vicar and the church wardens, but she kept a watchful eye on it herself; it was she who had seen to it that the girls were provided with plain, serviceable bonnets and the boys with jackets. It was she who visited the school to inspect the girls' needlework. A fine seamstress herself, she considered herself to be a strict but fair judge, dismissing with contemptuous eye and biting tongue the bungled efforts of the less skilful, so that they crept back to their desks with bowed heads, shamed into tears. But for a child who produced a particularly fine piece of work, evenly sewn with tiny stitches, her admiration was genuine and her praise instant as she made a mental note to see to it that the girl got a place as undernursemaid or lady's maid or some other position at the hall where her gift might be exploited.

She didn't visit the school so much now, of course, though she did go occasionally, pushed in her wheelchair by Witchart, the butler, or by Jimson, the head gardener, when she was doing a tour of the grounds. The garden was one of the few things about which she and her daughter-in-law disagreed. Elspeth loved informality, colour and exuberance in a garden in the modern fashion. But she was a dear girl and in every other respect deferred to her mother-in-law, indeed modelled herself upon her, so Lady Arndale had happily conceded that so long as the formal gardens remained near the house, nature could prevail beyond. Thus they divided the supervision between them and it suited her anyway, as she grew old and infirm, to confine herself to the area near the hall, to the parterres, the conservatory, the greenhouses, while Elspeth and her husband made decisions about the rest. Jimson understood the arrangement, as did his staff.

Elspeth was over at the piano now, accompanying the children as they sang, as she herself used to do in the old days. Elspeth was lovely in her pale pink teagown, especially so since she had only just discarded the mourning she had been in for the King's death. She herself had not altered her dress when King Edward died; there was no need since she was still in mourning for Queen Victoria.

6

The death of the King was sad, of course, but it was nothing to the shock that Queen Victoria's death had been. She herself had been born in the same year that the great queen had come to the throne and, like almost everyone else in Britain, had known no other monarch. She had not liked or approved of the Edwardian Age. Maybe all that high living had suited high society in London, but it was not at all the style which suited the country gentry. Fortunately George V seemed much more Victorian in his ways; not for him all that racing, that dashing off to foreign spas and having to do with immoral women. The court would set a better example, she thought approvingly, under a new king who was more like his grandmother, who loved the countryside as Queen Victoria had done, who was more of a family man and, according to Charles, an excellent shot.

It was a relief to her that Charles was her elder son. His younger brother, William, who lived with his fashionable wife in London, was very Edwardian in his ways. Unlike dear Charles, he hardly ever saw his own children, was out every night with his wife at dinners and balls and theatres. She was a beauty, of course, but that was no excuse for gadding about all day forever shopping and going to her dressmaker or attending matinees and, if she was at home, reading unsuitable books and letting the children read them too, even the girl. She'd come from nowhere, Selina had, and without a penny too. She, Lady Arndale, knew an adventuress when she saw one, even if poor innocent young William didn't. She tried not to think about them, or their impending arrival next month.

She turned her mind instead to the much pleasanter prospect of Charles' family, relaxing as she thought of dear Teddy, doing so well at school, cast in his father's mould he was. Looking ahead she could see, as clearly as any ancient prophetess might have done, his future mapped out before him. He would leave school with honour, a credit to his family, he would go up to Oxford – when would that be, 1914 or 1915? – and study some subject, she was not sure what but certainly something suitable for a young gentleman.

Then in the fullness of time, he would return home to learn

7

from his father all he needed to know about the estate, gradually taking over more and more of the burden of responsibility, as Charles had once taken over from *his* father, until the time came when Teddy would take over altogether. Charles and Elspeth would continue to give him advice, of course, as she had always done and intended to go on doing while life was in her. Not that her advice was always taken, she thought, grim again for a moment.

She hadn't approved of young Diana being sent to that place in France. It was all very well for them to say that it was a *Protestant* convent, she still felt in her bones that words like convent and prioress smacked of popery. She sensed too that there was an obstinate streak in her granddaughter that irked her. She didn't know where the girl got it from, certainly not from her mother, the amenable Elspeth.

As for the two youngest, it was too early to tell. Rupert was said to be argumentative, but certainly he never argued with *her*. His father had never been difficult so it couldn't be in Rupert's blood. Anyway if he did show signs of rebelliousness no doubt boarding school would soon knock it out of him, if Nanny hadn't already done so.

Then there was little Laura, such a sweet little girl with her huge watchful eyes taking everything in. Untidy, alas, with her unruly hair and with stockings that never seemed to stay up, but time and Nanny and her devoted mamma would put everything right, Lady Arndale thought, relaxed now as she thought affectionately of Charles' children.

She must have dropped off for a moment, for she awoke with a start when Nanny came in to collect Rupert and Laura. They came over to her, as she knew they would, to give her a goodnight kiss; she gave them her blessing and refrained from inviting them to recite their twelve times table.

Meanwhile Nanny had one of her quick words with her mistress concerning the children's wish to go and see the Pastes' new baby.

'But of course, Nanny,' Elspeth said. 'We always encourage them to play with the estate children. So long as they don't get too familiar, of course. I suppose . . . ?' She glanced at the children and touched her hair significantly.

It was a gesture which Nanny interpreted correctly. 'Quite safe, ma'am,' she confirmed. 'No lice in the Paste family.'

They were very nearly late to bed that night, delayed by their father who came into the hall just as they were going upstairs. The children rushed up to him, Laura reaching him first, to be swept up in his arms and swung up high. Rupert had a more reserved embrace as befitted his age and sex.

Nanny watched, impassive. Nobody looking at her could have guessed how her heart delighted to see her Mr Charles playing with his children. He had been just under a year old when she had come here, aged thirteen, as undernurse to old Nanny Bradshaw. She had been here ever since and looked after his children as she had once looked after him. She had lifted him on to the same rocking horse, washed him in the same bath tub in front of the fire, she had heard him say the same prayers.

'Nanny,' he was saying now, 'I haven't seen you for nearly a week. How is everything in the nursery? Off you go, you two. Upstairs. Nanny will follow in a moment.'

'Well, Mr Charles,' she said, when they were out of earshot, 'I think Rupert is getting restless.'

He nodded.

'Yes, I've noticed. He should be at school, of course, but they insist on another term off. He was so very ill with the diphtheria, you remember.'

Remember? Would she ever forget it? She'd thought they'd lose him, as they'd lost little Louise with it forty years ago.

'He might have been better off in the schoolroom, but with Teddy away at school and Diana abroad, it would have been a bit intense for him. Dr Portly says it's important in such cases not to overtax the brain. Physical exercise is of course excellent for him.'

'He gets plenty of that. He goes out on his pony and he loves bicycling round the estate. He needs occupation.'

'I'll ask Thomson to make time to take him out shooting. He was very good with Teddy.'

She nodded. She trusted the keeper absolutely. He knew

about keeping boys in order as well as getting them to shoot straight.

'And I'll take him around with me whenever it's suitable.'

'He'll enjoy that. There's nothing he likes better than going round the estate with you, Mr Charles.'

'Yes, they've all taken splendidly to it. I've much to be grateful for. Well, I'd better let you go up now, Nanny,' he said, touching her hand in a little gesture that unconsciously conveyed that if she'd been his mother, granny to his little ones, it would have been a kiss. Not that she would ever have allowed such a thought even to form in her head, much less express it. Any more than he would.

The children were playing funerals when she got back into the day nursery. Rupert had spread a rug over his sister, who was lying under the table, and was chanting:

> Ashes to ashes,
> Dust to dust,
> If God doesn't take you,
> The devil must.

'That's not a very nice game, Rupert,' she told him. 'Now, wash hands before supper.'

'Everybody said the King's funeral was splendid, Nanny,' Rupert objected, as his sister went obediently towards the washstand. 'And even if they aren't nice, we can't do without them. What would have happened to King Edward if there weren't any funerals? He'd still just be lying about, wouldn't he?'

'Hands, Rupert,' Nanny repeated, ignoring what he said, and going to open the door. 'I can hear the supper being brought upstairs now.'

Mary-Ann, small for her fourteen years, was carrying a tray which was so wide she could only just spread her arms far enough out to grasp the sides of it. She was flushed and breathing hard after climbing the five flights of stairs from basement to nursery.

She was very new to the job and so unused to the ways

10

of the hall that she dropped a little curtsey when Nanny thanked her.

'No need for that, my girl,' Nanny told her. 'Put the tray on that table.'

'Yes, ma'am. Sorry, ma'am. I mean . . .' And she fled.

They always had cocoa and plates of bread and butter for supper, but tonight there was a currant bun apiece as well.

'Very kind of Cook, I'm sure,' Nanny said. 'But not to be touched until the bread is all eaten.'

She spoke grimly. Only plain food at night was one of her rules and she saw this infringement as an attempt to undermine her authority, just another skirmish in the war ceaselessly waged between kitchen and nursery. But she could manage them, she'd seen cooks come and go, though not as frequently as the tutors and governesses with whom she'd likewise done battle over the years. They were better educated than she was, she'd never be foolish enough to deny it, but they didn't have the control that she had. Where children were concerned the final decision was always hers.

'And don't gobble, Rupert, or you'll get tummy ache and need medicine.'

She glanced significantly at the remedies on the shelf: formamint, pommadavine and, most dreaded, castor oil, next to *Nursing Notes* and a well-worn *Handbook of Instruction on the Care of Children*. Rupert's jaws moved more slowly, knowing that Nanny's favourite quotation from that book was, 'The bowels should be kept well open.'

Since his brief sojourn at school, Rupert had been promoted to having his own room, one floor down. He washed there while Nanny saw to the filling of the brown bath in the night nursery for his sister. When she was little, Laura's favourite moment of the day, second only to the precious hour with Mamma, was being lifted out of the bath on to a big towel, previously warmed over the tall fender round the fire and spread across Nanny's capacious lap.

'Who's a newborn baby?' Nanny used to half chant, half yodel, because she wasn't much good at singing, and she'd wrap her in the warm thickness of the towel, rocking her to and fro. This happened every night unless Nanny was cross

11

over some misdeed, so Laura had learned to be especially good from tea time onwards; nursery memory tended to be blessedly short.

She was too big for anything like that now, of course, but still when Nanny handed her the thick bath towel from the fender there was something comforting about the warm fluffiness of it, which lingered even now as she methodically dried herself while Nanny emptied the bath water into two buckets for the kitchen staff to remove. Usually this chore was left to the nursemaid but it was her day off and Nanny didn't believe in leaving work for her to do when she came in. This she explained to Laura so that she would learn from it consideration for others.

'Just like your mother sees that as little work as possible is done on a Sunday so that the staff can rest and worship. And now time for your hair.'

Every night the long fair hair was brushed and combed and tied up in rags to make it curly for the next day. In dry weather it sometimes stayed curly, but usually the curls dropped out by mid-morning. Rupert said it was stupid and if she had any sense she'd refuse to have it done as he would if he was a girl. She told him he wasn't and she didn't and that was that. And he told her that she sounded just like Nanny.

On Thursday nights her mother heard her prayers. She came in tonight just as her hair was finished; it was always like that, as if everyone knew to the minute what everyone else was doing. Nanny left them to go and have her own supper and Laura knelt by her bedside. First the Lord's Prayer, which she got through without a mistake, and then 'God Bless all Her Relations', whom she named in order of seniority starting with Grandmama, then, since she was allowed to add on any extra she chose, she offered up the kitchen cat, a pet rabbit and the Pastes' new baby for blessing. Her mother, changed now from her teagown into her dinnerdress, sat quietly in the armchair, listening. Then she hugged her daughter, kissed her goodnight, told her to sleep tight and tip-toed out, as if sleep might already have come.

Sleep did not come easily to Laura; she was still awake when Nanny came up. Her bed was on the other side of the

12

night nursery and she had a thin screen behind which she prepared for the night. The lamplight shone dimly through it, illuminating her shadowy figure as she undressed with her back to Laura contriving to keep herself completely covered until she was into her nightdress.

Laura watched fascinated, as first of all she spread her nightdress on the bed and took off her apron and cuffs. Then her hands disappeared up her skirts and came out holding a stocking which was placed on the chair. The other one followed, then her drawers, then her flannel petticoat, then, very slowly and with much twisting and turning, her stays. And now she hunched up her shoulders and eased her arms out of the sleeves of her dress, pushing it upwards until it covered her head and hung like a tent over her body.

Her arms were free now and reached out to take the nightdress off the bed. Hidden under the tentlike covering of her dress she manoeuvred herself into the nightgown and not until it covered her completely from head to foot did she remove her black bombazine.

Reassured by this familiar ritual, bemused with watching the firelight as it made flickering patterns on the ceiling, Laura's eyelids grew heavy and at last she slept.

While Laura was watching Nanny's shadow contorting itself in the interest of modesty, her parents and grandmother were, unusually for them, dining alone. It seemed to Lady Arndale therefore an ideal evening to broach the subject of the school once the meal was over and the servants out of earshot.

'I hear,' she said, after they had solicitously seated her by the fire in the drawing room, having taken her stick and propped it up against her chair, 'that you have been having talks about the future of my school – I should say the *estate* school.'

Charles smiled, his good-natured smile. 'In a real sense it is your school, Mamma – and I am delighted that Elspeth has carried on in the same tradition but there are now only eight pupils left where once there were as many as forty. And Miss Poole is nearly sixty years old.'

'Millicent Poole is perfectly strong and able to continue. It suits her well to live so conveniently in her cottage adjoining the school—'

'Which of course she would continue to do in her retirement,' her son interrupted.

'Of course. As for numbers, they have always fluctuated, Charles. I remember the time after the typhoid epidemic when they were very low. They may well rise again.'

'I think not, Mamma, if you will forgive me. Some of the children are going to the National School and some to the one the Braithwaites have started in Stanham. It has certificated teachers and the children learn a wider range of subjects than Miss Poole can manage.'

'What do they want with a wider range?' his mother demanded. 'It will only lead to discontent. What the Braithwaites are doing seems to me to smack of radicalism.'

'Ideas about education have changed, Mamma,' he began soothingly.

'But we are not discussing educational theory, Charles. That is not what the estate school is about. It has always been about the estate, about loyalty to the estate, about equipping the sons and daughters of the workers to take their place on estate lands or in the house, so that the girls will have good deportment and a pleasing manner and be good with the needle. And the boys . . .' she was less sure about the boys so hesitated for a moment before going on '. . . the boys will be able to read and to understand orders and do their sums and learn obedience.'

'I quite agree with you, Mamma, and I'm sure that Elspeth does too . . .' he paused to give his wife the opportunity to nod her acquiescence '. . . but we really do have to look at the financial aspect of it too. You see, to run a school for eight children is almost as expensive as running it for forty. Miss Poole is still paid her six pounds and fifteen shillings a quarter, however many children there are. The churchwardens tell me that the education of forty children costs twenty-five pounds a year, that is about twelve and sixpence per child. Now they estimate that for eight children the cost would still be nearly twenty pounds a year and that is two pounds and ten shillings per child.'

'It is a great deal of money, I agree.'

'But Charles,' Elspeth put in, 'perhaps it isn't so very much when you consider that each of our boys' education costs nearly a hundred and fifty pounds a year.'

It was an unfortunate remark and they both looked at her with disapproval, her husband because what she had said appeared to undermine his argument, and her mother-in-law because she considered it a most gross comparison. By unspoken agreement they dropped the subject and talked of other things.

Two

M iss Poole stood in the porch and rang the school bell. She was a slightly built woman, pale and sharply featured. Her thin grey hair was drawn back into a tight little knot skewered with hair pins to keep it in place at the nape of her neck. Nonetheless she swung the heavy brass bell up and down with all the vigour of someone half her age and twice as muscular. She had done it every school day since she first came here forty-five years ago at the age of fifteen.

The children, who had been chattering under the beech tree where they gathered each morning, were instantly silent and came forward to form themselves into two lines, boys on one side, girls on the other.

'Good morning, children.'

'Good morning, ma'am.'

'You may enter.'

There were five rows of desks in the schoolroom, each with a seat attached. Miss Poole, who had put down the bell and taken up the cane, pointed with it to indicate that they were to sit down. She watched as they squeezed themselves into the front row, girls on one side of the narrow aisle, boys on the other. There was plenty of space in the rows behind, but these were the seats they had been allocated and it didn't occur to them to question the arrangement.

Miss Poole watched, saying nothing, then took up the register and read out their names, each child standing as their name was called and saying, 'Present, ma'am.'

'Our Father,' began Miss Poole and their voices, some mumbling, some whispering, some, like Dicky Paste, lagging behind, took up the familiar words.

'Ahfather, Witchart in 'eaven, arold be thy name. They

16

kingum come, they willbedone, as tis in 'eaven. Gie us thisday our dailybread anforgivus are trespusses as we forgiven that tressspus aginus. For thine is the kingum, poweranthe glory, frever anever. Amen.'

'You may stand to sing our hymn,' she told them.

They stood as the harmonium wheezed out the tune of *All Things Bright and Beautiful*. If Lady Arndale had happened to be passing the school at that moment, she would have been reassured by the sound of their singing:

> The rich man in his castle,
> The poor man at his gate,'
> God made them, high or lowly,
> And order'd their estate.

They did not sing with much relish, for they were subdued by the knowledge that the inspector was due this morning. To make it worse, they did not know exactly when he would come, so their dread increased with the passing of each minute. Miss Poole said it would be towards the end of the morning. 'So,' she said, 'we shall start on our usual Monday morning lessons.'

Monday morning's lessons always began with chanting the alphabet, twice forwards and then twice backwards. The one who had most difficulty with this was Edith Paste whose mother had been in service in a clergyman's house in London and had picked up scholarly ways there. She wrote letters for her neighbours in a fine copperplate hand and had books in the house which her former mistress had given her and continued to send. So she had taught her daughter to read, long before she started school, by pointing out words. Edith hadn't learned the alphabet, and although she had picked it up as she went along, she wasn't used to the idea of reciting it and in fact found it easier when they chanted it backwards as it seemed to rhyme better that way round. When they had to read in turn she did as the others did, spelling out each monosyllabic word slowly as Miss Poole pointed to the letters; 'C–A–T' she would conscientiously intone, not wanting to get into trouble for being different. Safely back home she would settle to reading a novel by Mr Dickens or Mr Thackeray. She never took to Mr Scott.

The other one who had difficulty with the alphabet, though for different reasons, was her brother, Dicky. Miss Poole made allowances for him; he wasn't exactly simple, it was just that he didn't know – and never would know – how many pennies make a shilling. But he was a good-natured lad, ready to smile, to apologize as he stumbled through his lessons. She did not cane him for mistakes which in the others might have merited a stroke across the hand – not that she used the cane much, she didn't need to; its very presence, combined with the look in her eye that bowed the will, was enough to control even the most wayward child.

Next they had geography, which Dicky enjoyed because they were allowed to turn in their seats and look at the maps on the wall while Miss Poole talked about them. The biggest one showed the whole world with much of it coloured pink, which, Miss Poole explained, meant that it belonged to us. That was something to be very proud of, she told them. Imagine what it would be like to have been born in some unfortunate country that didn't have such an empire! And we had clever men to go out there and rule the people who lived in these pink-coloured lands, she explained, and brave soldiers to fight any that were wicked or ignorant enough not to want to be ruled by us. That is why there were wars in places in Africa and in ones which were more difficult to spell, like Afghanistan. If you ever went to a great city such as Gloucester or Salisbury, Miss Poole said, you could see the flags of the regiments of men who had died out there fighting for their Queen – or King, as it was now and had been for nine years, but she still forgot sometimes – and country. Oh yes, the children must be very grateful for being born in a country with such an empire and of course grateful too to the Arndale family who had built this school for them and provided the beautiful maps which hung on the walls.

There were other less pleasant things on the walls, which Dicky didn't like to look at: the backboard leant there, a great wooden board with a pole projecting out of it on each side. If you slouched over your work you had to sit with it against your back, your arms hooked over the poles, forcing you upright. It wasn't often used and when it was it was mostly on the girls because it was important for them to have something called deportment if they were to work in the big house which was what all their mothers wanted for them. When Dicky saw anyone fixed to the backboard it made him think of Christ skewered on the cross and he felt fear and horror and wanted to run outside.

It was mainly the boys who were punished with the finger stocks that were also on the wall, on a little shelf. The strips of wood had holes for your fingers and a strap to go round your wrist, so you couldn't fidget. His sister, Edith, said that the boys had their fingers put in the stocks more often than the girls, because the girls had more to do with their fingers, sewing and doing the cross stitch and seemed handier with their pen too, whereas the boys never seemed to know what to do with their hands when they were shut up indoors, so no wonder they fidgeted.

The greatest threat, though, came from outside. Through the window he could see the holly bush, planted years ago so that if you didn't hold your head up you could have a collar of holly put round your neck to encourage you to keep your chin raised. 'Do not mutter, child,' Miss Poole would say. 'Raise your head up when you speak or it will be a necklace of holly for you.'

It wasn't a threat she ever carried out; Edith said it was because it would have been as painful for Miss Poole to make the collar as it would have been for them to wear it. She was clever, was his sister, Edith; he would never have thought of that.

They were just starting on sums when there was a loud knocking at the door. Only the inspector knocked like that. Miss Poole, nervous herself because a bad report could mean a cut in her salary, went to open it.

A retired clergyman, dressed entirely in black, the inspector strode into the room. Immensely tall, he towered over the children who stood to greet him, eyes downcast, too frightened to look up at him. They knew him of old, a terrifying figure, huge in his black garb, which, combined with his sharp beak of a nose, made him look like some great bird of prey. His face was red and angry-looking with dark and penetrating eyes that scared you so much you couldn't speak straight and forgot everything you knew.

'I have heard,' the booming voice began, reverberating so that it seemed the very walls shook as well as the children, 'that there are children in this parish who do not know their catechism. So we shall begin by reciting it.'

Their catechism used to be tested by the vicar, a gentler man but one who had been ill for some time. They prayed for his speedy recovery nowadays more fervently than they prayed for anything else.

The first part was easy, just saying your name and the bit about godparents. A lucky boy called Sidney was called out to recite that piece. He went and stood on the chalked cross at the front of the class which the inspector had drawn, rattled it all off without a mistake and was allowed to go and sit down again.

The next part was easy too; they chanted the creed unhesitatingly, all being familiar with it from church each Sunday. The commandments followed; again familiar with it from church, they had no difficulty in promising not to make themselves graven images, nor to take the Lord's name in vain, to keep holy the sabbath, honour their parents, not commit murder, adultery or theft, not to bear false witness and refrain from coveting their neighbour's wife, servant, maid, ox or ass.

Clever Jane Bradley got the next question and recited her duty towards God without a single mistake. The inspector nodded, Miss Poole smiled and Jane went back to her place, envied by the rest of them.

The inspector looked at the row of boys and pointed his cane at Dicky. Dicky Paste, small for his years and awkward in his cut-down trousers which hung stiffly about his skinny legs, extricated himself from the narrow confines of the desk and bench and went to stand on the chalk cross. His chapped, red hands, disproportionately large, were trembling even as they hung limply by his side.

'What is thy duty towards thy neighbour?' the inspector asked, his voice seeming to come from so high up that it might have been Jehovah himself who was doing the interrogation.

'My duty towards my neighbour is to love him as myself,' Dicky began.

He stopped; the next bit always confused him.

'Come along, boy,' Jehovah prompted.

'And to do to all men as I should . . . would . . . unto they . . . me do . . .'

There was a sharp intake of breath from the deity above, but Dicky stumbled on: 'To love, honour and something my father and my mother, to honour the King and obey and—'

'Stop this at once,' the inspector roared. 'Do you not know it is blasphemous thus to mangle the catechism?'

Dicky hung his head.

'Answer me, boy.'

Dicky nodded.

'Speak up, yes or no.'

Dicky managed to raise his head a little.

'Yes,' he whispered.

'Then if you know it is blasphemous, why do it? You have one more chance to get it right and then I think you can guess what your punishment will be.'

Without this threat he might have managed to get the words out in the right order, as he had eventually done for Miss Poole the day before, but with this unknown threat hanging over him, his mind emptied itself of all coherent thought. He started again and did even worse than the first time.

He had never had the cane before; the vicar never used it and until now he'd always been lucky in escaping the inspector's notice.

He held out his hand.

He was surprised how loud was the swishing sound it made as it came down and at the sudden sharp pain of it. It was a cutting kind of pain and he almost expected to see his hand sliced in two. Seeing it still intact, he smiled with relief as he made himself look up at the inspector.

'How dare you grin at me, boy?'

There was such an expression of outrage on the great red face that glared down at him, its eyes blazing, its mouth working with anger, that Dicky trembled to think how great must have been his own sin to have provoked such wrath. When the great voice boomed, 'You shall have another stroke for your impudence,' he knew he must have deserved it, but he didn't know why.

This time the cane came down with greater force, so that Dicky cried out and blood spurted up in a dotted line across his big and clumsy hand.

'Go back to your place, coward,' the inspector told him in a voice whose icy coldness was somehow more terrifying than his former hot fury.

As Dicky shuffled back to the bench, he saw that his sister, on the other side of the aisle, was sitting, white-faced, stiff and immobile. Her eyes were full of tears. He knew that he had let her down; more than anything he wanted to put it right, to comfort her but, even if he had dared, he didn't know how.

The rest of the duty of the neighbour was left to little Lily Patterson, daughter of the labourer who lived next door to the Pastes, to recite.

'To submit myself to all my governors, teachers, spiritual pastors and masters,' she piped in a monotonous sing-song. 'To order myself lowly and reverently to all my betters.'

'Stop a moment,' she was ordered and stood, terrified that she had done something wrong, but the inspector only wanted to add his word to that of the Lord.

'Now who are your betters?'

Timid hands were about to be raised, but the question was rhetorical. The inspector proceeded to answer it himself.

'I will tell you who your betters are,' he boomed. 'They are the governors of this school, its teacher, all clergymen and, as the catechism says, all those who have been set in authority over you so that you may do your duty in that state of life to which it has pleased God to call you. Above all you must do your duty to your great benefactors who have graciously bestowed this place of learning upon you. I speak of course of the Arndales of Northrop, who give employment to your parents, without which you would all starve, and education to you children, although some of you do not always appreciate it, and should be deeply ashamed of your ingratitude and ask God's pardon for it. Remember always that those who do not seek forgiveness shall burn for ever in the everlasting fires of hell.'

The children sat horrified at this prospect, so cowed by now that when he told Lily to continue and she recited, 'To hurt no body by word or deed,' it did not even enter their minds to wonder if the inspector too had once made these promises.

Three

It was Nanny who taught catechism in the nursery, it having been agreed that the governess, being French, could not be expected to inculcate Christian doctrine into her charges.

'For I, the Lord thy God, am a jealous God,' Nanny prompted now.

'You shouldn't be jealous,' Rupert interrupted. 'Papa said so yesterday morning when we were talking about a pony.'

'God's jealousy is different,' Nanny explained, unperturbed by this outburst. '*He*'s not jealous because His cousin has a new pony or because He gets less pocket money. Oh dear me, no. Jealousy here means that God won't put up with any other God being worshipped.'

There was something wrong in her logic, Rupert thought, but before he could work out what it was, his sister interrupted with, 'And what did you say adultery was? I keep forgetting.'

Nanny was used to this question; she fielded it easily.

'It means having babies without getting married.'

'Like the Virgin Mary?'

'No, not at all like that.'

'But it's not fair. I mean it's not your fault if you have a baby. You just wake up in the morning and there's the baby in the bed and Mamma says it's a lovely surprise.'

''Course it's not fair,' Rupert joined in, ever the champion of the unjustly treated. 'You find this baby in the bed and then you realize you're not married and it spoils everything because of adultery and you've broken the commandment and God's angry.'

'What happens to you if you break a commandment? What does God do about it?'

24

'If you're sorry, Laura, he forgives you.'

'And if you're not?'

'You go to hell.'

They knew about hell; the vicar warned them in nearly every sermon about the flames that awaited them, flames that burnt for ever and ever in a great fiery furnace. Once they had both held their fingers in a candle flame to see how long they could bear it, Rupert intending to time it with his new watch. But they couldn't bear it long enough to time it even for a moment. Ever since the experiment they had been able to imagine how it would feel if they had been burning all over, not just a finger, and if it had gone on for ever and ever, not just a split second. And all the time there would be devils leaping in the flames, mocking them in their agony, and their ears would be filled with the roar of fire and sounds of people screaming.

Even Rupert was silent; hell was not a thing to be trifled with.

At last Laura said, '*We*'re safe though, aren't we, Nanny? I mean, I don't think I'd steal or murder someone or covet my neighbour's ass.'

'Don't be silly,' Rupert told her. 'We don't have a neighbour with an ass. In fact we don't even have a neighbour.'

'Of course we do. Think of all the cottages on the estate. Oh, when can we go and see the Pastes' new baby?'

The Pastes' cottage was about a quarter of a mile from Northrop Hall. The children made their way slowly, going round the back of the hall to the yard so that they could look in at the stables, where old Dyer was forking straw, while his son, young Dyer, was polishing tack in the harness room next door.

'It ain't me and the 'osses you be after seeing,' old Dyer said. 'It's the motor cars, ain't it?'

'Yes, that's right,' Rupert said, while simultaneously his sister said, 'Oh, no. We like to see you too.'

She wasn't just being polite; she loved the atmosphere of the stables, the warm sweet smell of straw and horses. The aroma clung to old Dyer even when he was outside; if you were standing near enough to him you could smell horses and

25

leather, mixed with something else, sharp and acrid. She'd have happily lingered here with him, but Rupert had already gone off to the motor stables, a new block built alongside the old.

After the warmth of the stables it seemed a cold and heartless place which housed the three motor cars. Here there was no straw on the floor, just bare concrete, no smell of living creatures, just machinery and the whiff of petrol. But Rupert loved it and was already talking about motors to Slater, the coachman turned chauffeur, who was washing the running board of the Daimler.

Normally a taciturn man, Slater could talk endlessly about cars. He had a good audience in Rupert.

'The late King favoured the Mercedes,' he confided, 'painted lovely claret red, they were. I don't know what the new King fancies. Of these three, I still minds the Panhard.'

'Why? Why do you like it better than the Rolls-Royce or the Daimler?'

Slater scratched his head.

'Sentiment,' he admitted. 'It was one of the first I ever saw, to get a proper look at, like. You had to climb in from the back under the hood and sit on a bracket seat attached to the door. And there was an umbrella-holder on the outside so the gentry would have somewhere to put their umbrellas when they got into the motor, because of course they never went out without an umbrella. Very nice the holder was, made of wicker with brass fittings.'

'When did you see it, like you said, for the first time you got a proper look?'

Slater thought for a while, scratching his head again as if to stimulate the thinking process. 'It was in the old Queen's time when I was still a lad. 1896, it must have been, the year they raised the speed limit from four to twelve miles an hour. It was because of one of them motors that my father's employer had a visit from the police the year before, because he was driving at six miles an hour and didn't have a man with a red flag walking ahead.'

'Did they put him into prison?'

Slater laughed.

'Nay, he wasn't the sort to be put in prison, but he had to

show them his carriage licence and they wrote his name down in a book.'

'And just for going at six miles an hour! How fast can you go, Slater?'

'Oh, four or five times that, Master Rupert. But I go steady out of care of the passengers. And you see the roads are that bad, all lumps and potholes, you can't go too fast. There used to be lovely roads in the days of the stagecoach, but they neglected 'em something shameful when everyone took to the railways. Soon nobody will need roads, they said.'

'And now the motors need them.'

'Well, there's them as say it's only a rich man's sport and it'll never catch on, this motoring.'

'Oh, I do hope it does, catch on, I mean.'

'There's others as say that there'll soon be thousands and thousands of them and that even people who never kept a horse, will get a motor.'

'But if they haven't a horse, they won't have a stable, will they? So where'll they keep the motor?'

'Oh, they'll find a way. Mind you, I don't know which way to think, but that's what some of the motor servants are saying, as I've talked to. But I say 'ow can any but the rich afford it what with the price they are and tyres costing twenty-four pounds a pair and always bursting?'

'Yes, that's the problem,' Rupert agreed, in his father's voice.

'But when you think of it, folks said the same about bicycles.'

'Bicycles?'

'Oh, I remember the first one coming down the hill in the village and how we all trembled, so afeard he'd fall off. A gentleman it was and how he kept up and balanced on that great wheel at the front and the tiny one at the back, we couldn't make out. We never thought it would catch on, just a toy for gentlefolk everyone said. And whenever one passed by, us boys would stare and the lassies would shriek and jump out of the way.'

'Girls do, rather,' Rupert agreed.

'That's not true, I never shriek,' Laura burst in. 'You

27

shouldn't say I shriek, it's lying and slandering to say I shriek.'

'You're shrieking now.'

'No, I'm not.'

'Oh, do be quiet. I'm talking to Slater.'

'That's very rude. I shall go and see the baby.'

She stalked off, but not too fast, wanting him to catch up later.

'Go on, Slater, about the bicycles.'

'Well, I was just saying like, as 'ow we thought they'd never catch on and now look at 'em all. You and all your brothers and sisters, all with your bicycles and quite a few of the estate workers too. Bicycles used to be very 'eavy and hexpensive you see, but now they're cheap enough. Even people in Littleton village 'ave them, men go to work on 'em and women go into market on 'em. Yes, even in the village.'

He looked down on people in Littleton village. They were worse paid and worse housed than the estate workers; rougher folk they were who didn't mind their manners.

'But now I think you'd better be following your sister, Master Rupert.'

Rupert sighed, touched the gleaming lamp of the Daimler in a little gesture of farewell, as he might have stroked a horse, and set off after Laura.

The Pastes' cottage was one of a pair, reached by going through a shared gate and walking down a brick path past the door and windows of the one next door. The children kept their eyes down as they walked past, Nanny having told them that it is very rude to look in other people's windows.

The door of the Pastes' house was wide open so they couldn't help seeing straight into the living room, as they stood on the doorstep and knocked. A pot was boiling on the fire and there was a smell of cabbage and what could be bacon. Through the open door at the back they could see Mrs Paste in the kitchen, possing clothes.

She looked up from the tub when she heard them, wiped her hands on her apron and came to the door. She was a tall, handsome woman, who did not drop a little curtsey at the sight of them as some of the cottagers did.

'How are you, Mrs Paste?' Laura enquired, in her best grown-up manner. 'And please may we see the baby?' she asked, forgetting to wait for a reply.

'He's in the baby carriage out the back with our Edith,' she told them. 'She's going to push him about for a bit. You can go along with her if you want.'

They had never seen such a tiny baby before and found him an awesome sight. His little face was wrinkled like a prune and his miniature hands spread out like starfish. His eyes were open but didn't seem to look straight at you, as if they were too loosely moored in his head, reminding Laura of a china doll she had whose eyes kept swivelling about because the wires that secured them must have come loose.

Edith, standing by the wicker baby carriage, seemed strangely unaffected by this miniature marvel.

'You can hold him if you like,' she said casually to Laura, 'but he'll likely wet you.'

Laura declined the offer, not out of fear of getting wet but because she was terrified of hurting this fragile assemblage of flesh which already had a somewhat bruised look. Or she might drop him, for he didn't seem very good at keeping still; he kept jerking his arms about in convulsive little movements, groping blindly in front of him as if clutching at invisible objects or weaving complicated patterns in the air, his mouth working and twisting like an old man trying to find his words.

'Our meyther doesn't like babies tightly swaddled,' Edith said as they pushed the baby carriage around the side of the house, bumped their way up the brick path and set off along the dusty road. 'She says it's best for them to be free to develop their muscles.'

Laura couldn't see that he had any muscles to develop, but she bowed to Edith's superior wisdom, for since she had so many brothers and sisters she must know a lot about babies.

They walked aimlessly along the dusty roads and down footpaths which led across fields and into little copses. Rupert was soon bored with talk of babies and ran ahead.

'Our Dicky'll be coming along this way soon,' Edith said

as they came back to the road towards their house. 'He's been working in the fields all day.'

'Didn't he have to go to school?'

Edith shrugged.

'It's potato picking week,' she said. 'So the lads go off. He's better working than at school. He's ever so good at making things, is our Dicky, and grand with animals. He's too soft with them, Feyther says, but he'll learn.'

Rupert held open the gate for her so she could push the baby carriage through. As they entered the little wood they heard a sound, a kind of high-pitched scream. They looked at each other.

'Sounds like a rabbit,' Edith said and began to run forward, the baby bouncing up and down, Laura panting to keep up with them.

Round the corner the trees gave way to a grassy patch in which they saw Dicky, bending down, trying to release a rabbit from a snare. It was a simple loop of wire attached to a stick pushed into the ground. The rabbit was meant to run into it and be strangled as the wire tightened round its neck, but this was a baby one which must have been small enough to run through the loop only to be caught by its leg. It was hurling itself frantically backwards and forwards trying to free itself. The screams which tore out of it seemed too loud for its tiny body; they mingled with Dicky's sobs of pity and frustration.

'Hold still, will you, oh please hold still,' he was saying as he tried to get a grip on it as it flung itself from one side to the other. 'You'll only make the wire tighter.'

Laura stared in horror. It was Rupert who ran to help. 'You hold it, Dicky, while I pull the stake out of the ground.'

Between them they managed it and Dicky was holding the terrified animal, the wire and stake still attached to its leg, the wire cutting deeply into its flesh.

'Can't let it go like this, got to get the wire off,' Dicky said.

He always spoke slowly, gruffly, and now more so than usual.

'We need something to prise it off,' Rupert told him. 'Something to get between his leg and the wire.'

30

They tried pieces of stick but they broke, they tried the tip of a penknife but it was too thick.

'We need something thin enough to slide between—'

'Slide? I've got a hairslide,' Laura offered, snatching it out of her unruly hair.

Very gently, holding the frightened little animal in his big red hands, Dicky eased the end of the hairslide under the wire, pressing it into the bloodstained fur. The rabbit, which had been quiet as it lay there trembling, screamed again. But the wire was gradually pulled up and away. Very carefully, very smoothly Dicky slackened the wire until he could lift it off and the stake with it.

'Them's cruel things,' he said, throwing it down in disgust and he made off with the rabbit across the field.

'He knows where there's a warren up there,' Edith told them. 'He'll likely set it down by one of the burrows. I don't know what our feyther would say if he knew,' she went on as they pushed their way back towards the road. 'He hates rabbits, like all gardeners do. He's too soft-hearted is our Dicky. If it hadn't been for him, I'd have taken it home to Meyther to put in the pot.'

Four

'Do we have to go to Northrop, William?' Selina asked. 'It's so incredibly tedious.'

Her husband smiled down at her; part of him was always puzzled that his wife didn't enjoy the annual holiday in the country. It was so beautiful, this part of Gloucestershire where he had spent his boyhood. He didn't envy Charles for inheriting the estate – he himself would never have wanted to run it – but still he loved the place. Of course, it was different for Selina, he told himself. She hadn't been brought up in Northrop, didn't feel at home there even after all these years. So, puzzling though her attitude sometimes seemed, he knew it behoved him to show all the tolerance and understanding that she deserved.

'You know we have to go, my darling,' he told her, in the indulgent voice of one humouring a beloved if wayward child. 'Mamma expects it.'

He stood looking down at her as she lay nested among her pillows, her long hair framing a face whose beauty still astonished him. Her features were so flawless, so classically symmetrical, that worship seemed the only possible reaction to them.

'We need only stay two weeks,' he conceded. 'I'll find a reason.'

She rewarded him with a smile, a slow smile that warmed those languid, rather heavy-lidded brown eyes and opened the lips to show the very even, white teeth, so that his heart stirred and he longed not to be standing here dressed for the city, but to be down there with her among the pillows.

'Careful!' she warned as he made a sudden movement to kiss her. 'Mind the tray.'

He moved her breakfast tray on to a table, sat down on the bed and took her in his arms.

'You must go,' she said. 'You'll be late.'

'What are you going to do today?' he asked, delaying departure.

She stretched and yawned, moving slightly away from him.

'I'm going to a fitting with Madame Gagneux, then having lunch with Fiona. And we thought we'd go down to the law courts. I know you think it's naughty of us, darling, but we do so enjoy listening to a good divorce case.'

'So long as it doesn't put ideas into your head.'

'Darling, as if anything could! That was a horrid thing to say.'

'There, I take it back,' he told her, kissing her while taking in his breath, so that his words, with her lips, were drawn into his mouth.

'Go to work, wicked man,' she ordered.

Reluctantly he got off the bed.

'I shan't have time to see the children this morning,' he said, glancing at his watch. 'Tom won't mind but tell Celia that I'm sorry.'

'I expect she'll be out with Nanny by the time I'm up,' she told him.

'Well, tell her at teatime.'

'Oh, I shan't see the children then. I'll be in such a rush to change. You haven't forgotten about dinner and the opera?'

'Of course not. I shall be home by six, ready to escort my beautiful wife.'

She rewarded him again with that wondrous smile and he stood in the doorway gazing back at her and thinking that, but for the lack of a blue robe and the trace of a halo behind her head, she was the image of a Raphael Madonna.

As far as the children were concerned the best thing about the holiday in Northrop in October was getting there.

'Shall we have a coach on the train all to ourselves again, Papa?' Tom asked the day before they left.

It was one of the rare occasions on which they were all

together in the drawing room and Tom wanted to make the most of it to get in as many questions as possible.

'Of course we shall. So long as you buy ten tickets you have a coach to yourself.'

'Will it be in two rooms, with a lavatory in between like last time?' Celia joined in. More than anything else she had been bedazzled by the travelling lavatory.

'Just the same as last time,' he assured her.

'Oh, *everything* will be just the same as last time,' his wife put in and sighed deeply.

'Don't you want to go, Mamma?'

'Of course your mamma wants to go,' William pre-empted, putting his arm around his wife and murmuring in her ear, '*Pas devant*, darling, I beg you.'

'Run along, both of you,' she said to her children. 'Nanny will be waiting.'

'No, she won't,' Tom told her. 'She said we could have an hour with you.'

'Don't contradict your mother, Tom. Mamma and I are going out this evening, so we must change now.'

'Ooh, will you wear the new hobble dress?'

'Of course, darling,' her mother told her giving her a little kiss, for she was always delighted with anyone who showed an interest in her clothes. 'And from now on all my clothes will be hobbled.'

'Even your drawers and stays?'

'That will do, Tom,' his father told him severely, but Selina only laughed and, kissing her son, told him to be off upstairs.

'I think he needs more disciplining,' William said, when the children had left.

'Oh, he's all right, darling. Besides, discipline is Nanny's job. That's what we pay her for.'

'I hope he doesn't come out with such remarks at Northrop. I think you should rebuke him when he speaks to you like that.'

She gave a little pout.

'Don't be angry, William. I truly do think it's Nanny's job. I mean do you really want me to get all cross and wrinkled from behaving like a governess?'

34

She pulled a scowling face, wrinkling the smooth white brow and pulling down the luscious lips he loved to kiss. She was a good actress and for a moment did manage to give to her lovely face a touch of the virago.

'Don't, please don't,' he said, laughing and drawing her to him. 'Anything rather than that.'

'I don't think Mamma does want to go,' Tom whispered to his sister the next day as they sat on the train, the four of them in the front room of the coach, the servants and luggage at the back.

'No, you could tell by the way Papa spoke.'

'Silly, really. Everyone knows that *pas devant* is meant for servants, not children.'

Their mother was sitting looking very bored, a neglected novel in one gloved hand as she stared out of the window.

The children weren't bored. They loved to watch the countryside rush by, were thrilled when the train noisily entered a tunnel and Papa jumped up to close the windows, too late because the smoke had already blown in and Nanny had to come round to wipe the soot off their faces. Their mother pulled down the veil of her fashionable hat but all the same there were little black specks on her face.

It all made a wonderful change from life in a London square. Even the maids looked different, hardly recognizable without their caps on their heads as they served the picnic lunch. And to dine as you moved so fast through the landscape with little houses and trees and streams flashing past was like being allowed to eat in a cinematograph show. Once some children looked up from picking late blackberries in a hedge and waved at the train. They wanted to wave back but Nanny said it was vulgar.

But on the whole, Nanny was in a good mood as she nearly always was; they liked her casual ways, for she was not a bit like some of their friends' nannies who were very strict and never smiled. Nanny Tubmorton came from Scotland, laughed a lot and spoke differently from the undernursemaid who came from Yorkshire and the housemaid who came from London – not from their part of London but from the bit called cockney.

The French governess spoke differently again. And to have the four of them so close together talking their different tongues was an added excitement. They would have been quite happy to have a journey twice as long.

The train stopped especially for them at the little halt near Northrop. Three motor cars awaited them, their uncle driving one, Slater another and somebody they didn't know the third. Uncle drove off first with their mother and Nanny, they followed with their father in Slater's car. The maids came in the third car and their man Phipps stayed with the luggage at the station to be collected later.

It was nearly dark as they drove towards the hall, the dust rising from the road so that it seemed darker still.

'It's not dusty like this in London when we drive in our motor,' Celia said.

'Don't grumble.'

'I'm not grumbling, Tom, I'm just saying.'

'The reason it's not so dusty in London is that the roads are macadamized,' their father explained. 'Something will have to be done about these roads, eh Slater?'

'Yes, sir.'

Their father made a few other attempts to talk to Slater but the chauffeur's replies remained monosyllabic either out of natural taciturnity or fear of losing concentration, for the roads were not only blindingly dusty but also winding and rutted. So they made their way in silence until at last they turned up the drive, through the lodge gates and up to the hall.

Nanny Stone did not approve of Nanny Tubmorton but did her duty in giving her the right kind of courteous welcome as good manners required. Lady Arndale did not approve of her daughter-in-law, but offered her cheek to be kissed as nobility obliged. The young cousins all liked each other very much and were soon quarrelling happily.

They had their supper together and then Nanny Tubmorton took her two charges away to the visitors' wing, Rupert was sent off to his room and Laura, having said her prayers, lay wideawake with the excitement of it all until Nanny

36

Stone came up and performed her nightly ritual of veiled undressing.

Meanwhile the adults dined together and while the two brothers remained at the table for a glass of port – Lady Arndale not approving of their having more than one glass – the ladies withdrew to the drawing room.

Installed in her chair by the fire, Lady Arndale began her habitual cross-examination. 'And when I say cross-examination,' Selina reported to her husband later, 'I really mean examine crossly.'

'Come over here, my dear,' Lady Arndale began, indicating a chair. Selina moved across obediently, but without any intention of being intimidated.

'Tell me your news,' Lady Arndale requested. 'What arrangements are you making for my grandchildren's education?'

'Tom and Celia?' Selina asked, as if uncertain if they were Lady Arndale's grandchildren or not.

'Of course,' Lady Arndale told her, simultaneously biting back irritation at the girl's impertinence and giving thanks that she was merely the wife of the younger son.

'Well, we haven't really made up our minds yet. There are some very good day schools in London now, you know.'

She spoke only to annoy; she and William had already decided which public school Tom should go to, despite his protests, when he left his preparatory school. She certainly couldn't do with having him at home.

'*Day school?* For Thomas?'

'Yes, that *is* what I said,' Selina replied coolly, for all the world as if she thought Lady Arndale's hearing equipment might be in question.

'But one hears such terrible tales. You have no control about the class of boy Thomas might meet there. Indeed make friends of. I am told rich Jews now send their sons to such places.'

Selina shrugged her beautiful white shoulders in a gesture which could only be construed as one of indifference.

'Disraeli was a Jew,' she said.

'There are different rules for politicians,' Lady Arndale snapped. 'I shall discuss the matter with William in the morning. Tonight I am tired and shall bid you all goodnight. Be so kind as to ring for Patchet.'

And I shall tell William that you misunderstood everything I said, Selina thought as she watched Elspeth and Patchet escort her mother-in-law out of the room.

Five

I t was Lady Arndale's custom after lunch on Sunday to show all visitors round the estate. So, in a chill, damp wind, they set off, her ladyship leading the way in her wheelchair, well wrapped up in rugs, as the other women enviously observed as they followed behind her in their fashionable but less than windproof coats, their stride restricted by the tight skirts beneath.

The children followed their elders and the London servants brought up the rear, bemused but obedient to the ways of this strange household.

'We shall go first to see the horses and then to the motor stables,' Lady Arndale explained.

'Oh, good. Can we look at the cars in the garage, Grandmama?' Tom asked.

'Not *garage*, Tom, *motor stable*. Garage is a vulgar term imported from France.'

'Oh, is it? We always say . . . what's the matter, Papa?'

'If we ask Slater he might let you crank up the engine,' their uncle put in.

'No, Charles. Not on Sunday. Sunday is the servants' day of rest, apart from essential cooking and cleaning.'

'She means emptying the chamber pots,' Rupert said and the children giggled.

Elspeth heard and frowned. Selina heard and laughed.

After the stables they toured the gardens, then walked down to the lake. With sinking heart they all realized that they were expected to walk around the perimeter, a distance that would add at least another mile to their tour of inspection. By the time they were halfway round, the rain was falling in a steady, businesslike way. Lady Arndale kept dry under the hood of her chariot, the others did the best they could with flimsy shawls, as they shivered and dreamed of fires and hot-water jugs.

By the time they got back to the house they were all, except Lady Arndale, cold and wet. The ladies went upstairs to hand their mud-stained skirts to their maids for restoration, and changed into teagowns. The nannies took charge of the children and the adults assembled for tea in the drawing room, where later the children were all allowed to join them and were treated to lemonade and biscuits.

'Next week,' Lady Arndale told her two sons and their wives, who were seated around her chair, 'there will be the bonfire party in the far paddock. You remember I pointed out to you the pile of timber the men are preparing? All the estate families will come, of course.'

'It used to be an old custom, here, the burning of the guy,' William told Selina. 'I used to love it when I was a boy, but it's been dropped in the last few years.'

'We stopped when the Queen died,' his mother explained. 'I thought any kind of celebration was inappropriate after such a tragic loss.'

'So now we are reviving it,' Charles said. 'Thomson will be in charge of everything, so you can be sure the children will be safe. There will be fireworks too, of course.'

'Oh, the children will love that,' William exclaimed. 'Ours have never been out for Guy Fawkes night, have they, Selina?'

His wife shook her head.

'I don't know if it will be very tactful to ask our Roman Catholic governess to celebrate the burning of her co-religionist,' she said.

'Nonsense,' Lady Arndale told her, rightly sensing that her daughter-in-law didn't care at all about the feelings of the governess and was speaking solely to annoy.

Elspeth, not sensing it, said, 'Perhaps it would be a kindness to find some other amusement for her that evening?'

How kind she is, Charles thought and supported her with: 'Well, you know, Mamma, I do sometimes think it is time to let bygones be bygones as far as the Roman Catholics are concerned.'

'My father, your grandfather,' Lady Arndale proclaimed,

'always said that he would never forgive Sir Robert Peel for giving the vote to Roman Catholics. He said it would result in the decline of the nation and Empire.'

'And did it?' Selina asked innocently.

Charles glanced at her; a straightforward man, he was always puzzled by his sister-in-law and now found himself wondering how anyone who looked so wise and good could say such a thing.

'People nowadays just burn a guy, Selina,' he said. 'I don't think that much religious feeling attaches to it any more. I remember during the Boer war how they burnt effigies of Kruger.'

'Yes,' Selina agreed, 'and some people are talking of burning an effigy of the Kaiser this year.'

'Burn the Kaiser?' Lady Arndale exclaimed. 'Burn the Queen's grandson?'

Selina laughed.

'I don't think Queen Mary has any grandchildren,' she said.

'I refer of course to Queen Victoria,' Lady Arndale told her sharply, 'who was always on the best of terms with the Germans. She would not at all have approved of this modern alliance with the French.'

'Selina dear, shall we go and see how the children are managing?' intercepted Elspeth, drawing her sister-in-law aside and leading her towards the table where the children were having their lemonade and biscuits.

'We have to be a little careful what we say to Mamma on certain topics,' she confided. 'She didn't really approve of King Edward, though, of course, she was always totally loyal to him,' she added hastily. 'It was just that she could not approve of some of his ways.'

'Oh, dear, did he have *ways*?' Selina asked, all wide-eyed innocence.

'Well, you know, he did have a reputation for consorting with unsuitable women. And Mamma didn't like the way he went abroad so much.'

'Is she against travel for everyone, or just for royalty?'

'Well, there was a story that somewhere abroad,' she said,

41

dropping her voice to a whisper, which made Laura, who was standing nearby and was always sensitive to the sound of a whispering adult, stand very still, holding her drink in mid-air, as she listened, 'that a woman danced naked in front of the king.'

'Oh, that's quite untrue,' Selina told her confidently. 'I know for a fact that she was wearing two oyster shells and a five franc piece.'

The air was sharp and clear on bonfire night. The stars shone brilliantly, hard splinters of light in the deep blackness of the sky.

'It's a shame Teddy and Diana aren't here to enjoy it,' Elspeth remarked as she walked with Selina towards the paddock. 'But of course Teddy can't ask for leave off school when his examinations are so near and Diana won't be home before Christmas.'

'Oh, education is such a bother, isn't it?' Selina agreed. 'It does seem to get in the way of so much pleasure for the young nowadays.'

'Oh, I didn't mean that,' Elspeth assured her. 'Of course Teddy must keep at his work.'

'I don't think we were ever so solemn about it.'

'Well, of course it's different for girls.'

'I don't think my brother let it bother him too much. But admittedly he was rather a *scamp*,' Selina said, somehow contriving to make it sound like a word of praise.

'I worry a little about Diana,' Elspeth confided. 'I hope she won't find England too, well, *ordinary* after France.'

Selina stopped and turned to her.

'I've been thinking about her recently,' she told her sister-in-law. 'I wonder if she would like to come and stay with us for a while? I'd simply adore to have her, and I could show her around, take her to a few parties and theatres, you know the kind of thing.'

The idea of having the companionship of a young girl had only just occurred to her. It would be fun and an excuse to get about even more than she usually did. She warmed to the idea.

42

'Do say yes,' she urged, as Elspeth hesitated.

'Well, it's very kind. It's just that I'm not sure what Mamma and Charles would think of the idea.'

She couldn't really say that they might not consider her aunt Selina as the most suitable influence on a young and impressionable girl like Diana.

'Frightened of the evil influence of London?' Selina asked, laughing. 'Even though you let her go to France?'

'Ah, but it was rather different. The institution is well known to Mademoiselle and supervision is very strict.'

'You mean I'm a less reliable institution?' Selina asked, laughing but managing at the same time to put a little gentle reproof into the remark.

'Oh, of course not. Forgive me, I certainly meant nothing of the kind.'

'Good. Well, let's regard it as settled. You know,' she went on a little plaintively, 'you are so good at inviting us here and I do sometimes feel under an obligation, because you visit us so rarely.'

Again Elspeth felt apologetic, as she was meant to do.

'I'll speak to Charles tonight,' she said, taking her sister-in-law's arm. 'For myself, I think it's a lovely idea. Goodness, look how far ahead the children are.'

Rupert had run ahead to the bonfire. Nanny and Laura had reached the gap in the hedge by the croft.

'Nanny,' Laura was saying, 'how big is a five franc piece?'

'Oh, about so big, I should think,' Nanny said, making a circle with the thumb and first finger of her gloved right hand, as she wondered whatever had made the child ask such a strange question.

The estate children had brought candles in jam jars or encased in turnips after their mothers had scooped out the insides and cooked them for dinner. They were shadowy figures, indistinguishable from the gentry and the indoor servants, as they came and went in the firelight, sometimes brightly lit as the fire blazed up, then suddenly invisible as they backed away into the night, for the heat from the great pile was intense; old railway sleepers burned there, cut-offs from the carpenter's shop, woodwormy furniture, anything combustible had been heaped up for the past two weeks and now made this great blazing mountain in the paddock.

The fire seemed to draw everyone together; it was hard to make out workers from employers, staff from masters, under servants from upper servants as figures came and went, in and out of the flickering shadows. Fathers hoisted little children up on to their shoulders, mothers clutched older children by the hand, warning them not to get too close.

And on top of the bonfire was perched a figure so lifelike that it was hard to believe he was stuffed with straw as he sat up there in his shirt and trousers, shoes on his feet, flaxen hair escaping from under his hat. As the flames reached him, a cheer went up from the family at the hall, in which the estate children joined, but their mothers were heard to say, 'It's a sin and a shame to waste good clothes like that.'

Then Thomson and some of his men, who had been busy with stands and timbers, roped away from the rest, began their amazing display. Rockets blazed up far into the night sky, exploding into myriad crimson and gold stars, putting the Milky Way to shame. A great gasp of amazement went up from children and adults alike. Rocket after rocket soared up into the air, which was filled with cracks and bangs and an unaccustomed sulphurous smell.

It stopped suddenly and instead, lower down, Catherine wheels, which had been pinned to a wooden frame, began to whirl round, first one, then another and another. Silently they whirred, scattering their stars into the night air. Then again the rockets went up so that both high and low there were explosions of colour, stars which mounted and mounted and then gracefully cascaded down in their showers of gold and orange and red, diminishing, dying, leaving only their strange acrid smell.

Adults marvelled, but to the estate children it was something beyond belief. They had never seen anything so beautiful and knew they would never see its like again. They pointed out each marvel of sound and colour to anyone who would listen, tugging at each other in case somebody missed a moment of this wonder. In the excitement and the darkness, nobody noticed that Dicky Paste had vanished.

44

Although they had told him what was to happen that night, he had not imagined anything like this. He had not understood that there could be such a blazing, fiery furnace, had thought it would be an outdoor version of the fire in the grate at home. This was more like the hellfire of the sermons. And the figures drifting about, some of the men with pitchforks stirring the blazing timbers, looked like devils when the flames turned them red. And that lost soul on the top burning and burning, twisting in agony.

He moved away, tried to hide from it behind the crowds. Then the explosions started: at the first great bang he screamed with terror but the sound was lost in the applause of the others. As explosion followed explosion and the sky was filled with what seemed unnatural colours and strange fumes, panic seized him and he began to run, he didn't know where so long as it was away from this terrible thing. He ran until he crashed into a hedge where he lay down in the ditch, curling up so that he could cover his head in his arms, his eyes tight shut, moaning as he rocked himself. There at last he fell asleep and wasn't found until his frantic parents stumbled over him in the morning.

Six

Activity suited Selina; she could shop all day, dance all night and never feel tired. But boredom exhausted her. By the end of her stay in Northrop she was almost too weary to get out of bed.

'At least in November we don't have to play croquet,' she remarked to William as they returned home from church on their last Sunday and prepared to go down to luncheon.

Lady Arndale sat at one end of the table, Charles at the other, the two wives on one side with the vicar, William and the vicar's wife on the other. These Sunday invitations were a source of great satisfaction to the vicar and of terror to his wife, who nibbled at her food like a frightened rabbit and spoke scarcely a word.

Selina almost fell asleep as the family talked of hunting, which she loathed, and estate matters which she didn't understand.

Somebody had said something to her about horses, which she hadn't heard since she was miles away planning wonderful outings next week in London.

'Horses?' she repeated. 'Well, there's not much point in having them now that we have motor cars, is there?'

After the stunned silence which followed, William diverted the conversation by asking his mother about the school.

'Such a shame if it has to close,' he said. 'It's such a pretty little building.'

'It isn't the prettiness of the building which is important,' she told him, 'but what goes on within its walls.'

'If it is closed,' the vicar said, 'might I suggest, Your Ladyship, that we shall need to think about who will teach the children their catechism? Of course I can examine them from time to time, but the learning must be a daily task.'

'In our household it is their mother and their nanny's duty,' Charles said.

'Ah, but I am not speaking of households such as yours, alas.'

'Perhaps I might try to er . . .,' the vicar's wife began but her voice trailed off. She was so terrified of Lady Arndale that she could never get out a complete sentence in her presence.

'How do you arrange things in London?' Lady Arndale enquired, ignoring her and looking first at her younger son and then at his wife.

Selina shrugged.

'Oh, I leave it to Nanny,' she said. Then she brightened: 'But I have been myself to one or two or those revivalist meetings. You know, the Americans who come over? They are quite fashionable now and really I found them quite amusing.'

'Amusing?'

'Well, lively, you know.'

'You're surely not saying, Selina,' her mother-in-law put in, outraged, 'that you would take religious instruction from a band of rebellious colonialists?'

Remembering that Lady Arndale had strong feelings about Americans, Selina placated her with, 'Well, there are one or two British ones as well, you know. Unfortunately the best one was killed by a fellow Christian who threw a spanner at him. Or it may have been a chisel.'

'He committed murder?'

'He didn't intend to. He just intended a fraternal reprimand, you see.'

'Murder is murder, Selina.'

'Ah, but surely it's the intention that counts.'

They were distracted by the arrival of pudding.

'I expect you have abundant plans for when you return home,' the vicar said to Selina, hovering over her as she reclined on a chaise longue. She saw that he was about to launch into one of his long, rambling, boring monologues and wondered if she could stay awake. 'Delightful though it has been to see you here,' he was saying, 'especially in church, and no doubt a great joy to Lady Arndale –' he genuflected slightly towards the great lady as he spoke her name – 'and her family to have you staying with them, no doubt you will have much to do on your return. There is much for the young to see and learn in London, though I am afraid I am not myself well acquainted with the great metropolis.'

'Oh, there's plenty for children to do here,' Elspeth put in, coming up to offer bonbons because the servants were freed now from duty. 'In many ways there is more for them to do in the country.'

'Oh, of course. I did not in any way intend to suggest any inferiority here in Northrop,' the vicar said, horrified that she should have thought such a thing possible. 'Far from it, dear Mrs Arndale. What possibly could surpass life at Northrop Hall?'

'What was that about Northrop Hall, Charles?' Lady Arndale demanded of her son. 'What are they discussing? People mutter so nowadays one cannot make them out.'

'Mamma would like to know what you are discussing,' her elder son called dutifully to the others.

'We are talking of town and country, Mamma,' Elspeth explained, raising her voice.

Lady Arndale tossed her head and made a sound which in a lesser mortal might have been described as a snort.

'Your father and I always regarded towns as places where people less fortunate than ourselves had to go to earn their living.'

'Oh, come, Mamma,' William cajoled. 'There are plenty of good things in London, different from country pleasures, but equally good. Take theatres, for example—'

'Which reminds me, darling,' Selina interrupted, 'that we owe Tom a treat. We were taking him to see the *Yeomen of the Guard*,' she explained to the others, 'at the Savoy Theatre on the night of his birthday in May, but of course it was cancelled. I thought it was really mean to close the theatres just because the King had died.'

'*Just because the King had died*,' Lady Arndale repeated, outraged. 'This is treason.'

48

'Oh, no, I was sorry he'd died, of course,' Selina told her. 'I just wish he hadn't done it on my son's birthday.'

'If you will all excuse me, I shall go to my rest,' her mother-in-law said. 'Please be so good as to call Patchet.'

After she had left them and the vicar and his trembling wife had taken their leave, the rest of them sat on, none of them wanting to be the first to break up the remains of the family party, but all wanting to be elsewhere, Edward mindful of his promise to take Rupert out on the lake despite the weather, Elspeth feeling guilty because she hadn't heard Laura say her catechism for some time, Selina and William just wanting to go to bed.

'You will be sure to come to Mamma's great celebration, won't you?' Charles remarked. 'I know it's a long way off but we do want to have all the family.'

'Her seventy-fifth birthday you mean?'

'More than that. She wants to mark the seventy-fifth anniversary of Queen Victoria's accession, which of course is on the same day, as you know. She insists that that is what should be celebrated.'

'Even though she's dead?' Selina asked, and shivered.

'Especially since she's dead,' William told her drily.

'What are you going to do?'

'Oh, plans are still rather vague. There is to be a reception in the conservatory and then luncheon. If the weather is fine we shall be outside. You know how Mamma loves to show people the grounds. I think she might like to lead a procession round the lake. Of course it partly depends on how well she is.'

Selina, who couldn't imagine that her mother-in-law would be in anything except her usual rude health and anyway thought that, even if she wasn't, it didn't take much energy to be pushed in a wheelchair while everybody else had to walk, made no comment on this fact, but instead said, 'Of course Diana will be home by then, won't she, so she'll be able to join in.'

'Oh yes, and Teddy too, since it's such a special occasion.'

'Have you had a chance to talk to Charles yet about Diana coming to stay?'

Hearing his name being spoken, Charles came over to them.

'What's this about me?' he asked, smiling at his wife.

'Do you remember I told you that Selina has most kindly invited Diana to stay when she gets back?'

Charles did remember, of course. He also remembered, as she did, that neither of them had been very enthusiastic about the idea.

'You see,' Selina went on, 'she can come out in London; we can take her about in a way which I know you would find difficult.'

This argument appealed to Elspeth who, like many of the country gentry, found the problem of a daughter coming out into society an irksome business. If they had a place in London themselves, of course, it would be different, but neither of them wanted that.

Seeing that she was wavering, Selina concentrated on Charles.

'I think it really is a very important part of her education,' she said. 'Young ladies too must be equipped to live in the twentieth century. And after all you have let her go abroad which is much more hazardous than London, surely.'

'Oh no, she has been scrupulously cared for in the Anglican convent. We would never have let her go if the establishment had not been very well known to our previous mademoiselle.'

'I assure you, Charles, that she will be equally well cared for, chaperoned, indeed *cherished* in your brother's home.'

She spoke solemnly, her Madonna-like face looking up at him with such an air of kindly concern that he wondered why he had been so hesitant.

'It's most kind of you,' he agreed. 'Elspeth will be writing to her this evening, won't you, darling, so you can mention it?'

'And I shall write her a little note of my own, assuring her of my welcome,' Selina said. 'I always think these things should be properly done,' she added with reassuring emphasis, as if to show that propriety was for her an overriding consideration.

Seven

'It's going to be wonderful,' Selina assured her niece. 'We shall go everywhere, see everything. I can't tell you how much I'm looking forward to being your chaperone.'

She meant it. She was easily bored, constantly on the lookout for diversion and now here was this young creature to be formed, to be like the younger sister she had never had. She would transform her from child to woman. The idea excited her, she would really surprise the family at Northrop with what she would make of their elder daughter. 'But first,' she went on, 'we must do something about your clothes.'

They were in Selina's boudoir, a pretty little room with many flounces, mirrors and bowls of flowers. She was lying back on her chaise longue, one arm behind her, encircling her head, her fingers playing with her hair. Her lovely face had an appraising look as she observed her niece.

The girl sitting opposite to her still wore her hair down her back, under the tam-o'-shanter. That, and the plain pleated skirt and rather shapeless jacket, made her seem much less than her seventeen years.

'You look as if you've come straight from the schoolroom,' she said, but she spoke kindly.

'I *have* come straight from the schoolroom,' Diana told her.

Selina laughed.

'But soon you will be eighteen and the time has come to put your hair up and your skirts down,' she told her, getting up from the chaise longue. 'So if you've finished your tea let's go and look at the rest of your wardrobe. The maid will have unpacked by now.'

Diana followed her along the corridor, past the head of the

51

stairs, up the half landing and along to her own room on the other corridor. The house was not as large as Northrop Hall but it seemed more spacious, with its well-proportioned, high-ceilinged rooms, wide corridors and beautiful grand staircase. Most of the ground floor was taken up with the ballroom, where the dance in her honour would soon be held.

The house was less homely than Northrop Hall, she thought, but certainly more modern. As well as the elegant staircase with the curved balustrade which had been constructed in the days when room had to be made for the ladies' hooped skirts, there was a lift which could take you up from the basement to the second floor, which Diana knew she would never dare use on her own.

There was a proper bathroom at the end of each corridor and Uncle William was thinking of putting in a system of pipes so that the water could come out of taps instead of being carried up by the servants.

Her bedroom, like her aunt's boudoir, was a very feminine room, with flounces round the washstand, a thick carpet on the floor and pictures on the walls of gardens with pretty ladies, whereas her room at home had linoleum on the floor and the pictures were of dogs and horses.

The maid had unpacked the clothes and put them all away, but Selina looked them over with a merciless eye: the little sailor suits, the pinafores, the pleated skirts, the childish yoked frocks with sashes.

'What's this?' she asked, holding up a long white shiftlike garment. 'Surely not a nightgown?'

'Oh, it shouldn't have been packed,' Diana told her. 'It's the shift we had to wear at the convent when we had a bath.'

'You wore it *in* the bath?'

'Yes.'

'Whatever for?'

'So we wouldn't see our bodies.'

Selina looked at her with disbelief, then began to laugh. She had a surprisingly deep, throaty laugh.

'Why ever shouldn't you see your own body?' she asked, sitting down and waving to Diana to do the same. 'I'm sure you have a very nice little body.'

'The nuns said it would give us unholy thoughts.'

'What else did they tell you?'

'Oh, lots of things. And of course we studied French every day and—'

'No, I meant about unholy thoughts.'

'Oh well, they said we shouldn't think too much about clothes and appearance because it might tempt men to sin and then it would be all our fault.'

'Very convenient for the men,' Selina said drily. 'And what else?'

'Not much else. Well, we had to keep our eyes down and be demure. And not have our shoes too highly polished.'

'Your shoes? I'd have thought nuns would want you to have clean shoes.'

'Clean, yes. But they said that if your shoes were highly polished a man might look into them and see the reflection of well, you know, like a looking glass.'

Again the throaty laugh.

'Diana, darling, have you ever tried to look at yourself in a boot instead of a looking glass?'

'No, and I don't think you'd see much, but they were just warning us that if it did happen and the man had sinful thoughts it would be our fault for wearing shiny shoes.'

'I think,' Selina told her, 'that you have much to unlearn as well as much to learn, my dear.'

She lay back in her chair and took up the same pose as before, her slender white arm embracing her head, her fingers occasionally entwining a lock of hair.

'We shall start with a visit to my dressmaker, Madame Gagneux,' she said. 'Your mamma did tell me that she and your papa are quite agreeable to that. They know that you will do better here than at home.'

Diana nodded.

'Then I have lots of things planned for the evenings,' her aunt went on, 'and during the day there is so much to do in London. We shall go to the law courts, of course. Oh, if only you'd been here for the Crippen trial two years ago! I'm afraid there'll be nothing as exciting as that. I suppose you read all about it in the papers, but it's not quite the same as actually being there in court.'

'Oh, no, I didn't read anything. Mamma doesn't allow us to read newspapers in case we see anything unsuitable, so I haven't heard of it.'

'Haven't heard of it?' Selina repeated.

She could hardly believe it. She knew her own children had followed it avidly. On the other hand it was a great opportunity to repeat the tale herself.

'Crippen murdered his wife,' she began, 'and ran off with Ethel le Neve, his mistress.'

'His teacher?'

'No, not a teacher. The woman he wanted to live with.'

'Oh, I see,' Diana said, but she didn't really. She'd once had a mademoiselle called Elene la Neige to teach her French who had lived with them but she supposed that was somehow different.

'They ran away in disguise on a boat to Canada,' her aunt was saying, 'and he called himself Mr Robinson and she was supposed to be his son.'

She paused, unwound her arm and reached for a bowl of grapes, selected a little bunch and snipped them off with the silver grape scissors. She offered some to Diana who shook her head and said, 'Please do go on about Mr Crippen.'

Selina laid the grapes aside, flattered to have such an eager audience.

'You've heard of the radio?' she asked. 'Well, this trans-atlantic radio means you can send messages across the sea. It works like the telegraph, I *think*, though I don't really understand it. It's all very modern. Anyway they used it to tell the Canadian police, who met Crippen and his mistress off the boat. That was in the July and the trial was in October.'

'And you went there? To the trial? Weren't you frightened? I mean with him being a murderer?'

'Goodness, no. Plenty of society ladies go to trials. But I'll tell you this. When the trial started, on the very first day, one of the jurymen fainted. It was when they described how Crippen had chopped up his wife.'

'He chopped her up?'

54

'Didn't I tell you? No, I didn't, did I? It's the sort of thing most people know. Well, this juryman collapsed at the horror of it and they had to postpone the trial until the afternoon, but the point is that not one of the ladies in the public gallery fainted. I think,' she added, with a knowing little look, 'that women are actually in some ways much stronger than men. But it doesn't do to tell them so.'

'So what happened in the end?'

'Well, he was hanged of course but not his mistress, though she must have known all about it. They put the bits of his wife together and they were buried by the members of the Music Hall Ladies' Guild, of which she was a member, you see.'

Again Diana nodded, though she didn't really see. The whole tale had been so extraordinary that in a way nothing about it could surprise her, not even this Ladies' Guild burying the reassembled body of poor Mrs Crippen. Her mother helped to run some sort of Ladies' Guild at Northrop but she couldn't imagine they would have anything to do with the likes of the Crippen family.

Outside in the corridor a gong was ringing.

'Time to dress for dinner,' Selina said.

She looked at her niece's wardrobe, shaking her head.

'Perhaps for tonight just wear this,' she suggested, choosing a pale blue yoked dress with a dark blue sash and tight cuffs. 'Then tomorrow we'll go and consult Madame Gagneux.'

Diana, who had imagined that the dressmaking would take place in the same brisk and matter-of-fact way as it had done in the nursery at home, was amazed by Madame Gagneux's salon. It was a huge room, thickly carpeted and hung about with silks and satins which Madame seized and draped over her, nodding and muttering the while. Long looking-glasses swung in frames all around the room, so that she could see herself from a bewildering number of angles and everywhere there were books of patterns and paintings and photographs of fashionable women. Assistants waited anxiously in the background, ready to rush forward at Madame's behest.

Madame herself was surprisingly small. An imperious little woman, very dark-skinned, with a prominent jaw and huge brown eyes, liquid and expressive; it was impossible not to think of a monkey when you looked at her, an impression which was increased by the thin little pink hands which darted about Diana's body, tugging, adjusting, pinning, shortening, lengthening, putting in a dart here, some ruching there. Her mouth dangerously spiked with pins, Madame would suddenly snatch the tape, which was always round her neck, to check a measurement, scowling anxiously the while. And all this was only to make what she called the toile, a plain cotton pattern on which she would base the future garment. No, it had not been thus with the Northrop seamstress.

Her aunt took a great interest in all that was going on, in fact seemed more concerned with the perfection of the clothes than was Diana herself, making suggestions, walking around her niece as she stood there in her chemise, remarking on her figure, on her small waist and ample bosom in a way which her mother would never have done and which Diana found embarrassing, although she knew it was kindly meant. She couldn't help wondering what the nuns would have said.

Every day for nearly a week they came to the salon because, as Selina explained to Madame Gagneux, it was not just a garment or two they were having made but a whole wardrobe. There were simple morning frocks, dresses to change into for luncheon, more elegant tea gowns and even more elegant dinner gowns. All these, of course, were the kind of clothes her mother wore at home, but they were somehow more stylish, and as for the ball gown it was beyond imagining. And there was another one in the making.

'You shall have my Milly to do your hair,' Selina told her the day before the first ball. 'And I shall come up to look at you before I am got ready myself.'

For what seemed like hours, Milly worked on her hair, pinning it up in great coils, rolling it on the curling tongs, even putting in a little frame at the back to hold it in place for the long evening ahead. Most ladies needed extra pieces they called rats, she said, but Diana had no need for one, her hair was so thick, she explained as she backcombed, twisted and pinned. The big mistake was to wash it too often; washed hair was soft hair, and soft hair wouldn't stay up however hard you tried. You could easily see which ladies foolishly washed their hair once a month, it was so floppy, falling all over the place. Hair needs a bit of dirt to keep it in place.

'Madame said I could bring you some of her fuller's earth for your cheeks and some pink salve for your lips,' Milly offered. Then, seeing Diana's startled look, added, 'Only if you wish it, of course.'

'No, thank you,' Diana told her, remembering remarks she had heard her mother make about painted ladies and wondering what the nuns would have said if they'd heard the suggestion that one of their girls should put such things on her face.

'Well, you don't need none of it, Miss Diana,' Milly said. 'You've a very fine complexion left as nature intended. And now I'll go and fetch Madame.'

Selina had expected to see her niece greatly improved, fit now to be seen in society from which she had tended to shield her this past week. But she had not expected such a transformation. She had never considered Diana particularly attractive. There was something too direct about her gaze, too down-to-earth, for her ever to be a languid beauty or light-hearted flirt. She was too utterly unselfconscious for that. A woman needs a little guile, a little playfulness, a certain self-awareness, if a man is to flirt with her, Selina thought, and that was simply not in her niece's character.

It was still there, that direct look, but now it seemed attractive, arresting; the face beneath the piled-up hair, the face above those perfect white shoulders, gazed back at her with a frankness, a simplicity which had a beauty all its own. Looking at her now, Selina found herself thinking that Diana might not be a woman who would bewitch men, but she would be one whom men would admire and want for a friend and later for something more.

'Darling, you look absolutely divine,' she said, planting a kiss very carefully on one cheek in order not to disturb the dress or the hair. 'Come along with me while I get ready.'

So Milly collected up the combs and brushes, the spirit stove and curling tongs and all the tools of her trade and they went together back to Selina's dressing room.

As she sat at her dressing table, with Milly brushing out her hair, it occurred to Selina that it was one thing to have a niece who looked like a rather gauche school child and quite another to have a niece who looked like an attractive young woman.

'I think, Diana,' she said, 'that you should simply call me Selina. It's absurd to call me aunt when we are so near in age.'

'If that's what you really want, Aunt,' Diana replied.

She knew that her aunt had married very young and had had Tom when she was still only eighteen, but she had never thought of her as being near herself in age. And besides, wouldn't her mother think it was an impertinence?

'Perhaps just while we're in London,' she added.

It was the first of many things the knowledge of which was to be confined to London.

Her cousin Tom came home for the ball, timed for the first day of his holidays. She hadn't seen him when he arrived in the afternoon, but he came to his mother's room now, knocked loudly on the door and walked in before she had time to respond, which surprised Diana, used as she was to waiting until her mother requested her to enter.

He rushed across the room and embraced Selina who said, 'Darling, do be careful of my hair, you dreadful boy,' laughed and pushed him away.

But he just smiled and kissed her again, though this time more carefully on the cheek. Taller than Diana remembered him, his shoulders broader, his face fuller, he looked much more than his thirteen years. There was something eager, restless about the way he moved; he gave an impression of great energy looking for somewhere to expend itself.

'You haven't greeted your cousin,' his mother rebuked, and Diana, who had been standing unobserved by the window, moved forward.

He turned, seeing her for the first time. For a moment he seemed not to know who it was.

'Is that really our cousin Di?' he asked, genuinely astonished.

Then he kissed her and, still holding her hands, held her at arm's length, looking her up and down.

'Golly,' he said. 'You look ripping.'

'It's only because of the dress Madame Gagneux's made for me,' she told him candidly. 'And Milly has put my hair up.'

'I didn't recognize you, honestly at first I didn't.'

'I hardly recognize myself,' she told him.

Selina watched them and smiled and thought what a handsome young man her son was going to be. One day he would break a few hearts. As she had done.

Which reminded her of something.

'We shall be seeing one of your school fellows this evening,' she told him.

'Oh, no,' her son exclaimed, not at all liking the idea of any meeting between the world of school and the world of home. 'Who, Mamma?'

'Crawley, he's called, and—'

'Oh, no, not that loathsome Creepy Crawley, little chap with red hair and—'

'Not at all like that, darling,' his mother interrupted, laughing, as she remembered the handsome young eighteen-year-old whom she had so recently bewitched. 'Sebastian is Lady Crawley's son and he has dark hair and—'

'*Sebastian Crawley!*'

He seemed to think that this was even worse news.

'Mamma, you must not, absolutely must not, refer to him as a school fellow of mine, please—'

'Whyever not, foolish boy?'

'Because Sebastian Crawley is in the sixth form and he plays cricket *and* rugby for the school and *please* don't talk to him about me or say anything *awful*. I mean, he probably hasn't even *heard* of me. He'd think it was the most fearful cheek.'

'Don't worry, darling,' Selina told him, laughing and kissing him lightly on the forehead. 'I shall be the soul of discretion. I shan't even mention that you hero-worship him.'

'I *don't*, Mamma,' he objected, blushing furiously. 'It's just that he's the most famous chap in the whole school.'

'Of course. And I wouldn't dream of embarrassing you in any way,' Selina reassured him. Then, glancing at her watch, added, 'Now we really should be going down. You must lead your cousin in the first dance, Tom. Make sure you write it on her card. And it would be nice if you would take her into supper.'

'I don't need to be told, Mamma,' he said petulantly. 'Of course I want to dance with my cousin but it does rather take the fun out of things if a chap's *told* to do them.'

'I think we know from your headmaster that you seem to prefer the things you're told *not* to do,' she remarked.

'Oh, don't start on that. I've had enough of that from Papa.'

'All right, dear boy,' she conceded indulgently. 'It's in the past. Now shall we go down?'

The ball was different from anything Diana had been to before or ever imagined. There had been dances in Northrop, of course. She had galloped up and down many a ballroom doing the Sir Roger de Coverley with her father, danced the lancers with local acquaintances and with Teddy's schoolfriends when they came to stay. She had been taught Scottish reels and even the sword dance. But these dances were different, these one-steps and waltzes where your partner held you close and asked, 'Do you reverse?' which wasn't a question she understood until Selina explained.

It was thanks to Sebastian Crawley that she managed the new dances so well. Immediately they arrived, his parents brought him over to be introduced to her, remarking that he and Diana were the only very young people here, apart from Tom who didn't really count, being the son of the house.

She liked Sebastian immediately; he was tall but not too tall, she thought, dark but not too dark, amusing but not silly like some of Teddy's friends. And he danced so well that she was guided without any difficulty through all the unfamiliar steps. All the same, she had to concentrate on what her feet were doing, so left most of the talking to him.

He didn't seem to mind and chatted away very easily. He talked about school, which he would be leaving next year and going up to Cambridge. She was careful not to mention Tom, which was silly because he had obviously recognized him and in fact they got on very well.

'It was all right with you,' Tom confided later, as the three of them went into supper together. 'I just didn't want Mamma saying something awful. I knew *you* wouldn't.'

She found the two boys easier to talk to than some of the women. What women they were! She had never seen people like them. They were not just elegant but so sophisticated, almost brittle, as if enamelled in their magnificent dresses. And their voices were special too, as if they had left their everyday voices at home. And the things they said never seemed quite serious, so you didn't know how to take them. But they were all very kind and made a great fuss of her and told her how lovely she looked and how lucky she was to have the beautiful Selina to chaperone her.

Selina, watching her niece, observed how she glowed, positively shone, in all this admiration. Turning to her husband she said with some satisfaction, 'Don't you think you should congratulate me on turning our ugly little duckling into a swan?'

For once he did not agree with her. He shook his head as he told her, 'No, you have merely helped the butterfly to emerge from the chrysalis. It would have happened anyway.'

She pouted at this, not liking her role to be so diminished, for what was the point of transforming the girl if some of the glory didn't reflect upon herself?

Nearly every evening after that there was a dance or dinner to go to, a theatre or an opera. Sometimes Sebastian was one of the party, sometimes not. Then there were tea parties at which sophisticated ladies talked knowledgeably about the Diaghilev ballet and Impressionist paintings. Diana had heard of none of these things. Her entertainment at Northrop had been on the croquet lawn or tennis court in the summer with walks and bicycle rides and picnics, while in the winter there were charades, dumb crambo, games of spillikins by the schoolroom fire and books to be read and sometimes, as a special treat, a magic lantern show put on by her father, with a sheet over the window and her father telling a story as he put plates into the magic box to produce images which were frequently upside down.

It was all a far cry from the social round in Billington Square, where arrangements were constantly being made, sometimes frantically remade, notes being distributed among friends by messenger boys in blue uniforms with little pillar box hats on the side of their heads at sixpence a time.

She didn't see much of either Tom or his younger sister. Celia had gone to the seaside with her nanny and a holiday tutor had been engaged for Tom and they always seemed to be away somewhere.

'All the chaps at school know why their parents get them these holiday tutors,' Tom told her. 'It's so that they needn't bother with us in the vacations any more than they do in term time.'

'Oh, it's not true, Tom,' she'd protested. 'Both Aunt and Uncle love you very much.'

'Oh, yes, I'm sure they do. I expect they'd be fearfully cut up if we died. But that isn't the same thing as wanting to be with us, is it?'

She nodded, but all the same what he had said worried her.

'You do love Tom, don't you?' she enquired now in her direct way, as her hair was being brushed by Milly, in front of whom Selina always spoke as if she was a deaf mute. Diana thought that her mother would have considered this very indiscreet and she wondered sometimes if it meant that her aunt was very trusting or just that she regarded Milly as less than human, a machine who existed to carry out certain tasks, attend to her whims and had no other existence. Whatever the reason, she found that she herself was now doing the same, talking in front of her with no embarrassment.

'Of course I love Tom, what a funny question!' Selina replied. 'Naturally I get cross with him sometimes, but who wouldn't? He's such a scamp, a handsome scamp. A real Bumfontein.'

'Bumfontein?'

'His grandfather, my father, another very handsome scamp.'

'But I thought your father's name was Barnfountain?'

'It was, of course.'

She hesitated in the manner of one who has made a slip and seeks a way to put it right. 'My mother changed her name, well, altered it a little, when she brought me over here, my papa having sadly departed this world.'

Diana nodded, sympathetic.

'It was hard for my mamma, very hard. And you see . . .' again she hesitated '. . . I can trust you, my dear?'

Diana nodded, aware that this was going to be another piece of information to be confined to London.

'Not wishing to distress your grandmama, who had strong views about what she still thought of as rebellious colonials, we decided not to mention, when it became clear that your uncle William and I were destined for each other, that a little of the blood which flowed in my veins was American.'

Fifty percent of it to be precise, but why confuse the sweet girl with percentages?

'Do you think, darling, that I might take Diana to the courts to hear the Countess of Fairleigh's divorce case?' Selina enquired of her husband one day.

'Oh, no, surely that would be most unsuitable for a young girl?'

'But I do so want to go myself. But far more important than that is that I do believe that a modern girl should be aware of these things.'

She looked at him earnestly, her eyes luminous with sincerity.

'There have been nearly seven hundred divorces in the past five years,' she went on. 'A girl should know this and what better way than being taken to hear a case by a fond relation who is also a close and trusted friend, as I am to her?'

It was so patently obvious that her only concern was the proper education of her niece that William didn't demur. It is women, after all, he thought, who must know what is best for other women.

So Diana went with her aunt and sat among the row of fashionable ladies who were listening with relish to the accusations against the countess by her husband's lawyers and to the counter-accusations against him by hers.

'You must learn from this, Diana,' Selina told her when they got home and were sitting in the little boudoir drinking tea, 'that a lady must never cause a scandal, whatever anybody does, there must never be a scandal.'

'I'm sure I should never want to cause a scandal,' Diana told her.

'In this case it was all the fault of the duchess.'

'Duchess?'

'Yes, she was the hostess at the Friday-to-Monday house party, which the countess's lawyers referred to. As such it was her duty to see that the guests were put into appropriate bedrooms. She failed to do this. She should have known to put the countess in a room adjoining Sir Frederick's.'

She paused to cut herself a little bunch of grapes and offer one to Diana, before going on: 'Of course, it was not her fault that the servant responsible for ringing the warning bell at six o'clock in the morning should have died of a heart attack as he climbed the stairs. That is not something which even the most diligent hostess can foresee. But, alas, it meant that at this crucial hour very few of the guests got back into their official bedrooms on time, including the unfortunate countess who has such a horrid husband.'

'Is he really horrid?'

'Oh, such a country bumpkin. You know what some of these squires are like. He once told the bishop that his duty towards his neighbour was to give him a good place on his shoot, never look over his hand at cards, lend him money if he needed it and kill him if he committed adultery with his wife.'

'Well, at least he hasn't done that,' Diana pointed out.

'It might have been better if he had. To be divorced is so much worse for the countess than having her lover shot.'

She took a sip of tea and added, 'Such a shame about the postponement of the next hearing. Tomorrow I shall take you to the House of Commons instead. Do have another Marie biscuit, darling.'

As the days in London turned to weeks, Diana was increasingly aware that her aunt moved among two distinct circles of people; there was the set which belonged to her husband and his colleagues and their wives, and a quite different one which she seemed only to be on the fringes of, but in whom she

64

took a profound interest. There had been a group of very grand people, apparently, who called themselves the Souls, she told Diana, very old now, but their children formed a coterie and she did actually know some of them, or at least knew people who knew them. Their lovers were known and recognized in the same way as husbands were recognized among her own friends and any children born of these liaisons were brought up with the rest of the children in their mother's household and nobody minded. Quite recently Lord Caster's daughter had been told that she wasn't his child and in fact her father was Lord Plaister, to which she had replied, 'As long as I am brought up in a lord's household, I don't mind at all which one is my father.'

Selina seemed to admire such tolerance, be fascinated by the ways of these people, but it all seemed to Diana quite astonishing; she couldn't imagine her mother putting up with such behaviour nor imagine how the nuns would have felt about it. But when she said as much, her aunt only suggested that in that case it might be better not to mention it at home.

'Of course your mamma and I would be completely of the same mind about this, Diana. She would agree with me that no woman should ever seek divorce. A woman who does that will lose her children to her husband and, worse still, all her property as well. So she will be not only disgraced but also penniless.'

'How dreadful!'

'And quite avoidable if only she'd observed the rules laid down by society. And when I say society I mean High Society, not the kind of society you have in Northrop. Which is why it is as well not to speak of such things there,' she added, giving her niece a meaningful look.

'You have to understand,' she went on, 'that these matters are managed with the utmost discretion. The perfect example was set by the late King Edward. Ladies like Lillie Langtry and Mrs Keppel and the Duchess of Warwick were all married and no longer very young. He only seduced married women and would never have so much as flirted with an unmarried girl. He would have regarded that as quite immoral. Morality is so very important, Diana,' she told her niece with solemn emphasis. 'It is always upheld in the great households. If a maid is found to have been too familiar with, say, a footman, the slut will be sacked at once, shown the door and without a reference too. Examples must be made if morality is to be maintained. And now it really is time to go and get ready for the dance.'

Diana was more excited than usual about the dance, for it was at the Crawleys' mansion. Sebastian had told her all about it, how wooden flooring had been put on the lawn so they could dance in the garden and it was all going to be made pretty with lanterns, and how he was going to stand with his parents to greet the guests, but how once she arrived he would leave them and stay with her and how he hoped he could dance every dance with her. She had laughed at his enthusiasm but had been happy to promise that it should be so.

There had been no need to promise really because hadn't she danced nearly every dance with him anyway whenever they were at the same party? She had got used to seeing his face looking anxiously out for her, to seeing it light up when he recognized her, to the way he wanted to please her. It was very strange, this feeling that she could grant or withhold a favour and thereby make another human being either happy or sad. She had never felt like this, never felt so happy, so light-hearted, so alive. She just knew that nothing would ever be boring ever again. She didn't of course say a word about this to anyone, but hugged the secret of it like some precious jewel that must be kept out of sight, brought out only to gaze upon in secret, in the privacy of the night.

He kept his promise; he was there waiting for her, standing beside his parents, but he left them when she arrived and soon they were dancing together, both thrilled with the knowledge that it was only the start of a whole, long evening together. He looked down at her, smiling, and she looked up at him, glowing, as they danced and danced.

His parents watched them with approval. Not so Selina. All last year she had indulged this handsome boy, flirting with him, enjoying the youthfulness of him. She, who had stayed so young herself, loved the freshness of his skin, the exuberance of his hair. William was by no means old, not even middle-aged yet, but he had already lost that youthful glow. His skin was coarser, the hair which she had loved to stroke, and slowly run her fingers through, was thinner now and dryer, not so lush.

Sebastian had once had eyes only for her. Now he had eyes only for Diana, she observed, as William and she watched the couple dance by.

'Youth calls to youth,' William remarked, smiling.

He put his arm around her waist and led her on to the dance floor. And she told herself what a dear man William was, worth a thousand foolish boys. But it irked her all the same.

'Come and see what we've done in the garden,' Sebastian said after supper. 'Let's dance outside.'

It was a mild night, as they danced through the wide open doors and out into the garden. There were little lanterns in the trees, casting shadows, making it all seem bigger and stranger.

'Oh, how pretty,' she exclaimed. 'It's really like fairyland, isn't it?'

'I'm so glad you like it,' he said. 'It's really just for you.'

She nodded and smiled for she understood what he meant; he wasn't saying that it had really all been done for her, just that it was of herself that he had been thinking when he watched the work being done. It's like that with real friends, she thought, you reach the meaning behind the words.

Other couples danced in and out of the garden, coming and going, but they stayed there, entranced. There had been light clouds in the warm night sky, but they cleared now and the stars shone brilliantly. The moon was almost full as it hung there above them as they waltzed.

When the music stopped, he kept holding her hand.

'Are you warm enough? Would you rather go inside for the next dance?' he asked.

She shook her head.

'No, it's lovely out here.'

'There's a bench we could sit on while we wait,' he told

her, looking about. 'Oh, they've moved it back there to make more room for dancing.'

'I'm all right, really.'

But he led her to the seat all the same and they sat together, companionably silent for a while.

Then: 'We have a little wood at home,' Diana remarked. 'And in the summer evenings we scare each other by playing hide-and-seek among the trees when it's just beginning to get dark.'

'I don't think this one could be very frightening,' he said, laughing. 'Nobody could get lost in our little garden. You go and hide,' he added, 'and I'll count up to ten and come and find you.'

'You have to shut your eyes and count slowly,' she told him. 'And no peeping.'

'I promise I won't peep.'

It was fun to play a childish game again, after having to be so grown-up in London. She got up and made her way quickly down one of the little paths between the trees. It was much darker here among the thick foliage lit only by glimmering lanterns. Moving as silently as she could she went and stood behind a sweet-smelling mock orange bush, breathing in the heavy fragrance as she stood, holding her full skirt close against her body and keeping quite still.

He passed the tree once, as he made for a more obvious hiding place behind a large rhododendron. Then she heard him coming back. She dared not try to see exactly where he was, fearful of making a sound which would attract his attention. It was a game which they had always taken very seriously at Northrop Hall.

As she stood very still, he came up behind her, and said, 'There, I've caught you.'

'Oh, and I thought you were over there and . . .' she said laughing, then stopped for he had looped his arms around her.

'There now, see if you can escape,' he said.

She tried but the encircling arms were too strong; they felt like a band of iron around her.

'I can't,' she said, smiling up at him.

'Try,' he teased.

And she did try, but in vain, so she leant back against his arms instead.

'You are not like any other girl I've ever known,' he said, his voice suddenly hushed and serious. 'I wish I could keep you here like this for ever.'

Then slowly he leant forward and kissed her.

Just a kiss, a little kiss, a touch on her lips, but the thrill of it ran through her, soft but all pervasive. Then quite of its own accord, it seemed, her head swayed and went to rest on his shoulder. She felt one of his hands come up and lie gently on her hair. They stayed very still for what seemed a long time, wrapped up in their own little world; a quite different world it was, from the world of a few minutes ago, as the two of them clung together in the moonlit garden with its shadows and sweet scents.

Suddenly the music started up again and somebody was calling her name. It was Selina, who had watched them go out.

'We're here, Mrs Arndale,' Sebastian explained, leading the way and moving quickly out into the open. 'We were just resting between the dances.'

So they returned to the other world and danced for the rest of the evening and Diana tried to look as if nothing had happened, as if her life had not been somehow wonderfully transformed. But she could not help her mouth smiling, her cheeks glowing and her eyes from seeking his.

'You looked like a little princess tonight,' her Uncle William told her kindly as they said goodnight.

But her aunt made no comment.

Diana kissed them both and went quickly to bed. She couldn't wait to be alone, to relive the evening.

She lay for a long time, wideawake. She started with the moment they had arrived and she had seen Sebastian waiting, she recalled each dance in turn, making sure she could remember what kind of dance it was and what music had been played. She remembered all that they had eaten at supper and everything he had said, consciously dawdling over these preliminaries the longer to savour what had followed until she reached the point when they had danced out into the garden.

Oh, she could see it all again in her mind's eye, the mystery of the trees, the shadows and the lanterns, and then the moon coming out from behind the clouds, huge and ancient as if it knew all their little human secrets.

It had all been so magical, even the childish game of hide-and-seek, which had cast its spell over them. She felt again his arms looped about her, how strong he felt as she pretended to try to break away. She saw again his teasing smile and the fondness in his eyes. She heard again his soft laugh, heard him say that she was different from any other girl he had ever known, that he wanted to stay like this for ever.

Then at last she reached the kiss; it seemed now as if everything had led up to that moment, but of course it hadn't been like that at the time. It had all just happened. The kiss. Her first kiss ever. Well, not exactly her first kiss *ever* – the family regularly kissed each other and Teddy's friends had occasionally pecked her cheek – but her first kiss *of that kind*.

Reliving it in her mind, she found to her infinite joy that night made her body relive it too. So her treasure was safely stored.

It was almost dawn when at last she fell asleep, but she got up at nine, far too restless with happiness to lie abed. As she went downstairs, Milly stopped her with a message to say would she please go and see Selina, who always had her breakfast in bed.

'Of course,' she said, 'I'll go along now.'

She was singing to herself as she made her way along the corridor to Selina's boudoir.

Selina was sitting up against a bank of pillows, the breakfast tray set aside, a few letters scattered across the bed. She was looking lovely, as always, her long hair unpinned, framing her face, curls escaping to lie against her breast, which was very visible through her flimsy froth of nightgown.

But yet, Diana observed, she was looking very serious.

'Good morning, darling,' she said. 'I thought it was time we had a little talk. Would you like some hot chocolate? There is plenty in the jug.'

'No, thank you, Aunt.'

'*Selina,*' her aunt corrected.

'I'm sorry, Selina.'

'No need to be sorry, darling. I know it wasn't intentional.'

She paused, as if considering the best way to broach the next topic.

'You know, I am sure,' she began, 'that I take my duty as your chaperone very seriously, very seriously indeed.'

'Yes, of course. And you've been wonderful.'

'If I failed in my duty I should feel I was breaking my solemn promise to your mamma. You do understand that, don't you?'

'Yes.'

'Good, so we understand each other. You will know that my motive in what I have to say springs entirely from the need to do my duty as your chaperone.'

She paused, then went on: 'We all make mistakes when we are young, dear child. Often they are not intentional. I'm sure you, for example, don't know when you have made one.'

'Oh, I think I would know, Aunt, I mean Selina—'

'Please do not interrupt,' her aunt said quite sharply.

'But what have I done?' Diana asked, now suddenly alarmed. 'Have I done something wrong?'

Selina looked at her and smiled. She reached out and touched her niece's hand.

'Only inadvertently,' she said. 'I am sure you had no intention of doing so. But I do feel I must talk to you about this because, as I say, I take very seriously my duties as your chaperone.'

Again she paused, as if seeking the right words before going on: 'You see, what may seem perfectly all right to you may not appear to be so in the eyes of the world. Society has very high standards by which it judges us all. I'm sure you know now what I am referring to.'

Diana shook her head, genuinely baffled, unable to see how anything she had done could possibly offend Society.

'Then I must tell you. It is about your behaviour with Sebastian Crawley.'

Diana blushed; even to hear his name brought the blood rushing to her face.

'Ah, I thought so,' Selina remarked, observing this. 'Others than myself must have seen how much you have danced with him recently. It is far from proper for a young girl to make her preference so obvious. Then last night you were out alone with him in the garden.'

'But other people went out to dance. They were meant to.'

'Lady Crawley's garden is very ill-lit.'

'I'm sorry, Aunt, I really had no idea—'

'I don't blame you, you poor child. Sebastian was very much to blame for taking you out there. He is older and knows more about the world than you do. Yes, he is much to be blamed for leading you astray.'

'That's not fair,' Diana burst out.

Unjust criticism of Sebastian brought out all that rebelliousness in her which her grandmother had observed from nursery days onwards.

'It wasn't his fault,' she contradicted angrily. 'I agreed quite willingly to go outside to dance. And other people went too. If it was improper they should have put up a notice saying: No Dancing in the Garden. By Order.'

Selina looked at her niece, too surprised to reply.

'And,' Diana went on, 'you say it's all right for all these society people to have lovers and be really wicked and yet when Sebastian and I do nothing wrong, just dance in the garden, we get all this blame. It's so unfair.'

Selina did not reply, but allowed herself to look very hurt.

'I'm sorry you feel we have treated you so badly, Diana,' she said, speaking more in sorrow than in anger. 'Ingratitude is hard to bear. I am sure that on reflection you will realize that what may be permitted in older, married women is absolutely forbidden to an unmarried girl. I'm sure that you will realize that Society, which welcomed you and showed you every kindness, should be respected; you should not reward it by behaving with wantonness.'

Wantonness! What had she done to deserve this accusation? But there was something very convincing about the way her aunt had spoken, with a solemnity that she had not heard in her before. And it was true, what she said; everyone had been kind to her, her aunt and uncle especially. To be ungrateful as well as wanton! Anger left her; guilt took its place. Oh, what would they say, her father and mother, if she was sent home in disgrace?

The very thought of them brought tears to her eyes.

'I'm so sorry,' she choked. 'You won't say anything to Mamma and Papa, will you?'

'No, dear,' Selina said, observing with satisfaction these signs of contrition. 'On condition you drop this unfortunate friendship with Sebastian. We shall regard it as a sad but small mistake, a very minor incident which only upset for a little moment our lovely life together in London. There, you are forgiven and I shall never refer to it again. Give me a kiss to show that we are friends,' she added holding up her lovely face to her niece. 'And then I must get up. I have plans to see to for our little party tonight.'

Back in her bedroom, Diana wept a little and then began to pace her room, unable to believe that a few hours ago she had been so happy. It was all such a muddle; she had accepted the nuns' teaching, then revised it when her aunt had mocked, and she'd enjoyed so much all these parties and dances which the nuns wouldn't have approved of, nor perhaps her mamma. And now it had all gone wrong. It seemed suddenly as if she didn't know what was right and what was wrong. She longed for the old nursery rules, the certainties of Northrop. And what was she going to say to Sebastian? At least she knew that he wouldn't be at the party tonight, because the Crawleys had gone into the country for three days. So that gave her a little time to think.

'It's quite an informal evening we're having tonight, Diana darling,' Selina told her that afternoon. 'I think the cherry dress would be suitable, it's so light and summery.'

'You'll look very pretty, Diana, whatever you wear,' William told her.

He had come home early this evening and the three of them were having tea together in the drawing room. Her aunt was being exceptionally sweet to her; grateful that the discord was over, Diana tried not to think about Sebastian.

'By the way,' her uncle was saying, 'there was a note in the hall from the Bramleys apologizing that they won't be able to come after all. Dr Bramley has an urgent case on hand. Of course I wrote a note asking her to come just the same.'

Selina frowned. Above all things she hated having spare women around. Spare men were a different matter.

'I don't think she should come alone,' she said. She paused trying to think of a justification for this statement. 'I think your mother would not think it quite respectable for a woman to go out alone without her husband,' she went on. 'I should not like to be responsible for any damage to Mrs Bramley's reputation.'

'But this is, as you said, an informal occasion, though your doubts do you great credit, my dear,' he said gently, taking her hand. 'I think, however, that Mamma would quite approve of her coming alone,' he added.

'Your mamma would never have invited a doctor and his wife in the first place,' she told him.

That was true and put him on the defensive.

'He is becoming quite eminent as a surgeon,' he said. 'And doctors no longer have to use the tradesmen's entrance. Times are changing; we have to change with them.'

His wife shrugged.

'Perhaps it doesn't matter as I'm not sure if Mrs Bramley is respectable anyway. Lady Parsons said she'd been seen in a restaurant.'

'Oh, I can't believe that! How could Lady Parsons possibly know such a thing? She would never go into such a public place herself.'

Selina shrugged again. She was pouting a little by now.

'I only repeat what I was told,' she said. 'You must doubt my word if you please to do so.'

He put his arms around her.

'Of course I would never doubt your word, my angel,' he said, kissing her.

Diana watched in some embarrassment. Her parents did not have such public disagreements nor such reconciliations.

'I shall go and remove the note,' William said, releasing his wife. 'I don't expect it will have gone yet.'

But the messenger boy had already taken it, hopped on his

bike and, sixpence in his pocket and pill box hat aslant on his head, pedalled off with it to Cadogan Place.

It was, as her aunt had promised, an informal occasion. More of a *conversazione* she had said, with a buffet supper and a little dancing. It was a warm evening and the doors were open for people to sit out in the garden.

Diana was introduced to Mrs Bramley and saw that her aunt did not like the lady very much, although she greeted her with apparent kindness.

'I am so sorry,' she said, 'that you have had the inconvenience of coming alone.'

'It was good of you and Mr Arndale to allow me,' the other replied, smiling. 'And I haven't come alone as Mrs Porter kindly invited me to accompany them. And they will take me home. They live just across the square from us.'

As Selina was distracted by the arrival of more guests, Diana walked with Mrs Bramley out into the garden. She was surprised at how lovely Mrs Bramley was. It was a different kind of beauty from her aunt's, more vivacious, more a matter of expression than of feature. From the intense way she listened you could tell that she was more interested in other people than in herself.

'And tell me, my dear, what you have seen and done in your time in London?' she was asking now.

Diana began to tell her about the dress fittings and the parties and the dances and suddenly she felt she didn't want any more of them. In a totally unexpected rush of homesickness, she looked at the little London garden, paved and ornamented with flowers in baskets and urns, and longed for the open space and long vistas of a proper garden. She'd had enough of pavements and town houses, of London squares and traffic; she wanted the green fields and meadows of Northrop, the mossy pools and little chattering streams, the quiet villages and stone-roofed cottages, the grassy lanes, the woods and valleys and the unpeopled quietness of it all.

Her voice trailed off and her eyes filled with tears.

Mrs Bramley moved slightly to shield her from view.

'What is it, my dear?' she asked. 'Something is troubling you.'

To her horror, Diana felt her lips trembling as she said, 'I think I want to go home.'

Mrs Bramley held out a glass of champagne.

'Drink it,' she said. 'I haven't touched it.'

'Oh, I just have the fruit cup.'

'Take this as medicine ordered by your doctor,' the doctor's wife instructed.

So she gulped it down and whether it was the champagne or the kindness of her new friend, she didn't know, but she felt better and was able to talk sensibly about how she couldn't bear to stay any longer in London. She didn't mention Sebastian.

'I think you have been wanting to go home for some time,' Mrs Bramley said when she had heard her out, 'but have only just realized it. After all, you have been here a very long while and it is natural that you should miss your own home, however kind your aunt and uncle have been. I think you should tell them that you are ready now to leave.'

'I don't want to seem ungrateful.'

'They will understand. Talk to them tomorrow.'

Selina was sitting up in bed finishing her breakfast when Diana broached the subject of her departure. She was surprised that her aunt didn't raise more objections.

'I'm afraid you'll find it very quiet in Northrop after being here,' was all she said, smearing a little butter on to a thin piece of toast.

The truth was that she was getting bored with the project of bringing her niece out in society. Even apart from the little trouble with the Crawley boy, it was no longer particularly amusing and she was ready for another diversion. So she added, without too much enthusiasm, 'You do know that you can stay as long as you like, don't you, darling?'

'Thank you, but I want to go home now, truly I do. I mean,' she added hastily, 'I've enjoyed it very much and you and Uncle William have been so kind, but I think I'm ready to go back.'

She had lain awake last night thinking about it. Of course it had all been very exciting and different but she'd had enough of it. It wasn't just because of the upset over Sebastian – though it still hurt to think his name and she knew how disappointed he would be when he came back to London to find that she had left, but she would leave him a note and he could write to her, so that would be all right. No, she realized that she'd felt homesick before all that, even though she'd never admitted it. It wasn't just the countryside that she was missing, but the familiar old house with its routines, and her parents and Laura and Rupert and Teddy, to say nothing of Nanny and the horses and even the birds in the dovecote.

'You can come back any time, you know,' Selina assured her, as she was leaving two days later. 'We shall miss you. I wonder when we shall meet again?'

'We shall all be together for Grandmama's birthday celebrations, shan't we?'

'Oh, yes, I'd forgotten about that,' Selina said, sounding less than thrilled at being reminded of an event which she knew would involve spending a great deal of time wandering through gardens, plodding around a lake and admiring a lot of boring vegetation in a conservatory.

Eight

A dam Paste lifted the tropical maidenhair fern into the sack-lined wheelbarrow and pushed it cautiously up the path, through the yard, round the back of the house, up the side and paused at last outside the great conservatory, so called to distinguish it from the smaller one leading off from the dining room, which the family used for everyday.

It would have been quicker to go directly across the front of the house, but Lady Arndale had strict rules about the gardeners remaining as invisible as possible, so that herbaceous beds, lawns, arbours and rockeries should seem like a natural gift of the creator, not something toiled over by working men in overalls.

Every plant that he had set up in this conservatory in readiness for the great day was a prize specimen. For weeks he had washed and polished the leaves of the great palms, repotted ferns that he thought might possibly outgrow their pots by June 20th, tied jasmine grandiflora, whose flowers were so much bigger than the outdoor variety, to delicate frameworks of split canes, kept plants like the New Zealand tree fern in a special humid house of their own, had rejected any plant which was unbalanced, removed every leaf which was marked, never mind how slightly. He had mulched, fed, watered and loved each and every one, and knew them like he knew his own children; better perhaps because, his hours being long, he saw more of them than he did of his family.

His son Dicky had a way with plants, no doubt about it, he loved them and got them growing but he'd never make his way as a gardener, never get the names sorted. He wasn't simple, it was just that he'd never know an amaryllis from an agapanthus, let alone this *Nephrolepis exaltata*, with its amazing spread of pale green fronds, from *Adiantum cuneatum* 'Gracillimum' with its triangular fronds, upright when young and gracefully bending as the plant matured. Or rather, Dicky would recognize the plants, tell them apart easy as anything, but he'd never get the names right. And that was something you had to do on an estate like this. No, Dicky was not the stuff of which head gardeners were made.

He hadn't been much older than Dicky himself when he'd started here and even when he still lived with the other lads in the bothy, before he left to live in the cottage when he was married, he had studied to get to know the long names, found ways of remembering them although he had never had much schooling. Self-taught, he was, though, to be fair, Mr Jimson had helped him a lot as he always did help and encourage any of them who wanted to get on.

The first step up was when he put him in charge of melons and grapes, though Mr Jimson kept a careful watch. He did more work in those days, did Mr Jimson. He was getting on now and liked nothing so much as showing the gentry round the grounds, picking them a buttonhole, a rose maybe or a carnation and perhaps a little bouquet of pinks for the children. The other lads laughed a bit behind his back, but he'd worked hard in the past, so why shouldn't he take it easy now? The family trusted him, you could see that by the way Lady Arndale listened to him when he showed her round the glass houses so she could pick and choose plants for the house, but really it was Mr Jimson who did the choosing. Mind you, the lads laughed about that too, said that like Queen Victoria had had her John Brown so Lady Arndale had her James Jimson. But Adam didn't hold with that sort of talk and told the lads they should show more respect for their betters.

One day, he could be a head gardener himself, Mr Jimson had told him, if he worked hard and kept up the learning. He had a way with plants, no doubt about it, Mr Jimson had said, when he put him in charge of the conservatory plants.

The conservatory was looking magnificent now. It was a lovely building, everything done perfectly, even the heating pipes concealed under brass gratings and not just the usual iron ones that most people had. They'd made alterations to the conservatory, just for this party, leaving all the big plants, like the oleanders and myrtles, acacias and eucalyptus, which grew in beds round the outside but taking out the middle bed, to make more space for the guests. Instead they'd made stands round the sides, the carpenters had, so that the plants could be arranged in tiers, the tallest reaching right up to the roof.

The pillars were still there, of course, with ipomoeas and passion flowers climbing up them and the magnificent wistaria whose long grey stems he'd trained to go under the rafters and give shade to the camellias beneath. It flowered twice this one did, he looked after it so well, he reflected now with satisfaction, as he looked up at the soft blue tassels.

Of course Lady Arndale favoured green, she'd really have liked to have nothing but palms and ferns in all their beautiful delicate shades. Too much colour offended her, she found it vulgar. Orchids were allowed because she said it was natural to them to be among ferns and palms and besides, she said, they were exotic without being showy. She said the same of hibiscus and bougainvillea, but would on no account have anthurium lilies in the conservatory. Frangipani was allowed and now sweetly scented the air.

All week he had been busy arranging the plants on their stands and shelves, moving a croton here, a cordyline there to catch the light at midday, which was the time the guests would arrive tomorrow. He noted that the *Agapetes macrantha*, which he had brought in yesterday from one of the other houses, was looking its best, its pink flowers reminding him of waxy little lanterns. He was a bit worried about the *Calathea zebrina* whose velvety leaves must be kept fairly cool. Deep green they were with pale bands above and purple below. After some thought he moved it to the other side, where he found a home for it in what he thought would be a cooler spot. In its place he put the little *Syagrus weddeliana* with its terminal crown of leaves, its slender stem netted with black fibres, most elegant of all the small palms, he thought. Well set off by the little Seville orange tree alongside.

He took one last look at it, before closing the door behind him, imagining how it would look tomorrow when the colour of the ladies' dresses was added to the picture; like tropical birds they'd be, amid all this luxuriant foliage. It was perfect, nothing he could do could possibly improve it. He wished, as he pushed the empty wheelbarrow back to the shed, that Lady Arndale could see it now, but she was spending the day resting in bed in order to be at her best for the great day. He hoped for everyone's sake that it would be fine, but mostly he hoped it for the plants' sake, for they would surely look their best in spring sunshine. The signs were good, he thought, glancing once again up at the sky, which was calm, with a few delicate clouds and streaks of pink. Red sky at night, he said to himself; the omens for tomorrow were good.

He arrived early at work the next morning, knowing that Lady Arndale would be up betimes on this great day. It was a glorious morning, lawns and beds basking in early sunshine. Mr Jimson was there already in the shed which was his office. He looked up as the undergardener came in but did not return his cheerful greeting.

'Your presence is required up at the hall, in the great conservatory,' he said. 'Lady Arndale's orders.'

Adam was taken aback, then, straightening his jacket and smoothing his hair with his hands, he set off to walk the circuitous route round the house to the conservatory, thinking that perhaps she wanted an urn moved, a plant trimmed, a hanging basket rehung, something of the kind. But there had been a strangeness in Mr Jimson's manner that was a bit disturbing. Still maybe even he was feeling the strain of this great day; he'd be expected to be available to answer the guests' questions whereas the other gardeners, like himself, would neither have to be heard nor seen.

Lady Arndale was standing in the conservatory, leaning on her stick. Her face was always stern, but now it was fierce with rage.

'How dare you,' she spat rather than said, 'how dare you present this, this –' she was hardly able to get out the words she was so angry – 'this *mockery*?'

Adam Paste was not looking at her; he was staring at his plants, at the maidenhair ferns, all drooping and woebegone, at the frangipani which had turned quite black, at the palm

81

whose dull leaves hung limply down, where a few short hours ago they had reached out, glossy and strong, at the calathea whose velvety leaves hung limp along the stem. It was a picture of sad, neglected plants, of plants which looked as if they had been put there a month ago and left untended, unwatered. He rubbed his eyes, unable to believe what they seemed to be showing him.

'Have you an explanation, man?'

'No, my lady,' Adam said, for he could think of none.

'Then take a week's notice but leave at once,' her ladyship said, regaining her usual control, her words cold and clear. 'But first send Jimson to me with all his team.'

'Yes, m'lady.'

'And never, never show your face here again.'

He walked back to the shed, trembling, unable to take it all in. What had happened to him was catastrophe enough, but what filled his mind was disbelief about the plants. What could have happened to them overnight? Not many years ago his grandparents would have blamed spells, witches, curses, but that was not the way of his mind, not now. Yet there seemed no other explanation, however hard he tried to think, no reason why or how all these healthy plants should have withered in a few hours. But there had to be a cause, there just had to be.

He realized immediately he stepped into the shed that Mr Jimson had known he'd be sacked. He could see it in his eyes. Besides he had the week's wages ready, the half sovereign and crown piece were there in his hand.

The head gardener didn't say he was sorry; it was certainly not his place to express regret about a decision made by his employer. And he knew his place, did Mr Jimson. He just handed over the wages, reminded Adam that he'd have to be out of the cottage in a week and said goodbye.

Elsie was feeding the baby when he got home. She had taken a stool out the back and set it on the path and was nursing the baby in the sunshine; Adam could see the spring flowers on one side of the path: tulips and narcissi, anemones and Granny's bonnets, which he'd learned to call aquilegias. On the other side were all his newly planted vegetables, just showing in their neat rows. And Elsie amongst it all, nursing the baby.

He stood looking out at it, this picture framed in the doorway, of his life as it had been until an hour ago. And now it was all to be lost. Then he moved forward, his shadow before him, so that she looked up, expecting a neighbour. She stared when she saw him; it was unheard of for him to come home during the day. And on this day, of all days. She saw his face, his grey, stricken face.

'You're ill,' she said, jumping up, still clutching the baby to her breast.

He just stood there, looking at her, shaking his head.

'Nay, I'm not ill,' he said. 'Finish feeding the babby and then I'll tell 'ee.'

It was Monday morning when the men came from the estate and put their furniture out in the road. Adam had asked for an extra day so that he could borrow a pony and trap to take them to the house which he had found to rent in Littleton village, but it hadn't been granted. And there was no other day on which the trap was free.

'We'll leave the sticks 'ere for a while,' Adam, who always referred to their furniture in this way, told his wife. 'We'll walk on now and carry what we can.'

So they set off along the dusty road to Littleton, Elsie carrying the baby and a bagful of clothes, while the five-year-old Patsy held on to her mother's skirt and struggled to keep up with her. Edith pushed the baby carriage with the three-year-old twins in it, perched on top of the precious books. Dicky had the cooking pot and some bits and pieces of china as well as a bag of clothes, while eight-year-old Jack, who was big for his age, carried their one upholstered chair upside down on his head and Adam took his garden tools and everything he could from the vegetable plot. The house in Littleton was smaller than this one but it did have a good-sized garden, so they wouldn't starve as long as he could dig, as he kept telling Elsie.

They didn't talk much as they walked the four miles; they had already said everything that was to be said, they had discussed their plans again and again. Adam had already started looking for work as a jobbing gardener, Dicky was old enough now to be taken on as a labourer by one of the farmers.

'Our Jack's a strong lad,' Adam remarked. 'Up to earning a few coppers at the farmhouse, running errands, rook scaring, pumping water, shoe-cleaning and the like. There's always work for a willing lad before school and after.'

It was brave talk, but his wife knew they couldn't manage. They only had two shillings left out of the half sovereign and crown. Food and rent had taken the rest. And that two shillings they would have to keep to pay for a wagon or else leave their stuff out in the road. They decided to leave the furniture where it was and keep the two shillings.

'I'll walk back later, when we've had a bite,' Adam told her. 'Dicky'll come wi' me and we'll carry that sack of taties an' all last winter's vegetables between us.'

'Take the baby carriage,' she told him. 'And take our Edith to push it.'

So after a meal of bread and lard, the three of them left Elsie and the three younger ones and walked the four miles back to their old home, where the furniture was still piled up outside in the dusty road, a sad little heap of beds, chairs and a big deal table, under which they had put all the rest of their belongings, in case it rained. These they now piled into the baby carriage or secured to Dicky's back, head and arms. Only the table, three hard chairs and four stools were left to be transported.

'I'd best take the chairs,' Adam said at last, after staring at his possessions for a while. 'That table's a two-man job. You and I'd best come back for it later, Dicky.'

If the thought of walking yet another eight miles after this trek was finished didn't appeal to him, Dicky knew better than to say so. He nodded, took up the coal scuttle and set off, his sister pushing the baby carriage alongside him.

Adam was going to follow with the chairs and stools when his neighbour, also a gardener, came back from work.

'Give 'ee a hand?' he asked for he was a man of few words.

'Ah'd be thankful.'

'Ah'll be back,' said the other, going into his own house.

His wife was a shrewish little woman who kept a neat and tidy home for him, spotless and joyless it was.

'Ah'm goin' to give next door Adam a lift with 'is sticks,' he told her now.

'Ah've told you not to meddle wi' 'em. You'll get yournself in trouble. And 'er ladyship'll be 'avin you out 'n the street just like they'm be.'

'Mebbe,' he said and left.

Outside the two men hoisted the table up on to their shoulders, balanced it carefully, picked up the chairs and made their way, crablike, along the Littleton road. Progress was slow; after a while, they paused, lowered the table and sat for a moment on the chairs by the roadside. That was when they talked of what had happened to the plants in the conservatory, that was when the truth of it was told.

When he had finished, his neighbour looked at Adam, waiting for response. Adam only nodded, looked thoughtful and said, 'Best be getting on afore 'tis dark.'

The children were well ahead of them, were home and in bed before the men struggled into the cottage, slid the table down and stood up, rubbing their aching backs.

'You'll be 'avin' something before you go back?' Elsie asked.

But he knew there was nothing they could spare, so he shook his head and departed.

Nine

'The numbers are down to six now, Mamma,' Charles told his mother. 'The estate manager and the churchwardens all advise that the school should be closed.'

'Six! Last month it was eight. They are so ungrateful. Very well. I can see your minds are made up.'

'I'm sorry, Mamma, I know how much it meant to you, but times change, you know.'

'For the worse, for the worse,' her doom-laden voice tolled like a funeral bell.

They were in her private drawing room sitting by the fire for although the day had been brilliant, she had insisted upon drawing the curtains to protect the carpet, so the warmth of the sun hadn't managed to penetrate.

'It was a nice touch, Miss Poole bringing them up to sing Happy Birthday last month,' he said, striving to cheer her.

'She does her best with poor material, poor soul,' she replied ungraciously.

'Oh, come, Mamma, they sang very well and the whole day was wonderful.'

'It started catastrophically enough,' she told him.

'But it worked out well in the end. I thought the flowers looked quite lovely.'

She shuddered at the memory of it, of all the drooping ferns and palms and exotic plants being carted away and replaced by such a vulgar display of pelargoniums and calceolarias, of gloxinias, and lumpy-headed hydrangeas, begonias and cinerarias all clashing horribly with each other and with the ladies' dresses.

'People admired them, Mamma, everyone remarked on the

brilliant display. I thought Jimson did very well to arrange things as he did.'

'He's a good and loyal servant of the estate,' she conceded. Then almost immediately asked, 'And when do you intend to close the school, Charles?'

'We thought next year at the end of the summer term, if you agree, Mamma.'

'That will be forty-five years since we founded it in 1868,' said Lady Arndale, who was always quick to detect an anniversary. 'I remember the day so clearly.'

'Then shall we say July 1913, Mamma, if you agree?'

'It will happen if I agree or not,' she told him drily.

'It would be nice to think we had your approval,' he told her smiling and taking her hand.

She softened.

'You must act as you think best. That is all I can ask now.'

'Thank you.'

'But I cannot but remember how when Lady Clarkson died all the children of the estate school followed her cortege. They were dressed entirely in black, black coats, bonnets, shoes, everything provided by her grieving family.'

'Yes, I'm sorry that you won't – I mean, it must have been very touching.'

'A very moving sight.'

'I must go now, Mamma. I promised I would join the children when they come down after tea. Will you come too?'

'Not today, I think. Nor shall I be coming down to dinner. So I shall say goodnight to you now.'

Her son kissed the proffered cheek and walked apologetically out of the room, wishing that his mother did not always induce in him such feelings of guilt.

He felt more cheerful as he approached the drawing room. He and Elspeth had been desperately worried about Rupert who had been ill again last term; this time it had been pneumonia which had sent him home from school to be nursed. But he had come through the crisis and was much better now, full of restless energy, just as he had been when he was recovering

87

from diphtheria, always wanting to know what he could do next. It was a good sign.

Diana had settled down too now and was quite her old self again. He'd worried about her when she first came back from that stay in London. She'd seemed altered, in fact more changed than she'd been by her stay in France. He couldn't quite put his finger on it, but there was a strangeness about her, a difference from her former self. She seemed older and it wasn't just all those elegant town clothes she'd brought back with her. It went deeper than that; although she was obviously glad to be home again, she'd looked more thoughtful, sadder even.

Elspeth had told him not to worry; the girl would soon settle down now she was back in her own family and a proper, sensible routine; she, Elspeth, didn't wish to be critical of her sister-in-law, of course, and it had been very kind of her and William to have Diana to stay, to show her London and to bring her out at various dances but no doubt the ways of Selina's household had been very different from theirs in Northrop. Diana, being well brought up, must of course have done her best to fit in there and it would take a little while for her to adjust to being at home again.

Elspeth had been right, of course; slowly Diana had slipped back into being part of the family, got back to enjoying all the old pursuits, found her old friends, in fact was staying now with their nearest neighbours, the Parmenters, for a few days. No doubt they'd all be riding together or going off on their bicycles and generally doing all those healthy things which she hadn't been able to do in London.

Nanny was coming down the stairs; he waited for her and they went together into the drawing room.

'Rupert's looking so much better, Nanny,' he remarked.

'I've been better for ages,' Rupert, overhearing, told him. 'When can I go back to school?'

'In September.'

'Don't you like being at home, darling?' his mother asked.

'It's all right,' he said, out of politeness. 'But what's jolly unfair is that when chaps go away to school they have dinner with the grown-ups in the holidays, but whenever I go away

I seem to have to come back and I'm not allowed to stay up for dinner because I'm not properly away.'

'When you come home at Christmas you shall come down with your brother.'

'Oh, ripping! Thank you, Papa.'

'And what about me?' Laura demanded. 'I'll be left up there all alone and—'

'Girls don't go away to school, so of course you don't stay up.'

'I don't see why not and I don't see why girls shouldn't go to school just as much as boys. And anyway—'

'Shh, Laura,' her father interrupted. 'Little girls have different sorts of brains from little boys. It wouldn't be kind to them to do the sort of work boys do at school. Any more than it would be kind to expect boys to do needlework.'

'But I hate needlework,' Laura protested. 'I hate it even more than lessons.'

'That's enough, Laura,' her father said. Then, turning to his son asked, 'How did you get on with Thomson today?'

'Oh, it was wonderful, Papa, much better than last time.'

Last time, hearing a bird, he had taken a shot into the trees and Thomson had lectured him on what a dangerous thing he had done, ordered him never to do anything so stupid again, and then he'd taken the gun from him, removed the cartridges, handed it back and made him carry an empty gun for the rest of the lesson, not allowing him another shot. It had been a humiliating experience. He had thought at the time that it was the worst thing that had ever happened to him in his whole life and that he would never recover from the shame of it, but this time all that was forgotten, though Thomson did make him recite the routine again and again, how to break the gun between drives, walk with it over your right forearm, always pointing down. And the final golden rule: never, never point a gun at anybody, even in fun.

'Thomson is very good at teaching,' he said. 'Better than some of the masters at school.'

'He thinks you'll be as good a shot as your brother if you keep cool and try not to get so excited.'

Rupert shook his head. He could tell, just by the way

Thomson looked when he spoke of Teddy, that he knew the elder brother was special.

'Thomson says Teddy has an instinct,' he told his father. 'Some people are like that, he says. They can just raise the gun and hardly seem to pause to take aim.'

'Yes, Teddy has a gift,' his father conceded, 'but if you persist you may acquire the skill he has by instinct. And even he has to work very hard at it. Practice, constant practice, my boy, that's the secret of success.'

'Oh, Papa,' Laura interjected. 'I had a letter from Teddy today. He says he's been promoted in the Officers' Training Corps. And he won a prize for small-bore shooting.'

Charles had already heard the same news from his son, but did not tell her. Laura adored her brother whose letters were very special to her. She loved to give the rest of the family news of him as if she was his special messenger.

'Will he be a general by the time he leaves school?'

'Not quite as grand as that,' her father told her, laughing, 'but he might well be a lieutenant in the OTC.'

'Lieutenant Teddy Arndale,' she rolled the words out.

'It might be more dignified to give him his proper name,' her father suggested.

'Lieutenant Edward Arndale,' she repeated.

'Like Grandpapa,' Rupert put in. 'Teddy was called Edward after him, wasn't he, Papa?'

'But he was a sir and not a lieutenant,' his sister pointed out, 'so they wouldn't get confused.'

'Since he's been dead for ages and ages it doesn't really matter,' Rupert said.

'Shh, Rupert, I'm sure Grandmama wouldn't like you to talk like that,' his mother told him.

'Well, she's not here, is she?'

'All the same, darling, you must show respect.'

'And,' Laura told him, 'you don't know how far she can hear now she's got that trumpet thing.'

Lady Arndale had taken recently to carrying with her a trumpet which she raised to her ear when she wanted to be sure of hearing you and ostentatiously set aside when she wanted you to know that whatever you had to say was of no possible interest.

She had become even more formidable since its acquisition; the servants found that it added to their terror of her and regarded it more as a sinister weapon than as a sign of disability.

'Papa, it's awfully important I get shooting practice if I'm to be as good as Teddy one day. Can I go out with Thomson again tomorrow?'

'If he has time.'

'Oh no,' Laura put in. 'Let's go and see the Pastes tomorrow. The baby will have grown a lot if we don't go again soon.'

Their father hesitated. If it had been his decision Adam Paste would not have been dismissed, but he hadn't had the strength to cross his mother on her birthday.

'The Pastes are no longer here,' he said.

'Not here? Where have they gone? On holiday?'

'No, people like the Pastes do not have holidays. They are living elsewhere.'

'But why?'

'I'm afraid Paste failed to do his duty at his job which greatly upset your grandmother.'

'So we shan't see them ever again? Not even Edith and the baby?'

'No.'

Laura cried that night as she lay in the dark waiting for Nanny to come to bed. She cried not because she understood what had happened to the Pastes but because Dicky and Edith had not thought to say goodbye and she had supposed that they were her friends.

Ten

O ver the next few weeks the Paste family settled into this
new way of life, of being in a village and not part of
an estate. It was strange, after years of living among estate
workers who looked down on the villagers, to find that here
the village people looked down on estate workers.

'They'm not independent as we do be,' they'd say. 'Mebbe
they'm better off but they'm like slaves and if they job goes,
they home goes wi'it.'

When, eventually, they learned why the Pastes had come
to the village, it only confirmed their worst fears of living
on estates.

'We don't go tuggin' forelocks and curtseying to nobody,'
they told Adam as they worked in the fields. 'Old Farmer
Bainton's a stickler and mean as they mek 'em, but 'e don't
own us, 'e can't turn us out of our 'omes.'

Their new home seemed a small place after their old one.
There was no range so the pot had to sit directly on to the fire
until Adam fixed a hook to sling it above the flames. Even so
most meals had a smoky taste. There was no proper staircase
either, just a ladder up from the one room to the two up above.
The little ones shared their parents' bed, the older ones had
the other room with an old sheet across the centre to divide
the girls from the boys for decency's sake. They'd had the
same arrangement in their old house, but the bedrooms had
been bigger there.

Downstairs everything had to be done in the one room,
which was sitting room, kitchen and nursery. It was a big
room though and all right on fine days, but when it rained
and the clothes had to dry indoors, the place was filled with
steam. Elsie Paste made the best of it, gradually improving the

place and refusing to part with her books even when they were short of money for food. They were a present, she couldn't sell them, she told Adam, and besides neither of them knew how to go about selling them anyway.

Adam joined the labourers in the village, walking two miles each morning to a farm to follow the plough. After he had walked the two miles home, he went straight into the garden, digging, planting, hoeing. As he planted parsnips and turnips, potatoes and cabbage, he thought of the time when he had tended grapes and orchids and it seemed as if it must have been in a different world. At first he trained himself to remember all those long names in the hope that one day he might get back to the old life, but slowly they became harder and harder to recall and at last slipped away into oblivion, just as his ambition to become a head gardener was lost beyond recall.

Dicky was the one who was happiest with the move: it meant no more school. It meant doing proper work in the fields with other young lads; he felt like a grown man as he collected his four shillings a week, which he was proud to hand to his mother who gave him twopence back for himself, just as she gave his father back a shilling when he handed her his wages.

Above all he loved to be out in the open and never cooped up in a school room, not understanding what was wanted of him. He knew what the farmer wanted of him: he wanted him to pick stones, pull weeds, top and tail turnips. He understood that, he enjoyed doing it. He grew strong doing it, his shoulders broadened and he could heave a sixty-pound sack up on his back and hardly notice. But when they broke off at twelve o'clock to sit under the hedge and eat bread-and-pickle sandwiches, he loved just to lie back and look across at the meadows, filled now with cornflowers and kingcups, and gaze up into the sky and hear the larks singing while the others talked and joked and scuffled in mock fights with each other.

They didn't include him in their talk but they didn't bully him; he was Dicky Paste, a harmless lad, a hard worker, not exactly simple but one who didn't know how many ha'peth made a shilling. At potato picking time, when they were paid by the sack, he was the only one who didn't put in a few stones and clods of earth to make up the weight. He picked slowly, wiping the soil off every potato before putting it away. It took him twice as long as they did to fill a sack. The others observed this and smiled, but didn't mock. He was all right was young Dicky, they said, just that he didn't know how many potatoes made a hundredweight.

It was different for Edith. There might always be work for the boys in the village and they were encouraged to stay at home as breadwinners, but there was nothing here for the girls. Their beds were needed for younger brothers and sisters, there were other mouths to be fed, so they were sent away to go into service and be provided with bed and board elsewhere.

'It's not what I be wanting for our Edith,' Elsie told her husband one night, as they sat by the fire, the children all in bed. 'It'd be different going up to the big house, if we'd still been at Northrop but that's all past now. And I don't fancy her going miles away with her box, but she can't bide here, not earning, after next year, that's certain.'

'So what can be done wi'our Edith?'

'She could be going another two year to the National School. She'd profit by it.'

She was ambitious for her daughter, wanted something for her better for her than service in an ordinary household, some nice genteel place, like she'd had herself.

'And you don't have to pay a penny a week for heat and light like we had to at Miss Poole's.'

Adam nodded, respecting, as he always did, his wife's views on anything connected with schooling.

The National School seemed enormous to Edith, bustling and noisy after the tiny one on the estate with its eight or nine children. Here, to her amazement, there were more than a hundred pupils and three teachers. There were no backboards or finger stocks, no catechism but a bewildering number of different subjects to be learned. Her teacher, Miss Calne, young, pretty and quite plump, seemed to belong to a different species from angular old Miss Poole. Everything was different here; only the desks were the same, with their benches attached and the same little porcelain inkwells which had to be filled every week from the same kind of enamel jug.

Because she was new, Miss Calne appointed Edith as ink monitress to give her, she said kindly, something to do. It was her duty to collect all the empty inkwells and carry them on a tin tray to the big walk-in cupboard where Miss Calne, having filled the enamel jug from a big raffia-covered glass bottle, carefully decanted its contents into the little white ink pots, which Edith then carried back into the classroom to drop them, one by one, into the blue-rimmed holes in the desks, taking care not to let the contents splash out.

From that first day she loved her new school, begged to be allowed to stay until she was thirteen, which was what the law said but most of the parents in the village ignored. And hadn't Miss Calne said she might stay on as a pupil teacher and even that she might one day train to be a proper teacher herself and be paid?

All this she repeated, at the end of her first year there, to her father, who was now inclined to be suspicious of all interference from his betters.

'Mind that she's not stuffin' your 'ead with nonsense,' he warned. 'They can mislead you into being too ambitious, them folks can.'

Her mother was more encouraging.

'It'd be grand if it could be done, but it would cost money.'

'How much is there in there?' Adam asked, jerking his chin in the direction of the mantelshelf.

'Fifteen shillings and sixpence halfpenny, not a penny farthing more,' she told him. 'But at least we've started saving again.'

The cracked old teapot, handed on by Elsie's former employer, had never been used for its original purpose since tea was far too expensive to be brewed in this household; Elsie's home-made beer brewed from blackcurrants was cheaply made and, she said, better for them. Besides beer could be carried out to the fields and tea would have got cold. So the original purpose of the old teapot had long ago been forgotten; it was seen now only as a bank and, as such, occupied a prominent position on the shelf over the fireplace.

It was true, what she'd said about saving, Adam reflected.

They'd managed better after that first hard year. He had an allotment now as well as the garden plot and by their second autumn had grown enough vegetables to keep them going through the winter; potatoes were sacked up, carrots stored in boxes of sand, beans salted, fresh greens picked all the year round. And enough to spare for Elsie to take to the market. They had a pig too which gave them bacon for the year and dung to nourish the soil. Then at harvest time Elsie had gone gleaning with the other women and found, to her amazement, that the harvesters had left a generous amount of ears of wheat, something that would never have been allowed at Northrop. They threshed it at home and when she took it to the miller she was astonished to find it made enough flour to last them for nine months.

'I don't regret it now, this move from Northrop,' she said one evening. 'I wouldn't fancy going back.'

'Ay, it's worked out, but it was terrible that first year,' he told her, and she nodded, remembering those hungry months when she could see the bitterness gnawing at him as he endured the ruination of all his plans.

So Edith stayed on at school and did so well that when Miss Dewey, the postmistress, needed extra help in the shop at busy times like Christmas, she was taken on for odd jobs. She wasn't allowed to do any of the official business like pensions because she wasn't signed on and anyway you had to be a lot older, but she did what Miss Dewey called the running about, the fetching and carrying and sometimes went on the rounds with the postman if there was a lot to carry. She'd have liked to help with the telegram deliveries because sometimes two telegrams came in close together to be delivered in opposite directions and old Tommy Tawser had to decide which one would have to be taken late. But Miss Dewey said no, she wouldn't be allowed to help with that as you had to be signed on and take an oath and she wasn't responsible enough. Secretly she thought she was just as responsible as old Tom, who had once dropped a telegram in a horse trough where he'd stopped for a drink, but of course didn't say so. She was just thankful to be allowed, for the time being, to help in the shop and earn a few shillings for her mother.

For the long run though, she had other plans. Miss Dewey was getting on and one day they'd have to find another postmistress and who better than herself if she got herself in the way of running things? So she watched and learned, found out how the telegraph machine worked, got familiar with the numbers on the forms and with the government instructions, which were sometimes couched in language which others found difficult, but she could usually make out quite easily. The adding up was no problem either; she'd always been good at mental arithmetic.

Besides, she liked talking to the customers, especially on Mondays when the old people came to collect their pensions. It was four years since they'd started, these old age pensions, but the old people from the village still rejoiced when they collected their five shillings. 'No more work'ouse for us,' they'd say, shaking their heads in wonder.

'I wish my mother 'ad lived to see it,' one of them would say. 'If she and my father 'ad 'ad their seven-and-six they'd not 'ave died as they did.'

And they all nodded, for everyone in the village knew about the old Strattons; Jane and Jonas had been married for seventy-three years and had known each other from childhood, indeed from babyhood, for they'd been born in cottages next door to each other and old Jonas used to tell how he'd looked after the baby Jane when he was not much more than a toddler himself and how she used to look up at him from her cradle and he'd fallen for her lovely eyes there and then, and they'd always known they'd marry when they were of age.

By the time they were in their eighties only their youngest child survived and she couldn't afford to take them in; she could scarcely survive herself. So Jonas struggled to do odd jobs and Jane still went stone-picking in the fields, but it was only coppers that they could earn now and the day came when their few savings were used up.

They knew it was the workhouse for them and for all people like them. And the workhouse meant separation for it wasn't allowed for men and women to be together there; it wouldn't be moral, the Guardians said. When the man from the council came, they clung together, they pleaded not to be torn apart,

Jane wept, but he said they must go the next day, the landlord must have the cottage back now they couldn't pay the rent.

They were found the next day, lying by the empty grate, the poison having done its work. In death they were not divided; they were entwined together, like two gnarled old trees whose roots have grown together so that their branches cannot be parted.

The old people in the village still talked about it, as they gathered together at the post office to collect the pensions that allowed them to stay together at home now they were too old to work. And they'd often say God Bless Lord George and if, as Edith once did, anyone tried to explain that Lloyd was his name and he wasn't a lord, they'd just say of course he was a lord, how could anyone who had done such a wonderful thing *not* be a lord?

Eleven

After the children had been dismissed for the last time, Miss Poole looked around the empty school room, at the familiar rows of desks, at the maps on the wall, the backboard and the finger stocks, the slates, the cane in the corner, the register on her desk. Three bonnets still hung from the pegs on the right of the door, two jackets on the left. Everything was in its final resting place.

She took the key from its hook, closed the door and locked it behind her. Then she stood outside on the gravel path which drove a straight line through the luscious summer grass and for a moment saw again the fifteen-year-old girl that she had been when she first came to Northrop School. She was not, however, much given to introspection; forty-five years of drilling necessary facts into unwilling heads, of teaching by rote, of maintaining the relentless discipline required to keep country lads in order had cured her of any tendency towards contemplation. Instead she looked ahead to tea and gingerbread in her parlour.

As she turned towards the schoolmistress's house where these good things awaited her, she saw approaching from the direction of the hall, Lady Arndale, magnificent in her new wheelchair, being pushed by the dignified figure of Mr Jimson, the head gardener. They approached slowly so she had time to regard the grandeur of the old lady who day by day looked more like Queen Victoria, in her black dress, widow's cap, her jet beads and above all the look of rigid determination on her formidable face, the absolute authority in her eye.

The only possible reaction was to curtsey.

'Well, Poole,' Lady Arndale said, 'I hear you have retired.'

'Yes, M'Lady. That is so. Today, I have retired.'

'But you will be allowed to remain in your house.'

'Yes, M'Lady. I'm very thankful for it.'

'So you should be.'

'Oh, I am indeed, M'Lady. Might I ask what will become of the school?'

'Become of it? It will remain as it is. One day it may be reopened.'

Miss Poole wondered if, in that case, she would return to work there, or would someone younger come and in that case would she have to leave the schoolhouse, but she did not have the courage to raise such trivial matters to such a great personage, so stood in silence until she felt herself dismissed, when Lady Arndale told Jimson to continue with her walk.

'We will take the route through the woods to the lake, Jimson,' Lady Arndale instructed. 'Since it is so dry. You may leave me there for an hour.'

It was a perfect July day and the countryside was at its best. The banks were bright with Queen Anne's lace, with cornflowers and poppies and beyond them she could see the fields of ripening corn. She passed trim cottage gardens, saw trees laden with fruit. The cottages, under thatch or stone tiles, were in good repair, hedges were trimmed, ditches cleared. She took great satisfaction in all this, seeing it as the achievement of her lifetime's work, ever since the great decision to move south had been made fifty years ago. Yes, exactly fifty years, because they had moved here in eighteen sixty-three and now it was 1913. And it had been, above all, her own achievement, aided by her consort and, of course, God's guiding hand.

When she had first lost Edward she had thought she could not survive, but she had striven, as the great Queen-Empress had striven when she lost her dear Albert, and had conquered grief and continued the work as he would have wished. She had passed this estate to her son, and it would pass to his son and, like the British Empire of which the Queen had been the great mother, the estate would continue happy and glorious for generations to come.

She had no doubt of this and so was in a serene mood by the time they reached the lake, contented with her lot, satisfied with the changelessness of things. It might be 1913, she thought, as she sat alone after Jimson had left her with instructions to return in an hour, and there might have been many changes, but the right way of ordering one's estate did not change with the decades and never would.

She regarded the lake as one of her greatest achievements. It had been a patch of swampy ground when they came, which nobody knew what to do with, but she had seen what could be made of it, had brought in landscape gardeners who specialized in such work and now, fifty years on, it lay before her, a beautiful expanse of water, shining out there in the open, glinting here in the dappled shadow of the trees. The banks had grown muddy but had recently been cleared so that the pebbled shore dropped steeply down to the clear water. Nearby a little stream emptied itself into the lake, bringing with it eddies and ripples. On the far side a pair of swans moved majestically through the water.

The sun was hot on her face, having slipped out of the shade of the trees. She would move the chair a little, perhaps even go a short distance along the path round the lake. She enjoyed the freedom the new chair gave her to propel herself, though of course on the whole she preferred to have the propelling done by Jimson.

She released the brake and the chair began to roll forward. She turned the steering rod to direct it along the path, but since the banks had been cleared, the incline was too steep for it to respond. It gathered speed, it plunged towards the water. She clutched at the wheel, turned it the wrong way so that it accelerated instead of braking.

The chair plunged into the lake, the impact throwing her forward. Face down she lay in the water, the chair tumbling over on its side. The little tide created by the stream pushed her gently along towards deeper water, buoyed up at first by her voluminous skirts so that she floated like some ancient sea monster now long extinct. Then slowly, as the bombazine dress and flannel petticoats absorbed the water, Lady Arndale began to sink.

Twelve

'I really do think, darling,' William said, as he watched her letting down her hair in front of the looking glass, 'that we should go back to Northrop soon. We haven't been since Mamma's funeral last year.'

Selina shuddered and ran her fingers through her long hair. If there was anything she really disliked it was a funeral. And of all the funerals she had ever been to, her mother-in-law's had been quite the most dreadful.

'It's an end of an era,' people had said solemnly, dabbing their eyes.

And a good thing too, she had thought to herself, but hadn't, of course, said.

She had tried, for darling William's sake, to behave decorously. She had donned the black veil as the other ladies had done, and actually the black silk dress with the hobble skirt which hugged her figure had suited her wonderfully and she would have worn it more since but it brought back such awful memories just to look at it, much less put it on.

The family had gone on so; Elspeth repeating endlessly how she had rushed down to the lake when Jimson raised the alarm, the entire household following her, but not Charles who was away somewhere and nobody could find him, so she had had to take over. It was she who had instructed the men and watched as they hauled the lifeless body out of the water. The best thing had seemed to be to put it into the wheelchair where it just lay – at this point Elspeth's voice would break and Selina would tell her to hush, not distress herself and she could imagine it for herself. Of course she could imagine it: her mother-in-law flopped like some stranded whale in her wheelchair, dripping all the way up to the house where the doctor awaited, for Elspeth had thought of that too, sending Slater to bring the doctor immediately Jimson had come gasping to her with the news.

Then there was endless waiting, hanging about before the funeral could be arranged. There might have been longer delays about an inquest, but fortunately Charles' position enabled him to expedite all that. William had left her at Northrop for a few days as he had work to see to; she had wanted to return to London with him, but he said no, she must stay here to give the others her moral support. She pleaded that her own children needed her in London but he said they were perfectly happy with Nanny, an argument which she had used too often herself to be able to refute it now.

The funeral procession had seemed endless, miles of black-coated figures trailing along the dusty summer road to the church, the cottage windows shuttered or curtained, workers standing with bowed heads, Miss Poole and a tiny band of children marching along in their new mourning garments, the girls looking like ebony toadstools under their great black hats.

It was all so lugubrious and depressing; after all, she wanted to say, her mother-in-law was a very old lady and she'd lived longer than most, so what's all this commotion about? And if she was so pious, so strict in her religious duties as they all kept saying, surely she'd gone to heaven and they should be pleased for her, not go wailing on as if they thought she'd gone to the other place?

Most depressing of all, in the weeks that followed, was the change in Elspeth. She seemed to be turning more like her mother-in-law every day. She seemed to think that the burden of the estate now fell on her shoulders, though clearly she should leave it all to Charles who actually liked all that sort of thing.

So now, when William was on about returning to Northrop, she brushed back her hair and said, 'I just find it so depressing there, darling. I can't think why they don't cheer up and get on with life.'

103

'I'm sure they're trying to, darling. I thought Diana seemed very mature in the way that she was supporting her mother. Her parents must be very grateful to you for all the useful instruction you gave her in town.'

Selina shrugged. Actually she thought Diana had reverted somewhat. Of course she still looked much more grown-up in her London clothes but wore them somehow with less style in Northrop and often put on quite old things when she was playing with the younger children who had to be kept constantly amused to spare Elspeth's nerves.

'Perhaps we should ask her to stay again sometime when they can spare her from Northrop?' William suggested.

'Yes, perhaps.'

She spoke without enthusiasm. Transforming Diana had been one of her passing fancies. It hadn't been a total success, she had to admit to herself. And anyway she had a new diversion now, having met two suffragette ladies who had had some amazing adventures and invited her to go to meetings with them next month. She wasn't very interested in their political ambitions but the way they set about getting what they wanted was absolutely enthralling. It seemed to her like a new fashion which quite a lot of society ladies were following. But she knew how furious Lady Arndale had been when votes for women was mentioned and how she'd quoted the Great Queen's abhorrence of the very idea. It smacked of democracy, she said. No doubt Elspeth would feel the same; it might be courting disaster to involve Diana.

So she just smiled and added, 'Next year perhaps we'll ask her to stay,' and began scooping up her hair in her fingers, drawing it back from her face and sweeping it up into wings just above her ears. Some people were wearing it like that now. She would get Milly to try it properly tomorrow, she decided, letting it fall back on to her shoulders.

'As you know,' William was saying, 'I've promised we'll go to Northrop for a month in July, but I do think perhaps we should go there for a few days at Easter, just to lend moral support.'

'Oh, darling, I had hoped we might go to Paris at Easter,

104

just the two of us. It would be so cheerful there compared with Northrop which I do find somewhat depressing.'

She looked up at him, her eyes dark with anxiety.

He came across and stood by her.

'We can't have that,' he said, looking down at her. 'And after all I do think Charles seems quite back to normal. He's busy managing the estate, as he always was. I'm sure he misses Mamma as we all do, but I wouldn't say he was depressed – or depressing to other people.'

'No, to be honest, darling, it's Elspeth that I do find just a little bit wearing on my nerves.'

The great eyes that gazed up at him now were penitent, because she wanted him to know she hated to seem disloyal to her sister-in-law whom, actually, she quite liked.

He came across to her. Her head, as she sat there on the padded stool, reached only to the top of his legs. He leaned over her and held it to him.

'She seems to be getting so like your Mamma,' she said, her voice a little muffled in the folds of his silk dressing gown.

'I know what you mean,' he said, stroking her hair, pressing her head and shoulders against his body. 'I've noticed it too. I suppose she feels she must continue the role.'

'She needn't be so sanctimonious about it,' Selina said petulantly, forgetting for a moment about not wanting to be disloyal.

'She'll get over it. You'll see. Give her time.'

'It's odd really,' she said, moving slightly away so that she could look up at him. 'I mean, women are supposed to grow like their mothers as they get older, aren't they? I don't think they're supposed to grow like their mothers-in-law.'

He laughed and took her in his arms, drawing her up from the stool.

'I love you when you look so puzzled,' he said, kissing her. 'And anyway we don't know what her mother was like, do we? She may have been very like Mamma.'

'Heaven forbid. Oh, I'm sorry, darling. I shouldn't have

105

said that. I am truly sorry. After all she is your mother. I mean was.'

Her penitence was irresistible.

'Come to bed,' he said and after that no further mention was made of visiting Northrop at Easter.

Thirteen

'Well, I think it's absolute nonsense,' Charles declaimed. 'What are we supposed to be fighting for, I'd like to know. Nobody's invaded my land or any other part of the British Empire as far as I am aware.'

They all looked up at him, alarmed by his unwonted anger. What had come over their usually easy-going father, Teddy, Diana, Rupert and Laura all wondered, especially as the boys were just back from school when usually nothing but rejoicing filled the house.

Laura was particularly hurt; she just wanted to sit and to listen to Teddy, whose homecoming she always longed for from the day he went back to school at the beginning of term. What she particularly loved about her elder brother was that he never treated her like a child even though he was so tall and clever and excelled at school, not just at lessons, but in the Officers' Training Corps where he'd done so well that they'd made him a second lieutenant. And now her father was spoiling everything by going on about this war.

Diana too couldn't see the point of talking about a war which might never happen, but she grieved for her father's grief. She loved him more than ever now, realizing how much she had missed him when she was in France and then in London. It seemed a strange interruption in her life, that time in Billington Square, now that she was home and back to normal.

She tried to think of Sebastian as just part of a funny interlude; that was the only way she could bear it. She had been so sure that he would write. She hadn't, she realized later, put her home address on the note she'd left for him, but of course he could easily find it out. She kept remembering how he'd told her he was longing to see her again, hated the thought of being away from her even for three days. So he *must* have been disappointed, terribly disappointed, to find that she'd left. But then why, oh why, didn't he write?

She had taken to going down early in the morning so that she would be the first to look through the post on the hall table. She used to imagine how she would find it, among all the other ordinary letters, her own precious one, how she would carry it upstairs to read in secret. Many times she imagined herself doing these things, many times she ran downstairs to hunt through the pile of letters – a new day, new hope – and many times she turned and walked empty away.

So the anxious days had passed until one morning her father came into the hall, just as she was going miserably back upstairs.

'Would you like to come round the estate with me today, darling?' he asked. 'Blake's away so I shall be on my own. There are one or two things I want to look at. And you haven't been out with me for so long, have you?'

She had been about to refuse when suddenly she'd looked up at him, saw the concern, the love in his eyes.

'Yes, please, Papa,' she'd said, running over to him.

That was the moment when she'd realized she had to try to get back into her old life, here at Northrop where she belonged. She reminded herself how she had longed for home, for the estate and the meadows and lanes, for the little streams, for the familiar villages and stone-roofed cottages, above all for her home and family. She must try to forget about that interlude in London; it was unreal – and so was Sebastian who had been part of it. He was probably dancing with somebody else now.

Determined to act as if nothing had changed, she had thrown herself into playing with the younger children, taking them on walks and cycle rides, helping her mother and Nanny, sometimes going with her father round the estate, riding with her friends, just as she used to do, telling herself that this was where she belonged, this was her world.

At first she was acting a part but the strange thing was that she had moved imperceptibly from pretending to be happy to actually being happy. She couldn't tell exactly when it happened; it was just that one day she realized that she wasn't putting on an act any more, she really was enjoying being back in the old routine.

She was so lucky, she thought now, not to have parents like Aunt Selina and Uncle William who hardly ever saw their children. For wasn't it her father who had saved her that morning, when she was so miserable, and taken her out with him, though actually, she suspected, he hadn't really been planning to ride round the estate that day. He was a much more reliable friend than any Sebastian, she told herself.

All the same, she felt that her father was being unreasonable now and wished, for everyone's sake, that he'd talk about something else.

Celia and Tom too looked embarrassed, never having known their uncle be so ratty. William glanced anxiously at his brother, and Selina decided that Elspeth must be getting the poor man down. Really, to be still in full mourning after a whole year, it was so dreary, so Victorian. No wonder Charles was so jumpy; probably not getting enough sex. She wondered idly if wearing black all day made you frigid by night time.

'We're not at war yet, Charles,' William put in. 'I went to listen to a debate in the House last week and they were all talking about the Irish problem—'

'William,' Charles interrupted. 'War is coming and none of us knows why. What's it got to do with us if Serbia's been invaded?'

Nobody seemed able to tell him. They sat in uncomfortable silence round the dining-room table, Laura wishing that she hadn't insisted upon being counted as a grown-up and being allowed up for dinner, if this was the way the adults talked.

'I never thought it made sense for Disraeli to broker that ridiculous Treaty of Berlin which made Serbia so great,' her father was saying, 'and I don't see why I should defend a bunch of Serbian savages now. And as for France, after all this rivalry from her in Africa, why should we keep up the alliance?'

'There is the question of Belgian neutrality, Father,' Teddy put in. 'We learned about that in history and it does seem we should intervene if it's broken.'

'History! You've chosen the right word, Teddy. When that

treaty was made nobody thought that by the end of the century Belgium would be challenging us in Africa. And look at how she's behaved in the Congo.'

Laura wondered where the Congo was and if it was one of the pink bits on the map. Selina stifled a yawn. Even croquet would be better than this.

She hadn't been able to postpone a visit to Northrop any longer. William had insisted that they accept the invitation from Elspeth and Charles to stay for July and early August, to get away from the heat of London, which must be quite appalling in the summer, they said. She sometimes thought that Charles and Elspeth must be the only people in the land who didn't know that everyone who was anyone went to London for the summer season, didn't run away from it to the boring countryside. She stifled another yawn and thought of the ball she was missing tonight, the opera she had missed last night and the dinner she might perhaps have given tomorrow.

'Well, if it's war, I shan't be going up to Oxford next term,' Teddy said. 'I shall enlist straightaway. I suppose I'm sure of a commission, aren't I, Father?'

'That's no way to talk,' his father told him.

'Oh, I hope it lasts long enough for me to enlist,' Rupert said.

'If it's a war, it'll be a short one,' his uncle assured him. 'Sorry to disappoint you, Rupert, but everyone says that if there is a war it will be over by Christmas.'

'Well, I for one,' Elspeth suddenly cut in, speaking for the first time, 'am very proud that my sons should be so ready to fight for their country.'

The two boys looked at her gratefully, but Charles looked at her as if he was seeing her for the first time.

It was the hottest summer anyone could remember. Flowers drooped in their beds, leaves hung limply on trees and the grass rustled as they walked across the croquet lawn.

It was the last game of the tournament, thank God, Selina thought to herself as she trailed slowly across the dry grass to join her partner. She was playing with Elspeth against Tom and Laura, who had just beaten Diana and Teddy, and was wondering if it would be better to play so badly that Tom and Laura would win quickly and get the wretched business over or if it might be better to go for a quick win. She wasn't very good at the game, but had mastered the art of absentmindedly covering the ball with her skirts and then gently pushing it along to a more favourable position in front of the hoop.

The trouble was that Laura was so very good. Left alone when Diana was away and her two brothers had gone back to school, she used to spend hours playing croquet against herself, using two mallets and two balls. Sometimes she even invented three other players and played imaginary partners. In this way she became the best player in the family, far better at croquet than she was at tennis which she couldn't practise on her own.

She was not at her best today, however, and Elspeth was playing well, whacking the ball, her sister-in-law noticed, as if she was firing it into some miscreant enemy of the Empire. Selina decided to go for a quick win, constantly nudging her ball along under her skirts, once even moving her partner's ball very slightly, so that it could just squeeze through the hoop. A difficult shot, but Elspeth managed it, not having noticed that the ball was at a slightly easier angle to the hoop than it had originally been.

They were winning now; she had an easy shot to hit Laura's ball and the game was theirs. She missed it by a hair's breadth. Undeterred, she moved across to take her second shot; the others were all further away than she was and probably hadn't seen.

'I thought you missed, Mamma,' Tom called out.

'No, Tom, I just managed to graze it on the side.'

'I didn't see my ball move,' Laura objected.

'It hardly did. You wouldn't see from there. But I heard a little tap as it touched. Didn't you, Elspeth?'

'Well, I can't say really. But you were the nearest, Selina, so you would know.'

It was so unthinkable that anyone would cheat at a game that she gave her sister-in-law the benefit of the doubt, as Selina had known that she would.

Thus they won, dropped their mallets on the ground for the

servants to put away and walked towards the shade of the trees where Diana, Rupert and Teddy were waiting and where tea would soon be served.

'You are very good at croquet, Laura', Selina said kindly to her niece. 'You really deserved to win. Such bad luck.'

'It's in her blood,' Elspeth remarked. 'Dear Grandmama was very good at croquet when she was younger. She was of a standard to play at the All England Croquet Club at Wimbledon had she so wished. But then of course they changed it to include having tennis there which she didn't approve of.'

'I thought Wimbledon was always for tennis.'

'No, Rupert, it was originally introduced as a sideshow for the lower orders who might not appreciate the more serious game. She considered it vulgar.'

'But we played tennis here and she didn't mind, 'Laura pointed out.

'That was just at home. It was people watching that she objected to.'

'Well, they watched croquet.'

'That's different, darling,' Elspeth told her. 'Ladies don't have to run about and stretch in the same unladylike way. Croquet is a more dignified game,' she pronounced, sounding, Selina thought, more like her mother-in-law every minute.

'Could we go for a picnic tomorrow, Mamma?' Rupert asked as Witchart appeared with the footman bearing trays of sandwiches and cakes, silver teapots and hot-water jugs, biscuits and lemonade.

'Yes, that's an excellent idea. It really is too hot for games.'

'A picnic by the lake?' Selina enquired.

Elspeth shuddered. It was a year since that dreadful event but still she could not bear the thought of having a picnic in the place where her mother-in-law had gone to her watery grave.

'I thought you might like to go further afield,' she said. 'Furzebridge perhaps?'

'Oh, yes, please. We can swim in the pool downstream.'

'And the girls can paddle.'

'Can we cycle there?' Tom asked.

'Yes, if your parents agree.'

Selina nodded; she would agree to anything concerning the picnic so long as she didn't have to go on it.

'And Laura and Celia can go in the pony cart with Nanny if she wants to come. She may send Nursie instead.'

Nursie was the name they had given to Mary-Ann when she was promoted to nursery maid.

'You mean because Nanny's too old?'

'Of course not, don't be rude. Nanny may be busy with other things.'

'Why is it rude to say someone's old if they *are* old? I mean Grandmama was very old and—'

'That's enough, Rupert.'

Rupert was silent after that. In fact none of them had much energy for talking as the heat grew more intense in the stillness of the mid-afternoon and they sipped tea, nibbled at cucumber sandwiches and thought about tomorrow's picnic.

'I shall go in and discuss the menu for it with Cook,' Elspeth said, getting up out of her chair. 'We'll only go if the weather holds, of course,' she added.

'Oh, it will hold,' Rupert assured her. 'Thomson said it would reach ninety tomorrow.'

'How does he know?' Laura demanded. 'You believe everything he says, you boys do. And you never believe anything I say.'

'Of course not, you're only a girl.'

'You'd think he was a prophet like in the Bible, the way you believe in him.'

'He *is* a prophet. A weather prophet, silly.'

And so, hot and quarrelsome, they made their way back to the house.

The cyclists set off first.

'Oh, can't I go on my bicycle too, Mamma?' Laura begged.

'No, darling. It's quite a long way to Furzebridge, you know. You'd get there all hot and tired.'

So she had to stand and watch as the boys and Diana mounted their machines.

'Aren't you going to wear a veiled hat, Diana?' Selina asked. 'Your hair will be ruined.'

'No, Aunt, I like to feel the air blow through it, 'Diana called back as she followed her brothers and Tom down the lane.

Dust rose in individual columns behind each of the cyclists, then merged into a single thick grey cloud in which they were lost to view. Selina and Elspeth watched until they were out of sight.

'I do hope you enjoy the picnic,' Elspeth said to her sister-in-law. 'I'm afraid I am needed here.'

Selina hesitated, seeking the best excuse not to go.

'I'm afraid,' she said, 'that I must forgo the pleasure. I'm feeling a little unwell this morning.'

'Oh, dear. I am sorry. And I'd thought you might keep an eye on the children for me.'

'There is nothing I should have loved more,' Selina assured her, eyes wide with regret, 'but the truth is that I may possibly be in a delicate condition so must take no risks.'

'Of course not. Oh, Selina, how lovely. I am pleased.'

'Well, it's only a *possibility*, as I said,' Selina told her, knowing that anything is possible even if this particular thing was highly improbable and that when it turned out to be a false alarm, her sister-in-law would not be suspicious, only sympathetic.

So they went back into the house, Elspeth to have a last word with Cook, Selina to find William and tell him the good news that they had the day to themselves.

In the nursery, Nanny was giving last minute instructions to Mary-Ann.

'Take an extra sun bonnet for Laura and put in a spare one for Celia,' she ordered, 'because she never seems to have everything she needs now that they don't have a nanny any more, not that that Tubmorton was what I'd call a nanny.'

She spoke to Mary-Ann almost as an equal now. The girl had come on wonderfully since her arrival, fearful and trembling, four years ago, as a mere tweeny. But even then Nanny had observed her clean and tidy ways with approval. She was good with the needle too, so it wasn't long before she had seen that she was promoted to nursery maid. She was much more confident now, had filled out and grown taller. She was a rosy-cheeked, well-rounded girl, still quiet and amenable, but firm with the children and well-spoken too.

She had the makings of a nanny, the girl did. Well, no doubt Miss Diana would be marrying before long and the time would come when Master Teddy would do the same and then there would be more babies at Northrop Hall to be looked after, the next generation of Arndales to be cherished. And she, Nanny Stone, would one day have to retire to the cottage Mr Charles had promised her on the estate, so if the girl had ambition and minded her p's and q's the position might well be hers.

She wouldn't have entrusted some nursemaids with this outing to Furzebridge but she was confident that Mary-Ann would see that everything was done as it should be done. So with a final instruction to keep the sun off young faces and make sure that the children had the special salad without any of that oil and vinegar dressing with which Cook liked to cover summer vegetables, although it was a well-known fact that vinegar caused acid stomach in young people and that oil got on to everything, she handed over her charges to Mary-Ann, knowing that she herself would have a peaceful day at home, mending and ironing, seeing to one or two things of her own, perhaps enjoying an afternoon nap because she did find nowadays that after lunch her eyelids grew very heavy.

So she stood and saw them off, standing alongside Mrs Arndale who waved while the children waved back, and she herself kept her hands clasped in front of her on her stomach, as was right and proper. Then she returned to the house, climbed the back stairs and settled herself in the nursery with a pile of stockings to mend on one side of her and a small glass of port on the other for the good of her health.

The cyclists got there first, hurtling down the narrow lane and on to the steep track which in turn became a narrow path which led to the tree-fringed stream. The boys threw down their bicycles under a beech tree, left Diana in charge of them and dashed away down to the pool.

Years ago this part of the stream had been dammed to make a deep pool for dipping sheep. Its original purpose had been long forgotten, but the pool remained, deep and clear with brown boulders visible among the sand and gravel at the bottom.

They pulled off their clothes and jumped in, the water icy against their warm bodies as they splashed and swam, ducking, fighting, shouting with the sheer animal exuberance of it and the joy of being cool at last. Overhead hung willow branches on which they swung, dropping into the water, landing on each other, until at last, exhausted, they climbed out, the water which glistened on their shoulders, soon drying in the sun.

'Brilliant,' Tom said, rubbing his hair vigorously on his shirt. 'Pity it's not deep enough for diving.'

'We could dam it some more,' Teddy told him. 'It used to be deeper, but the dam's not been maintained.'

'Let's work on it after lunch. There are plenty of loose stones down there on the bottom – and on the banks.'

'Yes. And we could raise the bank here too.'

They talked about how it could be done as they put on their clothes, stopping, half-dressed, to assess the weight of stones, to argue about methods of damming or just to squinny into the water if one of them thought he saw a trout lurking beneath a boulder.

Meanwhile Diana sat under her tree and thought how unfair it was that the boys could rush downstream, strip off their few clothes and jump into the water, while she had to sit here in all these stupid garments, laced into stays, weighed down with skirts, and with these horrible bones in her collar which dug into her neck. Some girls were allowed bloomers for cycling but her mamma wouldn't hear of it. Oh, how she'd love to jump in the water as the boys did. At best she'd be able to take off her shoes and stockings and paddle when the others arrived.

She wished they'd hurry up. Papa had said a motor couldn't get down these steep and narrow lanes, so it had to be the slow old pony cart and wagon. Still, it was quite pleasant to lie here under the tree, the mossy ground still cool, while the stream chattered ceaselessly as it rippled past, as if it could go on for ever. It was a relief that all that talk of war yesterday seemed to have been blessedly forgotten; nobody had even mentioned it at breakfast time. Uncle William said these scares had happened before and would no doubt happen again. There had been crises in places like Agadir, he said, and they'd all died down, as this Sarajevo business would. So she lay back enjoying with closed eyes the sense of peace and calm, until the shouts of the boys and the sound of cartwheels simultaneously aroused her.

The boys said they were starving, so it was agreed that luncheon would be early.

'Come on, we'll play hide-and-seek while they're getting it ready,' she told the others. 'I'll count to a hundred while you go and hide.'

So she leant against a tree, her eyes hidden, counting loudly while they ran off into the wood, Laura keeping close to Celia, she noticed, because despite her argumentative ways she was nervous of shadows and imaginary wolves.

'One hundred. Coming!' she shouted and looked about her.

She saw that the footman and driver had lifted the hampers down from the waggon and were handing them to the maids, who had already spread the tarpaulins on the grass and covered them with linen cloths. There was really only one direction in which the others could have gone to hide, so she turned her back on the preparations for the picnic and wandered into the woods. A sound made her look up; Tom had hidden up a tree, caught his trousers on a branch and was struggling to free himself while Rupert, watching from another tree, was struggling not to laugh. Both of them were making a lot of noise in the process.

'Spied Rupert and Tom,' she called out.

They scrambled down and joined her.

The others were more difficult to find. Teddy had managed to bury himself under a pile of last autumn's leaves and dead branches and she twice walked past without seeing him. Celia had cheated and kept moving but since she said she'd never played before and didn't know the rules they let her off, though it did seem hard to believe that anyone existed who had never played hide-and-seek.

'It's different in London, so don't quarrel about it. It's only a game,' Diana told them. 'But wherever is Laura? Luncheon will be ready by now.'

'She was with me at the beginning, but she turned back,' Celia said.

So they made their way back to the picnic place. Silver, crockery and glassware were laid out now on damask cloths, jugs of lemonade awaited them and there was even a bottle of wine in a cooler, which Rupert immediately noticed.

'I asked Papa if we might have wine and he said just this once,' Diana told him, 'for the older ones.'

'Tom and me are older, aren't we?' Rupert enquired anxiously.

'Tom and *I*,' his sister corrected him.

'I know *you* are,' Tom said, puzzled.

'Oh, never mind. Yes, you and Tom can have some, of course. But where is Laura?'

Mary-Ann came quietly up to her.

'Don't worry, Miss Diana,' she said. 'I won't give her away, but I promise you she's quite safe.'

Just then Laura, who couldn't bear the suspense any longer, jumped out of a pile of rugs by the wagon, crying out, 'I'm the last to be found. I've won, I've won.'

'I think it's a bit of a cheat not to go away and hide properly in the wood,' Celia objected.

'I'm not a cheat,' Laura told her, instantly furious. 'I'm not, I'm not.'

'Of course you're not,' Tom said. 'She's just jealous that she didn't think of it.'

'I'm not jealous,' Celia told him, enraged now in her turn. 'I had a much better place.'

'Stop quarrelling and come and have luncheon,' Diana told them, leading the way over to where the picnic was being spread.

'Isn't it nice not to have to go and wash our hands?' Laura whispered to Celia, keeping her voice low in case one of her elders heard and thought of a way of making them do so. Celia nodded and they were friends again.

For a while they chattered as the maids served the food, but then fell silent as they concentrated on the serious business of eating chicken and ham, crunchy meat pies and sausage rolls which Cook had made that morning, potato salads, lettuce and tomatoes. The maids filled their glasses with lemonade but Teddy poured the wine.

118

'Oh, I wish we could have a picnic for every meal,' Laura sighed. 'It's so much more fun than sitting round a table.'

'It wouldn't be much fun if it was raining,' Rupert pointed out.

'I didn't mean if it was raining, silly. Of course I didn't.'

'You said every time. Didn't she, Diana?'

'It's too hot for arguing,' his sister told him. 'Oh, look, strawberries.'

Cool and moist, the shining, dimpled fruit was piled up in crystal bowls.

'Can we eat them with our fingers?'

'Yes, if you don't have cream, Laura.'

Torn, Laura deliberated before saying at last, 'I shall eat half with my fingers and have cream on the rest.'

Afterwards they lay back, some in deck chairs, some on rugs. Only Tom wandered about restlessly; he went to inspect the pool and came back wanting to discuss the dam with Teddy, but his cousin was asleep. So he lay down beside him instead. None of them would have thought of breaking Nanny's ancient rule about not swimming for an hour after a meal. If you swam in under an hour after eating, she always pronounced, you got appendicitis. The late King had once nearly died of appendicitis.

'Had he been swimming, Nanny?' Rupert had once asked.

'No. But all the same,' Nanny had replied.

It was very still, lying there under the trees. Soporific was the word for it, Tom decided, as the heat built up. It felt as if the warmth of the afternoon sun was adding to the existing warmth of the morning and today's heat was piling up on yesterday's heat and it would just go on day after day getting hotter and hotter. Somewhere a bee was buzzing and above a pile of stones by the wagon he could see the heat visibly shimmering. He watched through half-closed eyes as the maids cleared away the remains of the meal, packing food into hampers, stacking dirty plates into containers, which the men carried over to the waggon. The maids wore their usual aprons for picnics but not their caps. It was quite strange to see their hair.

Nursie was returning with Laura who had presumably been answering a call of nature somewhere out of sight in the bushes.

119

Then she settled down with Laura alongside and began reading to her. She was so pretty, that nursery maid, with her dark curly hair and pink cheeks; her lavender coloured dress suited her colouring. She had big dark eyes, almost violet coloured they were, with the longest eyelashes Tom had ever seen except on a donkey. Once he wouldn't have noticed. Even last year he'd probably have preferred a donkey, but all that had changed now. Very suddenly too. Overnight he'd become bored with things he used to enjoy, excited by things he'd never noticed before, restless and much more inclined to want to be alone.

He found himself trying to describe the girl, as he watched her through half-closed eyes. You couldn't call her cheeks peachlike; peaches had that yellowish tinge while hers were flushed pink, more like a rose. But the texture was peachlike; he imagined her cheeks would be very soft to touch, different from his own hard jaw, he thought as surreptitiously he felt his chin. She had rolled up her sleeves; he could see the roundness of her arms. They would be soft to the touch too. As she lent forwards to turn a page, he could see the movement of her breast under the bodice of her dress. All of her was so rounded, so soft. He found himself imagining the feel of that too, as he lay there, warmed by the sun, replete from the meal, sleepy from the wine.

It wouldn't do; such thoughts brought embarrassment. He crossed his legs and tried to think of something else, something to distract his mind, something boring like working out how hot it would be if they were in France and the temperature was in centigrade. It was ninety in Fahrenheit, he thought, and you had to multiply by nine which would be eight hundred and ten and then divide by five which would be one hundred and sixty-two. Then you took off thirty-two which would make it a hundred and thirty centigrade. Which couldn't possibly be right. Perhaps he should have multiplied by five and divided by nine. Yes, of course, to get it smaller you'd have to do that. But he didn't bother because the exercise had served its purpose. He lay back, his legs outstretched in front of him, feeling virtuous as he looked up not at Mary-Ann but instead at the dark patterns the leaves and branches made against the bright blue of the sky.

When he woke up, the others had already bestirred themselves, the boys to return to the pool, the girls to paddle in the
stream. Diana was sitting on the bank, her legs dangling in the
water. Laura was sitting alongside her. Mary-Ann was standing
in the middle of the stream, holding up her skirts with one hand,
while with the other she held on to Celia who, her dress tucked
into her drawers, was wobbling uncertainly. What a baby she
is, Tom thought, I could swim when I was her age and she
can't even stand in the water without falling over. Still, she's
only a girl, so I suppose she can't help it, he added to himself
with a feeling midway between contempt and compassion.

He went and sat by Diana on the bank, watching the pair in
the stream. Water swirled gently around Mary-Ann's bare legs,
as she stood there, her dress bunched up around her, looking
down at Celia.

'I want to paddle too,' Laura announced and slithered down
the bank. She stood for a moment and then began to wade
out towards the others. She had almost reached them when
she caught her toes on a sharp stone, tripped, cried out and
made a grab for Mary-Ann, who, hampered by Celia, would
have fallen if Tom hadn't quickly jumped in and caught her.
They stood swaying for what seemed a long time, the two girls
clutching Mary-Ann, clinging to her like little plants seeking
support while Tom, his arm around Mary-Ann's waist, his
feet braced firmly on the bed of the stream, held the whole
uncertain structure in place.

It seemed to last a long time, this water ballet, but it must
only have been a minute before Diana, laughing, waded in,
caught hold of Laura and deposited her on the bank, where
she hopped up and down, saying her toes hurt and she was
surprised there wasn't any blood, she was sure there ought to
be because it hurt so much.

'I'm all right now, thank you, Master Thomas,' Mary-Ann
said, disengaging herself from his arm.

'I'm afraid your dress got wet.'

'It'll quickly dry in the sun.'

She spoke quietly, her voice was soft. He couldn't remember
if he had heard her talk before. No, he couldn't have, he'd have
remembered that sweet voice. She was so gentle, so composed.

121

He wasn't at all composed. He muttered something about the dam and went off downstream, in a turmoil as he remembered the feel of his arm around that little waist.

When Diana had told them that tea would be at half past four, they'd all said they wouldn't be able to eat another thing, but by four o'clock they were all saying they were starving, so the cloths were brought out again and laid with plates and knives and cups and saucers, which the men unloaded from more hampers, while the maids set out the sandwiches, cake and biscuits and fruit tarts. Mary-Ann, having put Cook's special custard pie to one side, to have last, knowing it was a favourite with the younger children, insisted that they ate a piece of plain bread and butter before anything else, as this was one of Nanny's rules.

'Where's Tom?' Diana asked, looking up from wiping Celia's fingers.

'He said he just wanted to finish his section of the dam. He'll be here in a minute.'

'It's bad manners to come to table late,' his younger sister virtuously informed them.

'I told him it would be all right, Celia. We're doing a third each and he had the most difficult part, where the bank kept falling in.'

'And it's not a table anyway,' Laura told her.

At that point Tom appeared. He lent over Diana and murmured an apology, since she was the most senior person there, then he sat down just behind her. He looked surprised and after a minute got up again. The remains of the custard pie was flattened in the grass. The rest of it was stuck to his trousers.

'He's sat in the pie,' Celia shrieked and she and Laura fell into each other's arms screaming with laughter.

'That's enough, it's not really funny,' Diana tried to say but had to stop because she was laughing too much. Soon they were all rolling on the grass, pointing and laughing.

Only Tom was not amused. He looked at Mary-Ann, horrified that she'd think him a silly child, but she, struggling not to laugh, was trying to think what Nanny would have said and done, but couldn't. So with twitching mouth, she cleared up as much of the yellow, crumby mess of custard and pastry as she could, while avoiding Tom's eye.

'You can have my other shorts, Tom,' Teddy offered. 'We're about the same size.'

Actually Teddy was taller, but Tom took the shorts and made off into the bushes, glad to get away from the whole giggling lot of them.

'There'd be room for the bicycles in the waggon, Master Teddy,' the driver said as they prepared to leave. 'If you want a ride back.'

'I think that's a good idea. It would be nice all to go back together. I'll ask the others.'

By this time they were all tired, glad to sit in the waggon or the trap and have a lazy journey home. The sun was low in the sky now, the light less harsh as they made their way slowly along winding lanes banked with dusty flowers; the white cow parsley was brighter now than the red poppies in the hedgerows, which had seemed so vivid earlier in the day. Evening had transformed the world they'd travelled through this morning.

They didn't talk much as they sat, their faces tingling from the long day's sunshine, their bodies lulled by the movement of the wheels. They were all pleasantly sleepy as they turned past the lodge and up the drive of Northrop Hall. Celia and Laura were both clutching bunches of wild flowers, picked for their respective mothers at Mary-Ann's suggestion, so their hands were sticky from the juicy stems as they clambered down.

The grown-ups met them in the hall, Celia and Laura were taken off to bed, their floral offerings having been, it seemed to them, rather unenthusiastically received by their mothers, who appeared to be thinking of something else.

'What is it?' Teddy asked, when the little ones had gone.

'We sent for news to London,' his father told him. 'It seems that if no answer to our ultimatum to Germany is received by midnight, we shall be at war.'

The four of them looked at him with disbelief. They had forgotten all about the crisis. Now it was upon them, present and frightening, and the day which had seemed so real was suddenly an idyll of the past.

'I think we'll go up,' William said, and he and Selina led the way upstairs, Tom and Rupert following, but Teddy and Diana stayed in the hall with their parents.

'I'm going to wait up,' Charles said.

He sounded weary and anxious and looked suddenly much older.

'We'll stay with you,' the others told him and went with him into the drawing room.

And so it was that at midnight, with the windows wide open to the airless night, they heard the church clock striking twelve.

Afterwards they always associated the outbreak of war with standing together that sultry evening listening to the striking of the hour. But the younger children remembered it as the day they had the picnic at Furzebridge and Tom sat in the custard pie.

Fourteen

Teddy volunteered immediately war was declared.

'Promise you'll write to me,' Laura begged. 'And soon, because if it's over by Christmas there won't be much time.'

All the servants had lined up to see him off, Witchart had shaken him by the hand and then the family had gone to the station to see him on to the train. He was resplendent in his new uniform; he had gone back to London with the cousins the week before to see to everything and buy all his kit.

'It's a bit like going away to school and having everything new, isn't it?' Rupert put in.

'It is not at all like that,' Charles told him sharply. 'Your brother is going to war, not some peaceful place of education.'

Rupert was silent, hurt by this unaccustomed asperity.

'Sorry,' he muttered. 'Didn't mean it,' but he did really and couldn't wait until it was his turn to go.

They watched as Teddy got on to the train, shook hands with his father out of the window, blew kisses to the others, then he was lost in a cloud of smoke and steam.

They stood on the deserted platform, feeling sad and left behind after he had gone, then Charles put his arm on his younger son's shoulder to show he still loved him despite that rebuke, and Rupert glanced up at him and smiled. Diana observed all this and felt glad. Elspeth did not; she was still standing watching until there was no wisp of smoke visible from the departed train. Then she turned to the others and said, 'Oh, doesn't it make you proud?'

She looked younger now that she had abandoned her mourning; patriotism demanded a more cheerful look, she had decided, and felt sure that Lady Arndale would have understood. It was as if the war had given her not so much a new lease of life as an injection of energy into the old one. She had already begun organizing bandage-rolling mornings for other ladies of the county and comforts mornings at which they knitted for the soldiers. In October she appointed a retired nurse to teach First Aid to the young ladies of the neighbourhood and commandeered a few bewildered estate children to come and have bandaging practised on them.

'Selina, my darling,' William said. 'I need to talk to you very seriously.'

She was sitting at her dressing table in her nightgown, brushing her hair.

'Oh dear, you sound very solemn,' she said, turning towards him. 'Have I done something *very* bad?'

'Of course not, my love. As if you ever could!'

He came across and stood behind her, looking at her in the glass.

He hesitated, not able to find the right words for what he had to say. She waited, wondering what it could be. In the end he just blurted out, 'I feel I must enlist.'

Whatever she had expected, it certainly was not this.

'Enlist?' she repeated. 'You?'

'Yes.'

'But you're not a young man. You're a husband and a father,' she pointed out, bewildered.

'Many of the men fighting out there are husbands and fathers.'

She had put down the brush and was staring at him, wide-eyed.

'I know I'm not young,' he admitted, 'but I'm not too old either. And if they do introduce conscription it will be for men between eighteen and forty-one and I'm quite a long way off that still.'

She put her hands on top of his, which were resting on her shoulders. Her eyes were full of tears.

He was half alarmed, half touchingly pleased by her concern.

'I don't expect they'll put old chaps like me in the front line,' he said, trying to reassure her, 'but I can probably be quite useful taking up supplies or something.'

126

'Couldn't you be useful at home somehow?' she suggested persuasively, 'so we can be together,' she added, rubbing her cheek against his right hand, then moving it down on to her breast.

But he took it away and said firmly, 'I'd be ashamed not to go, Selina.'

There was something in his tone that made her feel that neither reasoned argument or feminine wiles would move him.

'Now, what we have to discuss is where you and the children should go while I'm away. Tom, of course, will still be at school, but I suggest that we close this house and you and Celia go down to Northrop. You will be safe and well looked after there. I shouldn't need to have any anxiety about you if you were with Elspeth.'

The idea that she should be put into Northrop Hall in order to spare him anxiety almost made her throw the hairbrush across the room. But she controlled herself and said, 'I think not, William,' for she knew she would prefer anything – Germans, air raids, the arrival of the Kaiser himself, or any other horror – in preference to slow death by boredom with her sister-in-law in Gloucestershire.

On an impulse, she said, 'I shall stay here and help with the war effort.'

She had suddenly realized that a great new diversion was being offered to her. Her suffragette friends had told her that the fight with the government was off for the duration of the war. It was time now to unite to fight the common enemy. Women, they said, could serve in all manner of ways. They could train as nurses, they could be VADs, they could join various voluntary organizations being set up all over the country, they could offer hospitality to soldiers who were on leave, soldiers who were waiting to go abroad, soldiers recovering from injuries.

Nursing did not appeal to her, but the idea of entertaining all these fighting men thrilled her. Yes, that was what she, Selina Arndale, would do, she would devote her time and energy to comforting soldiers in London. What better excuse could there be for not going to Northrop?

* * *

Teddy kept his promise and wrote long letters to Laura from his training camp in the north of England. What she loved about him was that he wrote as if to an adult, he never talked down to her just because she was only eleven. He told her about the shortage of equipment and instructors, about how messages were still sent by messengers on horseback as if it were 1814 and the telephone hadn't been invented. What are they thinking of, he demanded, why even the local post office at Northrop had telegraph equipment years ago. There should be field telephones, there should be radio transmission, he raged, telling her all these things just as if she wasn't still a child, and a girl at that.

She asked her father about it, read books in his library so that she could reply to Teddy's letters in a way that would be worthy of them. And he rewarded her with more letters; from his training camp in England he told her what was going on in France, describing to her the movements of the British Expeditionary Force, the retreat from Mons, and then how it was the Germans who were retreating, which she didn't quite understand but didn't like to ask. He told her how they had stopped and dug themselves into trenches and so long as they stayed behind their defences, none of the usual methods of attack could get them out. He told her how our side had dug similar trenches and were lined up opposite them. It was unlike any kind of warfare that ever men had fought, he said, this trench warfare.

It was the first time she'd heard that word and she thought they must be something like the ditches that ran below many of the hedges on the estate. Later she understood better. Telling her about the battle of Ypres, he wrote, 'Don't think of battles being like the ones in history books. Men don't run out into the field and fight until one side runs away so it's all settled in a few hours. It isn't going to be like that any more. Both sides will just dig themselves in, shoot each other until the artillery runs out, but if it doesn't, then this could go on and on.'

So Uncle William had been wrong; the war wouldn't be over by Christmas.

After Christmas Teddy was no longer reporting other men's

experiences; he was out there himself and sent them letters which their mother read aloud.

'The arrangements for post are amazing,' he wrote. 'Yours reach me in four days. Imagine it – Northrop to Picardy in four days! And just with the name and regiment, nothing else to go by, and yet they find their way to the billets and hospitals and even to the trenches. I can't tell you what letters from home mean to the men. You should see their faces when a letter comes for them, hear their glee when they've got two or even three. It's not the quality of the letters that seems to matter most, it's the *quantity*!'

His letters always started with thanks for the parcels they had sent: every week they sent hampers from Fortnum and Mason, cakes made by Cook to recipes she knew he liked, his favourite cigarettes, biscuits and chocolate and all sorts of odd things that he requested like string, candles and even, once, sealing wax. Then he told them odd stories about the men and particularly about his servant, Miles, who, they could tell though he did not say it, was absolutely devoted to him. Evidently he had found favour with his commanding officer too, for he wrote and told them that the colonel had glanced through his papers and remarked, 'Ah, I see you're an excellent shot. That should make you useful for special duties.' Modestly he didn't take credit for this achievement. 'If I'm any good with a gun,' he said, 'it's all due to Thomson's instructions and then to the OTC training at school. I don't think I'd have made much headway without either of those.'

That's what she loved about him, Laura thought when these words were read to her; he was never boastful, never showed off, never got exasperated like Rupert. Somehow you could always tell how he'd react, which was very comforting, she thought, lovely, predictable Teddy.

Diana was a different matter. Her gentle sister, who used to be so compliant, seemed to have changed. Maybe it dated back to the time she stayed in London with William and Selina. And now here she was arguing with Mamma, which wasn't at all the sort of thing any of them had ever done.

'Mamma,' she said one morning after her father had left the breakfast table and the servants had finished clearing. 'I

129

have decided I should like to help the war effort. I should like to nurse.'

'But of course, darling,' her unsuspecting mother said. 'I am proud that you wish to serve as Teddy is doing in your own little way. You have done very well at the bandaging classes and I think you would profit by going to the Home Nursing course. I have always believed young ladies should learn something of nursing in order to be able to manage their family's health when the time comes.'

'No, Mamma. I don't mean that. I mean I should like to train properly in a Voluntary Aid Department. I could train at the military hospital in Shappenham.'

Her mother was silent, aghast, then burst out with, 'You poor, silly child, what are you thinking of? You have no idea of what life is like in such places, nor of the sort of women you might meet there.'

'I should meet other nurses—'

'Who would not be at all our sort of people.'

'And do you object to Teddy mixing with men who might not "be our sort of people"?'

'That is entirely different. And I have dreadful tales of young ladies who have volunteered as VADs being treated like skivvies by the trained nurses, who revel in ordering them about.'

'Of course one would take orders from qualified nurses, Mamma. One would expect to do so.'

'I will tell you something, Diana. It is shocking, but perhaps it will make clear to you the kind of treatment you might expect.'

She paused in the manner of a woman wondering if some enormity should, after all, be uttered.

'Lady Murray gave one of her houses to be used as a nursing home,' she began. 'Her daughter volunteered to work there as an auxiliary. One afternoon she was going upstairs to see the matron in her office, when a sister saw her and told her she must use the *back stairs*. This sister was the daughter of the local butcher.'

Diana shouldn't have laughed. She knew she shouldn't. But she couldn't help it.

Her mother said nothing. She glanced pointedly at Laura and then said, 'I suggest that you and I continue this conversation elsewhere, Diana.'

So Laura didn't hear the rest of it, didn't hear her mother raising every difficulty, nor Diana countering them. She didn't hear the gasp of horror from her mother when Diana said she would live in a nurses' home with the other girls, didn't hear the threat to summon her father, nor Diana's calm rejoinder that when she had mentioned it to him he had seemed to think it a good idea.

Not, Diana knew, that her father's casual agreement meant very much. He had always left such matters to his wife and was now very distracted by what was going on in the estate, suffering as it was for the first time from shortage of workers.

The problem, it seemed, was that many of the staff had taken it into their heads to volunteer. Both he and his wife deemed it very inconsiderate.

'But,' Diana pointed out, 'if it's good that Teddy enlists, then surely it's good for the gardeners and grooms and everybody else to enlist?'

'Nonsense,' her mother said sharply. 'They won't be officers.' And even her usually kindly, tolerant father said she was too young to understand these things and that a gentleman had his honour to consider which didn't apply to these other men, who should just stay here to do their duty.

'Yes,' her mother put in. 'You remember your catechism and how you learned about doing your duty in that state of life to which it has pleased God to call you? Well, it pleased God to call them to be workers on the estate and they should not shirk that duty by running off to France.'

She sighed and her face had taken on a martyred look as she went on: 'They have let us down badly. You children may not realize it but from next month we shall have no menservants within doors, apart from Witchart who is elderly. For the rest we depend entirely on women and I for one do not enjoy seeing them struggle with work that is too heavy for them.'

'It's worse out on the estate,' her father agreed. 'The fences go unmended and we just have to let go anything

131

that isn't urgent. Your mother has to bear seeing the gardens go wild.'

'Jimson does his best, but he's an old man now and just has the one boy to help.'

'If there's conscription—'

'Oh, I'm all in favour of conscription,' his wife interrupted. 'That will catch the scroungers and cowards.'

'If there is conscription,' he continued as if she hadn't spoken, 'Blake will have to go, and for the first time the estate will be without an agent.'

She was silent for a moment and then said, 'Well, I'm sure you'll find a way of managing, as we all must.'

All the same Elspeth increasingly sensed doom all around her as she watched the crumbling of her immaculate world, saw the weeds among the roses, the convolvulus and couch grass creeping in the herbaceous border, saw the unpruned fruit trees and the dishevelled topiary work that no longer looked like peacocks or unicorns. She was glad Lady Arndale had not lived to see it. She knew that her husband felt the same dismay as he looked at neglected barns, untrimmed hedges and clogged ditches and wondered if it could ever be put together again.

Fifteen

If there was any of that ill will towards VADs that her mother had warned her about, Diana was too busy to notice it. She seemed to be always rushing, rushing to get up in the morning at the unaccustomed hour of six, her cold fingers struggling with the buttons and studs of the unfamiliar uniform, without a maid to help her, she who was used to having a fire in her bedroom and a jug of hot water on the washstand. She thought of Nanny and often longed for her reassuring presence as she battled with the stiff apron and starched cuffs by the pale light of dawn.

At first she seemed to do nothing but clean: rubber sheets had to be scrubbed, glass trolleys wiped, sterilizers had to be polished until you could see your face in them, though she was not tempted to do so since the cape did not suit her and she had trained herself not to look in the four square inches of looking glass which hung by a piece of string on a nail in her bedroom. It's a far cry, she thought, smiling to herself, from Madame Gagneux's salon.

When she was not scrubbing and washing she seemed to be walking down endless stone corridors, tramping between surgical kitchens, sink rooms and wards. She fell into bed at night aching all over from the heavy lifting, her feet painful and her chapped hands itching and sore.

But the odd thing was that she had never felt happier in her life. It puzzled her, this contentment that she felt. She had never known anything like the physical discomfort of these days, but she had never felt so free. It was the first time she had gone anywhere unchaperoned. It had been unthinkable in the past for her ever to be alone with a man; now it no longer mattered so long as the woman was a nurse and the man a wounded soldier. In her free time, a blessed hour or two each day, she could go off and do whatever she wanted unchaperoned. And when she was promoted to doing proper nursing she realized that for the first time in her life she was doing something useful.

Her only fear now was of being found wanting, of being squeamish, of fainting, as some young lady volunteers had been said to do at their first operation. In fact she found it so intriguing that she wouldn't have missed any of it by losing consciousness. Besides, the fact that the patients were anaesthetized and knew nothing of what was going on, reduced the horror of what was being done to them. She found the dressings much more horrible to observe, the patients aware, stricken, embarrassed, heartbreakingly stoical.

The other strange thing was that, although she never saw him now, she felt much nearer to Teddy, for through these men she got to know what his life must be like on the front where he was fighting. He must have realized this and wrote to her freely, knowing that there was no need to pretend with her as he did with the rest of the family.

They had always got on easily, she and Teddy, but they had never been particularly close, why should they be? But now in their letters they were closer than they had ever been at home. They wrote to each other intimately, with understanding, with shared anxiety and grief. He didn't need to protect her from the knowledge of what the war was doing to men's bodies; she saw the consequences for herself when the remains of them reached hospital, after being briefly patched up at the base hospital in France. But he also knew that when he talked of home, she would understand because they shared an unspoken love of the countryside in which they had roamed as children.

'Sometimes when we first landed and marched through a land that was relatively unscathed,' he wrote in his early days in France, 'I was reminded of home. Of course it wasn't really like home, the smells were different for a start. You'd be amazed how the scent of herbs rises from the ground in the evening as we crush them under our boots as we march! But just sometimes there's a moment of breathtaking similarity and I'm carried back to a different life in the green valleys and little

134

woods of Northrop and imagine myself back at home. We had billets in a chateau last week, pretty battered and deserted now, but it reminded me of home with its granary and stables and dovecote. It had a vinery too, of course. Apparently it had suffered in the Franco-Prussian war and the owners had never been able to afford to restore it. But it had grace and charm and there was a kind of sad beauty about it. I first saw it in the moonlight on a mild, clear night.'

She had never had such letters from him before; he had written to the family from school of course: the compulsory Sunday letter had arrived each week recounting house matches, cricket scores, modest references to prizes for shooting, to OTC exercises. There had never been anything about what he was thinking or feeling.

As he moved nearer the front and the scenery was more scarred, the letters were less idyllic.

'I find myself looking at a ruined village and imagining how it must have looked before the war, when these blackened stumps were leafy trees and these piles of rubble were houses, along streets where children walked to school and the women went to market and looked after the cottages which are now just a heap of stones.'

He wrote long letters to the family, but often wrote separately to her, as if he needed to tell her things that he didn't care for the rest of the family to hear.

'Don't tell this to Mamma,' he wrote in the summer, 'but sometimes I feel utter despair. The new recruits come out so full of idealism and hope and deserve so much better equipment, so much better billets. Some of the barns and sheds we put them into are hardly fit for cattle to bed down. Imagine, no drains, no disinfectant, and so many men crowded together. Sometimes they're worse than the trenches. I've heard men say they were glad to get back to them after a spell in the billets.'

To the rest of the family he wrote cheerfully of life in the trenches. 'It's a cushy life in here,' he said. 'We dig ourselves in and although it's a bit noisy out there in no-man's-land, we're safe behind our earthworks. It's the men who have to bring up supplies that I'm sorry for. Compared with them, your son is having a pretty easy time.'

135

But to her he wrote more fully of the trials of the men who had to walk that road.

'It's a holed and muddy way, Diana, along which mules drag the supplies and soldiers march with reinforcements. On that exposed road, they have nowhere to hide from enemy fire, they have no earthworks to protect them. The enemy sights them easily for the Germans know the road well; they were tramping along it themselves not so long ago! So they keep up the shelling, killing ambulance men, waggon-drivers, ammunition carriers, men bringing cartloads of stones to fill up the holes in the road, as well as soldiers on the march. Yet such a little time ago this was a peaceful country highway along which people travelled in safety, surrounded by fields and orchards as they went about their everyday affairs. And now it has all been reduced to this desolate wreckage of rubble and filth and mud by this pointless war.'

At Christmas he wrote, 'Do you remember how last year the men gave themselves a truce? One still hears such strange stories from all along the line. One regiment saw that the Germans had put a Christmas tree in their trench and decorated the top of the parapet with Chinese lanterns and were shouting out an invitation to come over and join the party. One man accepted and one by one the others followed so they all stood on no-man's-land exchanging presents, swapping cigarettes for jam and so on. Further up the line our men realized that the enemy fire was diminishing and finally stopped, so they did the same. The two sets of trenches were only a few yards apart so both sides could see the other, standing on the top repairing the trenches, digging extensions, mending wire quite openly with nobody firing. It seemed a sensible arrangement to let each other get on with such work in safety. One Yorkshire regiment reported no fighting for several days until they got an urgent message from the Germans saying that their general was paying a visit that afternoon, so the British had better keep their heads down as the general would want to see a little fighting!

'A Scottish regiment actually had a football match with a Saxon one on the other side. They used their caps to mark the goal, kept all the rules and played for an hour. Then the commanders found out and stopped play. The score was three to two to the Germans. There were many stories like these and it seems that all along the line the men managed to talk and with a bit of broken English on one side and broken German on the other conveyed that they didn't want to kill each other. Of course it couldn't last; the "high-ups" wouldn't allow it.

'Well, this year precautions were taken well in advance and we were told that there must be no repetition of the "regrettable occurrences" of last year. So we had to keep firing all day, though there were some who ignored the order. A battalion of the Coldstream Guards were approached by German soldiers walking across unarmed, so went out to meet them and exchanged souvenirs. But the officers had had their instructions about this sort of thing so they ordered the artillery to fire into no-man's-land which brought the celebrations to a pretty quick end.

'I wonder if it is the first time that commanders have been afraid that their men might get too friendly with the enemy? Isn't it strange to think that if the men had refused to end their impromptu truce the war would simply have come to an end? Maybe the staff who keep so far away behind the front line would have come puffing up to shoot at each other.'

At Easter he was going to be given leave.

'We shall celebrate in the old way,' his mother told her husband, 'despite having to manage with so few servants.' She was always having to try to cheer Charles up, he seemed so low in spirits since the war started, constantly harping on the waste of it, oblivious of the glory.

The three of them were sitting by the fire in the drawing room after dinner. She had founded a Ladies' Knitting for Victory club, so half a scarf dangled from knitting needles on her lap, for she liked to show a good example. Charles was sitting staring gloomily into the fire, a newspaper abandoned by his side. Diana was sitting a little apart, reading a nursing textbook.

'It's a shame we can't have William's family to share in our celebrations,' she went on, 'don't you think, dear?'

'William's out there, where maybe I ought to be.'

'Oh, Charles, that's absurd! You are well over the age.'

'It's the old men who are sending the young ones out to die,' he pointed out. 'Maybe it would stop if some of the old fellows went out there to see for themselves.'

'That is what William is doing and when he has leave you must talk to him. I'm sure that would make you see things differently.'

The knitting needles clicked for a while, then she laid the scarf down and said, 'You know I can't help but feel ashamed when I remember how I once misjudged dear Selina. She seemed just a little too, well, pleasure-loving and I know your Mamma mistrusted her. But how she has risen to the occasion! Nothing will make her leave London, not even an invitation to come and enjoy a far easier life with us here. Her duty is to comfort the soldiers, she insists, and nothing will make her forsake that sacred task. She is an example to us all.'

She sat quietly for a moment, the knitting needles at rest, as if in silent homage to her sister-in-law. Then she turned to Diana and said, 'You, of course, will be at home for Teddy's leave, Diana.'

'Certainly I can get home for part of the time,' Diana said, raising her eyes from her book.

'For *all* the time, Diana. I insist. You must tell them that your brother will be home from the war.'

Diana smiled.

'Other nurses have brothers in the war, Mamma.'

'I'm sure that if *I* have a word with Matron.'

'No.'

There was no mistaking the authority in her voice. Her mother did not argue with it. After the war, she thought, everything will get back to normal; servants will know their place and daughters will obey their mothers.

Teddy had been home for two days of his week's leave before she was able to join them. She saw at once that he was strained and tired and had the look of grey exhaustion which she had seen on the faces of the men coming home from the front, those young men who seemed to go away as eager schoolboys and come back as disillusioned veterans. Would it be as easy, she wondered, to talk to him as it had been to write? Or would they have to revert to the kind of superficial friendliness of pre-war days?

Clearly her mother had striven to re-establish the jollity of the school holidays.

'If this lovely weather holds we might have one of our family picnics,' she suggested at breakfast.

Charles nodded.

'Perhaps you'd like to come with me round the estate first, Teddy,' he suggested. 'You'll be horrified when you see it, though. We just can't keep it up any more without the men. You'll be really shocked, I'm afraid. You'll think it's gone to ruin.'

Teddy just looked at him, shook his head and said nothing. Diana knew, as clearly as if he had spoken, that he was thinking of the derelict farms and the deserted villages of France. He was remembering the real ruins. There was nothing here that could shock him after what he had seen and endured out there.

'Tomorrow perhaps,' he said. 'I've one or two things to see to this morning,' and he went up to his room.

'He needs young company,' his mother said after he had gone. 'We must invite people over while he is here. A dinner party and a little dancing is just what he needs.'

Later Diana went and tapped on the door.

'I was hoping you'd come,' he said. 'Do you think we could slip away for a walk?'

It was a perfect spring morning as they set off towards the lake, not talking as they walked briskly between the fresh green of hedgerows newly in leaf. On the far side of the lake they sat down on a bench and she knew how much he wanted to talk, but couldn't find the words.

'Is it worse, in a way, coming back?' she asked at last.

He nodded.

'You know, Di, when you're in a filthy trench, soaking wet, covered in mud because a shell has just sent up a shower of earth, you just think that heaven would be a hot bath and clean clothes and a quiet bed.'

He paused.

'Oh, I know it sounds ungrateful and they're trying to give me a wonderful time, but it's all so *unreal*, Di. And back there it's going on just the same and here they've no idea what it's like. No idea at all.'

He pointed across to a glade, a little clearing in the trees, a few yards wide.

'You see that cleared patch, there, Di? Imagine our trenches here and the German trenches over there on the far side. And between us a sea of mud. Because it's not like ordinary mud, you know, it's a foul, polluted liquid which lies in stagnant pools, it flows like a thick river and when a shell bursts it sends up this awful liquid mud like a geyser, spraying everyone. And it gets into your rifle, it stops it working. And we had to order the men over the top, into the enemy fire and I lost nearly every man in my company. For what? Just to try to capture a bit of wasteland. Which we failed to do. Not that it matters because it had no strategic value, as the men knew. It's as if some force has taken over which drives both sides on in this insanity and nothing, not reason, not common sense, not humanity, can stop it.'

He was silent for a while, staring across the lake.

'I feel such a hypocrite sometimes when I write to the relations of the men who've been killed. I say that they've been buried in the field. I don't tell them the obvious, that when the shells explode afterwards we're all showered with mud and with bits of that shallowly buried body. There is no dignity in death out there. Sometimes as you walk or sit you feel a kind of bouncing in the ground and you know that underneath there's a gas-filled body which has ballooned and you move away and try not to think about it. Some people get immune to it all, but I don't seem able to.'

He shook his head, remembering, then went on: 'I had a nice lad in my company, Sanders he was called, one of those fresh-complexioned, clean-looking chaps, always managed to look less filthy than the rest even in the trenches. The men used to rag him a bit. I saw him go over the top. Next time I saw him there was this cat beside him, chewing. You know the way cats put their heads on one side and chew? Sanders' head had been blown half off and it was his brains that the cat was chewing.'

140

He stopped and turned to her.

'I'm sorry, Di, I shouldn't inflict these horrors on you.'

'It's all right. It helps to talk. And remember I've seen the horrors too. I know what they look like, feel like, smell like.'

'Don't you sometimes think it's quite pointless, all this misery? I do, though I wouldn't admit it to anyone else.'

'There are conscientious objectors, aren't there?' she suggested tentatively.

'That's not the answer. If you opt out, you don't stop the thing going on. So you might as well stay in with the rest of them.'

'And of course you can be shot if you don't stay.'

'Don't say that, don't say it,' he suddenly cried out and jumping up off the seat, began to stride along by the lake.

She ran after him.

'Oh, Teddy, I'm sorry. What have I said?'

'Don't ask me, don't ask me about it.'

He spoke fiercely, savagely even. Then he stopped in his tracks and, stooping forward, clutched his head in his hands and began to sway rhythmically from side to side. She had seen shell-shocked men rock themselves like that.

'Teddy,' she said, very firmly. 'Come and sit down again. You are going to tell me what is wrong.'

She took his arm and led him back to the bench, as she might have led one of the walking wounded.

He didn't speak for a while, then very slowly he began.

'Di, do you remember, I think I told you in a letter to the family, that when I first went out I was congratulated for being a good shot? I'd passed this musketry range test—'

'I remember. You said it was all thanks to the OTC and Thomson.'

'Did I?' He gave a sardonic smile. 'Well, thanks to whoever or whatever it was, I had this skill, I'd earned this reputation. And when the commanding officer mentioned it, of course I was rather pleased with myself. Oh, yes, quite proud of myself, I was, when he said I'd be useful for occasional special duty.'

He couldn't go on.

She waited. She took his hand in hers.

'There is an Army Act, Di, which lists twenty-five offences for which one of our men can be shot, things like throwing down his arms, desertion in the face of the enemy, behaving in a cowardly manner.'

'Yes.'

'Somebody has to do the shooting. Preferably a good marksman.'

'Oh, no,' was all she could say, suddenly understanding.

'All soldiers are afraid, Di. All of us. It's just that some of them can take it better than others, and some can take it for a while, but get worn down. And you see the men who drew up these rules were thinking of battles in the past which lasted two days or so. This war is absolutely different. It's not men fighting other men, it's men being mown down by machines, worn down by the ceaseless thunder of gunfire. I've seen them try to escape the bombardment by clawing their way into the earth. Literally they tear at it with their fingers, push their heads into it, desperate to hide in mother earth. They try to burrow into it like animals. Of course that's what we all are, just terrified animals. But I was trying to tell you something, wasn't I?'

He stopped speaking and seemed to need time to make himself go on.

'The first man I had to help to kill was one of my own men, a pathetic lad who'd volunteered early on and gone to pieces after two years in the trenches. We had to be there at dawn. Twelve of us there were. It was all very secret, quite cut off, as if it was known to be a shameful thing that we were doing. He was brought out by two military policemen and tied to a post, hands behind his back. They put a white rag over his heart. That was our target. A fellow countryman's heart. An exhausted young fellow, Di, at the end of his tether after two years of fighting for King and Empire.'

He couldn't go on, shedding the tears now, that he had not shed then.

She waited, saying nothing. He had taken his hand from hers and rubbed it across his face.

'Nobody wanted to shoot. I think some aimed wild on purpose. Some had drunk to get their courage up. He was one of their mates, Di. I don't know whether we killed him first time round. A senior officer marched up to him, put a gun to his temple and blew his brains out.'

She put her arms around him, held him close. She wept with him, knowing that whatever happened to him in battle now, this was a wound which would never heal.

'Next time Teddy is home,' her mother proclaimed at dinner on the last day of his leave, raising her glass in his direction, 'it will be for good.'

Diana had managed to dissuade her mother from inviting guests and giving dances, so the family was alone.

'What do you think, Teddy?' his father asked. 'Will there be a breakthrough soon?'

'It's no good asking soldiers from the front,' Teddy told him. 'We don't know what goes on until they tell us. But the rumour is that we're building up for a big attack in the summer.'

'Now that we have conscription,' his father suggested. 'I suppose that will give Haig the necessary manpower?'

He spoke hesitantly; he was much less confident and bellicose than his wife.

'One only hopes that these scroungers will fight as well as men like Teddy,' Elspeth said, looking fondly at her son.

He rewarded her with a look of exasperation, of anger which only years of instruction in gentlemanly good manners enabled him to hold back.

'Even before conscription, Mamma, I wondered at the courage of our men. And still do now. After all, what are they fighting for?'

'I'm sure I don't know what you mean, Teddy.'

'I know what *I'm* fighting for. I'm fighting for the land I know, for the estate which I'll inherit, for all this lovely Cotswold countryside. Of course people like me want to defend our country. But some of the men, Mamma, what are they fighting for? To defend a miserable slum in the foul centre of an industrial city?'

'If it's what they're used to, I suppose they don't know anything different,' his mother suggested.

'It's all they have,' he went on, ignoring her. 'Yet still they'll fight and die. That's true patriotism because there's nothing in it for them. And they are so stoical, so full of humour. And they suffer more, not just because their conditions are worse but because they start out less fit. It's not just undernourishment, rickets and so on, the doctors say you can even tell by the feet which men have worn good boots from childhood and which have not.'

'Teddy,' his mother told him severely, 'this really is somewhat revolutionary talk. I don't know what your grandmother would have said.'

Before he could reply, Rupert, who hadn't been paying much attention to the conversation, cut in with, 'Have you seen any aviators fighting, Teddy?'

'He's mad about these new air machines,' their father explained, glad at the change the conversation had taken.

'Well, yes, they use them quite a lot for reconnaissance. They use balloons too.'

'Those things like sausages?'

'That's right, they're weird things.'

'Go on, tell.'

'Well, they're tethered to the ground of course and then winched up to over a thousand feet. Two men sit in a basket underneath so they can survey the land with magnifying glasses. They can see the German trenches which are quite invisible to us on the ground even though we're only a few yards away.'

'Oh, I'd love to go up in a basket like that. What do the Germans do? Shoot them down?'

'They try. I saw one get hit not long ago. It just exploded in flames, but the two observers parachuted out. One landed in a tree and another in the mud, but they were all right.'

He didn't speak of the ones that had been incinerated in their burning balloon.

Diana watched him, admiring the way he was making an effort to speak cheerfully of the war to Rupert, choosing subjects that would be of technical interest to his younger brother, avoiding the horror.

'And the aviators?'

144

'Oh yes, they fly over the enemy lines too to take photographs. And they fight too, of course, shooting at each other round the fuselage. It's pretty dangerous.'

'That's what I'd like to do,' Rupert told him. 'If only the war lasts long enough.'

'Well, they say they feel safer up there than being stuck in some trench. What we envy, of course, is that after a stint they fly back to a hot meal and warm bed.'

'Speaking of which,' Diana put in, 'I think it would be wise to go up early tonight, Teddy, since you're off so soon.'

He glanced at her gratefully. 'Yes, Nurse,' he said.

It wasn't until William had gone abroad that Selina had taken seriously to comforting the soldiers.

While he was still at home, in fact immediately he had enlisted, she had joined with other society ladies in organizing parties for officers in London. Mainly these were in the ladies' own homes but some were in clubs and public places where they never would have ventured before. Sometimes William was with her, sometimes not. Either way she relished the excitement and novelty of it.

Then he was sent abroad and she missed him dreadfully. It wasn't so much that she feared for his life – he had, as he'd foretold, been posted with the staff officers well behind the lines – but she missed his reassuring presence. She was one who desperately needed admiration, couldn't flourish without it; for years his unfailing adoration had kept her confident and serene. And now he was gone.

She felt herself wilting without his support and at the same time she was getting tired of all those committee ladies with their tedious discussions; it would be better, it seemed to her, to do much more entertaining on her own. So she took to opening her house several times a week to officers who were without exception young, charming and very grateful. They provided all the attention and admiration that William was no longer there to supply. She still had servants to see to everything as before, plenty of time to prepare and beautify herself. Really, she thought, it was just like giving a pre-war party except that there were no women.

There were some special cases of course, like dear Major Trent whose wife had left him for his commanding officer. Dreadful for the poor man; he needed extra comfort. Then there was the American who had volunteered to fight with the British in France. He was very ashamed of his country for not joining in the war on the side of the allies.

'I feel,' he said, late one night as he stayed on having a whisky and soda after the others had left, 'that I must apologize on behalf of my government for not being here alongside our British comrades.'

'It must be hard for them to decide,' she told him, looking up at him with her big innocent eyes, Madonna-like in her forgiveness of the American administration.

'Dear lady, it should not be hard. My grandparents came out from England to settle in the States, my father was born there as I was but we still feel we belong here, where our roots are.'

He took a long drink. Then he sighed.

'I suppose if your grandparents had come out from Germany you might have felt differently?' Selina suggested in an attempt to cheer him.

'No, ma'am,' he said emphatically. 'You are the kindest, sweetest lady but there is no excuse. None whatsoever.'

He sounded so depressed about his country that she realized he needed comforting every bit as much as a wounded soldier. It was a matter of great satisfaction to her that he looked so much more cheerful when he left the next morning.

Sixteen

There had always been soldiers around Littleton, militia-men or men back from far-flung parts of the Empire who told tales of tropical sun and jungles which nobody quite believed. Dicky knew some of the lads who had gone off for a bit of soldiering but it had nothing to do with fighting, more like looking after those foreign parts that were coloured pink on the map. That's the peaceful sort of thing he'd thought soldiering was about and it had nothing at all to do with him.

But it was different now. Everywhere there was this picture of the man saying Your Country Needs You. Even in Littleton, there he was, pointing his finger. And whichever way you looked it seemed to be you he was pointing at. And his eyes followed you. Some of the lads from the village had volunteered and there were tales of women handing out white feathers to men who hadn't enlisted.

One day when he had walked into Shappenham to get a binding knife repaired, a strange woman stopped him and asked why a young man like him wasn't in the army. It was different, she said, in France. Her husband, who was out there at this very moment, had told her that there was nobody left in the villages over there except women and children, all the men had gone off to fight for their country. It was shameful that our men weren't doing the same and she'd take him to the recruiting office herself, she would. She wasn't a village woman, she was a proper lady who talked as if she expected to be obeyed, so he just followed her and she left him at the door, after telling him that he'd be given a shilling for enlisting. He could hardly believe it – a whole shilling and for doing nothing except enlist; such a thing had never happened to him in his life. So he walked in and joined the queue behind the others.

The officer looked at him, a bit strange like, and asked him how old he was. He said nineteen because that's what the other lads had told him to say, and he couldn't see that it mattered. And that seemed to be all there was to it.

Except that his parents were very put out when the OHMS envelope arrived. 'What's this then?' his father demanded, for letters were a rarity and letters with OHMS quite unknown. 'Get on and open it so we can see.'

The letter told him to report to the Drill Hall at Halpenford.

'You've never joined, have you?' His mother was disbelieving. 'Stop, him, Adam. Tell them it's a mistake.'

Adam scratched his head.

'I don't know as we can,' he said. 'It'll be official now. Signed and legal, like.'

'But there's others can go.'

'And a lot have,' Adam told her.

'And we need his wages at home.'

'He'll get as much, more mebbe. He's made his decision and must abide by it, I reckon. If you make your bed, you lie on it. Besides they're talking of bringing in conscription soon so he'd have to go anyway.'

And so he had reported, been seen by an elderly doctor who said he wasn't very big, was he, but had a strong pair of shoulders on him, didn't he, so he'd pass muster, wouldn't he. He'd then been given a packet of food and a rail voucher and gone by train to an army base where there were a lot of tents. It was night by then and a pile of blankets and a dozen men were counted off into each straw-carpeted tent. Some thought it crowded, but it didn't bother Dicky who was used to being close to other bodies at night and found the smell of straw homely and comforting.

He was less at home with the drilling that followed and lasted for several weeks. He'd never been much good at telling left from right and sudden orders to perform quite simple manoeuvres confused him; he needed time to think such things out. He didn't like them jumped on him. Worst of all was trying to make out maps; he couldn't see why there was all this need to locate sites; long-sighted as he was, he never had any trouble locating destinations. He still envisaged a battlefield as something like the fields at home, across which you'd shoot at Germans who would be on the other side.

But he always did well on the route marches and really enjoyed the field exercises. He was sorry for some of his mates who had come from towns and weren't fit; true there was a grave digger with muscles on his arms and shoulders that made you think he could have lifted a horse, but most weren't like that. There were a couple of clerks who could hardly lift their kit up on to their backs; he'd help them if the sergeant wasn't looking. He got on well with all of them and was soon known as one who would lend a hand if you were in trouble. Not very quick on the uptake, our Dicky, they'd say, not exactly simple but a bit too trusting maybe, like the time he'd left the socks his mother had knitted for him just lying about and seemed astonished that someone had nicked them. They'd shaken their heads and laughed at such naivety.

When at last they marched to Southampton for embarkation, the sight of the Channel amazed him. Cotswold born and bred, he had never before seen the sea and could only stand and marvel at it. And the crowds too, what a sight they were, these hundreds of people who had gathered to see them off. When he heard their cheering he knew he'd done right to enlist and was grateful to the lady who'd told him that's what he should do.

They left in darkness, tightly packed together in the boat but at early dawn he managed to stand at the rails and gaze out across the vast expanse of water and watch the way the gulls followed the ship, sometimes taking a ride on it, like a man hopping on a passing cart as he trudges down a long lane. Then the wind got up and soon he was being violently sick along with a thousand others and longing for home and dry land.

They staggered off the boat filthy and exhausted and heard one of the officers waiting on the shore say, 'They're sending us the dregs now.' So they called themselves The Dregs, some of the lads did, and had a good laugh.

They were billeted that night in barns and sheds that were surprisingly like the ones at home. It was warm enough but the filth that soon accumulated offended him; it was worse after they'd had their rations and the remains of the meal

149

lay about and flies gathered in swarms on empty bully beef tins, on eggshells and bits of stale bread. He thought of home, so spotless and nothing wasted. Those egg shells would have been crushed and put on the compost heap at home.

Some of the villages they marched through in the days that followed also reminded him of home, which surprised him; he'd thought abroad would be different. As they got nearer the front, it shocked him to see unpicked fruit and unharvested corn, then, as they marched even nearer, there were ruins to be seen instead of houses, and burnt stumps instead of trees.

They stopped to camp in a village which the Germans had just left; every house was gutted or burnt and it wasn't like anything he'd ever seen before. Sometimes there would be half a house; he could hardly take his eyes off one whose side seemed to have been chopped off. He could see the life that had been going on there before it was hit: an onion half sliced on the table and some bits of meat and a dish with pastry lying across it and a rolling pin just like his mother used, everything ready for making a pie. There were dishes ready for washing in the sink and a shawl lying across a chair as if the woman had got too hot as she cooked and had thrown it off as he'd seen his mother do. Nobody was in the kitchen now yet all these things were so real, so familiar to him, so alive as if they had outlived their owners. He stood staring, until he was ordered to get a move on.

Slowly they explored the deserted village, moving cautiously down its narrow streets. The smell was terrible. He couldn't think what it was until he saw the piles of bodies, men lying where they had fallen in the street, charred remains of women and children among the rubble of their homes. And everywhere the smell of death; a stench unlike anything he'd ever known. But they had to stay, had to billet here among the dead, and set about burying them. When, after a week of horror, they were told they were moving up to the front the next day, he felt nothing but relief; anything, he thought, would be better than this terrible place.

They'd told him about the trenches, but he was never able to imagine real things from words so was never prepared. They were much deeper than he'd expected, though of course, he told himself, he should have realized they'd have to be at least seven feet deep to hide a man. Some were very narrow, especially the ones they called communication trenches, only three feet at the most and he kept bumping into the sides at first and wondered how anyone fat would have managed, but they told him that only the generals were fat and they didn't come near the front line anyway.

He was amazed at the way the men had made homes of them, furnished them, made little rooms within them. He saw tables and chairs grander than anything they had at home, which had been taken from abandoned houses. Some of the old hands said the Germans had even grander trenches with mirrors and even gramophones. They were just a few hundred yards away, these German trenches, behind their great screen of barbed wire.

At first he found it hard to credit that the Germans were really there. There seemed to be no sign of them, yet there they all were, waiting. It was eerie, this stillness, this waiting. The old hands said it meant there'd be an attack soon, but none came and they went back to billets after their week's trench duty without seeing any action.

The attack must have come soon after they left – and the rain. When they went back it was to a different world and to reach it they had to cross a bog land scattered with deep craters filled with liquid mud. He'd heard about the Flanders mud and had imagined it like the muddy Cotswold lanes in winter, mud deep enough to come over your boots and even overtop the pattens that some old women still wore. But this mud was different; it was liquid earth, a seething quagmire, treacherous as quicksands. The sappers had laid down duckboards for them to march along, but they too were slippery with mud and there was a long stretch between two huge mud-filled craters, whose sides were crumbling, encroaching on their path which was already so narrow that it was only the width of the duckboard along which they crept. He kept his head down, staring at the boots of the man in front, not letting himself look to right or left. But all the time he was remembering tales of men who had slid off into the great pools of slime and sunk slowly, horribly, as their mates tried in vain to pull them back. Kinder to shoot them in the head as they sank, some said, rather than have them

151

slowly choke to death as they were sucked beneath the mud of Flanders.

The trenches they returned to were hardly recognizable; one whole section had been taken by the Germans and then retaken. Parts of the rest had been broken and flooded, sometimes with water several feet deep in which rats swam, as they dined off the bodies that floated in it. Other bodies, that had been buried in shallow trenches after earlier attacks, were thrown up by the shelling. Rats scrambled about in the empty rib cages of the long dead and feasted on the brains of those who had died more recently. These were the biggest, fattest rats he had ever seen.

The silence of it all was even more eerie now; they moved quietly about in working parties, repairing the damaged walls, removing the bodies, clearing the drains, carrying away the debris, venturing out into no-man's-land to rescue the wounded, bringing in the dead. But they could not retrieve the men who had been entangled on the enemy wire; their bodies still hung there like rags on a clothes' line.

What puzzled Dicky was that he still saw so little of the enemy; so far he'd hardly seen any German soldiers, only the result of their actions. It made them seem a bit unreal. Sometimes as he peered out at their line, when he was on guard duty, he caught a glimpse of a figure moving quickly past a gap, most likely just the cap on a man's head, sometimes he heard them singing, sometimes one of their bullets flew out and he heard a thud as it hit its target. But for the most part there was this strange stillness.

They were wet the whole time now. Their uniforms were heavy with water, the puttees that bound their legs tightened so much with the moisture that it felt as if the blood couldn't reach their frozen feet. But worse than this to Dicky was the dirt and the lice. They hadn't washed for days and all of them were covered in lice. He'd never had them before; lice would never have been allowed in his mother's well-scrubbed home and he hated them, but some of the men seemed quite accustomed and didn't seem to mind the filthy things.

Soon it became a routine, this strange life in the trenches, moving back to billets, returning to the trenches, strengthening them, extending the communication trenches, repairing the wire, as spring moved into summer. There were long stretches when there was nothing much to be done except sit around the brazier, if you were lucky, and warm up the tins of bully beef which were otherwise eaten cold. And he would think of the cauldron his mother set on the fire with the piece of bacon in it and the dumplings and then the vegetables which she added last of all so when you came in from the fields there was this wonderful smell which filled the house, a mixture of cabbage and ham, all with a smokiness about it.

Men used these quiet times to write letters home. He'd never in his life written a letter until he joined the army and hardly knew how to set about it. It hadn't mattered much in England but the family, especially Edith, had said he must write when he got to France otherwise how'd they know if he was dead or alive. There were these Field Service Post cards you could fill in, with lists of messages and you crossed out the ones you didn't want to send, but he thought his family deserved better than that and the cards must be really meant for people who couldn't write at all which, thanks to Miss Poole, he could, even if he wasn't much of a one with a pen. So he sat now writing, struggling with the words, thinking he wouldn't tell them about the horrible things, just about, well, some of the things that weren't so bad. Sometimes larks flew down into the trenches to peck at crumbs and suchlike, much tamer than any at home. So he told them about the birds and not about the rats. Other men wrote asking for stuff to be sent but he knew there wasn't anything to spare at home, so in his letters he asked for nothing.

They had some good times too, the men joked a lot and made up nicknames for themselves and for the officers and even for the battalions and they sang music hall songs which he'd never heard before but soon he was singing *Gilbert the Filbert* with the best of them. Sometimes when the other men opened their parcels they offered him a cigarette or a piece of chocolate, for they liked him. They shook their heads over the way he never asked for anything to be sent, thought it was a bit daft of him when everyone knew that mothers, sisters and girlfriends

153

couldn't wait to send you anything you asked for. He wasn't exactly simple, they thought, he did his work all right, it was just that he didn't seem to know how many cigarettes make a packet.

Seventeen

Officially nurses weren't allowed to serve abroad until they were twenty-three, but nobody questioned Diana when she volunteered to go to France. Hospitals there were already understaffed and with the great push planned for the summer, they knew they would need every nurse they could get.

It was seeing Teddy on leave that had made her determined to go; she just knew that she wanted to be out there with him, in the same country if he was wounded. Her matron having agreed to part with her, she prepared to do battle at home. This time, however, her mother didn't protest as much.

'You'll probably be safer out there than here now that we have these dreadful Zeppelin raids,' was all she said. 'I cannot think why we don't kill all the German prisoners we take. If we retaliated like that they'd soon stop dropping bombs on London.'

'Or maybe they'd just kill our prisoners in counter-retaliation?' Diana suggested.

'I do wish you wouldn't always look on the dark side,' her mother said.

It all took longer to arrange than Diana had expected.

'All these formalities!' she grumbled to Rupert. 'I've done the necessary qualifying service in an English hospital, I've got the certificates in first aid and home nursing, I've had my interview with Matron, I've sent off all the papers to the selection board and now they tell me I should have put in a reference from "a magistrate or person of position".'

'Papa's a magistrate, isn't he?'

'I don't think parents count.'

'Try the vicar. I don't know if being a vicar counts as a

position exactly, but he's always obliging in a rather horrible way.'

In the end it was all done and she was passed by the selection
board to sail to Boulogne with the next draft of nurses.

Rupert went with her to Victoria station.

'Oh, I do envy you so,' he said, impatient on the platform.
'Next year I'll be over there. Oh, do keep the war going
until then.'

He sounded just like the other young lads who had sailed
for France, full of patriotic fervour and the conviction that
they'd beat the Hun and bring the war to an end in a way
their elder brothers had somehow failed to do. She shook her
head at him.

'Oh Rupert, that's the last thing anyone should wish,' she
reproved, but somehow she found his childish enthusiasm was
less offensive than her mother's jingoism; she couldn't think
why it should be so, only knew that it was. Perhaps it was
because boys like him were after all risking their own lives, not
volunteering other people's. Either way, she loved and forgave
him and would have hugged him if she hadn't realized how
embarrassing he'd have found it.

A gale was blowing that afternoon when she crossed with the
rest of the draft of VADs and arrived, dishevelled and seasick,
at Boulogne.

They were led across the windswept town to a hotel where
they were ushered into a gloomy dining room full of dark and
heavy antique furniture. They sat themselves down at long
tables, which reminded her of the convent refectory, except
that it wasn't nuns but ancient waiters who tottered around
putting out plates of pâté and bowls of radishes, followed
by a thin and tepid stew. Everything felt chill and damp; the
tables and chairs and even the cutlery was cold to the touch
and misted over with condensation.

They didn't eat much and talked even less, subdued by the
rough crossing and the strangeness of everything and, above
all, the knowledge that they were now at last in France, in
the land of battlefields. Her neighbour, Susie, was the only
talkative one. She knew France well, she told Diana, from

family holidays before the war. When it was announced that their draft of VADs were to go to Etaples on the river Conche, she was delighted. 'It's a lovely place,' she said, 'well-known for its picturesque harbour and main square with lots of cafés.'

The VAD sitting opposite shook her head. 'Not now, it isn't,' she said. 'Now it's known for its huge army camp, its railway and its hospital. My sister has worked there for a year. What possessed the military to put a hospital so near the railway line, nobody knows. The Germans are bound to attack it – it's the main line from Boulogne to Paris.'

'So we'll go on by train now?'

'Sorry, no, we're to go on motor lorries.'

'I don't mind what we go on,' Diana said. 'So long as it's not a boat.'

They laughed and made their way to the square where the lorries awaited them and then for twenty-three miles they bumped and rattled along the uneven, pot-holed road in a ramshackle vehicle, through driving rain. It was still pouring when they reached Etaples and evidently had been for some time because everywhere was awash with slimy mud. So this is the famous mud they speak of, she thought, glad that she'd taken Teddy's advice to bring wellington boots.

She wasn't sure what she expected the hospital to be like, but certainly not this: a huge conglomeration of huts and tents, linked by muddy paths. She should have realized that it was bound to be made of temporary buildings, but she'd still had in the back of her mind an idea that there would be a solid, brick hospital somewhere amongst it.

By chance she and Susie had been allocated the same hut, so she squelched towards it in her rubber boots while Susie followed in her rather less suitable flimsy footwear.

The hut looked anything but permanent, in fact it looked considerably less solid than any of the gardeners' huts at home. Still, it was a haven from the wind and rain, she thought gratefully as, shutting the rickety door behind them, they dumped their belongings down, looked around the bare little hut, which was to be their home for they didn't know how long, and began to unpack. She was glad that she'd followed

Teddy's advice not to bring much kit. Susie, who evidently hadn't been given or taken such advice, had to leave most of hers in her case and in various bags which she pushed under her camp bed, before lying down on it.

'I'll go and wash now,' Diana told her. 'We passed the washhouse about three huts back.'

Susie looked at her, nodded and yawned.

'I can't bring myself to go out again,' she said. 'I'd rather stay dirty.'

To Diana, brought up by Nanny to believe that cleanliness was next to godliness, the idea of going to bed unwashed was still shocking. Besides, she thought as she put on her nightie and then her raincoat and gathered her washing things together, the idea of a nice hot bath was pure luxury and hospitals always had plenty of hot water, didn't they?

This one didn't. In the damp and chilly washhouse she had to make do with a tepid wash. Her teeth were chattering as she rubbed herself dry, put her clothes back on and set off for the hut. It was very dark now, clouds completely obscuring the moon and stars and, although she had a torch with her, she was afraid of using it in case it was against army rules. So she did not see the piece of wood lying in the mud, tripped over it and fell flat into a puddle.

'I think I returned dirtier than when I set out,' she wrote to Teddy the following evening. 'And when I got back into the hut, there was Susie sound asleep in her bed while I had to set about getting rid of my newly acquired dirt.

'We are astonishly near the railway line which lies between us and the sea. The trains seem to miss our hut by inches, rattling away day and night and emitting shrieks and whistles as they pass. I can't say I got much sleep but it didn't seem to matter as I was so busy today that I'd no time to feel tired. I've been on the wards doing dressings all day. The wounds are dreadful, but there is no need to tell you that, I know.'

Her letters were censored, unlike Teddy's, who, as an officer, censored his own, whereas she knew that every word she wrote would be read by Matron. It wasn't that she wanted to say anything subversive, it was just that, especially at first, she found it inhibiting to feel that other eyes than his would scan

158

her words. It prevented her from referring to the conversations they had had when he was on leave.

Teddy wrote without any such inhibitions.

'You remember the awful business we talked about, you and I? Or rather that I talked about and you listened. Four times I've had to do it, Di. Under orders. It's such a shaming thing. And, do you know, I've discovered that the Germans don't do this, although of course their men have the same problem. They don't shoot the poor fellows. They send them back to do work behind the lines. It's awful to think that we are less civilized, less compassionate in this than the Germans are. And another thing I've found out is this: the Australians refused to allow Haig the right to shoot any of their men. He wanted to and said he'd use this ultimate punishment sparingly, but they wouldn't have any of it. Good for them! They've got a reputation for being pretty casual about regulations. Some people criticize them for it, but I think they've got the right attitude. They say they've come over to fight and that's what they'll do and to hell with all the rules and regulations.

'I often think of how we talked that day, that lovely spring day, Di. When I talked about the awful wastage of this war, I don't want you to think I would want to be out of it. It has to be fought. And this present attack has to be made. Somehow we have to take the pressure off the French at Verdun; the Germans are attacking them there so hard. And if we are successful here it will ease the pressure on the Russians on the Eastern front. Poor devils, they are suffering as we are, but in a much more dreadful climate. We had to put up with intense cold last winter, but they froze to death. And their organization is even worse than ours because they're so short of educated men. The tsars have seen to that.

'There's a sense now of building up for the offensive which it's rumoured will start at the end of this month, certainly before July anyway. We're bombarding like mad, the idea being to destroy their artillery and flatten their wire. We've been told not to rush across no-man's-land, just take it easy and walk in a leisurely kind of way because Rawlinson, who's in charge of the operation, thinks that the inexperienced battalions of Kitchener's New Armies might fall apart in a rush attack! They say it'll be perfectly safe because the enemy artillery will have been knocked out by then. My God, Di, I hope they're right.'

Clearly he had doubts. Two days before the attack on the first of July, he wrote, 'It'll take a lot to flatten their wire, Di. I've often inspected it and it's ferocious stuff. Ours is galvanized and looks grey. Theirs rusts and turns black. It's yards deep and has barbs at every inch. Then they have a trip wire just above the ground and that, combined with an iron spike dug into the ground with about a foot protruding, ensures that if our men trip on the wire, they fall back and are spiked. They make a nice easy target for the Hun.'

That was the last letter Diana had from him before the attack. But from the casualties which poured into the hospital she knew what a disaster it had been. The men – thirteen divisions of them – went over the top in wave after wave. And in wave after wave they were mown down by machine gun fire as they walked slowly uphill, for the enemy occupied the high ground. They just walked to their slaughter.

It was only afterwards that she was told that nineteen thousand young men had been killed on that first day and fifty-seven thousand wounded. At the time it was not a matter of statistics; it was trainload after trainload of mutilated men arriving at the hospital, it was having to move sick men out of their beds at night to make room for even worse cases which arrived straight from the front, roughly patched up by the field casualty stations. It was working day and night, snatching a few hours' sleep when she could. It was hearing all the time the groans of the wounded and the cries of the delirious. And always the fear that when she took the rough dressings off one of these hideously wounded men, revealing eyes burnt to blindness, or a mass of pulpy flesh which had once been a strong arm or leg, that man would be Teddy. Or see his name on the list of the dead. She didn't know which would be worse.

It was nearly a fortnight before she had news of him.

'I don't know how or why I'm still on this earth, Di. But I am and hope this message gets to you as you will know by now that the so-called great breakthrough was simply a mass slaughter. Haig promised that if it failed, the campaign would be called off, but I think it will continue, this hopeless throwing of men against guns. I am in a reserve trench at the moment, which, with the one third of my men who are still alive and are now merged with B and C company who have lost their officers, we're repairing in readiness for God knows what. I can't write more, just wanted to tell you I'm alive and as well as anybody can be in this hell on earth we call the Somme.'

For the first time since she had come to France, Diana wept. Tears of relief seemed to stream of their own volition down her cheeks as she sat on the camp bed in her hut, clutching the letter in her hand. She read and reread it through her tears, then she put it into the small case which contained all her belongings and went quickly back to the ward, not allowing herself to think that just because you get a letter from somebody it doesn't necessarily mean that they are still alive.

Eighteen

Tom had looked forward to his visit to Northrop mainly because he wanted to talk to his cousin Teddy who had been given a week's leave. He himself would be in the army in less than a month and the prospect thrilled him; to be a soldier instead of a schoolboy, to march with other men, what greater glory could there be? Perhaps to die. That didn't worry him, indeed the thought of dying a hero's death thrilled him even more.

But to die a virgin, that was a terrible thought; to die not having known what it was to be truly a man, to die wondering what it would have been like, that great experience that they so often talked about at school.

It was all right for labourers and people like that; they were marrying in their droves before they enlisted. Even if they only had one night with their wives, they said, they would be content to risk dying. But gentlemen's sons can't do that. He couldn't possibly ask someone to marry him at such short notice. Girls like his cousin Diana needed months of preparations to get married and anyway their parents wouldn't allow it.

He did think of asking his father's advice, but soon dismissed the idea. Once, years ago, he'd been close to his father; as a child he'd confided everything to him, much more than to his mother. And how he'd missed him when he'd first been sent away to school, how he'd howled in the lavatory, how he'd blubbed as quietly as he could into his pillow at night! How he'd longed to pour out all his misery to him. Later, when he'd settled in and was no longer homesick, he still wanted to share his thoughts and feelings with him.

He knew, however, that that wasn't what preparatory school was about. He felt sure that his father would be proud of him

162

only if he kept a stiff upper lip, put a brave face on things and above all conformed to the standards of other boys. So he wrote letters which detailed cricket scores, told of house matches won or lost, gave dull reports of visiting teams. And his father read them sadly, remembering the impetuous little boy who used to write him funny letters when he was away on holiday with Nanny Tubmorton, full of incident and ideas. He sometimes wished that there was some way of educating the sons of gentlemen without destroying their originality and spontaneity.

So they grew apart and Tom knew he couldn't speak to his father about this troublesome matter. Instead he asked a returning old boy visiting school at the end of term. Sodbury his name was. Tom had never liked him, but always thought him very knowledgeable and worldly-wise.

'Sex?' Sodbury had drawled. 'Well, in my day there was usually a kitchenmaid who would oblige if a chap was desperate, but the smell you know was a bit ripe. "While greasy Joan doth keel the pot," and all that, don't you know.'

Tom didn't know. None the wiser he went to Northrop Hall in the hope of having a word with Teddy, who after all must have been in the same predicament. But Teddy had been remote, unapproachable somehow; perfectly polite, as always, but definitely unapproachable. And suddenly it seemed too trivial a thing to mention to a man who'd been fighting for two years, however urgent it seemed to himself.

After Teddy had left, his aunt and uncle pressed him to stay on.

'There's plenty you can do to help,' his uncle said. 'Everyone helps now, you know. But of course you may just want to go home and rest before joining your regiment, though your mother was quite insistent that you should stay.'

'Oh, I'd like to stay. Just tell me what needs doing and I'll help all right.'

He meant it. He was full of energy, impatient with life and wanted to be doing something active all the time; there was far more chance of that here than in London. He'd cycle over to Furzebridge and work on the dam, if there was any spare time. Anything was better than sitting around in Billington Square.

He was as bored in London as his mother always was in the country.

'There's a tree needs felling in the orchard, only a small apple tree but it's diseased, Jimson says,' his uncle told him. 'He'll show you how to set about it.'

'And Cook keeps asking for help fruit-picking. Mary-Ann has been helping and I did some myself, but I really did find it too hot and I've so much else to see to. It's a shame to let all that fruit go to waste now that food is so difficult. Cook wants to bottle as much as possible and of course make jam, though sugar is getting scarce.'

'I'll help with that, I'll help with anything.'

So he spent the next morning in the orchard felling the tree, sawing up logs, enjoying the hard physical labour.

As he passed the walled garden, he glimpsed Mary-Ann coming out of the fruit cage, carrying two big baskets of fruit.

'They're too heavy for you,' he said, taking them from her.

'Yes, I was struggling,' she admitted candidly. 'Thank you, Master Thomas. If you could hand them to Cook, I'll take them back to fill again.'

'I've been told to help you,' he explained, returning with her to the fruit garden.

'It's blackcurrants now and then redcurrants,' she told him. 'And Cook says this time to top and tail them before we take them into the kitchen.'

So they squatted on the grass by one of the bushes, picking the soft black fruit. The sun was warm on their backs, but only pleasantly so. He had on an old straw hat of his uncle's and Mary-Ann was wearing a sunhat, from which the dark hair, which she now wore up, escaped and lay against the bodice of her dress. Her face was flushed with the sun, and her arms had turned a lovely honey colour. All this he noticed as he did his picking. And all the time they talked easily as they picked and even when they were silent it was not an awkward silence.

When the basket was full they took it up to the steps where they sat, each with a pair of scissors provided by

Cook, snipping off the stalks and putting the fruit into a big brass preserving pan.

'You can leave the other end on,' she told him. 'It helps the set of the jam.'

'Are we allowed to eat some?'

She laughed.

'If we're not, I don't know how you got those purple stains on your lips, Master Thomas,' she told him.

She had a lovely laugh, soft but somehow bubbly. He didn't mind a bit if she laughed at him. He could have listened to her laughter for ever, which was odd because usually he didn't care for being laughed at.

They agreed that when there was an exceptionally big berry – and the big berries were always sweet, Mary-Ann told him – it was allowable not to put it in the pan but to eat it instead. So their lips were soon as stained as their fingers.

'Better wipe our mouths before Cook sees,' he said, when they had finished and prepared to take the baskets back into the house.

'Oh, she won't mind.'

Tom laughed.

'I think I'm more frightened of her than you are,' he said. 'We used to be really scared of her when we were little. Sometimes we could just stroll into the kitchen and she'd spoil us with buns fresh from the oven but other times she'd get so cross that we'd all bump into each other trying to get out through the door.'

'Oh, she's easier now, despite hard times and not much help. And things are done more simply.'

'All the same, better wipe up,' he said, handing her his handkerchief.

She took it and thanked him. He watched as she rubbed her lips and round her mouth. And when she missed a streak down her left cheek, he wiped it off for her. Then he took the handkerchief back and wiped his own face with it.

Cook was impressed by the amount of fruit they'd brought in.

'I'm grateful for your help, Master Thomas,' she said.

165

'Oh, there's lots more fruit out there. The bushes are laden. I'll come back this afternoon.'

'Thank you. Madam said you could have your lunch when you fancied, Master Thomas. She knows you're busy helping here. I've a salad prepared for you. And, Mary-Ann, yours will be ready soon to have with Nanny.'

He'd have liked to suggest they had it together, a picnic out there in the walled garden perhaps, but knew that would be a shocking suggestion. War had made it all right for master and maid to work together, but not eat together. So they went their separate ways.

'Do you need me for any indoor tasks this afternoon?' Mary-Ann asked Nanny as they ate their lunch together in the schoolroom. 'If not, Cook would like me to help with fruit-picking.'

'What about those two girls she's got in the kitchen?'

'She wants some scrubbing done and this afternoon they're to be busy with the vegetables. And she says they're clumsy with the fruit, crushing it with their heavy handling.'

'Well, then you can go,' Nanny conceded. 'There's a pile of mending, but I'll see to it. The fresh air's good for you. It puts colour in your cheeks, being outside does.'

She looked indulgently at the girl. Mary-Ann's prettiness was of that wholesome kind that appeals to women as well as to men. It had the unselfconscious attraction of small children which makes adult eyes linger and hands reach out to touch. So even Nanny, whose attitude towards looks was summed up in her maxim, 'Handsome is as handsome does', enjoyed looking at the nursery maid's bright eyes and delicately flushed cheeks as she went about her tasks, neat and light of foot.

'Redcurrants are worse to do than the blacks,' Mary-Ann told Tom, as they settled one each side of the bush, each with a basket alongside. 'You just pick off a whole bunch but then you have to fork them all off separately afterwards.'

Tom, who never liked being told how to do things, found it strangely agreeable to listen to her instructions. He would hold up a bunch, ask her to come and examine it to see if it was ripe for picking, pointing out that, though some of the berries on

166

the branch were bright red, others were still green. And she would have to come round to his side and it was pleasant to watch her frowning a little as she examined the berries and passed judgement and then smiled at him and went back to the other side of the bush, through whose green leaves they could glimpse each other and talk, while the delicate tracery made patterns of light and shade on her face. She didn't arouse in him the feelings he had had at the picnic, which he remembered with some shame and had to remind himself that he had at the time been a mere sixteen-year-old. No, this was a gentler feeling, more protective. He found her easier to talk to than other girls of his own class; he wanted to be her friend.

'How did you come to be working here?' he asked her. 'Do you live nearby?'

'No, my father was a sea captain, but he was drowned when I was seven. My mother died the next year, I think she had consumption.'

'Oh, Mary-Ann, how dreadful. I'm so sorry. Do you remember much about them?'

'It's funny but I never remember my mother moving about. She was very beautiful, I remember that, and she used to sit and read to me and she taught me early to read and write and sew, but I always remember her sitting or lying on a couch while we did these things. So I think now that she can never have been very strong and maybe my father's death was too much for her to bear. Anyway she died and I was put into a home.'

'Didn't you have any relations?'

'None that I knew of. I think my mother came from Scotland so they'd have been too far away. I remember there was an old lady called Mrs Beadles who was very kind to me. I think she'd have kept me with her if she could.'

'And what was it like in the home? Were they good to you?'

'No,' she told him sounding bitter, he thought, for the first time. 'People think it's hard in service working from six in the morning till ten at night, but it was worse in the home, I can tell you. And we were always hungry.'

She shook her head.

167

'They were cruel sometimes, when you think we were all orphans and could have done with a bit of kindness shown. Then when we were thirteen they began looking for work for us, the boys on the farms, the girls in service. And that's how I came here.'

'And yet your parents weren't poor?'

Her story had shocked him. He'd always supposed that servants were there, just as masters were there, all ready made, as it were. It hadn't occurred to him that they might have been created, that people could come down, as well as go up in the world, like two lifts alongside each other, one going up, one going down.

'No, they weren't poor,' she said. 'But they weren't rich either.'

She stood up suddenly, as if to mark the end of the conversation, and said, 'And now that these baskets are full, we can take them up to the steps to fork them, Master Thomas.'

'Please don't call me Master Thomas. Just call me Tom.'

'Oh, I couldn't do that, Master Thomas.'

'There you go again! I don't see why not when we're working like this together. And we are friends, aren't we?'

She smiled up at him, that lovely radiant but shy smile, her huge eyes lighting up, then the long lashes lowering over them, dark against the fair skin of her cheeks. He felt his heart lurch.

'I hope we are,' she said.

And so they sat on the steps, the sun warm but not too hot, the soft breeze gentle as they handled the fruit, their fingers occasionally touching in the basket among the bright red berries; anyone passing would have seen just two young people together and hardly have known that they were master and servant, war does such strange things.

Tom hardly saw her the next day. Apparently Jimson needed help with the pear trees.

'They're so heavy with fruit, Master Thomas, that we must tie up some of the branches or they'll break. Trouble is I didn't get round to thinning them as much as I should, there were more important jobs to see to and not enough hands to do them.'

168

So Tom spent the morning up the ladder, tying up the laden branches of the espalier pear trees, astonished at the abundance of the crop. He had never seen them growing before and was amazed by the way their long branches stretched so far along the wall, reaching out to touch the branches of the next one. And along the whole length of them, hung these huge pears, Conference, Williams, Doyenne du Comice, Jimson knew the names of all the varieties, but they just looked like pears to Tom. Unripe pears. By the end of a morning spent stretching up from the ladder to tie them up with thick string and raffia, while the sun beat down on his back and bounced off at him from the wall, he wouldn't have minded if he never saw another pear again.

'The Victorias are ready for picking,' Jimson told him.

Tom looked around, not knowing what a Victoria was, and then saw that Jimson was looking at a tree laden with plums. There were three such trees, all fan-trained against the brick wall.

'If we don't get them picked soon, they'll break the branches,' Jimson said. 'But best ask Cook first. It's time for the meal anyway.'

So they went up to the kitchen together.

Cook wasn't in one of her better moods.

'As if I hadn't got enough fruit to manage already,' she grumbled, pointing to baskets of berries on the table, pans of berries cooking on the fire, jars of berries being bottled.

'Then we'll let them rot on the trees, shall we?' Jimson said, turning to go.

'Oh, bring them in. I'll manage. And your luncheon's ready, Master Thomas,' she added sharply, 'in the dining room.'

Suddenly feeling like a ten-year-old again, Tom got out quickly.

He wasn't looking forward to an afternoon up the ladder with Jimson instructing him, but to his surprise when he went back into the walled garden, it was Mary-Ann who was there with the baskets.

'I've to pick the lower branches, while you go up the ladder,' she told him. 'Mister Jimson's busy with Mrs Arndale in the garden this afternoon. He says we used to just pick the plums as they ripened, but there's no time for that now, so we're to pick them all.'

So he climbed up the ladder, with one of the baskets on his left arm and with his right hand picked the plums, watching Mary-Ann out of the corner of his eye as she stooped to pick from the lower branches. Once he put his hand on a wasp which had settled on the plum he was picking and which, his eyes on the girl below him, he hadn't seen. Nor did he feel the sharp little pain of its sting. And so it went on until that tree was done and it was time to move the ladder along to the next one. And then the next, until the trees were bare of fruit and all the baskets were full.

Afterwards Tom always felt it was the peaches that did it.

When the plums were all gathered, Jimson came back and led them to a tall but not very productive fan-trained peach tree further along the wall, in the choicest of warm positions in the south-west corner.

'It hasn't been properly trained for two years now,' he told Tom dolefully, 'since we've been so short-staffed. All those replacement stems should've been tied in to keep the centre green, but it didn't get done so it's bare in the middle now and the fruit all at the ends of the branches. I'm ashamed to look at it,' he added, shaking his head.

He'd brought what he called his peach baskets, two trugs with soft linings to prevent the fruit from bruising.

'Very delicate, they are,' he told Tom. 'Need careful hand-ling. Mary-Ann knows how. Not that there's more than a few to pick. And we used to gather pounds.'

Few but perfect were the peaches. Ripe for the picking, they came away from the branch at the touch of Tom's hand.

After he'd eased them off he handed them down one by one to Mary-Ann, who stood waiting at the foot of the ladder. The plum picking had been a clumsy matter compared to the delicacy of this. Very gently he put the peach into the little hands that were reaching up for it and watched as she laid it carefully in the wicker basket. And of course every time she waited to take the fruit from him she had to look up and he looked down into her eyes, seeing the upturned face now from a different angle, such a sweet face, vulnerable and trusting as it looked up at him.

The bloom on her cheeks seemed to him as soft and downy as the bloom on the fruit and each time they looked at each other for a little longer, as if mesmerized. He wanted this to go on for ever and could hardly bring himself to pick the last peach. Having done so, he didn't hand it to her, but climbed down, still holding it and stood beside her. Then, instead of putting it into the hand she held out, he took that hand in his own and placed the peach in her palm, still holding her hand. Then he covered it with his other hand, enfolding both the peach and her fingers in his and it seemed the most natural thing that, holding her thus, he should lean forward and kiss her on the lips.

They stood unmoving for what seemed a very long time in the warm corner of the wall, rapture turning into hours what could in reality only have lasted for seconds.

Then: 'Oh, no, Master Thomas,' she managed to say. 'Oh, no,' and, breaking away from him, walked quickly towards the house. He followed her, confused and not knowing what to say. So they did not speak to each other again but silently delivered the baskets to Cook, who told Mary-Ann she could go off now to help Nanny.

As part of the war effort, family guests had been asked to make their own beds. Tom always meant to do so, but forgot. He'd go down to breakfast and when he went back to his room the bed had always been made by some servant or other. Thus he lost the precious handkerchief with which he'd wiped the juice from Mary-Ann's face and which he'd hidden under his pillow, intending to keep it for ever. It was returned to him after being washed but, although the stain hadn't been altogether removed, laundering had deprived it of the significance which the crumpled square of linen had had. Nonetheless he took it down to breakfast with him the morning after the peach-picking in the hope that it would be a kind of talisman to help him see Mary-Ann again.

'You've caught the sun, Tom,' his aunt said. 'You've really had an amazing week of sunshine, considering what a poor summer we've had. Charles and I are so grateful to you for all your hard work, dear, and we both think you deserve a day off. It is Saturday, after all, and you have to leave us on Monday.'

'Thank you, Aunt, but I really don't need a rest and I've promised Cook I'll help to finish the fruit-picking today. It's almost done now.'

'Well, if you're sure, dear. We should be very grateful. Cook and Nanny have been so wonderful since the housekeeper let us down.'

The housekeeper's mother had been killed in a Zeppelin raid and she'd had to leave to go and care for her disabled father. But she had been at Northrop Hall for twenty-five years so of course it seemed to Elspeth a clear case of desertion.

Tom went eagerly down to the kitchen after breakfast.

'The baskets are down there already, Master Thomas,' Cook told him. 'And she's been picking for an hour or more.'

He had to make himself not run, force himself to look unconcerned, but oh how he longed to see her again, how he ached for the sight of her, as he pushed his way into the fruit cage.

The baskets were there and beside them he made out the portly figure of Gertie, the kitchen maid. He almost stopped in horror, but remembering his manners, walked on and greeted her and for two hours picked fruit with her and tried to talk to her but since she responded mainly with nods and grunts, soon gave up. He could see what Cook meant about her ruining the fruit. She seemed to squash every berry she picked between her broad first finger and thumb. He could hardly bear to watch when he remembered Mary-Ann's quick little fingers.

Cook grumbled at their offering.

'I'll make them into jelly,' she said, giving the fruit a contemptuous glance. 'And Gertie you'd best go and get some potatoes. Tell the lad to dig them because you always put the fork through each and every one. But you can wash the soil off and bring them in to scrape. And carrots too, we'll be wanting. And radishes if they're any good. They never seem up to much after the first crop, whatever Mr Jimson does with them. Thank you, Master Thomas, I'm afraid you'll be on your own now. Madam had need of Mary-Ann indoors.'

The weather was on the change, Tom noticed as he went back outside. It was still hot but overcast now and sultry. This must be the most boring job in the world, he thought, tugging at the fruit with about as much finesse as Gertie had shown. For two pins I'd give up and go and look at the dam, he thought, or ask Jimson for something more interesting to do. He'd enjoyed taking that tree down; there must be others that needed to be felled. But he knew he couldn't give up on the fruit; he'd have to do his duty and stick at this boring task.

He heard someone approaching, a light step, and looking up saw Mary-Ann.

All thoughts of tree-felling and dam-building vanished from his mind.

'I'm sorry you've had no help,' she said. 'I was needed indoors.'

'You've come now,' he said. 'That's all that matters.'

And he meant it. At that moment it really was all that mattered to him. Never mind the war, never mind death, she was here in her lavender-coloured dress and her little sun hat which wasn't really necessary now that the sun had gone in and her dark eyes and long lashes and escaping hair, her pink cheeks and lovely lips which he mustn't think about, no really must not.

They didn't refer to what had happened the day before; they tried to behave as if that kiss had never been, but it was in both their minds. He did think of apologizing, but since he wasn't at all sorry, couldn't bring himself to tell her that he was.

They didn't pick on opposite sides of the bush now, but sat alongside each other, so that they could talk more easily. Sometimes they both reached for the same dark cluster of berries and their hands touched, so that they laughed and pretended to vie for it. And so the afternoon flew past.

'I have to go on Monday,' he said, as they sat on the steps picking the stalks off the last of the blackcurrants.'

'I know.'

'Shall we work together tomorrow?'

173

'No, there's church in the morning and no work allowed in the afternoon, even though there's the war.'

'Not even fruit-picking?'

She shook her head.

'Not even fruit-picking. Besides, it'll all be done by this evening,' she added, nodding towards the depleted bushes. 'There's only a couple of redcurrant bushes left to do.'

'Mary-Ann . . .' He hesitated.

'Yes?'

'What will you be doing tomorrow afternoon?'

'Me? Oh, my time's my own. I'll sort out my things and rest a while.'

'Do you want to rest? I mean are you so very tired?'

She laughed up at him.

'No, I'm never tired on a Sunday.'

'Do you cycle, Mary-Ann?'

She looked up at him, surprised at the sudden change of subject.

'Oh, yes, I have the use of one of the bicycles for going to the shops.'

'Do you remember how I cycled to Furzebridge two years ago? When you went with the girls in the waggon?'

'Of course I remember. It was a lovely picnic. And you sat in the custard pie.'

'And you laughed at me.'

'I never!'

'You wanted to.'

'Wanting's another matter.'

As they spoke, teasing, laughing, unconsciously they moved closer together. Suddenly he took her hand and said, 'Mary-Ann, would you cycle with me to Furzebridge tomorrow? I want to look at the dam before I go.'

She shook her head. Oh, it was so tempting, hadn't she been thinking of him all this past week, but no, it would never do.

'No, it wouldn't do,' she said aloud.

'But, Mary-Ann, we both went on that picnic together.'

'That was different, there were others there.'

'Well, they'd be here now if it weren't for the war,' he said, knowing it was a poor argument but needing to say

174

something. 'Would you like to come with me, *if* it was allowed, I mean?'

She nodded, eyes lowered.

Both of them were silent now, both thinking how wonderful it would be to cycle away, leave the hall behind, be free of it and everybody in it, be on their own, just the two of them, sailing downhill, pedalling uphill, arriving at the wood, paddling in the stream, she watching on the bank as he mended the dam.

Far apart in station, they were, but close together in their imaginings.

'It does you so much good, my girl, getting out in the garden,' Nanny said, looking approvingly at Mary-Ann's flushed cheeks as they had lunch together in the school room. 'You get quite pale when you're too long indoors.'

'Yes, I feel better for it.'

'You should get out more on your Sunday afternoons,' Nanny went on. 'Walking's not right on your own, I know, and I can't come with you, well, not far enough to count leastways. But you could take a bicycle ride; it's a good way to get fresh air.'

Mary-Ann could hardly believe it. It seemed, as she walked back to the garden that afternoon, that Nanny had been telling her to go to Furzebridge with Master Thomas. No, of course Nanny hadn't, she knew that perfectly well, but she had told her to go for a ride on a bicycle. Should she tell him? If she did, he would want her to go with him. But she couldn't not tell him. That wouldn't be right either.

So as they picked the redcurrants, not hurrying since there were so few left and there was no point in getting them done before the afternoon was over, she told him what Nanny had said.

It was worth it for the joy it put on his face.

'Oh, Mary-Ann, Mary-Ann,' he exclaimed. 'You *must* come now. Don't you see, there's no harm in it now that Nanny's suggested it?'

'She didn't suggest I go with *you*, just that I should have a ride in the fresh air for my health's sake.'

175

'But she'd know you'd be safer to go with me than to go alone.'

They talked about it, off and on, as they picked. And thought about it all the time. It seemed to both of them, though they didn't say so out loud, that it would be very unkind of her to deny him this one simple request when he was leaving so soon to go into the army.

By the time they parted it was arranged that she would leave by the back gate immediately after lunch and Tom would set off down the front drive a quarter of an hour later, overtaking her on the way. There couldn't possibly be any harm, Tom said, in such an accidental meeting.

Nineteen

The old hands, Dicky Paste realized, seemed to know in advance that an attack was going to be launched. He couldn't really believe it, there were always these stories and rumours, and he'd never been in an attack yet. But they were right this time. At last they were told officially and everything was arranged. They'd be attacking at dawn in two days' time.

It would start with a bombardment of the enemy's defences, and then they would go over the top under covering fire. He liked the expression; the idea of being covered was comforting to Dicky. Evidently they would go out, run across no-man's-land, find a way through the wire, which would have been destroyed, and all the time they'd be kept safe by this friendly covering fire. It was all prepared and organized and they just had to do their duty.

He hadn't known how deafening the bombardment would be until it started, the great booming, thudding bombardment into the enemy's lines, so loud he couldn't think or feel because it seemed to get right inside his head as he crouched with the others behind the wall of the trench, longing for the noise to stop, waiting for the whistle to blow even if it did mean that the moment had come to leave the safety of the trench and dash out there into the unknown of no-man's-land. Just so long as the roar of gunfire would stop, he'd be able to manage.

Suddenly it happened; the world went quieter, the whistle blew and they were all climbing up the fire step, jumping out of the trench, running across the wastes of no-man's-land towards the wire while enemy shells were falling among them, killing and wounding, tearing clods of earth out of the ground, spouting mud over the fallen men as they lay moaning in the agony of their wounds, twitching in their death throes. One of his mates fell beside him. He stopped, bent over him. 'Get on, man,' somebody shouted, and he remembered they weren't allowed to stop to help the wounded, they must be left where they had fallen until the stretcher bearers came, however long that might be.

So he ran on, almost blinded with the smoke that filled the air and the mud that sprayed down on them like a torrent of thick brown soup as the shells tore great holes in the earth. To his right and left men were falling and even if the man in front fell at your feet you just had to go on running as if he was not there.

He reached the wire; all around him men were trying to find a way through it. Some were tangled up in it, an easy target for enemy fire as they writhed and twisted to escape. The wounded who hung there contorted and groaning had to be left, adding to the decaying ranks of those who had gone before them days ago. Somehow he found himself through the wire with a little group of men and they were all running, he didn't know where for the air was full of smoke and all around him he could hear shrieks and groans of wounded men somehow audible through the ceaseless bombardment and the whistling sounds the shells made, the thud as they hit their target.

He didn't know if he was behind the enemy lines now, had somehow broken through or if he had veered off towards his own line. He couldn't see any of the men who had gone over the top with him, the figures which were lit up now and then by the flashes of gunfire were unrecognizable. If only the noise would stop maybe he'd be able to think, work out what it was his duty to do.

The noise was inside his head now, and he began to scream in a kind of rhythm with it. It was a relief to scream, made him part of all this terrible noise. A shell exploded nearby, sending up a shower of earth which fell on him, stunning him so that he fell to the ground and lay there, still screaming, while the earth heaved and rocked. He tried to claw his way into it, push his head into it, burrow into the safety of mother earth while all around him flashes of light pierced the smoke and figures dashed through it, leapt

178

as they were hit and fell to the ground, all screaming like souls in hell.

That was it: he was in hell. It was the night of the fireworks all over again, flares like Roman candles, shells sounding like rockets; only now it was not coloured lights from bursting fireworks that showered down, but deadly shards of red hot shrapnel that cascaded on to men and tore into their flesh. All he wanted was to find a ditch, as he had done that night when he was a child, and lie in it.

The thought calmed him; of course, yes, they had been taught about looking for cover. He raised his head a little and tried to look around him. Not too far away was a shell hole; half creeping, half wriggling on his belly, he began to crawl towards it. As he rolled down into it, a man jumped in alongside him. He grabbed at his rifle, saw that it was the second lieutenant, lowered his rifle. They looked at each other for a moment, then lowered their heads as the guns began to roar again and the shells to crack and thud.

He couldn't say how long it was before the young officer said, 'There's no way ahead. Got to try to make it back to our lines.'

'Yes, sir.'

'Follow me.'

He got up slowly, ready to crawl back, but then he heard it, a thin shriek like an animal and looking out of the hole he saw a man writhing and twisting as shells fell around him. The man was pinned down by his legs, he was trying to free himself but was badly wounded, didn't seem able to use his arms and was hurling his body backwards and forwards like a trapped animal.

Dicky was suddenly quite calm, all his terror fell from him; there was something out there to be saved.

'It looks like a heavy weight, there on his leg, sir. If one of us could lift it, t'other could move 'im out of the way, we could manage between us.'

The officer looked across at the man, observed the shells which fell around him.

'He'd be dead by the time we reached him.'

Dicky looked at him. He knew officers were there to be

obeyed, but he knew that he couldn't leave the injured man, pinioned down like that, like a trapped animal.

'Come on, man.'

He shook his head, but the officer didn't see, he was already crawling back.

Dicky hesitated and then began to crawl in the opposite direction, into the fire that surrounded the wounded man. Shrapnel and clods of earth flew up as shells screeched and crashed all around him, but now he moved quietly, purposefully forward, knowing where he had to go and why.

It was a great piece of mangled iron that lay across the man's legs, some kind of girder, that had hurtled down on him as he fell.

The man stared up at him

'Thank God,' was all he said.

'There now, don't you be a-worrying, we'll soon 'ave this nasty old thing a-lifted off,' Dicky told him, in the soothing voice he would use to an animal, trying to sound confident though he didn't know how he'd have the strength to shift it. He lay down and got his shoulder under the metal until it was far enough off the ground for him to grasp it. He raised it, terrified that he'd let it fall, crash back on the crippled limbs. If only there was someone else to help, to move the crushed and helpless legs while he had them free. With a superhuman effort he raised the metal higher and flung it out of the way, like tossing the caber in the old days, in that different world of home.

He lay for a moment, exhausted, alongside the unconscious man. A shell landed a little distance away but close enough to shower them both with mud which flowed into the man's open wounds. There was a low moan, the mouth gaped. Suddenly he remembered the water bottle in his pack, found it and poured water on the man's face, on his lips, tried to get some down him. The eyes opened. Only a lad really, a brown-eyed lad.

'Now if you can just raise yourself a bit, and get yourself over my shoulder I can carry you easy. No more'n sack of taties and I've carried many of 'em. Now then, up you come. Dicky'll carry you like a sack of taties.'

The lad could hardly help himself, but somehow Dicky got him up and over his shoulder, then crouching, sometimes running, sometimes crawling on his knees, he made his way through the fire and smoke in the direction he thought the lieutenant had taken. But he was soon lost in the greyness and the terrible, confusing din. Shells were falling all around him, shrapnel flying; he couldn't tell if one had struck the burden of flesh on his back, no way of knowing, just keep going, Dicky Paste.

It was by mere chance that he stumbled towards a field casualty station, one of several that had been put up near the front line. There was noise and confusion in there too, but an orderly saw him and came over. He shook his head when he saw the injured man and it was only when they had got him on to a stretcher that Dick realized how badly he was wounded.

'Well done all the same,' the weary orderly said. 'Though I – well, we'll do what we can.' Then he looked at him narrowly. 'You look all in yourself. We've got a rush on but if you sit over there I'll get someone to have a look at you later.'

He shook his head; he must find his way to his regiment, he'd disobeyed that officer, something you weren't supposed to do in the army, must get back as soon as possible, must explain. He set off in the way he'd come and it was quiet at first, but then it started again and suddenly he was in the midst of it, the noise and fury, the pounding of guns, the screaming of shells and the dim figures of other lost souls briefly lit in the shellfire or the weird yellow flares, as they ran, shooting, throwing hand grenades, yelling, crying out when hit. He lost all sense of direction or place, he no longer knew if it was day or night, because smoke darkened the day and the firing lit up the night. Bewildered, he began to run, screaming now, either towards the German or the British lines, he didn't know which and in all this bedlam he no longer cared.

Suddenly he ran into a wall. He felt along it, moving hand over hand and found a door, hanging off its hinges. He went inside. It seemed to be a ruined stable. There was a pile of straw, a man already asleep on it. Not caring if it was friend or foe, he fell down beside him and was lost to the world.

Twenty

O n the Sunday after Tom had left, Mary-Ann again set off on her bicycle for Furzebridge. All week she had longed to go back there, to be on her own there, to indulge in remembering all that had happened there. She cycled quickly now along the road which she and Tom had travelled at a more leisurely pace, side by side, getting off to walk up the steep hills which now she pedalled up furiously, impatient to arrive.

As she left the bicycle under the trees and walked over to the stream it seemed suddenly quiet. Very lonely she felt as she sat on the bank where seven short days ago she had sat and watched Tom shifting the stones to improve the dam.

'Can you swim?' he had asked her and when she shook her head had taken her paddling instead, higher up the stream. Afterwards he had dried her feet on a handkerchief with fruit stains on it and told her how he had kept it and why.

'You should've given it to me to wash, Master Thomas,' she'd said. 'I'd have got the stains out.'

'But I didn't want them out,' he'd told her. 'And please don't call me Master Thomas. You know I hate it and you haven't called me it for days now.'

'I know. I haven't called you anything.'

'I've noticed. You've just avoided it, haven't you? But now you're going to call me Tom.'

He spoke firmly as he turned her face towards him and looked into her eyes.

She hesitated. She just couldn't bring herself to use the name his family and friends used, not after all these years of showing respect. Whatever would his parents say if they found out?

'Come on,' he said, his face close to hers. 'Whisper it in my ear.'

At last she managed to whisper his name.

Strange that one little monosyllable should have such great effect. At the sound of his name, so softly spoken, he reached out and took her in his arms.

'Say it again,' he told her and she repeated his name and he said hers and looking back on it now she thought it was rather strange and even ridiculous that they had sat there, clasping each other and repeating each other's names as if they couldn't have enough of hearing them.

Then, still holding her close, he had lain back on the grass under the trees and said, 'Oh, Mary-Ann, I do love you. I do love you so,' and there was such an ache in his voice like a child that needs comforting.

She loved him too but couldn't say it. And tomorrow he would go away and how would she bear it? Her eyes had filled with tears which he saw and understood.

'I shall be back soon,' he promised. 'The war can't last much longer. Do you know I used to want the war to last long enough for me to be in it, but now I just want it over and done with so that I can be with you like this for ever.'

She clung tightly to him, wanting to keep him close, keep him safe, returning embrace with embrace, kiss with kiss. For a moment she worried about him seeing her plain clothes underneath, not like ladies' silks, but then she forgot as she longed only to feel his flesh against hers, knowing that that was all he wanted too. It was as if all the stored up feelings of the past week, all the times their fingers had touched among the fruit, all the times they had glimpsed each other's faces through a tracery of leaves, all the yearning, all the longing were suddenly released. And it was gentle and sweet and as natural as sunlight and when it was all too wonderful to bear any longer she heard herself call out his name and it was like the cry of a bird, far away and not like her own voice at all.

And he, shuddering in her arms, was saying her name too, over and over again.

And afterwards as they lay together in the grass under the canopy of trees, looking into each other's eyes, she understood what people meant by lovelight, as he gazed at her, caressing her and saying that he loved her.

'You'll wait for me until the war's over, Mary-Ann?' he asked.

'Oh, I can't. It wouldn't do. Whatever would your family say?'

'Listen,' he said, sitting up to show that he was serious. 'Things will be different after the war. Lots of people say so. Sensible people, I mean, people who know about these things. Teddy says so and Teddy always knows a lot.'

She nodded.

'Yes, I like your cousin Teddy,' she said and Tom smiled and she knew that he was pleased that she hadn't said Master Edward. He thinks I'm learning, she'd said to herself, aware now that she often knew what he was thinking.

'Teddy says that the war has brought all different classes of people together and they've learned to respect each other, proper respect, he says, not just servants having to respect masters because they're richer than they are.'

She wanted to believe him but couldn't help but remember the number of times she'd heard Mrs Arndale talk about things getting back to normal after the war.

'Teddy says it's happening already. He says just think how rich people used to drive in carriages in London and the poor people had to walk, often barefoot. Now they mix together on omnibuses, meet and talk to each other in a way they never did before.'

'They won't when the rich all have motor cars and the poor people stay on the omnibuses,' she pointed out.

'Oh, don't you *want* to believe it, darling Mary-Ann? I agree with Teddy, it will change. It'll be like it says in the Bible about how there'll be no more rich and poor.'

Maybe in the Bible, she'd thought, but not in Northrop church, where the rich sat in the front pews, the farmers in the middle and the labourers and servants at the back, each in clothes to match their station. And they sang about the rich man in his castle, the poor man at his gate, God made them high or lowly and ordered their estate. Which was their way of making clear to God how they wanted things to be.

But she didn't say this to Tom, because it would be unkind

when he was trying so hard to reassure her. Besides she wanted to believe him.

'Where would we go, Tom?' she'd asked instead, to show that she took him seriously. 'Your mamma and papa wouldn't want us in London, would they?'

'I shall get a job. I'd like a job to do with building or engineering, I think. I'd enjoy building dams and things like that. I'll train for it when the war's over and we'll live in a little cottage somewhere, a pretty little cottage with roses round the door.'

She'd seen the inside of more cottages than he had and would have preferred to live in a proper house, but didn't say so, not wanting to spoil his dream.

So they had lain together and she remembered now how they had kept postponing having to get up and ride home and she had been the one who'd insisted that they must get back before people began looking for them and unwillingly, very unwillingly, he'd agreed.

Walking back to the bicycles he'd scratched his hand on a wild rose bush and she'd wiped the blood with her handkerchief. He'd taken it from her to keep and given her his own big one with the juice stains in exchange. Then he'd kissed her again for the last time, he said. Except that he'd stopped on the way home twice to kiss her again and then a third time as he left her at the back gate, but she didn't really enjoy that because she was too scared of being seen.

But nobody had seen them, she thought gratefully now as she stood by the stream and remembered it all. He'd said he would write to her, but she'd begged him not to. Somebody would be sure to notice and recognize his writing, she said. So, reluctantly, he'd agreed, not wanting to get her into trouble. If there was to be any trouble, he said, he wanted to be there by her side. And when he got leave he'd find a reason to come to Northrop and anyway the war would be over soon.

She could hear his voice in her head now and smiled as she remembered his words; it was comforting to sit on the bank and relive it all. She shivered with pleasure as she remembered their love-making. It puzzled her to think that this was the same thing of which she'd heard women talk of as a trouble, and ladies, who talked in front of you sometimes as if you weren't there, called a duty which they owed their husbands. Were they just pretending or did they really not know how lovely it was? What were all their fine clothes and jewels worth if they missed this great joy? For the first time she found herself feeling pity for them, as she took off her shoes and stockings and began to paddle in the stream.

She'd always looked forward to her free Sunday afternoons, but now she longed for them all week, impatient for the time when she could make her pilgrimage to Furzebridge, just be there on her own, recapturing the hours she'd spent there with Tom. The next Sunday it rained, but she went just the same, the bicycle wheels slipping on the muddy lane, rain pattering down on the leaves of the big beech tree, bouncing on the water like dancing beads. Her clothes were soaked and the water poured off her wet hair and ran in rivulets down her face, so that she could scarcely see as she cycled back to the hall.

The next Sunday she woke up feeling ill.

'I'll be better when my monthly comes,' she told herself. 'It's always worse beforehand.' Sick and dizzy, she excused herself from church and lay in bed thinking of Tom. It was a bare little room, just the truckle bed, a small chest of drawers, a hook behind the door for hanging dresses. There was a china candlestick too because the lights which the Arndales had installed in the rest of the house stopped at the landing below the servants' quarters, as did the carpet.

But she loved her room, despite its dim light and bare wooden floorboards. Before the war, she used to sleep in a big attic room with the other maids, but most of them had gone now. Their parents had taken them away, knowing they'd get much better wages working in the munitions factories and suchlike. But she'd no parents so she stayed on and the attic room was used for storage and she had this little room to herself. It was nice to lie here with the rest of the house so quiet because they were all out at church. She prayed too, prayed that she would be better by the afternoon.

She was afraid that if someone saw her they'd tell her that if she wasn't well enough for church she couldn't be well enough for cycling. Which would be untrue, because she felt quite better now. Anyway nobody saw her as she slipped quietly out of the back door into the brightness of the afternoon.

It was sunny, but with a touch of autumn sharpening the air as she sped along to Furzebridge. Like a homing pigeon, I am, she told herself, smiling as she thought she'd one day tell that to Tom. It was lovely by the stream today; she could have stayed for hours just watching the water ripple ceaselessly on its way, or staring down into the depths of the pool where a trout lay unmoving, a still dark shadow half hidden under one of the brown boulders which had been too heavy for Tom to shift.

Sometimes it seemed like yesterday that they had been together here, her and Tom, she thought, as she wandered back upstream. Sometimes it seemed years ago, sometimes she wondered if it had ever really happened. She looked down at the place where they had lain under the trees. The sight of the crushed grass, the reality of it, reassured her. She bent and stroked it with the palms of her hands, first one hand, then the other.

The next Sunday was much colder; it seemed as if autumn really had come now, it was so misty walking back from church. The hall was scarcely visible until you were nearly upon it. She'd not felt well but had been scared of asking to be excused again. In fact it seemed to be quite a pattern now, this not feeling well at the start of the day and then being better by the afternoon.

It was when she had left her bicycle propped up against the beech tree and was walking down to the stream that she realized. She stopped, her body suddenly rigid with shock. How had she not thought of it before, how had she so miscalculated? It was six weeks and she was never more than a day or two late. Never.

She began to walk up and down by the stream, frantically pacing there and back, there and back, between the pool and the place where she and Tom had lain, as if there must be some solution, if only she could find it by keeping moving.

'Oh, what shall I do?' she kept repeating to herself. 'They'll put me out and I've nowhere to go.'

She told herself to be calm. She took out Tom's handkerchief with the fruit stains and held it to her face, trying to take reassurance from it. Oh, if only he was here too, if only he had his arms around her, if only he could tell her what to do. She could write to him, she thought suddenly. But then she didn't have his address. How could she find it? His aunt and uncle did sometimes write to him, she thought, and if she could see an envelope put out for posting, it might be addressed to him. But she knew there was very little hope of that.

Panic, which seemed to come in waves, seized her again and she resumed the frantic walking. Then came a moment of calm as she found herself thinking that nothing need happen immediately. It wouldn't show for a few months yet; she had time. She could alter her dresses, she was clever with her needle. Tom might come on leave or perhaps his parents would come to visit and they'd be sure to be writing to him and she'd see the envelope and copy the address. Or something like that. Try not to think about it, Mary-Ann, just get on with your work and it will all come right in the end. Tom will see to that. He loves you, cling to that certain knowledge.

So with panic alternating with moments of calm, she paced up and down and all the time the stream chuckled heartlessly alongside her.

Twenty-One

D iana kept reminding herself of what Teddy had said of Haig's promise to abandon the attack if it failed. Surely, she thought, that first day was clear failure enough? But the attacks went on as if the war was a machine which ground on of its own volition, taking in the seemingly endless supply of raw recruits and crushing them in its maw.

So the battle of the Somme dragged on in a series of attacks, none so great as the first had been in July, but all ferocious and death-dealing. And the long grey hospital trains with the Red Cross mark rolled in, day after day, night after night, bringing the wounded from the clearing stations at the front.

'Matron wishes to see you, Arndale,' Sister told her one evening in September. 'You may go when you have finished that dressing.'

The man's face was badly mutilated, his nose half blown away and his eyes stuck together with gas burns. His breathing was laboured. 'It's my lungs,' he kept saying. 'Open my lungs.' Over and over again he said it. She finished the swabbing and dressing, bade him a gentle goodnight, knowing that he would not be alive in the morning. And glad of it, for his sake.

Her feelings towards Matron had moved from simple terror, to mere fear, to admiration and now to affection. She reminded Diana of a terrier, with her sharp pointed features and her greying red hair which had a wiry way of escaping from her cap. She was quite unlike the dignified matrons Diana had known in England, who seemed to glide from bed to bed as if on rollers. Marjorie Plaister certainly did not glide; she strode. And her stride, like everything else about her, was purposeful.

Knowing that she was not a woman to waste words or time,

Diana was surprised to find her sitting in her room offering tea and cake.

'This is to make sure you sit down for ten minutes,' she explained, as if kindness was something which required explanation.

Well, Diana thought as she thanked her, perhaps indulging in such comforts does have to be justified when we have wards full of dying men.

'You know that we have now a great preponderance of surgical cases,' she began. 'We need more help in the operating theatres. I am therefore proposing to move you from your present ward to help in the emergency theatres. This is only a temporary measure.'

Diana nodded.

'Yes, Matron,' she said.

'How would you feel about it?'

'I shall miss my ward. But obviously I'll go where I'm needed.'

'I thought you would say that.'

Then why ask, Diana thought, particularly as you don't need to.

'You will be working with Captain Bramley,' Matron went on as she poured the tea and handed the cake.

Diana nodded.

'You may have heard of him?'

'No, I don't think so.'

'He has been under considerable pressure of late, as have all our surgeons, of course. He needs the best possible people in his team.'

She smiled and added, 'People like yourself.'

Diana felt herself blushing; something she hadn't done for years.

'I'm sure you'll do very well,' Matron said, rising and holding out her hand. Like all good administrators she knew how to bring an interview to a swift conclusion.

'Captain Bramley?' one of the VADs repeated. 'Poor old you.'

'Why? What's wrong with him?'

'Nothing that we can't blame the Germans for, Diana. He's been out here too long, that's all.'

The system they were reduced to struck her as extraordinary. To get through more operations, two surgeons worked side by side, moving between four or even six patients, leaving stitching and the immediate post-operative dressing to people who weren't really qualified for the task. Even the anaesthetists were sometimes unqualified and had to learn from directions told to them as they went along.

'It's more like an abattoir than an operating theatre,' one sister protested. Others agreed with her.

Sensing their disquiet, Matron called them together. 'I know it is not what we would do in any hospital at home, but circumstances alter cases. If we followed correct procedures some of the men would not get treated at all. They would die.'

After that they stopped grumbling, for they all knew that enough men died already. The journey from the front to Etaples was too long; some of the men were dead, or almost dead, on arrival. The cemetery nearby was a constant reminder of that.

If ever she felt too tired to go on, Diana reminded herself of the hours Captain Bramley worked. He was supposed to operate for nineteen hours a day and then have five hours' sleep. He rarely took it and was said to have admitted that he had lost the knack of sleep and preferred to take the odd catnap. Many of the men who spent weeks in the trenches did the same, he said.

He was a big, brilliant, irascible man. Gentle with the patients, he railed against the system even while operating.

'Look at this gas wound,' he said one afternoon, after the patient had been anaesthetized and he was working on the wound. 'Nothing, of course, to do with gas in the usual sense. Gas warfare takes more forms than one. This is caused by anaerobic bacteria in the mud getting into the wound. During the journey here the bacteria has multiplied, hence this putrid mass. The bacillus creates gas, you see, and balloons up. No cure. We must cut away the diseased tissue. We must amputate, but that won't necessarily stop it spreading. We can but hope. It's not something any of us has ever seen before. There now,

Sister, he's ready for stitching.' And he moved on to the next patient.

She was so fascinated by this man that she wrote about him in her letters to Teddy. She described him as being like an overwound clock that never runs down, never stops. He was interested not just in every aspect of medicine, but also in all aspects of the men's lives.

'Clever chaps in laboratories are working on a bactericide,' he suddenly remarked in the middle of another operation, 'so by the next war we shall be able to kill off these anaerobic bacteria. Of course by then they'll have thought up some other horror to inflict on the human body. This foot will have to come off.'

The men suffered dreadfully from trench feet. Walking and standing for days in deep water, their feet became swollen and lost all feeling. Sometimes they were frostbitten. Their toes fell off so they couldn't walk. In the medical wards they were treated with warm oil, wrapped in cotton wool and oiled silk, but too often gangrene set in.

In some ways she found the medical wards often more distressing than the surgical. To see young men, crippled with rheumatism after living in the trenches, creeping around the ward like old men in their eighties, remembering how fit and confident they'd been when they came out fresh from England, was heartbreaking. To see them delirious with trench fever, breathless with bronchitis, that was heartbreaking too. Except that she mustn't allow it to be so. Just get on with the job, and don't criticize because we're all under army discipline.

Being under army discipline, however, didn't stop Captain Bramley railing against authority. 'Saw the general the other day. Had a huge roaring fire in his office. Asked him how he'd like to live in an open ditch when it was raining for weeks on end. Right, that's ready for stitching. That's one good thing for this poor fellow; we can classify him as wounded, I think, and not sick, don't you agree, Sister?'

The men who went home wounded would receive a pension; the ones who were disabled through sickness, would not.

Teddy wrote again from the front after another not very

profitable attack which lasted two days and in which a few yards of barren ground was gained, lost and regained.

'Di, I must say that I'm ashamed of myself for having to write to you as I am about to do. I've carried this awful thing within me for months now and feel I cannot bear it any more and must tell someone. Must tell you, I mean. If I was a braver person, I wouldn't tell you, but I need to, I can't keep the memory of it always to myself. After the first push on the Somme I was called again for that "special duty" which you know of. I wondered what would happen if I refused. No, I didn't wonder, I knew. In the army you cannot refuse. It was a last minute affair and the officer who should have stood by to give the coup de grace wasn't available. Maybe killed in the latest attack. So they ordered me to instead. In the middle of this terrible war against the Germans, time could still be made to kill one of our men, or rather organize his own mates to murder him.

'They said that he'd deserted, that he'd been found hiding in a barn with another deserter who had escaped for a while but was later found and shot. He didn't try to escape, he said he was looking for his company, that he'd gone to help a wounded man and then got lost. Of course they didn't believe him. His "trial", I found out later, had lasted less than twenty minutes and at it somebody had thought the man a little simple.

'So there he was, tied to a chair, blindfolded, a white rag on his heart. Twelve men of his platoon were lined up. They looked ready to mutiny. I knew from the start it would be worse than usual. None of them could have aimed properly. I shut my eyes and when I opened them he was still alive, blood all over the place, jumping around attached to the chair, trying to loosen his bonds, trying to escape. He cried out for his mother and another name. The men were totally demoralized. So I had to be the one to do it.

'I could stop there. I could just tell you that. But oh, Di, it was Dicky Paste and the name he called out was Edith.'

Twenty-Two

'You are well out of all this,' her mother wrote to Diana. 'Conditions here are quite dreadful. I thought 1916 was the most dreadful year ever but it seems as if 1917 is worse. I never would have thought I would see our once lovely grounds in such a state. What your grandmama would have had to say I just cannot imagine. The servant problem gets worse from day to day. Even the female staff have left us now. We still have Cook and Nanny, of course, and Mary-Ann is an excellent servant indoors and out, so they, with Witchart, have to manage as best they can with the help of two girls from the village, one of whom is simple. At least Nanny is getting on better with Cook. It looks as if hatchets are buried for the duration of the war.

'The food problem is terrible, though not as bad for us as it is in towns. We try to send what we can spare to Selina who is still doing valiant work in London providing comforts for our brave boys. Jimson produces good supplies of vegetables, helped by a village lad who is also a bit simple. All the useful young men have gone over to you in France and we are left with the crippled and the simple-minded, as far as I can see.

'Meat is very scarce and there is dreadful stuff called margarine which is supposed to do instead of butter. Of course, Cook does manage to get butter from the farmers, but sugar is another matter. And tea is so scarce that when some comes into the shop we have to send a maid to queue for it! Have you ever heard of such a thing? However, we are all agreed that difficult though life is, we are all very proud not to be having rationing like the Germans do. None of that state-controlled food for us British!'

Sometimes Diana found it hard not to tear up such letters.

How could her mother talk about food and servant problems when the men out here were dying so horribly? And they bore it all with such stoicism. She could never get over the way they joked about the most miserable billets and flooded, rat-infested trenches, giving them names like the Ritz and Bond Street and Piccadilly, the way they anglicized the names of towns so that Ypres became Wipers and Auchonvillers became Ocean Villas and an estaminet became a Just A Minute. They could laugh and make up mock-heroic songs; oh, she would never forget the way the walking wounded sang as they marched – hobbled really – back from the front. 'Take me back to dear old Blighty,' they would sing and rejoice in a wound which would take them home. Except that sometimes the wounds were healed, the men patched up and sent back to the front to be wounded again.

And she thought of the others, the thousands of others, who would never return and those whose minds were so scarred with what they had seen and heard out here that it was impossible to imagine them leading normal lives again. She tried to write to Teddy in reply to his last letter, but it was hard to find words which would get past Matron's censorship and yet manage to convey what she felt. He did not mention it again, but she felt that there was a despondency about him now that there had not been before. Where once there had been anger, there was now despair.

'All the old idealism has been lost,' he wrote to her. 'Now there is just a kind of grim determination to stick it out somehow or other. I've thought about you a lot this last week as I've been working among doctors and nurses. It came about like this. I was told to take the men from my section to a clearing station, the idea being to give them a break from fighting. At least that's the impression we were given. The truth was that they'd more wounded up there than they could manage. The arrangement was that our men should meet the ambulances bringing the wounded up from the front. Some were already dead. Others were dying. The doctors looked at them, one by one, as they passed by on their stretchers and said which ones were to be treated. They put a tab on the others, which showed us that they were to be taken to a big marquee to die. Then in the morning our men had to go with blankets into this tent, wrap up the dead bodies, sew them into these makeshift shrouds, load them up into wagons and take them down to be buried. They were just laid down in trenches, in a long line, and the burial service read over them.

'But, Di, imagine what it must have been like that night for the men with the red tabs in that great marquee, just left to die, untended. A scene from Dante's *Inferno*. If only there had been nurses there, just to be with them, but nobody could be spared. As the doctors said, "We have to work on the ones that can be saved." But it's inhuman all the same and I sometimes wonder how long the men's spirit will survive. There has been talk of mutiny, you know. Both by the Germans and the French.'

The astonishing thing was that mutiny, when it did come, was not at the front, but at Etaples. The first she knew that anything was amiss was when they were told they mustn't leave the hospital. They all thought that this was as a result of the bombing of Etaples by the Germans a week before, which had provoked outraged headlines in England about the Huns bombing the nurses and their patients, but actually most of them thought that since the army had seen fit to site the hospitals between a main railway line and an army camp it was surprising they hadn't been hit before.

Things became clearer when soldiers began to be brought in who were not from the front. Diana found herself nursing a private with a fractured arm and leg and a deep gash in his head, who was described as being one of the 'local sick', an appellation which puzzled her. He was a loquacious cockney and told her the story as she dressed his wounds.

'It was really the treatment of the men by them base-wallahs at the Etaples training camp that did it,' he said. 'Those instructors was every one a bastard, excuse me, Nurse. Sadists the lot of 'em. The men hated 'em. We called 'em "canaries" because they wore these yellow armbands. They'd get us up at five in the morning, give us one dog biscuit for breakfast and 'and us a slice of bread which was rations for the rest of the day. Then it was a four mile march with full kit and rifle up to the Bull Ring and they'd be a-cursing and a-swearing at us all the way.

'Then it was a ten hour training stint with nothing to eat but that one slice of bread. Training! It was just slow torture. And of course the Bull Ring's on the dunes by the sea so you're drilling in deep sand and you can't 'ardly get your feet out of it. And it got into everything, just murder when it's 'ot, drilling there in full sun, sand everywhere, weighed down by your kit and all for what?'

'But couldn't you have complained? Made a report to a senior officer.'

He laughed.

'My mate objected and was given non-stop jumping up and down on the spot with full pack on 'is back until 'e collapsed. Another one got the same because 'e took exception to being made to bayonet a sack of straw over and over again while this canary screamed at 'im. In the end 'e can't take it no more and 'e says, "I've been bayoneting Germans since I enlisted in 1914," 'e says. "And I don't expect you've seen a live German since the war started," 'e says. That made the instructor mad because you see 'e knew it was true. So 'e got what they call field punishment. They tie you to the fence and you just 'ave to stand there, tied by the wrists, rain or shine.

'Us old 'ands, well, we could take it, but it was awful to see what they did to the new lads fresh from 'ome and not as fit as us old 'ands. They met 'em at Boulogne, the canaries did, and marched 'em the twenty-three miles 'ere, bullying 'em all the way. And they was only a bunch of ignorant kids. You know there's always a 'orrible smell of burning flesh 'ere because they burn all the hospital stuff, amputated arms and legs and that, along wiv the rubbish? Well, I 'eard one lad ask what it were and the canary laughed at 'im and said it might be the lad's legs they'd smell the cookin' of when 'e come back from the lines and 'e was sick, the lad was, and the canary stood there laughing. They made you feel ashamed to be a soldier with all their 'umiliating, the canaries did.'

'But surely if the command had known what was going on, they'd have done something about it?'

He shook his head.

'There was an officer tried to 'elp. Sent a report to General Thomson, the gaffer of this lot. Yes, sent a report, 'e did.

198

They sent him to the front next day. The ones who really 'elped was the Australians. They just didn't go along with it. I've seen them untie one of the men what was on the fence for field punishment. They're great, they don't care. Without the Aussies I don't think there'd 'ave been a mutiny.'

'Mutiny?' she repeated, astonished.

'You didn't know, Miss?'

She shook her head.

'No, we've been confined to the hospital. We thought it was something to do with the bombing.'

'Cor, fancy you not knowing. And it's all bin 'appening just round the corner.'

From him and others, they gradually pieced the story together. It seemed that the men finally snapped and turned on their tormentors when one of the hated military police shot a corporal for chatting to one of the WAACs. Then all the suppressed rage erupted and thousands of men rose up, hunting down the military police and canaries and even managing to throw the camp commander, General Thomson, into the river.

Of all this they had been kept in ignorance and now that they knew, they were ordered to write nothing about it. They were under an oath of silence. So, she thought, I shall have to wait until after the war to tell Teddy that he was right to fear mutiny, but that it came from an unexpected quarter.

'General staff seem better at cover-ups than tactics, don't they?' another VAD remarked, as they snatched a ten-minute break one evening. 'Have you heard this? There's not a word got into the English newspapers and when an American correspondent arrived to cover the bombing story, he was in his hotel at Etaples, where he was being officially entertained, when the mutineers burst in and told him their story. Before he could send it back, the army command took him off to Headquarters to keep him safe, they said. And they kept him confined there for ten days! Would you believe that now?'

'They say the first casualty of war is Truth,' Diana remarked.

'Who said that? It's good.'

'An American senator, I think. I'm not sure, but I do know it's true. Did you see Haig's statement denying that any discontent exists in our ranks? When we've just had a riot that apparently went on for six days.'

'But it's bound to come out in the end. The men who saw these things will speak out, won't they? And General Thomson's been dismissed, hasn't he? Doesn't that say something?'

'Sister will be saying something if we don't get back.'

The mutiny was suppressed and the mutineers brought back into army discipline; in fact many died in the attack which was launched within a few days, an attack which began in late September and ended in November at Passchendaele, where the long campaign on the Somme finally sank in the mud. Four miles of devastated, crater-pocked mud land had been gained, giving the British a less secure salient than they'd had before, while the Germans had a shorter front to defend behind the Hindenburg line.

Then suddenly there was rejoicing in the hospital; news came of a great victory at Cambrai where, nearly fifty miles from Passchendaele, on hard ground, three hundred tanks, which had been useless in the mud, smashed through the German lines.

'We've taken 'em by surprise at last,' the men kept saying. And it was true. Only unfortunately the British high command was also taken by surprise and had no reinforcements prepared to follow up the victory. All that had been gained was lost when the Germans counter-attacked.

The effect on the men in the wards was disastrous. It had seemed that victory was in sight, it had seemed that so much sacrifice had not been in vain, it had seemed that they might finish the job off and go home. And their commanders had let the chance slip through their fingers. They were as bitter as the winter weather.

For this was a bitter winter which began early and ended late. It was so cold in her hut that she had to take her clothes into bed with her or they were too frozen to put on in the morning. Her hands were clumsy with chilblains and her feet swollen with them. Most of the nurses had chilblains, some had slipped on the icy paths between the buildings and had bandages on sprained ankles as they hobbled about the wards. But they knew that their sufferings were as nothing compared with the agony of the wounded who were jolted about in ambulances which lurched over the uneven, frozen mud.

They were so young, these wounded men. They had arrived from home, many of them straight from school, strong and manly in their soldiers' uniform. And yet when she drew the sheet up over their dead faces, it seemed to Diana that they looked like children. What are we doing to our people, she would ask herself, what are we doing to them?

'Look at them,' one of the officers remarked to another as they watched some new recruits march past. 'They're sending us school boys now and I shouldn't be surprised if half of them are under age.'

'Maybe, but you have to be proud of them,' his companion reproved. 'It's a great thing, the idealism of the young.'

'I'd rather have half their number of cynical old-timers,' the other told him.

Tom didn't hear these remarks as he marched past, leading his platoon with pride. It was great to be here at last, marching to the battle front. He couldn't get after the Boche fast enough, could have done with marching more quickly that morning, though by the afternoon he was glad of the slower pace. At the end of the day they were all dog-tired, but it was amazing how singing kept them going.

'It's a long way to Tipperary, it's a long way to go. It's a long way to Tipperary, to the sweetest girl I know,' they sang lustily and Tom joined in, thinking of Mary-Ann, the sweetest girl he knew. Then they sang, 'If you were the only girl in the world, and I was the only boy,' and he sang that too, thinking of Mary-Ann and the wonderful things they'd do when he got back to her.

The only old hand among them sang his own version which, as far as Tom could make out, went something like:

If you were the only Boche in the trench,
And I had the only bomb,
Nothing else would matter in the world that day,

201

I would blow you up into eternity,
A Chamber of Horrors made just for two,
With nothing to spoil our fun.
There would be such wonderful things to do,
I should get your rifle and bayonet too,
If you were the only Boche in the trench,
And I had the only gun.

The men picked up the words quickly and Tom thought the parody quite clever, but preferred the sentimental old music hall version himself.

By the end of the second day of marching they had almost caught up with the enemy and were marching through territory that had changed hands many times in the war. German as well as English boots had marched along these roads and the signs were written in both languages.

By evening they were marching on a road which had been laid down by the enemy only a few days before and led to a little village which the Germans had only just evacuated.

'We're to billet the men here tonight,' the captain told him. 'But first we search the place house by house. Tell your men to be on their guard for booby traps and stray snipers.'

It was a laborious business for tired men, moving cautiously through ruined houses, rifles at the ready, creeping down shattered alleyways, nerves stretched to breaking point. When really, Tom thought, you could see the Germans had done a bunk, cleared out lock, stock and barrel.

At last the officers were satisfied. The men were led into an old school, which was less damaged than most of the buildings, their rations were organized and he went with his captain into the schoolmaster's house which adjoined it.

'I'm just going to have a final look around,' the officer told him. 'You keep an eye on things here, the men will send round if there's anything to report.'

'Yes, sir.'

'Be on your guard.'

'Yes, sir, 'Tom said again and thought what a thorough sort of chap his captain was, which was quite right of course, but all the same it was good to relax when he had gone and have a look round.

Not a bad billet, this was, not bad at all. He eased his pack off his aching back, all sixty pounds of it, dumped it down in the corner and laid his rifle alongside it.

There was a rickety table and a couple of wooden chairs still more or less intact. There were a few empty tins by the wall with a mouse or two scuttling among them, but on the whole they'd left things quite tidy, the Huns had.

A fire was even laid in the grate on top of the ashes of a previous fire. And a pile of wood ready on the hearth, mostly of old ceiling laths which they must have taken from upstairs; they'd noticed the hole in the ceiling, he and the captain had, when they'd gone up there to inspect the building.

He went over to his pack and looked for matches. There they were in a pocket, next to Mary-Ann's little handkerchief, which he kept in an envelope. He lifted the little square of linen to his lips before replacing it. Darling Mary-Ann, he'd marry her when he got back and nobody, but nobody on this earth, would stop him.

He put the match to the piece of German newspaper conveniently left sticking out from under the kindling and the fire flared up beautifully. He'd never lit a fire in a grate before. Servants had always done it, but he had lit fires out of doors and they never blazed up as well as this one. The laths were very dry of course, he noticed, piling them up high. This would cheer the captain when he got back.

Even as he thought it, he heard him returning, and looked up. He could just make out the tall figure silhouetted in the doorway, but the night was very dark and he himself was blinded by the bright flames of the fire.

'Got a fire going, sir,' he said.

He was surprised that the captain didn't reply but appeared to take out a revolver and point it at him.

It was pretty bad form, he thought, remembering how

203

Thomson always said, 'Never point a gun at anyone, even in fun.'

He shook his head and smiled as he remembered Thomson and Northrop. He was still smiling when the German shot him through the heart.

Twenty-Three

'It's very thin material, that dress you're making,' Nanny remarked to Mary-Ann as they sat sewing in the old nursery one afternoon in late December.

They had almost finished the pile of darning and mending for the household and she'd told Mary-Ann she could do her own sewing now.

'I thought it would come in for the spring,' Mary-Ann said.

'You know what they say: "Never cast a clout till May is out",' Nanny told her.

'Does it mean May the month or may the blossom?'

'Either or both,' Nanny said.

They sewed in silence for a while, Mary-Ann stitching the hem, almost the last thing to be done to the dress.

'You've put a lot of fullness in the front,' Nanny remarked.

'Yes, I like a bit of gathering,' Mary-Ann told her.

'Well, it'll be handy if ever you put on weight,' Nanny said piling up the mending. 'I'll go along to put this lot in the cupboards.'

She was away a long time. Mary-Ann had finished the hem and sewn the buttons before she returned.

Her face was pale and she looked dreadful, Mary-Ann noticed, getting up as the older woman entered.

'It's very bad news downstairs,' Nanny said. 'Oh, the poor family! Master Thomas has been killed in action.'

Mary-Ann gave a dreadful cry, a terrible desolate cry.

'Tom,' she shrieked. 'Tom,' she heard herself cry out as if at a great distance. It wasn't like her own voice at all. It was as remote as the time she had cried out in ecstasy, only now it was a cry of despair and desolation.

205

Her face was drained of all colour, her eyes wide open and horror-stricken. She swayed and would have fallen, striking her head on the overmantel but Nanny, who through years of looking after children had developed a way of moving swiftly despite her bulk, ran and caught her just in time.

She laid her on the bed by the window, which she opened to let in the air. After a while the colour began to return to the girl's cheeks and she opened her eyes, but the expression in them was of unbearable grief. Nanny observed it all, the grief, the rounded belly, the frightened eyes and it was as clear to her as if Mary-Ann had told her the whole story herself.

She said nothing. Least said, soonest mended.

But she did report downstairs that Mary-Ann had been taken bad and needed the rest of the day in bed. She could stay there the next day too, being Sunday.

So Mary-Ann went up to her little room. There she undressed and got into bed, taking with her the only comfort she had, which was Tom's big handkerchief with the fruit stains. She held it to her face, all she had of him, and sobbed until it seemed she had no more tears left to shed, when she drifted into sleep.

She awoke very early, to the bitter cold of a December morning. She could think of no way out as she lay staring into the darkness before dawn. She'd have to kill herself, of that she was certain. But she had nothing to do it with. There'd be poison somewhere in the grounds, but she didn't know where it would be kept or how she could steal some. She could drown herself, she thought suddenly. She couldn't swim so would drown quite easily. She could do it in the lake. But then she remembered that Lady Arndale had drowned there and it seemed going a bit above her station to drown herself in the same lake as Lady Arndale.

Furzebridge would be more fitting; she would end her life in Tom's pool where she had watched him build the dam, near where they had lain together.

So just as dawn was beginning to streak the sky, she crept downstairs, before any of the household had stirred, let herself out of the back door and down to the shed where the bicycles were kept. It wasn't locked, just the bolts drawn.

206

It was very cold cycling along the lanes, but it didn't worry her. She welcomed the icy lash of the wind, nothing could hurt her now. She didn't feel the rose thorns sharp against her hands as she pushed her way through the bushes after she'd left the bicycle against the beech tree. She didn't feel the freezing cold of the water as she slipped down the bank and into the pool. She was aware of nothing except the pain, the unbelievable pain, of Tom's death.

She paused for a moment standing there, where the water was still quite shallow and only reached the top of her legs, before moving out into the deep, dark centre of the pool. Suddenly there was a lurch, a strange twisting lurch inside her. The baby was moving. She had felt it move before but never so strongly as this. Perhaps it had felt the cold, she thought, perhaps it was asking her not to hurt it. Instinctively she put her hands over her stomach to protect it. It was Tom's baby and he wasn't here to look after it. She couldn't let the poor little baby suffer. Oh, if only she could die and let the baby live, but she couldn't. If she killed herself she would kill Tom's baby too. She must not do it.

She was almost out of her depth now; she reached out towards the bank, but her foot slipped and she fell back, her head going under the water. Her skirts spread out round her, buoying her up for a moment, then as they filled with water, they began to drag her down. Frantic now to save the baby, she thrashed about this way and that, choking and spluttering as her head went under. In one last desperate effort she threw herself towards the bank; her hand struck a branch of a weeping willow tree. She clung to it and managed to grab a bigger branch with her other hand. Gripping both of them tightly, she heaved her body forwards and found herself in the shallower water, within reach of the bank.

She scrambled up it, shivering now with cold, and made her way back to the bicycle, but on the way she ran over to the place where they had lain under the trees and, standing there for a moment, silently promised Tom that somehow or other she'd save his baby and wouldn't kill herself until afterwards.

The house was stirring when she got back but she managed to get up to her room without being seen, dumped all her wet clothes in her bucket, rubbed her hair dry and crept into bed.

It wasn't long before she heard Nanny's slow, deliberate footsteps on the bare boards of the corridor.

'I've brought you a cup of tea,' she said, handing it over.

She hadn't been up to this room before and gave it a quick look which made it plain that she thought it a bare and miserable sort of place. Then she sat down on the chair by the bed.

After the tea had been drunk, Nanny said, 'It doesn't do to beat about the bush. How long is it till the baby's due?'

Mary-Ann knew it was pointless to deny or postpone.

'Four months.'

'And what do you intend to do about it?'

The girl shook her head.

'Madam must be told.'

'Oh, please no. She'll put me out.'

'You should have thought of that before, my girl.'

She stood up, taking the empty cup.

'You stay there, today. Nothing can be said to Madam until the family's had time to get over its grief. If you're well enough you can get up for work tomorrow.'

So it was three weeks, during which time Elspeth and Charles had been up to London to see Tom's parents, his father having been home on compassionate leave, before Nanny, who had been in charge of the household during their absence, went to report to her mistress.

'How are they, Mister William and Mrs Arndale?' she asked.

'They are very brave. I hope they are proud to have given their son as I should be proud to give mine.'

'And will Mister William go back to the war?'

'Yes, the colonel will return to duty and Mrs Arndale insists that she will stay in Billington Square to continue her war work with the Ladies' League of Comfort.'

She paused.

'My sister-in-law has shown herself to be a real stoic. I have told her she may come here any time, but she insists upon staying at her post. She has no help now except for a little

208

maid-of-all-work who comes in daily. She has closed off all the downstairs rooms because she can't manage to black them out sufficiently well without help, but simply lives upstairs. She explained to me that since her bedroom and boudoir both have shutters and heavy curtains, it is more practical to spend time upstairs.'

'One would imagine she would be nervous, Madam, being alone in that big house.'

'I asked her that and she just smiled and said she was not.'

'Not nervous or not alone?' Nanny queried.

'Not nervous, of course,' her employer replied, puzzled.

There was a pause, then she said, 'And have there been any difficulties while we have been away, Nanny?'

'No, Madam.'

'I don't know what we would do without you, Nanny,' Elspeth said, 'not since that housekeeper let us down so badly. I sometimes think, Nanny, that the whole household would fall apart without you.'

Nanny nodded in acknowledgement of this unusual expression of gratitude then, after a brief pause, she looked directly at her employer and spoke again.

'With your permission, Madam,' she said, 'I should like to speak to you about Mary-Ann.'

'What about her?'

'She is expecting, Madam.'

'Expecting?'

'Yes, Madam, she is expecting a baby in about three months' time.'

'How disgusting!' Elspeth Arndale rose to her feet and almost spat out the words. 'How *dare* she? And in this house too!'

Enraged she began to pace the room.

'She must go immediately, of course. The slut will be shown our door. She shall go without a reference.'

'What will become of her, Madam?'

'I neither know nor care. She may go on the streets for all I care. It's probably where she belongs.'

'The baby may have good blood in its veins,' Nanny said quietly.

Elspeth Arndale stopped dead and stared.

'You mean? The little hussy has been going with officers, leading innocent young men astray? She deserves prison, she should be put away. She must go by nightfall. Girls like that deserve to be put out into the snow.'

She looked up and saw that snow had started to fall. It seemed providential.

'Well, Nanny?'

Nanny Stone stood in front of her, solid in her black bombazine with the carved jet buttons, looking as she had looked for as long as Elspeth had known her, the embodiment of the family values of Northrop Hall. Then in the same flat tones, which brooked no contradiction, which over the years she had used to prescribe children with medicine, mouth washings, punishments and admonitions, she stated, 'If she goes, Madam, I go too.'

Twenty-Four

'I had a really warm Christmas,' Teddy wrote to Diana. 'We were sent back after an indescribable time at the front, when our trench was just an elongated series of shell holes in which men froze. I had a strange experience when we were sent back to look for anywhere to billet ourselves and suddenly there was this bomb attack and we got scattered. I was thrown down and knocked out for a bit, but I managed to stagger along and found the remains of a barn. There was a kind of porch and as I went in there was a man standing in the doorway, as if he was welcoming me. He was bowing a bit towards me, just like Witchart welcoming a guest. It was weird. I stood staring at him, then I saw his grey uniform and reached for my rifle. But he didn't move. Then I made out his face and saw he was dead. He was just standing there, dead. He didn't seem wounded, but there's no mistaking that terrible glassy stare. I wanted shelter desperately but I couldn't bring myself to go past that fearful butler, I, who have seen sights so much worse than this, terrible deaths, worst of all the faces of men who've been bayoneted, but I couldn't bring myself to go past him, this man who looked like Witchart and seemed to be welcoming me in.

'Well, it all ended happily, because we got ourselves reassembled and marched to an abandoned village, much blasted and bombed but with more buildings standing than is usual. We got a good fire going in one house and used the wood from the building next to it to keep ourselves warm. We spread all our clothes about the place to dry and we slept by the fire and it was heaven. We could warm up food on the fire and make ourselves hot drinks, unbelievable after days of cold bully and biscuits washed down with icy water. We kept a roaring fire going all night and slept around it. The men brought round chairs and tables from the abandoned house next door which we broke up and burnt. There wasn't much furniture so they took down the ceiling and brought in dry laths which made a wonderful roaring, crackling fire. Then we started on the upstairs furniture in our house. It was a rambling sort of place, part demolished by bombing, and I was looking for something else to burn before we started on the banisters when I found this little attic room and in it there was a rocking horse.

'Di, it was just like the one in the nursery at home and suddenly I realized that we were burning somebody else's home and furniture and everything they'd used and cared for. And I just stood there, looking at it and was horrified that we'd been doing this without any compunction. I really hadn't given a thought to anything except getting us warm after the hell of Passchendaele. It made me realize what war does to us, completely changes all ideas of right and wrong, makes us forget the ordinary decencies, dehumanizes us. Survival is all that matters.'

As far as Diana was concerned, she was simply glad that he'd had a warm Christmas. In the months that followed, when he was back on the front line and she didn't have letters from him for weeks on end, she clung to the thought that at least he had had a few days of warmth and comfort, of dry clothes and hot food between the horror of Passchendaele and the slaughter of the German offensive.

For in March, in dense fog, the enemy launched a surprise attack on the Somme, tearing through the British line, retaking all the land that they'd lost the year before. In a few days they had advanced forty miles. Fortified by the troops they could bring in from the Eastern front after the collapse of Russia, they wanted to make the most of their chance before the Americans arrived. As they swept westwards all the old familiar names were in the news again, all the places that had been fought over for months were retaken in days as they moved steadily westwards.

Suddenly defeat seemed possible. The unthinkable might happen; the Germans might soon arrive in Etaples, they might take the channel ports and cross to England. Then the villages and market towns of the Cotswolds and the Weald, of Kent and Surrey might become known, as towns and villages of France had become known, simply as the names of battlefields. Peronne, Bapaume, Arras, Passchendaele, Beaumont Hamel, Armentieres. Would it one day be the same for Littleton and Northrop, for Cirencester and Malmesbury, for Cricklade and Highworth? The desperately wounded men who were pouring in on the trains clearly feared so. 'We hadn't a chance,' they'd say. 'There were just so many of them. They've taken the town of Albert, they're shelling Paris.'

The front was so near that the wounded were no longer being treated at casualty clearing stations at the front, but brought direct to Etaples. In fact, Diana realized, Etaples itself was now a casualty clearing station, it was almost at the front. They arrived not just in trainloads but in any returning vehicles that would take them, lorries, ambulances or cattle trucks. They arrived with wounds still filthy, stuck to the stretchers with their congealed blood, blinded, delirious. They had to be dealt with swiftly for the next consignment would be arriving immediately behind them. So they were washed, their wounds dressed. Then they were either sent back to England or to the cemetery.

She tried to feel detached, knew that she could only help them if she kept a firm control over her emotions, something she had schooled herself to do over the years, but still there were times when some new horror overwhelmed her. She looked out one day and saw a group of blind soldiers approaching. They had been formed into a line and were stumbling up the road, each with his hands on the shoulders of the man in front, so they seemed to be strung together, led by a youth with his arm in a sling, who was so exhausted he could hardly walk. The pity of it, oh the pity of it, she kept thinking as tears streamed down her face.

She felt Captain Bramley's hand on her shoulder. He handed her a handkerchief, stayed by her for a moment, then moved away without speaking and didn't mention it next time they were together. And she wiped her eyes and went out to help lead in the blind men.

The Captain was again operating day and night and once

more she marvelled at the way he could keep up his constant talk as he worked away on these shattered bodies, sometimes giving impromptu lectures on what he was doing, sometimes inveighing against the authorities.

'Have you heard the latest from the sanitary lunatics?' he demanded one day. Like most of his questions it was rhetorical. '"Keep up the spraying," they say. "Spray the dead bodies if they can't be buried." Now what's the sense of that? Bodies lying out there because it's not safe to try to bring them in, but they've got the gall to say it's safe to go and spray them with disinfectant. And what good would that do? The stuff stops the body decaying, which is what we want it to do as quickly as possible. Try to keep the rats off, they say. Rubbish. Let the rats do their work. The sooner that body is reduced to nice bleached bones the better for everybody. Now then, this chap's ready for stitching and stump dressing.'

Teddy, in the midst of the fighting around Amiens, still managed to let her know he was alive, though sometimes only with a field postcard. At other times he wrote as he used to do, as if he needed to share his doubts and fears.

He also shared his bitter amusement at the outpourings of the propaganda machine at home. 'Lord Northcliffe's in charge of it, as you probably know, Di. One of the men was sent a copy of what his lordship has just written so he nailed it up by the fire step in our trench so that the men, as they wade past, up to their knees in foul water, cold, hungry and about to face unspeakable horrors, can read, "The open air life, the regular and plenteous feeding, the exercise, the freedom from care and responsibility keep the soldier extraordinarily fit and contented." Somebody nailed a dead rat, a nice plump trench rat, up next to it.

'One of the saddest things to me now, Di, is that there's much more hatred of the Hun now, hatred born of fear. It's always struck me up till now that the men are remarkably free of it, bear the Germans much less ill will than the people at home do. The men knew that the German soldiers were having as wretched a time as they were, though of course the officers had to rouse them. The last service I attended, oh I can't remember how long ago, the padre preached a text on "Love Your Enemy, do well to them that despitefully use you." And there was the colonel looking solemn and nodding his agreement and only the day before he'd been telling us of the advisability of using our bayonets. *His* text was, "Take no prisoners, dead men eat no rations and tell no tales."

'Speaking of tales, do you know the Germans say the same sort of things about us as we say about them? I talked to an American doctor last year. It was before America came into the war and he was here as a volunteer and had been taken by the Germans but allowed to treat our wounded – there'd been a truce for clearing the wounded and dead. He said they were very decent to him. Of course it was at a time when people still thought that the Americans might come in on the Germans' side, as they've got so many Germans in their population. Anyway what I was going to say was that the Germans told him to be careful of the water because they said, "The English poisoned the wells before they evacuated this place." Just what we say of them.'

There was a hasty postscript to this letter: 'Oh, I nearly forgot to tell you, Di, that I've once or twice come across a Captain Crawley, Sebastian Crawley. He says he met you in London. It must have been that time you stayed with Uncle William and Aunt Selina in Billington Square. We don't have much time together but I like what I've seen of him and we seem to agree about a lot of things. He's more of a romantic than I am and sees the war as a crusade against evil. I'm more cynical. I just want to get the whole beastly business over. But we get on well and I find I can talk easily to him about Northrop, about home and we're both impressed by the way our working-class men fight, when they have so little to fight for compared with us, and we want to try to make things better for them when the war's over. You probably don't remember him, you must have met so many people then. How long ago those days seem, don't they?'

How long ago indeed! she thought. That name had once meant so much to her and still reverberated, a sad little reminder of youth and innocence. Before the war, before all this horror. That carefree girl dancing in the garden with Sebastian belonged to a different world from this. Could they really be the same person, that girl in her ball dress who could have danced all night without getting tired, and the woman she now was, here at Etaples, exhausted, with work-worn hands and aching legs, trying not to show fear as she waited, with the others, for the Germans to march into the hospital?

Nurses from the abandoned clearing stations arrived, destitute, having fled before the enemy. It should have helped, having extra staff, but it seemed only to add to the confusion and sense of rising panic. Then the day came when they were all ordered to pack up their belongings and be ready to evacuate the hospital if the enemy arrived. They could see and hear the gunfire now, flashes filled the sky and the relentless thudding drummed in their ears day and night. Then one night both the camp and town of Etaples were bombed and the railway line smashed. It could only be a matter of days now before the Germans arrived.

But they didn't arrive; it was the Americans who arrived instead, twenty-seven divisions of them. She saw them marching from Etaples as she had so often seen columns of British troops arriving, but these were fresh, well-fed men, unwearied by war. They had come over in British ships, equipped with guns, tanks and aeroplanes from French and British factories. And the nurses watched them as they marched and cheered and cheered as these young Americans made their way towards the beleaguered front.

So Paris did not fall, nor were the Channel ports taken. Instead the German advance was reversed. She did not at first let herself believe it; there had been too many false dawns. But as the gunfire and the bombing ceased, hope began to grow. The wounded, who still arrived in trainloads from the front, brought news of rapid advances. ''E's on the run is the old Boche,' they called out from their stretchers. 'You won't be seeing 'em 'ere, nurse, not now you won't.'

Twenty-Five

'Why don't you go on leave a couple of days early?' William's commanding officer suggested. 'You've had a rough time and there really isn't much for you to do here now.'

He was anxious about the younger man who, since his boy was killed, looked much more than his forty-odd years.

William agreed; he knew he could be spared and in a way that only added to his sorrows. Since Tom's death he had been haunted by a sense of his own uselessness and by the feeling that he had somehow failed his son. There seemed to be this great blank, an empty space, a kind of no-life, between that eager little boy he had loved and the eighteen-year-old man who had gone off to war and never returned.

Where had all those years gone? he asked himself as, the channel crossing over, he boarded the train at Folkestone. Where had he himself been when Tom was living them? And what was there to show for them? A handful of school-boy letters, a few memories of admonishments delivered in the holidays when Tom had been up to some prank or other, of brief greetings at breakfast before he rushed off to work, of glimpses of his son in the evening as he and Selina hurried out.

They had been great years for him, William; he'd had the companionship of the most wonderful, amazing wife anybody ever had, but what had those years been for Tom, he now wondered, as he had never wondered then.

He'd thought they were doing the right things for Tom. Kind people had been put in charge of him in nursery and schoolroom, a good school had been chosen for him. They had bought for him everything he needed, so they thought, including a superior and expensive education. And yet, and yet. They had not given him generously of their time, their understanding. Why, he'd seen craftsmen on his brother's estate who were closer to their sons, as they taught them their trade, watched over them, guided them, closer than he had ever been to his son, he thought bitterly as the train made its slow way from Folkestone to London.

Give your children your ear, your love, your time, a voice inside him seemed to be saying rhythmically in time with the engine, for without that you give them nothing.

And so he thought of Celia. He must learn from this fearful lesson life had given him, he must make sure that she had her parents' companionship, their support. Once this dreadful war was over, as it seemed likely soon to be, they must be involved in her life in a way they never had been in Tom's.

He thought about his daughter, as he gazed out at the darkening countryside; the trouble was that he couldn't remember exactly where she was. Was she at Northrop at the moment or still with those northern relations of Selina's whom he had never met? Perhaps she was spending a little time with her mother in London, though they had agreed that she should stay away in case of air raids, even though Selina – his brave, determined Selina – remained sternly at her post.

Yes, even after poor Tom had been taken from them, she had insisted on staying in London. She lived mostly upstairs now, she said, because the blacking out of the great windows downstairs in accordance with government regulations had been too difficult. They weren't supposed to show any light at all which might attract the enemy planes, which of course was an impossible task without servants; it was much simpler to picnic and entertain upstairs. She just had one little maid-of-all-work who came in by day.

Selina was so brave about it, he thought, never complaining about the hardships of wartime living, as some wives did, always saying how lucky she was, how grateful for the presents people gave her: Elspeth sent fruit and vegetables and evidently the soldiers she helped to comfort were similarly generous with their gifts, particularly the Americans, who positively showered her with luxuries, she said. He thought of her as some romantic princess in a tower, as she lived there all alone, his uniquely brave wife.

Thinking of Selina always made him feel better. He pictured the welcome she would give him. He imagined her sitting at her dressing table, brushing her long dark hair, her huge violet eyes gazing serenely back at him in the glass as he stood behind her. Those great innocent eyes. He would hold her lovely head against him, quite still at first and then, and then. His thoughts merged with a dream of her as his head lolled against the upholstery and the twilit Kentish countryside rolled by, unseen.

It was dark when they drew into Victoria station. He looked for a cab but they all seemed to be taken. He joined a queue for one. How old the drivers seemed, he thought, used as he was to being surrounded with young men. In fact it seemed as if all the young men had gone to France, leaving the old and frail, the women and children behind. All those young men, like Tom, led away by the Pied Piper of War, he thought and his eyes prickled with unshed tears.

He gave up the idea of getting a cab. He'd walk. He hadn't much to carry. How much did young soldiers like Tom carry in their packs? Sixty pounds, wasn't it? Half a hundredweight. Ah, but they carried more than that; we burdened them with our mistakes. We bred them, we educated them, stuffed their heads with Greek and Latin and ideas of right and wrong, and then suddenly took them away from all that and ordered them off to die in order to clear up the mess that was not of their making.

He put his hand in his pocket to make sure he had the front door key. How good, how familiar it felt, how reassuring. He fondled it as he thought of Selina. 'C'est le clef du Paradis,' he had once heard a Frenchman say of his latchkey. That was how he felt about it too, he realized as he stood outside his home. He felt a great surge of joy at the thought of having Selina in his arms again, so that his plans for Celia and even his grief for his son and all his generation were momentarily forgotten.

The pitch darkness in the hall surprised him. He always used to come home to a blaze of light when he came in from work, especially when he'd had the electric lights installed to replace the gentler gas. He had forgotten all about blackout regulations. He fumbled about for the switches. He found the row of them and now the hall and staircase were flooded with brilliant light. He looked in at the drawing room and, turning on that light too, saw that the furniture was covered in dust sheets. How dreary life must be for poor Selina, he thought, how lonely her life must be here in this dark place, and yet she has never once complained, he thought as he mounted the stairs, turning on lights as he went. Eagerly he crossed the landing and went down the familiar passageway, full of the excitement which approaching her never ceased to arouse in him.

He couldn't remember where the switch was so walked down the corridor in darkness, led on by the light shining from under the bedroom door. So she was there, she was there ready for him. Dearest girl, he thought, what a surprise I shall give you, arriving two days early.

The first thing he noticed as he stood in the doorway was the khaki jacket lying on the bed and next to it a pair of matching trousers. Then he saw her, Selina, sitting at the dressing table, gazing into the glass at the reflection of the man who was standing behind her. He, presumably the owner of the soldier's uniform, was a tall man, naked and erect.

Nobody moved; they stood, deprived of speech and movement, like figures frozen in a tableau. There was no sound until suddenly the silence was broken by the noise of an aeroplane overhead. Attracted by the sudden blaze of light, its pilot homed in on it, hastily releasing his bombs, anxious to get back to Germany as quickly as possible.

It was a direct hit; the whole edifice of 5, Billington Square collapsed, its ballroom and its nursery, its old-fashioned staircase and its modern lift, its bedrooms and its drawing rooms, all shuddered and crumpled and finally collapsed as if its structure was as insubstantial as a house of cards.

Twenty-Six

'It looks as if it will soon be over, Di,' Teddy wrote from Amiens. 'Hard to believe, isn't it? How will we ever live any kind of normal life at home after this? I have two contrasting souvenirs for you. One is a German badge with *Gott mit Uns* on it. The other is a similar British one which says *Dieu et mon Droit*. So whose side *is* He on?'

The letter had been delivered just before she came on duty, so she only glanced at it briefly, meaning to read it properly later on. Captain Bramley saw that she was looking happy and guessed at the cause, except that he assumed that the letter was from her sweetheart. Thank God, he thought, as he worked alongside her, that this war is almost over and soon the young will live and love again in peace.

'Matron said could you go to her office?' an orderly requested.

'Thank you. Please tell her I'll come when I've finished with this patient,' Diana replied.

'Go now,' Captain Bramley told her. 'I'll see to the stitching.'

'But I—'

'Be off with you. Do you think I can't embroider as well as one of you ladies?'

He spoke lightly but everyone knew that summons to Matron often meant bad news.

The little terrier face that Diana had first feared and then come to love was furrowed with grief now.

'I can't tell you how sorry I am,' she said. 'My poor dear child. It's your brother.'

He had been killed by a stray bullet two days after he wrote that letter.

Diana looked at her blankly. She seemed to feel nothing. Except perhaps disbelief. It just was not possible that Teddy should have gone right through the war from August 1914 until now, October 1918, unhurt and now be dead. Not just wounded but dead, not existing any more. Not there. No more letters. No more talk. No more shared grief. Never again a shared joy. No more anything.

'Sit for a while, my dear. I'll make you some tea.'

'No thank you, Matron. I'll go back to the ward.'

'You may go to your hut and rest.'

'I don't want to rest, thank you.'

'You're very brave, my dear.'

She knew she wasn't brave, just numb, but didn't say anything. What was the point of saying anything?

Captain Bramley had finished his embroidery. He had a final word with his patient, dismissing thanks.

He came across to her.

'It's bad news, isn't it?'

She nodded.

'Come with me,' he told her and taking her by the arm led her out of the ward and over to her hut.

She let him guide her along the path, but once inside she said, 'No, I don't want to be here. I want to get back to work on the ward. I'm all right, you know.'

'I know nothing of the kind,' he told her. 'I know you may snap and when you do I don't want you doing it anywhere near one of my precious patients.'

It was so like him, this abrasive kindness, that she laughed. And went on laughing and couldn't stop laughing. She sat down on the chair at the table and laughed hysterically, then she began to thump her head on the little table and the relief was so great she wondered why she hadn't done it before.

'Now, now,' she heard him say. 'We can't have this,' and he took tight hold of her, so she couldn't throw herself about any more and she gradually subsided, gasping and sobbing, into a dull calmness of total exhaustion.

He took her over to the bed.

'Now, while I'm gone you get yourself undressed and

222

properly into bed. I'll be back in five minutes with something to settle you and a hot drink.'

She made some sort of feeble protest.

'I speak as your doctor,' he said.

She wondered later how she would have got through the next few days without him. He watched over her at work, insisted on her having periods of rest and, when they were both free, let her talk and talk about Teddy. She told him about the brother she had hardly known when he was away at school and how it was only during these last four years that they had grown close, each confiding only in the other. But these four years were a lifetime. She told him how he used to write telling her all he felt about the war, knowing she understood. But she did not tell Captain Bramley about the marksmanship at which he'd excelled and which he'd been made to put to such terrible use. No, she could not speak of that.

She told him about the happy times too, about the games they used to play, even about the picnic the day before the war started, when they had all gone to Furzebridge and the boys had built the dam and swum. And she'd minded about being a girl and not being allowed to do things the boys did. And she'd resented being made to wear such awful restrictive clothes.

'And now,' he said, 'women are driving cars and ambulances and omnibuses, making munitions and doing all the jobs men used to say they couldn't do.'

'And wearing easier clothes,' she pointed out.

'Do you think you'll go back to wearing clothes like that after the war?'

She shook her head.

'Never,' she said. 'Nothing will force us back into stays and boned collars. There's a new garment now, called a Liberty bodice, and it's just that.'

So they talked of all manner of things and she wondered how he had gained such a reputation for being brusque and difficult, as he slowly helped her back into some kind of normality and acceptance that she had to go on with life without the brother who had become everything to her since the war started.

223

The day peace was declared was perhaps the worst of all to bear. There were reports of such rejoicings at home, but out here there was very little jubilation. There were too many maimed, too many friends left behind.

'I used to think it was good to have the regiments all come from the same district,' Dr Bramley said one day. 'The intention was good, of course, local loyalty and all that but I wonder now. It's cruel enough when your mates are killed, men you've trained with, but when they're your childhood mates, lads from the same village, boys you were at school with, it's worse. It's dreadful to see them when they carry in their dead friends, brothers too sometimes. They didn't think of that, did they, when they talked of local loyalty.'

And when you're put on special duty to shoot one of your men for desertion, that man could be from your own village too, she thought, but did not say. Teddy could never speak of it now – and nor would she.

They were among the last to leave. The last train taking the wounded back to England had left, most of the nurses had gone too, only Matron, three doctors and a few nurses were left clearing the hospital with the help of soldiers impatient to get home.

On their last evening she asked him something she'd wanted to ask many times before.

'Did you live in Cadogan Place before the war and is your wife called Juliet?'

He looked startled.

'I did,' he said. 'And she was.'

'Was?'

He looked at her and was silent. Then he shook his head and said, 'The irony was that I thought that she and the children were in danger in London, so I insisted that she took them to an aunt in Scarborough.'

Scarborough, the first town to be hit.

'The children were only two and four. Yes, all three of them were killed. Only my aunt survived and she, poor soul, was pretty badly damaged. And the final irony was that no bombs ever came near our house in London.'

Diana hesitated, then she took his hand and said, 'She was

224

once very kind to me, your wife.' And she told him about their meeting in London. 'It seems such a trivial thing now, but I can remember feeling so miserable and homesick and ashamed because I was in front of all these people and I'd been trying so hard to be grown-up and there I was crying to go home. And she understood and told me what to do. And made me drink a whole glass of champagne in one go, like medicine. And I'd never had alcohol before.'

He laughed.

'That would make the medicine even more effective,' he said. 'I can just see her doing it, hear her voice telling you what you were to do. Oh, thank you for telling me that tale.'

He paused for a moment and then went on thoughtfully, 'You know, when you suffer a terrible loss, nothing seems to help, but actually to be told something about the loved one that you didn't know, any little thing, any trivial episode, it seems to make them alive again, add a little bit to their life. And that's a great comfort. Yes, that's something I have learned. Thank you, my dear.'

They were sitting in her hut. It was strictly against regulations for a man to be in a VAD's hut unless he was acting as a doctor to her, but nobody thought about the rules any more.

'What will you do when you get back? Go on with your practice in London?'

'Well, I've been doing some thinking in the past few days,' he began, speaking slowly, as if he was now thinking aloud. 'We have to leave the rehabilitation of the world to the politicians, but we can do something about the rehabilitation of these men. There are about half a million amputees as a result of this war. Thousands of men have been blinded, thousands dreadfully damaged by gas. Then there are the psychologically damaged, the shell-shocked. And it seems to me that those of us who've survived owe it to the rest to help them. I'm going to try to set up specialist rehabilitation homes with staff trained for their particular needs. I'd like to work in one myself,' he said, sounding more enthusiastic with every word he spoke. 'When I get back I'm going to see about raising the funds. I'm sure that there will be plenty of other people who feel the same, it's just a question of getting together and organizing it.'

It struck her that he was perhaps over-optimistic, but she didn't doubt that he would get things done. He'd always managed to get what he needed for his patients out here, surely he'd do the same back home?

'And what about you? Because I've been thinking,' he went on without giving her time to answer, 'that you might join me. I've worked alongside you, we know each other's ways. There's nobody I'd rather have to lead the nursing staff. Would you be interested?'

She hesitated.

'I don't know what my commitments will be at home. I hear from my mother that my father is in need of care. His mind seems to be going.'

She looked up at him; it was somehow difficult to talk about her father in this way.

'She writes that he seemed to get depressed from the start – he'd always hated the idea of the war – and then he didn't seem able to manage the estate after the agent had gone. Of course they were both living for the day Teddy came home. And now –' she shrugged helplessly – 'I think he may simply give up altogether.'

'Another casualty of the war,' he said. 'It has destroyed many of the old as well as the young.'

'And also, you see,' Diana went on after a few moments, 'I'm not properly qualified. I only did a short training.'

'I doubt if any training could be more rigorous than yours out here,' he told her. 'I've seen you do everything qualified nurses do.'

'We weren't supposed to.'

He laughed.

'I don't remember any objections being raised at the time,' he said drily. 'Well, promise me you'll think about it. We will keep in touch, won't we?' he added anxiously.

'Oh, but of course.'

The idea of not being in touch with this man she'd worked with so closely, who had been such a friend to her, was simply unthinkable.

He looked at her closely.

'Now that the war is over,' he said, 'I have to go back and face my grief. It will be the same for you, my dear.'

She nodded.

He reached out and took her face between his hands, looking into her eyes.

'May we face it together?' he asked.

For a moment she didn't understand, but when she did, she looked up and nodded.

Twenty-Seven

E lspeth was aware, as she sat knitting by the fire, that
Charles was watching her anxiously as he sat on the
other side of the hearth. She knew what he was going to say.

'Is everything locked up for the night?' he enquired.

'Yes, Charles. Witchart has seen to it.'

'Who?'

'Witchart.'

'Oh, yes of course. Witchart.'

Silence for a while except for the clicking of knitting
needles, then the anxious voice again.

'Is everything locked up for the night?' and again she told
him that it was.

'I think,' he said after a while, 'that I should go and make
sure that everything is locked up for the night.'

'Very well, my dear,' she answered wearily. 'If it will put
your mind at rest.'

It wouldn't put his mind at rest, she knew that. Nothing
could now that he lived in his own anxious little world.

She wondered, after twenty minutes, if she should go
and look for him. Sometimes he forgot why he had started
perambulating around the house and she would find him
searching in the library for a book whose name he couldn't
remember or at his desk poring over ledgers of figures he no
longer understood.

The figures had ceased to add up since Blake had left and the
whole burden of managing the estate had fallen on its owner.
For a while he went into the office but then began to stay at
home, sitting in the library, pottering in the garden. Tenant
farmers who had formerly been dealt with by Blake began to
come up to the house to see him. They left looking puzzled.

That was when she had first begun to fear that something more than absent-mindedness was wrong with Charles.

She had a suspicion that the tenant farmers were taking advantage of the situation. Certainly their manner was less deferential than it had been.

'My husband has so much on his mind,' she would tell them. 'After the war everything will get back to normal,' but she had said it with less and less conviction.

'My son will see to all these matters when he returns,' she had been able to promise until last month.

Oh, Teddy, Teddy, her eyes filled with tears at the memory of him, of Teddy going off to war, of Teddy going off to school, of Teddy at home on holiday, loving to follow his father around the fields and farms. Teddy had known everything about the estate.

Charles came back just as she was going to look for him.

'Where's Nanny?' he asked.

'In her cottage, Charles, but she will be up tomorrow.'

'I'll see her tomorrow?'

'Yes, I promise.'

Then at last he did seem to relax and sat staring into the fire, like a child making pictures in the crumbling embers.

Of all of them, Nanny alone had not changed and she knew she could not have managed without her. She was the only one, apart from herself, who could soothe Charles. Indeed she seemed to comfort him with her reassuring presence more even than she, his wife, could. Nanny was like a mother to him, more of a mother than Lady Arndale had ever been. Sometimes, in his dreadful confusion, he even called her Mamma, which was terrible to hear.

She wouldn't go on living in the house, though Elspeth had begged her to. She had moved into the cottage on the estate which Charles had long ago promised her and lived there with that girl and the baby. The girl came up in the mornings and did all that had to be done around the house, or rather round the few rooms they used now. She helped Cook in the kitchen, did the vegetables and the washing up, did a bit of gardening, saw to the hens, while Nanny minded the baby. Then in the afternoon she went back to the cottage while Nanny came up and did the sewing and mending, usually up in the nursery with Charles sitting by her, as he used to do as a child. That was when he seemed at his happiest. It gave Elspeth a few peaceful hours, free of his restless wandering.

She had objected to these arrangements at first when Nanny had suggested them. She didn't want Nanny to move out, didn't approve of the girl, said there would be scandal, but Nanny had said that people had other things on their mind in wartime and if it really worried Madam, then it was a simple thing to put a ring on the girl's wedding finger and she'd say she was her widowed niece. It had been done before and would no doubt be done again and nobody any the wiser. Especially not nowadays when so many young women were widows. With Nanny so adamant, what else could she do but give in? And admittedly the girl was very strong and a hard worker.

'Rupert's gone out, has he?' Charles enquired suddenly. 'Mustn't bolt the door against him.'

'No, dear. He's on his way to Australia. Do you remember?'

Charles shook his head.

It seemed incredible that he didn't remember, didn't remember Rupert's obsession with aviation, his admiration for the Anzacs. Especially as he'd shared it, which she never did. It had started when one of those daredevil pilots had crashed his plane into the fruit cage in the kitchen garden. He hadn't been hurt but the plane was damaged beyond repair. As was the fruit cage. But Charles and Rupert had entertained the pilot afterwards, invited his colleagues round to the hall, got involved with them all, helped in those fund-raising efforts when the planes had performed such terrifying feats with names like 'loop the loop' and 'falling leaf' and – what was it Rupert used to rave about? – 'Immerman's turn'. And the two of them had insisted on opening the hall grounds for all sorts of public shows so the place had been full of gawping peasantry who'd rarely seen a motor car let alone an aeroplane.

She'd thought that all this flying business would stop once the war was over and there was no more need to send planes to fight the Germans. But these young men who had captured her son's heart and imagination talked of using planes in

230

peacetime, even of people being transported in them. As if anyone in their right mind would risk such a thing.

So many of those young men had been killed. The daredevil who'd broken up the fruit cage had died a month later. Quite matter-of-factly Rupert had explained that his Sopwith Camel had got into a diving spin and that was usually fatal. He himself, he assured her, was in no danger because he didn't fly a plane with a rotary engine. He was fearless, went off to France, survived the war and then last month told them he had this chance of going to train in Australia. How could he do this, she'd asked, when he was the only one now to run the estate. Rupert only said he knew he'd be no good at estate management, but he did know he had a gift for flying. The young just did what they wanted nowadays, all sense of duty gone, it seemed to her.

'And Diana's coming home soon. That's good,' Charles said.

He had spoken in his normal voice. She looked up and smiled. She smiled because he had spoken so, not because the thought of what Diana was doing made her in the least happy. Her daughter's decision to marry an unknown doctor shocked her profoundly. That boys should ignore their parents' wishes was bad enough, but for a girl to rebel in this way, to engage herself without even consulting her mother, was unthinkable, or would have been in normal times. He was twenty years older than Diana, apparently; just the sort of man who would manage to seduce an inexperienced girl who was far away from home.

There was no comfort in thinking of her other daughter either. Little Laura, who as the younger daughter might have been expected to spend the rest of her days at home, was talking about going in for nursing, for which there could be no possible excuse now that the war was over. She said it would be her *career*. Whoever heard of a lady having a career?

She blamed herself for ever agreeing that Laura should go with Lady Hinchley's daughters to the academy in Shappenham, for that was when the trouble started. It had seemed a good idea at the time, when all the governesses had used the war as an excuse to abandon their duties in the schoolroom, leaving their

231

charges untaught. How was she to know that the respectable widow who had run the academy for many years would be replaced by one of those dreadful modern women who believed women should be educated just as if they were men?

Of course Laura was still only a child, but she was a determined child and the way she talked now boded ill for the future. She must have been influenced too by Diana, not that Diana would have done so consciously, but the very fact that she had broken the rules, in a way that would have been impossible before the war, must have put it into Laura's head that she could do the same. If it hadn't been for this dreadful war none of these things would have happened.

And now the war was over and they were talking of celebration. Rejoice, they cruelly said, rejoice. Oh yes, she had once been among them, the shallow ones who talked of the glory of war. She knew better now; she who had been so exultant when it started, what was she left with now? The war had ruined the estate, destroyed its master, killed its heir. It had taken her younger son to the other side of the world and prevented her two daughters from growing up into ladies. It had killed her husband's brother and his brave wife, who had stayed at her post until the end, and taken the life of their son. And it had turned her into an old woman before her time, a sad-eyed lady, grey of cheek and of hair.

'Where's Teddy?' Charles asked suddenly.

She couldn't reply, only shake her head.

After a little while she heard him weeping.

'Oh, Elspeth,' he said. 'How could I have forgotten, how could I?'

It was the lucid moments, when he knew what was happening to him, which were the hardest to bear. Sometimes she hoped, for his sake, that there would soon be no more of them and that he could be left to dwell in peace in his own twilight world, unaware and unremembering. She got up and crossed over to him, nursing his head against her breast.

'It's all right,' she said quietly. 'I'm here.'

Twenty-Eight

'I think you would be well advised,' the lawyer said, 'to sell the farms to those tenants who have offered to buy them. You see, the receipts from rents are simply not adequate for the upkeep of the estate. And . . .' he hesitated, knowing that what he had to say would not be well received '. . . I also think you should consider selling the hall.'

Once upon a time she would have said, 'Never,' and been outraged at the man's impertinence. Now she only said wistfully, 'Mr Sedgewick, it has been my home and my husband's home and my children's home for a very long time.'

They were sitting in Charles' study, surrounded by his books and leather-bound volumes of accounts. Once the solicitor would have felt much in awe of her and of his surroundings, now he felt only compassion for the prematurely aged woman sitting opposite to him who had lost one of her sons to the war and the other to the Antipodes.

'I do understand that, believe me, Mrs Arndale,' he said. 'I know how deeply attached you must be to Northrop Hall but the upkeep is very great and the kind of staff you need here is simply no longer available. Everybody is agreed about that. If you sold the farms and the hall, you could of course live very comfortably.'

'I have two daughters to provide for,' she pointed out.

'I should be more concerned for yourself and Mr Arndale,' he said. 'Young women nowadays are much more inclined to provide for themselves. I believe that Miss Arndale is engaged to be married?'

'She wrote from France to tell me so. She and Dr Bramley, the gentleman she has agreed to marry, will be arriving tomorrow.'

'And I believe that Miss Laura is considering training as a nurse?'

'Some such thing. But she would need a settlement if she married, as of course her sister must also have.'

He shook his head and explained that the days of dowries and settlements were over; Dr Bramley would certainly expect nothing to come with his bride.

She listened, bemused. You live for all your life with certain assumptions and then in so few years they are all overthrown.

'I must warn you that the hall may not be easy to sell,' the solicitor was saying.

That was something she could not accept.

'But it is a gem of an estate,' she told him indignantly. 'It is the kind of estate people long for. I have frequently been told that.'

'No longer, I'm afraid. The price of houses such as this is falling steadily. You would be wise not to wait too long if you decide to sell.'

'And you have told me that I must,' she said miserably.

Sometimes she wished she could join Charles in his dream world, except that his imaginary anxieties seemed to bring him as much wretchedness as her real ones did to her.

No dowry might be involved but Elspeth Arndale was determined to show her future son-in-law the kind of life to which her daughter was accustomed. Silver was brought out of the safe and polished as brightly as poor old Witchart's frail hands could manage. Cook and she discussed the menu at length and Mary-Ann went out on a frosty morning to pick Brussels sprouts, January King cabbages and dig parsnips out of the frozen soil.

They arrived by car which, to her mother's astonishment, Diana was driving.

'She needs the practice,' Dr Bramley explained after they had been introduced and she had remarked upon it. 'It's a necessary skill nowadays which everybody should have. We should teach Laura next,' and then diplomatically added, 'with your permission, of course.'

It was a long time since any of the family had deferred to her; she was immediately won over. She sensed that she might have an ally in her future son-in-law.

'Where is Papa?' Laura asked.

'He is up in the nursery with Nanny,' her mother explained. 'I think it would be better for you not all to go up at once. Perhaps if you go first, Laura, then that will give me a little time to talk to Diana and Dr Bramley.'

'James, please, do call me James, Mrs Arndale.'

So they sat for a while and talked and Diana noticed how gently he spoke to her mother and was grateful for it; she could hardly recognize the woman she had become. And when Laura came down she saw that she had been crying.

'I think we should go and dress for dinner now,' her mother said, but Diana managed to dress quickly and slip along to the nursery before dinner.

Her father seemed pleased to see her but was unsure who she was. 'Is it Louise?' he asked, naming his little sister who had died over forty years ago.

Nanny was quite unperturbed.

'We're having dinner up here, your father and I,' she said. 'Your mother thought it best.'

And her father nodded, for all the world as if he was still the little boy who was happy to have his meals upstairs.

Elspeth had not intended that anything concerning the estate should be discussed, particularly not in the presence of a man who was not yet one of the family. But Laura, who had always been inclined to jump in when a more discreet person would have hesitated, said, 'What are you going to do about the hall, Mamma? I don't expect you'll want to stay on here now, will you?'

'I hardly think this is the time to discuss it,' her mother rebuked.

'But it's the ideal time, Mamma. Now, when we're all together. And Rupert won't mind anyway.'

'Then I must tell you that Mr Sedgewick thinks it should be sold.'

'And what do *you* think?' James asked gently.

'Well, James, I hate the very idea of leaving here, seeing the estate go into other hands, but I fear it must happen.'

Diana and James looked at each other.

'You tell her, James,' Diana said.

'Well, the situation is this, Mrs Arndale,' he began. 'I and some of my colleagues have been trying to find suitable places for homes for men returning from the war. There will be a need for convalescent homes, rehabilitation centres, nursing homes. All should be in quiet places, not too remote or staffing will be difficult, but certainly in the country where the men can be helped to heal. If you think you might favour the idea, I could suggest that Northrop Hall would be ideally placed for such an institution.'

Institution! She did not like the word. Northrop Hall an institution!

'The grounds, from what little I have seen, would be wonderful for the men and the house too, of course.'

'Grandmama used to travel all over the place in her wheel-chair,' Laura put in.

Considering that their grandmama's travels had ended up in the lake, Diana considered her younger sister's remark somewhat tactless and tried to divert attention from it by saying, 'And the kitchens would be big enough for communal cooking, wouldn't they?'

Their mother, who did not take kindly to having younger members of the family disposing of her property, frowned as she asked, 'What sort of men would come, James?'

'Probably amputees and people with other physical injuries. We haven't yet decided if the blind should be in with the others or separate. Maybe they should have some initial training on their own. We wouldn't take psychological cases. They need quite different specialist treatment.'

She nodded, though actually that hadn't been what she meant.

'You have to understand that we are in the very early stages of planning. Nothing like this has been envisaged before.'

'There hasn't been the need before,' she pointed out.

'That is true. And of course it's entirely for you to decide.

236

But if you do decide to sell your lovely home, please do consider this idea.'

It seemed to Elspeth that the doctor was talking more decorously about the house than her own daughters, so she looked kindly upon him as she said, 'Yes, I shall certainly do so,' and, after they had had coffee, suggested that he might like to go up with her to visit Charles.

'You two do that,' Laura said. 'Di and I will wash up.'

'Mary-Ann is here to see to it,' her mother told her sharply. 'Nanny and she are staying here tonight to give extra help.'

'Oh, I expect she could do with a hand all the same.'

Laura spoke casually, then she added, 'I wouldn't mind working here myself if the doctor in charge would have me.'

Charles and Nanny had finished their dinner in the school-room and were sitting by the fire in the nursery when Elspeth took James up to meet him. Nanny had the usual pile of darning and mending by her side, Charles was looking at a picture book.

Elspeth explained to him that this was the man that their eldest daughter was going to marry and he seemed pleased and shook hands with all his old courtesy. With great dignity he said he hoped they would be very happy and perhaps he would one day meet the bride. He himself was very happy, he said.

They talked for a while and she noticed how carefully James observed him, how gentle he was with him and she thought what a reassuring person he would be to have nearby if it did work out that he took over the hall for his hospital, and that maybe there might be a pleasant house somewhere on the estate where she and Charles could live. And both girls nearby too. By the time she and James went downstairs, it had begun to seem as if selling Northrop Hall might be a very good idea indeed.

Twenty-Nine

'What exactly is a dower house, Nanny?' Laura asked one day as she was having tea with her in the cottage.

'It's the house set aside for a gentleman's widow to live in when her son inherits the estate, Miss Laura.'

'So why didn't Grandmama go and live in it when Grandpapa died?'

'Lady Arndale was not the sort of lady to go into a dower house,' Nanny told her.

'I see.'

She didn't see really, but there was no point in arguing with Nanny.

'It's a nice house,' she said instead. 'I think Mamma will be very comfortable in it.'

'And you'll stay with her, Miss Laura? No more talk of running off to Bristol or Cheltenham?'

'I'll have to go away for my training, Nanny,' Laura explained, as she had tried to do many times before. 'But I could always come back and work here for a while. I'd be much more use if I was a properly trained nurse and,' she went on warming to her theme, 'I could become a qualified member of the Society of Massage and Medical Gymnastics. I could even train in electrotherapy.'

Long words had never impressed Nanny.

'Fine words butter no parsnips,' she declared, wiping her mouth firmly to show she had no truck with expressions like Medical Gymnastics and electrotherapy. 'There was nothing wrong with good old-fashioned nursing.'

Laura didn't reply; it had just occurred to her that she might be a doctor, like James. There was a proper sixth form at the academy now; two girls had gone to the university last year. Why shouldn't she?

238

'Just don't do anything to worry your mother,' Nanny warned. 'Mrs Arndale's had a lot to attend to these past two years, peace or no peace.'

Once she had accepted that the house should be sold, Elspeth had wanted to get it all settled as soon as possible. Even so it had taken six months for the lawyers to negotiate the transfer – she didn't like the word sale – and another year before the basic alterations were sufficiently completed for the first patients to be allowed to arrive.

They couldn't decide what it was to be called.

'It's not a hospital,' her son-in-law explained to her over coffee after dinner. 'I think we should avoid calling it anything like a nursing home.'

'Can't we just call it a rehabilitation centre?' Laura asked.

'Shouldn't the word soldier come into it somewhere?'

'But, Diana, there might one day be aviators and sailors as well,' Laura pointed out.

'Then we could call it the Ex-servicemen's Rehabilitation Centre.'

'It's rather clumsy.'

'We've really got to settle it now. Apart from anything else we should have a board put up so that people know where to find us.'

'I don't understand,' Elspeth cut in, 'why it can't just be called Northrop Hall as it always has been. People will soon realize what it is for.'

She waited for objections, but her son-in-law turned to her and said, 'Brilliant. And simple. And it leaves it open for us to use it as the need arises without being limited by any labels.'

The more she saw of her son-in-law the more she liked him, had even forgiven him for that dreadful little wedding ceremony in the registry office. She smiled at him now as she said goodnight and they parted, she and Laura to the dower house, he and Diana to their flat upstairs.

'You're so good with her, darling,' she told him. 'Much more patient than I am.'

'We have to involve her, Diana, as much as possible.'

239

'You have. She's making preparations for her fund-raising fête already.'

'And she's an asset too. She knows so many people and everybody knows her. We don't want the place to be some kind of institution the locals vaguely mistrust. We want it to be something they support and are proud of. That's why I like the idea of keeping the familiar name.'

She looked up at him.

'And also because it pleased Mamma,' she told him.

He was such a mixture, could be such a softie and yet could be harsh and impatient. His anger was spectacular too. He had been enraged at the treatment of soldiers returning from the war.

'To see them begging in the streets, Di, it's intolerable. I saw a man today with no legs, propped up in a shop doorway on a piece of sacking and a board saying, "War wounded. Please help".'

'What did you do?'

'I got his name and I'll get him down here somehow or other. And those awful slums some of them are living in. Do you remember how they promised they'd build them houses fit for heroes to live in? Well, I can tell you, you'd have to be a hero to live in some of those places.'

He'd corresponded endlessly with the War Office, spent days in London, bullying ministers and civil servants, refusing ever to take no for an answer, demanding support from businesses which had thrived on making munitions, chivvying the complacent into taking action, fighting officialdom, alarming everyone with his indignation, persuading them with his charm, putting to shame those who had profited from the war and all those who had gloried in it.

'It infuriates me to remember,' he raged to Diana now, 'how they exulted in every victory, glossed over defeat, boosted their miserable little egos with their flag-flapping patriotism while men died in agony. And the number of suicides among soldiers since the war ended is dreadful. The Germans didn't kill them, but their own countrymen did. My God it makes me mad with rage.'

But she knew it wasn't so; his indignation was not mad but

240

always productive. Creative indignation, that's what he's got, Diana thought. She'd observed it at work as he saved men's lives in the war and now she saw it at work doing the same thing in peacetime. He got things done. He'd got this scheme going and roused others to act likewise. Without him there would have been more men, maimed and helpless, begging in doorways.

'There's a Peter Dawson to be met,' James told Diana one morning the following spring. 'Usual arrangements.'

He didn't meet the new patients himself when they arrived. He said it was better for their morale to be met by a pretty young woman than by a grey-haired old doctor. They didn't have to face him until the next morning when they'd got their strength up.

It was the orderly who talked about the man, as he lowered the wheelchair from the ambulance and pushed it towards the main entrance door, Diana walking alongside.

'We called 'im Persistent Peter back there at the 'ospital. Should of bin dead by rights, didn't you, mate? No right to be alive, 'e 'asn't. Taken in for dead in 1916, put in a tent ready for burying, wasn't you, mate? But some bright young spark of a nurse like yerself saw 'e was breavin' and 'ad a bit of life in 'im, not much mind, but enough, weren't it, mate? Got 'im into a train to Etaples, patched 'im up a bit and shipped 'im back to Blighty. A matter of a couple of broken legs, ditto arms and God knows what all in 'is inside and 'ere 'e is ready ter be re'abituated. Ain't that right, mate?'

The man in the wheelchair said nothing while all this was going on, clearly accustomed to being the orderly's conversation piece. He had the most patient smile, not just resigned but somehow loving and very gentle.

She accompanied him to see James the next day.

After examining and assessing him, James asked, 'What were you planning to do before the war?'

'I was going to teach,' he said. 'I'd just finished my three years' training.'

'And what were you going to teach?'

The man in the wheelchair looked up at him and smiled.

241

'Gymnastics,' he said. 'It was a physical training college.'

Diana felt that awful stab of misery that she always felt at the poignancy of these cases of wrecked lives. But James immediately replied cheerfully, 'That's excellent. You're just the man we need. We're in the throes of planning a gymnasium. With you here we shan't have to buy a lot of expensive advice from people who'd probably get it all wrong anyway.'

She left them discussing the possibility of getting patients to row on the lake.

'What's going to happen to the old school?' Laura asked her mother that evening as they sat by the fire in the dower house. Charles had gone on his nightly round of the doors, checking that everything was safe in this strange little house which only had five bedrooms and three reception rooms and a tiny patch of garden of no more than an acre.

'I don't know, Laura. Your grandmother would have liked it to be opened again after the war.'

'There's no chance of that now. Didn't you say that another school is being built in Littleton?'

'Yes, the Paste girl is going to be in charge.'

'Edith? Oh, I'm so pleased. I always liked the Pastes. But isn't she rather young for the job?'

'Miss Poole was fifteen when she took over.'

'But this will be much bigger than our little school. She'll have staff under her. Of course she always seemed very grown up, looking after all her brothers and sisters.'

She gazed into the fire, remembering.

'Once I went with Rupert to see their new baby and Edith picked it up just as if she was its mother. We were too scared to touch it in case it broke. I might push Peter over to Littleton tomorrow and find out about the school.'

'It's four miles. Really Laura, eight miles of pushing a wheelchair, it's too much for any lady.'

'Oh, it's nothing. I love helping and James says I'm quite strong and useful. And I'm always trying to find new places to take the men. I think this one might be interested in the school. He was going to teach before the war.'

*   *   *

242

Many of the roads round about were being macadamized to take the cars, but the way to Littleton was still the old dusty lane, rutted and stony. But it was a lovely day of bright sunshine and light breeze so they made their way cheerfully, chatting all the time. Peter seemed to have taken a new lease of life now that he was busy with plans for the new gymnasium.

He was interested in the Littleton school too. The foundations were finished, the outside walls going up.

'Let's be nosy,' she said, pushing the chair on to what was still a building site.

Someone else was looking around too.

'Edith!' Laura called out. 'It's Edith Paste, isn't it?'

The girl turned and saw them.

'I hope to God she doesn't call me Miss Laura,' Laura thought.

She didn't. She didn't call her anything. In fact for a moment Laura thought she was going to walk away, but she only hesitated for a second, then came across and was introduced to the man in the wheelchair.

'And will you have a gymnasium?' he asked.

'Yes, only a small one and it will have to be used for other things like assembly, but it will have wall bars and vaulting equipment. If you like I can show you the plans. I live nearby.'

They went together to the cottage and she spread the plans on the table for Peter to look at.

'I'll make a cup of tea,' she said. 'You must be thirsty after the walk.'

Laura followed her into the kitchen, offering to help.

'And how's Dicky?' she asked.'

'Killed in action in 1916.'

'Oh, I'm so sorry.'

'I heard your brother was killed too.'

She nodded and they looked at each other, silent because there were no suitable words.

'I always remember how Dicky freed that poor rabbit,' Laura said at last. 'Rupert and he took the snare off its leg.'

'With your hairslide,' Edith said and smiled.

243

More relaxed now, they gathered together cups and saucers and went back into the parlour where Peter was poring over the plans.

'So you'll be able to live here when you start work at the school?' Laura asked.

'Yes, I'll keep house for my father.'

'Your mother?'

'Dead,' Edith said briefly. Then she went on: 'They'd just moved here out of the last place we had. It's much bigger.'

'It's a lovely cottage. And the garden's beautiful,' Laura said, glancing out of the window which overlooked the ground at the back of the cottage.

'So it should be, my father being the good gardener that he is and always was,' Edith said with what seemed to Laura uncalled for sharpness.

'Perhaps we can look round it afterwards?' Peter suggested.

So after tea, she pushed him round the neat rows of vegetables and immaculate flower beds before beginning the journey back. Partly because they were tired, partly because there always seemed less to say on return journeys, they didn't talk much.

They were almost back at the hall, when Peter said, 'I love the soft local accent, don't you?'

'Yes, the Gloucestershire accent is very gentle on the ear.'

'I think I partly like it so much because it's so like the voice of the man who rescued me. I suppose he may have come from this area.'

'It's possible. So you weren't unconscious?'

'Off and on. But I remember him holding me and talking as if to a child. It was strange to hear it on the battlefield coming from a man, it sounded more like a mother talking to her little one, or to an animal. As if there was just the two of us alone.'

He was quiet for a while, then he went on: 'He must have been a really strong man, all the same. You see there was this fearful weight on my legs and I heard this voice saying, very soothingly, "There now, don't you be a-worrying, we'll soon have this nasty old thing a-lifted off".'

244

He made a not very successful attempt to imitate the accent, but it was recognizably local.

'And then he flung it away as if it was made of cardboard. Or so it seemed to me. And then he managed to get me up on his back and I can hear him now saying, "Now then, up you come. Dicky'll carry you like a sack of taties."'

'Dicky? He said his name was Dicky?'

'Yes, it's all so clear, that part of it.'

'I wonder,' she began and then decided to say no more until she'd had time to think about it and consult Diana.

'I could hardly bring myself to be civil to her at first,' Edith told her father when he came in from work that evening. 'When I thought what that family did to you.'

'Nay, it wasn't the lass, nor even her mother. It was the old lady,' though in his heart he knew there was one who was more culpable even than she was, but he'd been silent all these years so why break silence now?

Thirty

'Well, I think we should use some of this money to try to restore the grounds,' Diana said. 'We've already got enough put aside to convert the stables, so we don't have to finance any more building work.'

They were sitting round the table in what had formerly been the breakfast room and which they now used as a study. The father of one of the men, Captain Dowling, had died leaving a substantial bequest in memory of his son who had lived here for six months, seemed to make good progress but had suddenly succumbed to pneumonia.

'It's a very generous amount of money he's given you,' Elspeth said.

'I'd rather he'd visited his son more often during his lifetime,' Laura told her.

'Conscience money or not, we'll make good use of it,' James said. 'If we're allowed to.'

Now that the scheme had grown and developed, he got impatient with the number of people who had to be consulted: the government committees, the health specialists, the military gentlemen.

'They showed no enthusiasm at all at first when we could have done with support and now it's got off the ground they all want to be consulted about everything,' he grumbled.

'But, darling, since they're providing most of the money, it's only to be expected.'

She couldn't see that it mattered really, since James had devised this perfectly sensible way of consulting those most involved, like herself, for example, and Matron and staff, and the men themselves and then, with his mind made up, he'd go and tell the committees in London what needed to be done and invariably got his own way.

He was away so much now that she sometimes thought that these committee men saw more of him than she did.

'They made enough fuss about the stables project,' he reminded her. 'As if I was trying to hang on to men who were fit to go out into the world.'

His aim had always been to enable men to return to their own community; some had families to look after them, some had wives or had found them since the end of the war. But there were some who had nobody and weren't able to fend for themselves. He was adamant that they should not be destitute of care, left to sink down in some slum. If they needed a home they must be allowed to stay on here. And so it followed that outbuildings must be converted into places to live in, homes adapted for the disabled.

'You got your own way in the end,' Diana pointed out.

'After a fight.'

'You enjoy fighting bureaucracy,' she told him.

'So what about the gardens?' Laura put in impatiently.

'Right, what's your view, Laura?'

'I think that we should start with the conservatories and greenhouses.'

'I agree,' her sister said. 'We could grow plants to put in the rooms, much better than the ones we buy now. And it would be a wonderful place for the men to relax as well as work.'

'And of course with the plants being high up on the shelving it would be ideal for them to do the potting up and so on from wheelchairs.'

'Couldn't we have some raised beds outside as well?' Elspeth suggested.

'Wonderful idea,' James told her. 'Perhaps we could walk around afterwards and consider where we should site them? So many of the men are keen on gardening, I'm sure they could do a lot of the work themselves so long as we adapt things a bit for them, don't you think, Diana?'

'Oh, absolutely, it's wonderful for them. Do you remember how George Watson had such difficulty after he'd lost his right arm? He used to get so discouraged and give up until

I happened to ask if he knew how to prune roses and then there was no stopping him and he was wielding the secateurs with his left hand. It's all very well doing exercises but there's much more motive if you're doing something useful.'

'You would need someone in charge, a real gardener,' Elspeth pointed out. She sighed and added, 'Jimson would have been ideal. He was our head gardener, who died on Armistice Day,' she explained to James.

'And how many gardeners did he have under him before the war?' he asked Elspeth.

She shook her head.

'I don't think I ever counted,' she admitted.

'The only one I really remember is Adam Paste who used to do the conservatory. Edith and Dicky's father,' Diana told her husband. 'I wonder what he's doing now. Did Edith say, Laura?'

'Yes, she said he was working on a farm, but she didn't say much, we were just alone a few minutes getting the tea. It was when she told me about poor Dicky.'

She had told Diana how Dicky might have been the one who rescued Peter. In fact she had rushed to tell her immediately she was free but her sister's reaction had surprised her. She was pleased, of course, said she thought it must have been Dicky, but had seemed to have some reservation, had asked that nothing should be said about it until she'd had time to think it over.

'Mr Paste would be ideal,' she was saying now. 'He knows the place and he'd know what grew well in the soil and so on. Why did he leave, Mamma?'

'Your grandmother felt he had neglected her very special plants. I know your father wasn't happy about his being dismissed, but with his mother insisting what else could he do?'

'Do you think he'd come back? Or would he be too old?'

'Oh, he wouldn't be too old, Laura. He was quite a young man then and it's only seven or eight years since he left.'

Because the war has aged everybody, destroying youth, making those in the prime of life prematurely elderly, Diana

248

thought, it is easy to exaggerate the actual number of years that have passed, as Laura has just done.

'Well, I propose Laura goes and asks him, since she's the one who's made contact again with the family,' James suggested.

'I'll cycle over to Littleton tomorrow,' Laura promised.

'And I'll put all this to the men tomorrow at their meeting and see how many potential undergardeners we've got among them,' James said.

And so the meeting closed.

'Can we talk about what I told you Peter said, about Dicky?' Laura asked immediately she was alone with her sister.

She was much shorter than Diana, so her eager little face was upturned as she asked, her brown eyes bright with expectation. Everything about her showed impatience with her sister. Here was Dicky Paste, her childhood friend, lover of all country things, saviour of trapped animals and he'd done this heroic deed – well, *might* have done it – and they should be finding out, digging out the truth, telling the world. And yet Diana actually hesitated.

'You don't think it's true, do you?' she asked, suddenly miserable.

'Yes, I think it's true.'

Everything that Peter had said tallied with what Dicky had said at his trial.

'Well, then? Have you thought about it?'

'Yes, of course I've thought about it,' Diana told her.

She'd thought about it half the night, trying to think of a way of telling everyone she knew it was true, without saying how she knew it was true. She owed it to Teddy and Dicky to keep that shameful event secret for ever. The Pastes must never know how their son had died. But she owed it to them to tell of his bravery. She owed it to Peter too.

'How do you know it's true?' her sister asked suddenly.

'Teddy wrote to me something about it,' she replied slowly, choosing her words with care.

'You mean he'd seen it? Why didn't you say anything before?'

'No, he hadn't seen it, but he'd heard about it. You know how these stories get about at the front?'

'And you've got his letter still?' Laura was almost jumping with excitement.

'No, I didn't keep that one. It got lost, I think, when we were preparing to evacuate,' Diana lied, for she had all his letters still.

'Oh, Di, what a *shame*. If only the Pastes could have seen that letter!'

Thank God they never will, Diana thought.

But aloud she just said, 'Don't say anything to the Pastes, Laura. When the time comes that should be Peter's privilege. Promise?'

'I promise.'

Laura was silent for a moment and then burst out with, 'Look, there *must* be someone official who'd know. Teddy couldn't be the only one, could he? I mean it would be so wonderful for his family to hear of it officially, with more details, which Peter can't remember. I could go to London and ask to look at records, James would know how to set about it.'

'Oh, please, Laura, don't. Just leave it as it is.'

She ached for her sister, loved her for her loyalty, for her enthusiasm to find out all the facts to comfort her friend's family, but oh what awful destruction she could bring about with her well-intentioned zeal. For a moment she thought of telling her the truth, but she was protective of her younger sister, as well as often exasperated by her, and knew she must never let her know how Dicky had died or who had fired the last fatal shot.

Adam Paste was hoeing between rows of early potatoes when he saw Laura getting off her bicycle. She had timed her arrival for early evening, judging correctly that he'd have had time to come home, have tea and probably be out in the garden.

He stopped his hoeing and stood waiting, not recognizing who it was, but guessing it might be the girl Edith had told him about, who had come with the soldier in the wheelchair.

He listened in silence to what she had to say.

250

'It's a long time since I did what you might call proper gardening,' he said.

'Oh, but look at your own garden!' she exclaimed, astonished that he could say such a thing with so much evidence of his skill all around them.

'This is plain gardening. Not the fancy sort we did up at the hall,' he explained.

'But, Mr Paste, it wouldn't be anything fancy. We want to grow things like this, flowers and vegetables with the men doing as much work as possible but under your guidance. And use the conservatory and greenhouses for plants again.'

'I'd need to think on it,' he said, warily.

'Oh, would you? And then would you come and talk to Dr Bramley about it? He's in charge up there now. I expect evening would suit you best, after work.'

'There'd be a condition,' he said.

'Yes?'

'Is Mr Witchart still there?'

'Yes, but he doesn't work any more. He had a stroke and is very frail. He can get about but very slowly on two sticks. He lives in one of the cottages.'

'I'd need to see him before I agreed to come.'

'See Witchart?'

'He'll know why.'

Puzzled, she left him to cycle back to Northrop Hall.

Adam Paste turned back to his hoeing and kept steadily at it, hoeing first the potatoes and then between the feathery row of carrots, the lettuces that were just beginning to heart up, the peas beginning to twist their way up the twiggy peasticks, changing to a smaller hoe to get between the onions which were plumping up nicely.

It was almost too dark to see by the time he put away his tools and went indoors. The children were already in bed.

'Well, I think you should take it, Father,' Edith told him decisively. 'You're too good for the labouring you do now. And you've often said our Jack has a way with plants so there might be a beginning for him there too, so you could train him up.'

'Ay, I've thought of that,' he told her.

251

He'd thought too, as he'd done his hoeing, of the glasshouses he'd be in charge of and of all the plants he had thought he'd never be able to grow again.

The next day Edith went to the library and by the time he came home there was a pile of gardening books, like the ones they used to have in the gardener's office up at the hall in the old days, all waiting for him on the kitchen table.

'You've grown into a right little school marm, you have,' he told her, but he read the books well into the night and the next day he went up to the hall.

It seemed strange to him at first; even as he cycled up the long drive he saw how overgrown it all was, the shrubberies all straggly, hedges uncut, lawns mown but edges untrimmed. And then he came nearer and saw all these disabled men, bandaged, in wheelchairs, on crutches, all busying themselves as best they could trying to put the garden to rights. He stood and looked at them and he knew he would take this job.

'I have a condition, though,' he told Dr Bramley as he had told Laura.

'Yes, she told me. You want to see Mr Witchart before you give your answer.'

'That's right.'

'He lives in the cottage down there by the little bridge. There's a pair of them. His is the one on the right.'

'Thank you.'

It was his own cottage, the one he had lived in with his wife after they'd married and he'd left the bothy. The one from which they'd evicted him and his young family at a week's notice. The pain and humiliation of it came back to him as sharply as if it was yesterday, as he knocked at the door of what was now Mr Witchart's cottage.

Edith gave him his tea before she asked, 'Well, so what did you say to them?'

'I said yes.'

'Oh, I'm so glad. I saw Laura Arndale this evening on my way home and she said you were up there and had gone to see Mr Witchart.'

'There was no call for her to say that.'

252

'Well, I was wondering when you'd be back and she just mentioned she'd seen you going to his house.'

'Our old house.'

'What?'

She put down the tea she'd been drinking.

'Father,' she said. 'What's all this about? Why did you want to see our old house?'

'I didn't.'

Again he hesitated.

'I went to see him and he happened to be in our house,' he said at last.

'But why did you want to see him?'

He shook his head.

'It's all in the past, Edith. Put it out of our minds.'

'I can't, since I don't know what I'd be putting,' she told him, sounding just like her mother. 'Come on and tell me. Has it to do with when they put us out of the house?'

'Well, if you want to know, I'd best tell you,' he said. Even so he hesitated before he went on.

'I wanted an apology from him, that was all. I wanted him to own up to what he'd done.'

'And what had he done?'

He stretched his legs out in front of him, looking into the fire, remembering.

'I left the conservatory in perfect shape that night. Not a thing wrong with so much as a leaf or a stem. And by morning many was ruined. I made him tell me, word for word. And he did, I'll say that for him. Oh, he knew why I wanted to see him.'

'Go on, what did he say?'

'He told me how he'd gone down that evening and the place felt a bit cold and he took it into his head to warm the place up a bit. So he got a footman to carry in a paraffin heater, one of the sort you might use in an outhouse in very cold weather, but you'd never put near a plant because the fumes are so deadly. He'd meant to take it out after a couple of hours but forgot all about it, left it burning all night. Just forgot, he said.'

He paused, remembering the look of the plants in the

conservatory, a picture so engraved on his mind that he'd not forgotten it even after all these years.

'He came down early the next morning,' he went on, 'and saw what had happened to the plants so he just carted the heater off when there was nobody about to see and opened up the conservatory doors and windows to let a draught blow in and clear the fumes. It was still a bit frosty the way it often is before a hot spring day. So what damage wasn't done by the fumes was done by the cold air.'

'And he didn't admit it, even when he knew you were going to be dismissed and us all put out in the road?'

Her father shook his head.

'No, he said nothing.'

'And all these years you've not known the cause of what happened to the plants?'

'Oh, I've known all these years. Our neighbour told me that night when he helped me move our sticks to Littleton. He said a young footman had seen Mr Witchart carrying the heater out and hiding it away in one of his big store cupboards nobody else had the key of.'

'And you never told us, not even mother?'

'What was the point? It would only have made her angry and more upset than she already was.'

'But why didn't you say? Why didn't you tell them, Lady Arndale and the rest of them? Why let them blame you when it wasn't your fault and they were making your family homeless?'

He shook his head at her innocence.

'Edith love, you don't understand what it was like. Mr Witchart was the butler, he was the great man in charge of the whole household, above everybody. You don't think they'd have taken any notice of a mere undergardener who dared speak against him, do you? They'd never have blamed him, never. It would have made too much of an upset. And no footman would have dared denounce him. He was like a god up there.'

She nodded and smiled as she poured out some more tea.

'I remember our Dicky thought that the Lord's prayer went: "Our Father, Witchart in heaven, Harold be thy name". Lots

254

of the estate children did, they really thought God's name was Harold Witchart.'

'Well, he's a frail old pathetic bit of a thing now, walking with two sticks and his hands all twisted, so we must pity and forgive him.'

'And living in our old cottage, too. This house is much better. That old chimney used to smoke whenever the wind was in the east.'

'And the soil's better here.'

So they sat over their second cup of tea, counting their blessings and pitying the mighty fallen.

Thirty-One

D iana laid the table in their little dining room with loving
care. Doing everything with the deliberation of the
undomesticated, she tried to fold the two napkins to look
like the boat depicted in *The Perfect Hostess*, which lay open
on the sideboard. The instructions were hard to follow and in
the end she went for the easier option of water lilies.

Having gently ferried them across to the table, she put in
the centre the candelabra, which had been a wedding present
from her mother, selected from the silver stored away in the
butler's pantry. Alongside it she placed the box of matches,
ready to light the candles at the last minute.

'I don't know why you want candles now there's the
electric,' Nanny had remarked when she had seen her that
morning polishing the candelabra.

'But candlelight is so much prettier, Nanny.'

'That's as maybe but candles were always for poor people.
All the cottages had them, candles and oil lamps. A sign of
poverty, candles were, after gaslights came in.'

Knowing her own culinary limitations, Diana had sought
Nanny's advice about what to cook. Usually she and James
had whatever the kitchen had provided for the men, but for this
anniversary dinner she wanted to make something special. She
had pored over some of Cook's more elaborate recipes, all of
which seemed to require ingredients unobtainable in Northrop
or involved cooking procedures of which she was ignorant.

Nanny came down on the side of simplicity. There was
nothing nicer she said than a good stew on a cold evening.
The butcher could bring up some best beef in the morning and
carrots and onions had been stored from the garden. And she
remembered that Cook used to produce something she called

purée de pommes de terre, which was really just mashed potato with butter and cream added. Cabbage was the obvious green vegetable at this time of the year, Nanny said, and needed to be put in plenty of water and boiled for a long time to soften it and get the acid out.

Diana smiled at this, thinking how James would have disagreed. He'd once said that the way cabbage got cooked in England it would be better to drink the water and throw the cabbage away. But she had dutifully resolved to allow a good half hour for it to cook.

'And what about puddings, Nanny? There's a recipe here for syllabub which sounds quite easy.'

Nanny had shaken her head.

'Boys like apple dumpling, spotted dick or jam roly poly,' she said. 'Perhaps apple dumpling would be best because there's plenty of apples still in store, wanting to be used. Apple dumpling and custard, boys can never get enough of it, boys can't.'

As far as Nanny was concerned, James was just a little boy who had happened to grow up into a doctor. There was no reason why his taste in food should have been affected by this transformation.

Diana remembered this conversation now as she went into the kitchen to check that the pudding wasn't boiling dry. Then she came back and looked approvingly around the dining room. Firelight and lamplight softened everything. And when she heard James come in she would turn off the lamp and light the candles and it would look still more romantic.

Romantic. That was what she wanted it to be. How else could she convey to James what she missed in her marriage? Words were so hard. Words can sound critical when you don't mean them to be. He was so good, so altruistic, so hard-working. He was everything that she admired and respected.

And he had suffered so much; he had lost his wife and both his children in the war. For four dreadful years he had had to operate on men in appalling conditions, always racing against time to make way for the next batch of the injured to be summarily dealt with. The experience had marked him, however well he had hidden it at the time, and the horror of it would never leave him. She was sure of that from what had happened on their first wedding anniversary. Her mother had invited them all to the dower house for a meal. Cook had brought in a joint of roast beef. 'Nice and rare, Madam,' she'd said. 'It'll run nicely with the pink when cut into.'

Her mother had thanked her and turned to James, asking him to carve.

It struck her that she had never seen him carve before. As she watched, she saw him pick up the knife, drive it an inch into the flesh, then drop it suddenly and abruptly leave the room.

She went after him. He had gone back into the drawing room, was sitting there, ashen-faced and trembling. He looked up at her. He hid his face in his hands, rocking himself and saying, 'I can't, Diana, I can't. Don't ask me to.'

She put her arms around him. 'I know,' she said, 'I know.' For she saw it with his eyes: the knife, the flesh. Day and night he had carved into the flesh of young men, hacking off limbs. Half a million amputees.

She went back alone into the dining room, told them he had felt a bit dizzy but would be back in a minute and added that he wasn't much good at carving anyway.

Laura said she'd do it. Her mother objected that it was a man's job and perhaps James would feel hurt at its being taken over by a young woman and Laura said she didn't think he'd mind though you'd think that he, being a doctor, would be good at carving, wouldn't you?

She knew it was no good trying to explain. They hadn't been there, hadn't seen the butchery. She had been there; she understood.

It was nine o'clock when the telephone bell sounded. She went out into the hall and cautiously unhooked it from the wall; it was a recent acquisition and she wasn't yet quite at ease with it.

'Hello, is that you, Diana?' James' voice enquired, sounding strangely near, yet distant in an echoing way.

'Yes, where are you?'

'Still in London at the rehab centre, I'm afraid. It'll be after midnight when I'm back, so I just wanted to tell you

258

not to wait up. I'll creep in as quietly as I can and not wake you.'

'What about dinner?' she managed to ask.

'Oh, don't worry about that. They'll find me something up here. Food's the least of my problems just now. But I'll tell you all about it tomorrow. And I think we should have a management committee meeting in the afternoon. Can you arrange it?'

'Yes, I'll tell them.'

'All right, are you, Diana? Not too tired?'

'No, I'm fine, thank you.'

'Then I'd better get along. Goodnight. Sleep well.'

'Goodnight, James.'

She stood in the hall for a few minutes, despondent, not wanting to look at the prettily laid table, at the napkin lilies and the candelabra, not wanting to be reminded of how excited she'd felt such a short time ago at the idea of this anniversary dinner.

So he had forgotten. Completely forgotten. More urgent matters had replaced the memory of it. Pull yourself together, Diana; people do forget things and after all a little dinner for two is a small thing compared with the matters he has been dealing with, matters that will affect men's lives, give hope to the injured, get the lame to walk, save a man's family from starvation.

But, oh, it doesn't feel like that, she thought miserably as she cleared plates away, turned off the oven, put the untouched food into the meatsafe, for she couldn't bear to eat anything now, yet couldn't bring herself to waste good food. It *does* hurt that he has forgotten because he doesn't forget important things, things that really matter to him. This doesn't matter to him, as it does to me. He has done it all before; he has had his youth and his lovely wife, his time of romance as a young man when he must surely have prized and celebrated his wedding anniversaries?

It was different for her. The war had robbed her of her youth. She had moved from virtual schoolgirl to responsible adult. The years between eighteen and twenty-two had been spent in the charnel house of war, the years of her lost youth. The war which had taken so much from so many had taken something precious from her too.

And children, what of those? She had thought that after two years she would have started a baby. It worried her, but he said, never mind, don't fret, it will happen, you are only twenty-five. But he was forty-five and she did worry. Perhaps having had children, he didn't feel the need as she did? Perhaps that explained why he didn't mind these nights away at work, these nights when he crept late and exhausted into bed, trying not to disturb her? She tried to understand, not to be critical. Of course the love of a forty-five-year-old man, whom war has aged beyond his years, cannot be anything like the passionate ardour of a young man in his twenties.

But love it still is and she must not selfishly grieve. It was dreadful of her to complain, even to herself, when so many were dead, so many hideously maimed. She had been spared, she was strong and healthy and had all her limbs. She should be ashamed to feel hard done by, when she had so much, including a wonderful partnership with one of the best people she had ever known. It was a great partnership, everyone said so and it must remain so.

Thus Diana lectured herself, as she prepared for bed, looking determinedly forward to a life which would be full of interest and hard work, shared with a man whom everyone admired and whom she respected beyond all others. Yet, however much she tried to ignore it, she could feel an ache, an emptiness, and all the years to come, those useful and interesting years, seemed to stretch joylessly ahead of her without any appeal, any savour. As if, having lost her youth, all that remained was duty, that dreary word which she had so often heard on her grandmother's lips and on her mother's too. Would she end up being the third generation of Arndale women to live a life of joyless duty?

Thirty-Two

It was a bit late in the year really to be planting up seed boxes, but it seemed to Adam a good way to start the men off. He had several of them in the conservatory now, some sifting soil, the stronger ones using the garden riddles, others the lighter sieves which the nurses had managed to borrow from the kitchen. Later he'd show them how to tamp it down in seed boxes. Then they'd plant the seeds, give them a light scattering of soil to cover, put a piece of glass and brown paper over them, leave them in the warmth and hope for the best.

The old compost heaps round at the back had hardly been touched since the war started so the years had turned them into piles of fine crumbly soil, which he and Jack, who had been brought in when they realized they needed extra muscle power, pushed in barrowloads round to the conservatory.

'Why do you go such a long way round, Father?' Jack had asked him on their first journey.

'Habit,' he told his son, shaking his head at his own stupidity. Of course they could push their barrows in front of windows now. And get a wave from people indoors.

It took a bit of getting used to, he had to admit to himself. He'd been told to set himself up in Mr Jimson's big wooden shed, always known as his office, with its desk and high stool, its collection of *Gardener's Chronicles*, its copy of the *Index Kewensis* and other learned books like the Royal Horticultural Society's *The Garden*, to say nothing of Mr Jimson's old seed catalogues, spraying schedules and lists of plants, all ranged neatly on shelves.

At first he'd felt he shouldn't be sitting here in Mr Jimson's office, on Mr Jimson's stool, writing out orders for seeds or loads of sand on Mr Jimson's desk with all its compartments and little drawers, just as he shouldn't have pushed wheel-barrows in front of the hall's windows. But he'd been here a fortnight now and was beginning to get used to it. Besides, hadn't Mr Jimson always said he'd make a head gardener one day? And so he had, though not in quite the way Mr Jimson had imagined.

There wouldn't be much to show for all their work in the conservatory and greenhouses this year, that was not to be expected as he'd explained to the doctor, but once these little seedlings came up they'd plant potfuls of gloxinias, calceolarias, godetias and cinerarias and all the other colourful plants that Lady Arndale had so despised and which would brighten up the hall no end. He'd bring some cuttings of pelargoniums up from home too, brilliant red they were. Very vulgar she'd have said, but then they were cheerful with it and the men needed cheering.

He left Jack pushing the loads of soil and sand for the men to mix and went to see how the others were doing in the vegetable garden. They'd had to get outside help to dig it over, ready for levelling and planting. It should have been done in the autumn of course so that the weather could have got at it and broken it up in the winter. He'd see that it was done properly ready for next year, but for now they must make do.

There were six of them working on it, with two male nurses helping them. That young chap who was waiting to get his new arms was doing amazingly well, treading the soil down with what they used to call the gardener's dance, while his mate managed to work the hoe from his wheelchair. Not a perfect tilth, how could it be, but good enough for all that.

He went and told them so. They asked him about what would be planted and he had to tell them that it was too late to raise all their own vegetables from seed this year; they'd have to buy in plants for cabbages and suchlike. It was too late for potatoes too but next year they'd have earlies and main crop and they could all help plant them in the raised beds which the doctor promised to get done by the autumn. That's how it is in gardening, you're always looking forward.

When he returned to what he still thought of as Mr Jimson's

office, Laura was at the door with a young man in a wheel-chair.

'Mr Paste,' she said. 'This is Peter Dawson and he'd like to talk to you. I'll push the chair inside, shall I, so you won't be disturbed?'

Puzzled, he took the chair from her, manoeuvred it over the step and watched her walk away.

He turned to the young man.

'What can I do for you?' he asked, expecting some question about the garden.

'You are Dicky Paste's father?'

'That's right.'

'I've something I'd like to tell you, Mr Paste.'

'Go on then, tell me.'

So Adam sat on the stool and the boy in the wheelchair poured out the whole story of how Dicky had saved him, how he'd thrown the terrible weight off his legs and carried him on his back like a sack of potatoes, sometimes running, sometimes crawling, through the hellfire to the casualty station.

Adam knew that it was true. Even if the lad hadn't told him that Diana's brother had written to her about it, he'd have known that it was true because he recognized that the words were Dicky's as well as the actions.

'He was the bravest man I ever met,' the man in the wheelchair concluded, 'and there were a lot of brave men out there. It would have been so easy for him to run and save himself like the other one did. There'd have been no shame in that. It's what we were told to do.'

Suddenly his eyes filled with tears.

'And I've never been able to thank him,' he said.

'He wouldn't have wanted thanks.'

'But I needed to give them. Now I can thank you, and that's the next best thing.'

He looked up at Dicky's father.

'I'd like to shake you by the right hand, Mr Paste,' he said, 'if I had one.'

Instead Adam bent down and embraced him. For a moment they clung together, the young man in the wheelchair and the older man stooping over him, both fighting back tears.

263

The younger man quickly controlled himself and looking up said, 'And then he was killed in action so soon afterwards. Oh, Mr Paste, I am so sorry. He saved me but he couldn't save himself. It seems so unfair.'

'War is unfair. Life is unfair,' Adam told him. 'It hasn't been very fair to you either.'

There seemed to be no words for what they felt; they hardly spoke as Adam pushed him out of the shed, across the lawn and back into the hall.

'We'll speak more of it later,' he said as he left him. 'And no doubt you'll be helping me with the plants before long.'

He returned to the shed and sat for a while, remembering his son, going through again and again in his mind the young man's account of what Dicky had done. It was so like Dicky, he could see him doing it. When the young man spoke he had heard his son's voice in his ears, as if he was back here with him. How many times when he was a lad had he rebuked Dicky for being too soft; soft on moles, soft on pigeons, soft on rabbits, soft on all creatures, garden pests or not? And yet it was that pitying streak in him that had made him save a man's life at risk of his own.

Killed in action, killed in action. That's what the officer had written, but then they'd seen the death certificate: shot at dawn for cowardice. But he was the bravest man young Peter had ever met! What was the sense of it?

They'd never told anyone about that death certificate. But it had killed Dicky's mother, just as surely as if they'd shot her too. Oh, she'd been so angry, his gentle wife, she'd wanted to go out there and kill the men who had shot her son. But he'd told her again and again that it wasn't the men who were to blame. They were only carrying out orders as you must do in the army. It was the system that had killed him; you need a bit of craftiness to survive in a system like that and Dicky had none.

No, it didn't allow for people like Dicky, a simple lad without any guile in him.

Well, nobody knew how he'd been killed now except himself and he'd take that knowledge to the grave with him. With that thought he got up off his stool, tidied away the catalogues, left everything in order ready for tomorrow and set off for home.

Laura had noticed how quiet Peter seemed after talking to Adam. She thought how terrible it must be to be stuck in one place, unable to move after such a tumult of emotions as he must just have had. How he must long to stride about, as she always did when the world pressed too hard.

'Would you like a walk around the grounds?' she asked the next day, adding, 'not to talk, just to go quietly and enjoy the peacefulness of it? It won't be too cold, I think.'

He smiled and agreed. He knew that she was concerned for him, worried at the memories which talking to Dicky's father must have brought back, but the fact was that meeting him had brought more happiness than he'd known since he was wounded. Among all the terrible things he had seen men do to each other in the war, Dicky stood out as the one great reminder that there are also good men who do good things. People can be unselfish by instinct just as much as they can be cruel by instinct. And to talk to Adam, to hear the same tone of voice in the father as there had been in the son, had somehow confirmed that belief. Why it had been such a healing thing, he didn't fully understand, but only knew that he felt a glow of optimism for the human race, that had remained with him undiminished ever since. He knew that if he could just keep that flame of optimism alight, the troughs of despair into which he sometimes fell might become less deep, less frequent, less terrifying. And so it was with greater peace of mind than he had known for a long time that he allowed himself to be pushed along the paths and lanes of Northrop as autumn tinted the trees and the leaves began to fall.

Thirty-Three

'Y ou're pale, my dear,' James had said. 'You're too much indoors.'

It was true, Diana thought, as she stood at the French window of what had once been the breakfast room and was now known as the den; she had always been an out-of-doors sort of person, but now she spent hours indoors, organizing the running of the home or typing letters for James, who laughingly referred to her as his unpaid secretary.

The den was the warmest room in the house, where the men came to relax, to have a drink and smoke. Heating pipes had been installed here, while the rest of the house was still draughty and cold, for there were no longer cheap servants to lug cheap coal to the fires in every room, as they had once done.

One of the many things that James was trying to arrange while he was in London today was for a grant to extend the heating system to the rest of the house, especially the men's bedrooms. Meanwhile they congregated here in the den now that winter had come.

They were having their mid-morning break in the dining room now and she was standing alone in the stuffy, smoke-filled room looking longingly out at the garden. Suddenly she couldn't bear to be indoors a moment longer and almost ran into the hall. From the pegs where the servants used to hang the hats of visiting gentlemen, which were now draped with an assortment of raincoats and gardening clothes, she took down her long, woollen coat, old but very warm. From its pockets she pulled the gloves which Nanny had knitted; Fair Isle, they were, with long gauntlets that covered the cuffs of her coatsleeves.

It was very still outside, not a breath of wind disturbed the frozen world. Frost still lay thick on the part of the lawn shaded by the house; beyond it she could see a clear line where the sun had touched the grass, melting its whiteness into green. The stark and spiky stems of unpruned roses were dark against the whitened wall and beyond them the leafless branches of a single beech tree were etched on the bright blue sky.

She breathed deeply, as if absorbing it all; the sharp, clear air, the edge of frost on it, the silent beauty of the garden. The gravel where she stood was still white with frost. It crunched under her feet as she began to walk towards the path that led to the lake.

She heard a car coming up the drive. It would be Noakes, who used to bring his goods in a horse and cart, but now used a modern delivery van. She didn't turn back to greet him; he would know where to go round the back, and she didn't want anything to delay her walk.

A car door slammed and footsteps, noisy on the gravel, came towards her.

'Excuse me,' a man's voice said, 'this is Northrop Hall, isn't it? Where the Arndales used to live?'

She turned, looked up.

'My God,' the voice said. 'It's Diana.'

'*Sebastian*!'

Sebastian, from whom she had daily longed for a letter all those years ago, Sebastian who had forgotten her so quickly, Sebastian who hadn't even bothered to write her a little note, Sebastian whom she had managed to forget. Sebastian who had met Teddy during the war and who had been no more than a casual reference in a letter.

There was a moment's hesitation, then they shook hands.

'So you still live here, Diana?' he asked, shaking his head in disbelief.

She laughed.

'Not only *live*. I *work* here.'

'Oh, it is so good to see you again.'

He spoke the commonplace words with feeling, then went on more formally, 'But perhaps I'm interrupting you. You were going out—'

'No, I was giving myself an hour off for a walk. It's such a perfect morning it seemed wicked to stay indoors a minute longer.'

'May I come with you?'

'Of course. I was just going to walk down to the lake, keeping in the sun. But tell me how you come to be here. It's so unexpected.'

He fell into step alongside her.

'I don't know if Teddy told you how we met, in the last year of the war?' he began gently, obviously fearful that talking about Teddy might upset her.

'Oh, yes, of course he did,' she told him, looking up, eyes shining, delighted to think that he would be able to tell her more about Teddy, add to her store of knowledge of him.

'He used to talk about Northrop Hall, you know, and how he loved the estate and just wanted the wretched war over so he could come back to it.'

'Yes, I know that from his letters, but he didn't write much towards the end, just a few lines sometimes.'

'Oh, Diana, the fighting was just so awful by then, first the retreat and then the advance. We tried to send off a card or a few lines when we could, just to let our folks know we were alive really.'

'I know. But I did so miss hearing from him, he seemed so close to me in his letters, it was almost like talking to him. But go on.'

He could tell how thirsty she was for anything he could tell her about Teddy in that last year.

'He talked about plans for after the war. Well, we all did but he especially wanted things to be fairer. He was always amazed at the way men fought for a country which had done so little for them, let them live in poverty and, often, ignorance. Yet they fought as if they owned the land which they weren't even allowed to walk on.'

'The government's doing something about that now, but go on, about Teddy.'

'We used to get so angry when people at home talked about the glory of war. About as glorious as an abattoir, Teddy said, but I shouldn't talk to you like this—'

268

'I know what it was like,' she assured him. 'I was there. Towards the end the wounded were just sent straight to us. I *do* know, Sebastian. You needn't be afraid of talking about it to me.'

'Yes, he told me that, how he could tell you things he couldn't begin to tell the people at home. The war did such horrible things, not just to bodies but to minds.'

They walked in silence for a while, remembering terrible sights and sounds, while around them the world was beautiful and still.

'But you know, Diana,' Sebastian said at last, 'Teddy always kept a cheerful face to the outside world. He cheered the men, kept their spirits up, despite all.'

He wasn't cheerful in his letters to me, she thought, grateful now that he had been able to share some of the burden of grief with her, so that he could save his strength for the men.

They rounded the corner and the lake lay before them, sparkling in the bright sunshine, dazzling their eyes as they stood gazing at it.

She was expecting this sight, but it took him by surprise.

'It's beautiful,' he said awestruck. Then: 'So beautiful,' he added in a different tone, an edge of bitterness in his voice and she knew that he was contrasting this scene with the trenches, this silence with that din, this peace with that war.

'We'll sit here for a while,' she suggested, taking his hand for a moment to lead him towards the bench.

'It just seems so *unfair*,' he suddenly burst out, 'to be sitting here, in the sun and Teddy . . .' His voice broke and he couldn't go on.

'Oh, I know, I know, we've all felt that, all of us. Why some and not others—'

'But it's worse than that. I'm here by *his* lake in *his* grounds. And he's over there – dead and I'm alive.'

'Shh, Sebastian, it's not your fault. Teddy always said it was just chance, some would be lucky, some would be unlucky.'

'But you see we both thought we *were* lucky, Diana. Only a few weeks to go, the war clearly ending, the Boche in full retreat. We talked about how we'd miraculously escaped. The end was in sight; he said it, I said it, we all said it, all through

269

October. We were both the same then, Teddy and I, but now – God, how different.'

His head was in his hands. He moved them now, lifted his face towards her. 'I'm sorry, Diana, sorry to burden you with all this.'

'It's not a burden, Sebastian. You sound so like Teddy. It's almost like hearing him again. Tell me more about him. Were you together a lot towards the end?'

'Not really, we were both so busy with our own men, but when we did manage a few minutes together, he always talked of home. I remember once he gave me a piece of some special cake the cook had made for him and he said how scared of her you all were when she got in one of her moods.'

Diana smiled.

'The boys were more scared of her than I was! How strange to think of things like that in the middle of a battlefield. It's so good to hear you talk about him. You saw him when none of us could. It gives him extra life somehow to hear you speak of him. Go on.'

'That last time we talked a lot about the League of Nations, about making sure there was never another war.'

'You don't really think there could ever be another war in Europe, do you?' she asked, horrified. 'Everyone knows it was the war to end all wars.'

'I said that, that we'd all learned from this one. But Teddy was pessimistic; he said I was a romantic and that men are capable of endless stupidity and that even the most dreadful lessons are only learned for a generation.'

'I can't believe that.'

She shook her head, not wanting to believe it. Then, glancing at the scar on his brow, she changed the subject, saying, 'So when were you wounded?'

'Ah, you've noticed the mark! It was in the same scrap as Teddy, but I was lucky; it wasn't much really, the bullet grazed my forehead. An inch to one side and it would have been fatal. I'd have been dead like Teddy, but all it did was knock me out for a bit and I fell on to something that broke my leg. So I was shipped home on Armistice Day. Amazing what a difference an inch can make in a battle.'

270

'So you were in hospital in London?'

'For a while, then they moved me up north, then I went home to convalesce. I was very weak, very low. My parents were very patient with me. I couldn't talk to them about any of it and I couldn't rouse myself to do anything, go anywhere. I think that's why my father bought me the motor, to encourage me to get out and about. And I was driving around today and I saw that notice, Northrop Hall, and I thought that's Teddy's place. Then of course I realized it had been turned into a rehabilitation centre.'

'Who told you?'

'There was a gardener chappie working up by the lodge.'

'That would be Adam.'

'So that's how I come to be here, thanks to my parents really. Again I was lucky. Some of the chaps had nobody to go back to, or at least nobody who was any help to them.'

She nodded.

'I remember your parents very well,' she said, smiling. 'They were always so kind to me. And I remember that party they gave, with the lanterns among the trees.'

'And we played hide and seek. What children we were then! When you think what followed so soon after.'

He looked at her directly.

'I've never forgotten that evening, Diana. It was awful to come back and find you'd left. I couldn't make out what had happened.' He paused then added, with something of reproach in his voice, 'You'd never even mentioned you were leaving so soon.'

'I hadn't planned it. And I did leave you a note.'

'A note? There was no note for me when I got home.'

'It wasn't at your home. I left it with Aunt Selina.'

'Your aunt? Your *aunt*?' He was looking at her in disbelief. 'But I went round to see your aunt. She didn't say anything about a note. I'd taken a letter so she could give me your address but she said she couldn't remember it offhand, so would add it and post it for me. But you didn't reply.'

'Of course I didn't!' she said indignantly. 'Since I never got it. I suppose it got lost somewhere on the way. Letters do sometimes.'

'And then later, when she was talking to my mother, she mentioned that she'd been here on a visit and I asked after you and she laughed and said you were very happy and had a really charming beau.'

'A beau?'

'Yes, she said you were clearly very much smitten with him and the family were delighted and looking forward to an engagement. So after that I didn't write any more.'

She sat, speechless, just looking at him.

'Then later, of course, I met Teddy and mentioned your engagement and he laughed and said, "Whatever gave you that idea? She's never been engaged and she's out here, nursing in France".'

She was still looking at him, still unable to believe her aunt's treachery. How could she have said she didn't know the address offhand, when it was only Northrop Hall, Gloucestershire, and she'd been here plenty of times?

'Oh, Diana, I was so relieved, so happy, despite all the horror of the war. I knew I couldn't do anything then, but I vowed that if I came out of the foul war alive I'd go and find you. In all the darkness, that hope was like a light at the end of a long tunnel.'

They were sitting close together now and he had taken her gloved fingers in his hands.

'But then I was injured and when I got back I was depressed and I thought you'd be bound to hate me for surviving when Teddy was killed.'

She shook her head, but said nothing.

'I used to relive that night in the garden,' he went on. 'I used to imagine that we could be there together again, not be interrupted this time, and that I could kiss you properly.'

So saying, he reached out and drew her towards him, held her close and kissed her. They clung together and there was comfort as well as passion in his embrace for as she rested her head on his shoulder it seemed as if he was a brother as well as her long lost lover.

Suddenly she broke away from him, looked at him in horror.

'Diana, whatever—?'

'I can't, I can't, I mustn't. Oh, Sebastian, didn't you know? Of course you don't know. I'm married.'

'*Married?*'

He looked at her, stupefied.

'Diana,' he said at last. 'Tell me it's not true. It's a lie, like that engagement, isn't it? You just *can't* be married.'

'But I am. I am. Look,' and she pulled off her left glove, the Fair Isle glove which Nanny had knitted for her, to reveal the little gold band which James had given her.

The colour had left his face, his eyes were dead. He wore the face of despair.

'Oh, Sebastian, I am so sorry.'

Her words were scarcely audible.

'I'd better go,' he said, getting up.

So they walked in silence back to the house and she watched from the steps as he got into the car and drove away.

Thirty-Four

'Cold winter, hot summer,' Nanny had predicted in Feb-ruary and the weather had obeyed her rule. As the days lengthened so the skies cleared and sunshine prevailed. The men worked outside most of the day and relaxed in the grounds each evening. The heating system was finished in April and never needed to be used.

Nevertheless Nanny insisted that Tommy wore his jacket when he was playing out of doors, as he was now, with his mother in their little front garden.

'Don't cast a clout till May is out,' she'd said. 'And it's still only the twenty-ninth.'

It was five o'clock when she called them in for tea.

'Take your jacket off, Tommy, or you won't feel the benefit when you go out again,' she told him and watched as the three-year-old struggled with the sleeves and dropped the jacket on the floor.

'Now pick it up and fold it nicely. That's the way. If a job's worth doing it's worth doing properly. We don't want to grow up into the kind of person who spoils the ship for a ha'porth of tar, now do we?'

She watched as his mother lifted him up on to a chair where a cushion gave him precarious extra height.

Perched there he had the tea Nanny always prescribed: a piece of plain bread and butter before you were allowed anything else, then bread and butter with jam, then cake.

'Home-made blackcurrant jam,' Nanny said. 'It's very good for you. Cook made it last year for the soldiers and your mummy picked the fruit.'

The little boy munched contentedly. A fire burned low in the kitchen range which that morning Mary-Ann had black-leaded,

274

polishing the brass knobs so that they gleamed now in the sunlight which slanted through the western window. A vase of early marigolds shone in the centre of the table.

'You can have some grapes for a treat to end with, Tommy,' Nanny said. 'But mind you don't swallow the pips or they'll gather in your appendix.'

He didn't want any grapes, perhaps out of consideration for the organ which Nanny held in such awe, and began to slide off his chair.

'What do you say, Tommy?' his mother prompted.

'Thank-you-for-my-nice-dinner-and-please-may-I-get-down?' he recited.

'Well, *tea* really, but that's as maybe,' Nanny said, reaching for a cloth to wipe his hands.

After they had cleared away, Mary-Ann went and stood in the doorway.

'It's a lovely evening, Nanny,' she called back. 'I think I'll take him for a walk down to the lake. Do you want to come?'

Nanny nodded and went to fetch her bonnet.

They walked slowly, Nanny in her black bombazine, Mary-Ann in her cotton dress, the little boy between them, holding hands. It was a beautiful calm evening, the sun setting the western sky alight.

'Red sky at night, shepherds delight,' Nanny prophesied as they stood back a little to let two men on crutches go past.

'Never stare, Tommy,' she said after they'd gone round the corner, though actually he was so used to crutches and wheelchairs that he never did.

The lake lay before them now, as they stood at the top of the slope, and they paused for a moment, gazing down at the expanse of water, lit up on the far side by the setting sun, lapping less brightly over here in the dappled shade of the trees.

Benches had been put up along the side of the lake for the men to come and relax and enjoy the view. Three of them were sitting on one now, drinking beer, their crutches propped up against a little table.

'Your good health, ladies,' they said, raising their glasses and waving.

Tommy freed his hand and waved back, Mary-Ann smiled at them and Nanny moved her mouth a little to show that she was friendly but didn't approve of familiarity.

The lakeside path was wide and level, sandy and scattered with pine needles. Tommy ran ahead, eager to get to the little stream which emptied itself into the lake. There was a bench here too so the two women sat for a while watching him as he squatted by the water's edge, busying himself with waterweeds and pebbles, throwing in little sticks, lifting stones to see what strange creatures might be lurking beneath them.

'I remember Lady Arndale having this lake made,' Nanny said, forgetting for a moment that her former employer must have lived to regret it.

'You can't imagine it wasn't always here,' Mary-Ann remarked, tipping back her head to feel the warmth on her face, as the setting sun made a path of golden ripples on the lake. If only she could walk across it, she thought, walk down that golden path and find Tom.

Nanny produced a little bottle of lemonade and a mug.

'Fresh made this afternoon,' she told Tommy as she handed him the mug. 'Now what do you say?'

He hesitated.

'Your good health, ladies?' he suggested.

Peter, exhausted as always at the end of a day's physiotherapy which was slowly getting him to walk again, was being rewarded by being pushed around the lake. Laura enjoyed these outings as much as he did, told him, if he demurred at the effort he was putting her to, that she'd much rather do this than be landed with some boring indoor task and anyway they always had plenty to talk about, didn't they?

They were, as usual, deep in conversation when they rounded the last corner and saw the little trio by the stream.

'Hello, Tommy,' he said, for everyone knew Tommy, the only child about the place.

They paused on their walk, exchanging greetings.

'What do you think you'll be when you grow up, Tommy?' Laura asked and then realized it was a pretty silly thing to ask a child who was only just beginning to speak.

276

'He's going to be an engineer and build dams,' Mary-Ann answered for him.

'Then he'll be very useful,' the young man told her, looking up and smiling. 'We'll need chaps like that to rebuild the world.'

'You must take him to Furzebridge when he's older,' Laura said. 'Keeping that dam maintained is quite a family tradition.'

She saw a shadow pass Mary-Ann's face and she didn't reply. Then, remembering the picnic on the day war was declared, she too fell silent.

'At least there won't be a war to interrupt *his* studies, 'Peter said, but he spoke without bitterness, genuinely glad to think that he had fought in the war to end all wars, so that young lads like this would be sure to live out their lives in peace.

They walked back together, Mary-Ann pushing the chair so that Laura could walk behind and talk to Nanny.

'She's on duty up at the hall tonight, isn't she?' Laura asked, nodding towards Mary-Ann.

'Yes, she goes up every Thursday to help the sister on night duty.'

'It isn't too much for her?'

'No, she'll have a good sleep tomorrow. I take Tommy in with me so that she can go straight up to her room when she gets in at six tomorrow morning and sleep till noon. She finds it enough.'

'Well, it's only till we get another auxiliary helper. Mary-Ann's such a hard worker, isn't she? And so willing, we don't want to overdo her.'

'Yes, she's a good girl, I must admit,' Nanny conceded, though she was always cautious about giving praise, fearing it might corrupt. 'And a good mother, I'll say that for her.'

'I suppose we don't know who the father was?' Laura queried, dropping her voice.

'Ask no questions and you'll be told no lies,' Nanny told her.

They parted at the top of the path, Laura pushing Peter back towards the hall, Nanny and Mary-Ann taking a now very tired little boy back to the cottage.

'There now, you can have your supper by the fire for a treat,' Nanny told him, 'while your mother gets ready to go out to work. And tomorrow morning you're to be as quiet as a little mouse so she can have a good sleep. And, look, I've put some blackcurrant jam on your nice rice pudding.'

Mary-Ann came down just as he was finishing his supper.

'Wipe your mouth before you kiss your mother goodnight,' Nanny said, but she was too late, he was already in his mother's arms having a cuddle and giving her sticky kisses. So Nanny put the cloth down, shaking her head and saying she didn't know what the world was coming to, really she didn't.

Tommy was sound asleep when she went up to bed that night. He was lying with his arms outstretched above his head in a way she considered healthy and good for his lungs. He was wearing nightclothes which had belonged to Master Rupert, handed down from Master Teddy, for she had a cupboard full of old baby clothes which she had always kept well mended, washed and ironed. The linen on the little bed had first been sewn for Master Charles, bless him, and there was plenty of life left in it still. Waste not, want not, that's what she'd always said.

She stood for a moment looking down at the little boy as he slept. He had his mother's long eyelashes and her rosy cheeks, flushed now from a day in the sun. But his hair was fair and straight like his father's and his grandfather's. He stirred slightly as she tucked the blankets more firmly around him, his lips made a little sucking movement, then he sighed and returned to his dreams.

After she'd settled him for the night, she began to undress, not quite so circumspectly as she had once done, but still with some modesty as she prepared for bed in the presence of this representative of the third generation of Arndales whom she had trained and cherished.